DUEL WITH THE DRAGON

BOOK 2

THE FALLEN KNIGHT SERIES

PETER WACHT

Duel With the Dragon
By Peter Wacht

Book 2 of The Fallen Knight Series

This book is a work of fiction. Names, characters, places, and incidents are the product of the author's imagination or are used fictitiously. Any resemblance to actual events, locales, or persons, living or dead, is coincidental.

Copyright 2025 © by Peter Wacht

Cover design by Ebooklaunch.com

All rights reserved. In accordance with the U.S. Copyright Act of 1976, the scanning, uploading, and electronic sharing of any part of this book without the permission of the publisher constitute unlawful piracy and theft of the author's intellectual property.

Published in the United States by Kestrel Media Group LLC.

ISBN: 978-1-950236-56-5

eBook ISBN: 978-1-950236-55-8

Library of Congress Control Number: 2024920388

✿ Created with Vellum

ALSO BY PETER WACHT

THE FALLEN KNIGHT SERIES

The Death of the Dragon (short story)*

The Dragon Awakens

Duel With a Dragon

Beware the Dragon (Forthcoming)

The Dragon Returns (Forthcoming)

THE REALMS OF THE TALENT AND THE CURSE

THE TALES OF CALEDONIA

(Complete 7-Book Series)

Blood on the White Sand (short story)*

The Diamond Thief (short story)*

The Protector

The Protector's Quest

The Protector's Vengeance

The Protector's Sacrifice

The Protector's Reckoning

The Protector's Resolve

The Protector's Victory

THE TALES OF THE TERRITORIES

Stalking the Blood Ruby (short story)*

A Fate Worse Than Death (short story)*

Death on the Burnt Ocean

Monsters in the Mist

The Dance of the Daggers

Bloody Hunt for Freedom

A Spark of Rebellion

Shadows Made Real

Shadow's Reach

Storm in the Darkness (Forthcoming 2025)

THE SYLVAN CHRONICLES

(Complete 9-Book Series)

The Legend of the Kestrel

The Call of the Sylvana

The Raptor of the Highlands

The Makings of a Warrior

The Lord of the Highlands

The Lost Kestrel Found

The Claiming of the Highlands

The Fight Against the Dark

The Defender of the Light

THE RISE OF THE SYLVAN WARRIORS

*Through the Knife's Edge (short story)**

* Free stories can be downloaded from my author website at PeterWachtBooks.com. My books are also available on Amazon and other online retailers.

1

LATE-NIGHT VISITOR

Draig stood in the shadows, leaning his blackthorn shillelagh against his shoulder like it was a baseball bat.

He stared at the Book Nook. He had been for the past quarter hour. Still as a statue, just another piece of the darkness.

Not a sound to be heard. Not a whisper of movement. Not even a breeze, which was strange with the ocean just a few hundred yards to the east.

He was alone but for the smothering shadows, the streetlights reminiscent of Victorian London few and far between on Market Street.

Well past midnight, all was as it should be in Kraken Cove.

Although it wasn't as it should be in his bookstore.

Draig hadn't been planning on leaving his lighthouse and piloting his cabin cruiser back across Raptor Bay until later in the morning. When the sun was up.

He hadn't had a choice, though. A common theme these last few days. Ever since his adventure in Williamsburg, in fact.

He wasn't enjoying feeling as if he were one of the main characters in an online game, being moved this way and that.

Reacting, not acting.

Just like it had been when he served his father.

That was one of the reasons why he had come to Kraken Cove. So that he could make choices that had an impact on his life rather than allowing someone else to make them for him.

His displeasure at the sensation of being played with like a marionette on strings would have to wait.

The alarm for the Book Nook had awakened him, drawing him across the water. The alarm that would alert him, not Cerridwen or Seshat.

From where he was standing, all looked as it should in his bookshop. Just a few lights on toward the back and the front light on to counter the night.

He knew the truth, however.

He knew who was waiting for him.

Just to make sure that he wasn't in for any of her frequent surprises, he used the Grym to examine the store and its environs. Seeing what was obvious and not so obvious. Looking for what might be hidden. What might be lurking.

Draig pursed his lips, thinking for a moment.

All clear, which was out of character for her. She usually left a small gift at the very least.

But nothing this time.

He could wait a little longer, just to irritate her. But what was the point? She was hard enough to deal with as it was when she was in a good mood.

Draig walked across the street and stood in front of the door. Still wary, he sent a strand of the Grym beneath the frame, allowing the Power of the Ancients to slither its way through the shop like a snake.

Just because he knew who had decided to make a late-night visit didn't mean that he trusted her. She had given him little cause to do so in the past.

Especially since more often than not she tended to work against him. Taking a unique pleasure from doing so, in fact.

Once the stream of magic completed its circuit, working its way over every inch of the store, Draig's eyes tightened.

Definitely out of character for her. His use of the Grym confirming that there were no surprises or traps waiting for him, Draig placed his hand over the door lock.

He didn't have the key with him. He didn't need it. Because though the lock resembled a deadbolt, it was much more than that.

Murmuring a few words under his breath, the palm of his hand glowed softly for just a heartbeat, and then the lock snapped free, disarming the nasty surprises that Draig had woven into the wards set at all the entrances and exits to the store.

Pushing the door open on silent hinges, he stepped through and closed the oak slab just as quietly behind him.

Then he waited. Extending his senses. Wanting to check again. Examining every nook and cranny of his bookshop. Gaining a feel for what waited for him.

He smiled. He had to give her credit. She was good.

She had broken into his shop, avoided all the traps, and then reset all of his wards.

No one else, except perhaps his mother, could have done the same. Then again, she did have an advantage that few others could claim.

There was just the one snare that she had failed to avoid, and he assumed that wasn't an error on her part.

Draig sensed her passage. Where she had walked. Where she had trailed her fingers across the covers and the spines. Where she had hesitated.

Draig followed the same path, coming to a stop after a meandering journey through the aisles right where the two steel staircases that resembled the caduceus met at the very back of the shop.

He waited there for almost a minute. Still cautious. Then he decided that he was wasting his time. If she wanted to do something to him, she would have already tried.

Placing the tip of the shillelagh in the center of the circle he was standing within, almost invisible runes carved into the floor that had been worn down over the years flashed to life.

When he opened his eyes again, he still stood in the circle, although he was no longer in his shop. Or rather the shop reserved for most of his customers.

"It's not here, Eris," Draig said.

"I didn't think it would be, brother dear."

Eris didn't turn around. Her eyes were fixed on the almost transparent wall to her front. What looked like glass but wasn't, the slight shimmer giving away the magic in use.

Her reflection revealed that she was smiling. Draig wasn't surprised. His sister had a penchant for the unique. The hard to acquire. Just like someone else he had met recently.

"I always enjoy coming here," Eris murmured, transfixed by the packed shelves staring right back at her. "It's so ... relaxing. Enticing as well."

She licked her lips, thousands of priceless books and artifacts teasing her. The knowledge protected by that gleaming barrier gave off an almost imperceptible hum. The power that could be obtained by anyone able to acquire and make use of just one of those items?

It was beyond imagining.

She and her brother were quite different from one another. But in this respect, valuing knowledge, understanding how it could be used ... they were much alike.

"You did well getting into the shop. You won't be able to break through the barrier, however."

"I'm aware of that, because I've tried, more times than I care to mention, and I'm quite disappointed by my failure to do so." Eris snorted in amusement, then turned around. "You're quite proud of yourself, aren't you? A unique construction combining two distinct powers over which only you can exercise control. Not even mother has the strength or the cunning to do what you did here."

Draig shrugged. "Not proud. Just telling you the truth is all."

Eris' snort of laughter became a low chuckle. "And there's the brother I know." She shook her head in disappointment. "Always telling the truth. Always doing what he believes is right. Even when doing so could cost him in the end."

Draig's expression soured slightly. He had no desire to relive the argument that they had engaged in ever since they were children.

Draig always doing what was right. Always so boring. Never having any fun.

Eris doing what she wanted to do. Ignoring the rules. Always having fun.

To curb his rising irritation, he studied his half-sister. She seemed little different than when he last saw her.

In appearance, they were very similar. Taking after their mother. Tall. Lithe. Wiry. Dark hair.

The primary difference being the color of their eyes. Draig's an orange red that burned with a greater heat as his anger intensified. Eris' eyes an icy blue that only got colder.

Draig lifted his chin just a hair. There. In the back of Eris' sea-swept orbs. A hint of concern?

Strange and slightly worrisome.

Because it was out of character for her.

Usually she was only concerned about herself.

"You wanted to talk."

"I did," Eris confirmed with a nod, her smile turning into a smirk.

Even though she hadn't come here of her own volition,

Draig knew that she wasn't going to make this easy for him. If only because she so enjoyed trying to get under his skin. "You didn't want to talk in the Dragon Vault when we had the chance?"

"I thought it best not to interrupt. Father-son reunions tend to make me emotional." She crossed her arms and shifted her weight, her right hip sticking out, left leg extended. "Did you enjoy seeing the King Teg again? It must have been quite a shock for dear old dad, particularly since you're still alive."

"You wanted that to happen." It was his turn to shake his head in disappointment. "Even after I helped you out with that paramour of yours. What was his name again? The one who threatened to reveal your relationship to mom?"

She laughed softly, a hint of condescension radiating out from her. She sought to hide her discomfort by provoking him just as she had done when they were younger.

He had helped her, unexpectedly so. Draig had told her that he had done it for the reason he offered. To ensure that Eris' boyfriend couldn't reveal the relationship to their mother.

She knew the truth, however. Her lover at the time had gotten aggressive, and she was having a hard time dealing with that. She thought she was in love, ignoring the fact that he was abusing her, emotionally and in other ways.

Draig had ensured that her former lover would no longer be a problem for her ... or anyone else for that matter.

"I was quite curious about how he reacted when the son he believed he killed was instead standing before him, holding his favorite sword no less," Eris said, ignoring her brother's questions, refusing to allow him to knock her off track. "He wants Excalibur back, doesn't he?"

"My father has wanted Excalibur back ever since the sword chose me instead of him. I had nothing to do with it. And even if I wanted to give Excalibur back to him," Draig said, lifting the shillelagh off the ground, "it doesn't matter. It's up to Excalibur, not me. That's the way it's always been."

"What is it with boys and their swords?" mused Eris, shaking her head, as if slightly mystified, also clearly amused as revealed by the sparkle in her eyes. "I never understood the attraction. Very Freudian."

"You're losing focus again, Eris."

"Right, sorry about that," she replied, although she didn't sound the least bit contrite.

"Why did you bring my father and his Knights to the Dragon Vault?" he asked, trying to bring their conversation back to the primary topic. "Why did you want that to happen? Just so my father knew that I was still alive?"

"I didn't want that to happen," Eris replied. "In all honesty, I really didn't care. I had other plans that evening, but I had to change them."

Draig nodded, understanding dawning. "Mom."

"Mom," Eris confirmed.

"Why?" She had been the one who granted Draig sanctuary after he faked his own death, giving him the time to put in place the final pieces necessary for him to start fresh in Kraken Cove without needing to bear the chains thrown upon him by the King Teg.

"You know mom. She does things for her own reasons." Eris raised her arms to her shoulders, revealing her exasperation. "She doesn't tell me everything. In fact, she barely tells me anything at all. No more than I need to know."

Draig nodded. Their mother was tight-lipped to begin with, always keeping her cards close to her vest. He could understand why considering the demands placed upon her. "What did she tell you?"

"That you couldn't hide anymore. That your sabbatical was coming to an end. That you were needed once more."

"Why would she say that?"

"How long is this inquisition going to last?" Eris wondered. "I've got better ways to spend my time than serve as our mother's messenger."

"Eris!" Draig demanded sharply, his eyes flashing as his aggravation became more tangible. He took several deep breaths to calm himself. If he lost his temper with his sister, it would serve her purposes and not his.

"You'd have to ask her," Eris replied, giving him a shrug that suggested she had little interest in her mother's designs. Seeing how Draig's eyes flashed again, she realized that continuing to push her brother when he was like this was a bad idea. She did like to tease him. But she had no desire to make him angry. Because she knew what could happen if she did. "As I said, she doesn't tell me everything."

"That's all she had to say?"

Rather than reply right away, Eris examined her brother. Ignoring her better instincts, just as she usually did, she spoke in a voice normally reserved for a mother speaking with her young child. "Do you miss your mommy, Axel? Do you need a hug?"

In a flash, Draig stood right in front of Eris, no more than a blur as he shot through the twenty feet that separated them.

Eris tried to step back, her eyes widening slightly, having forgotten just how dangerous he could be, but she couldn't. The shimmering barrier behind her prevented it.

"Do you really want to test me now, Eris?" he asked in a very quiet voice that made her entire body prickle as if she had been struck by an icy gust. "Do you really want to push me?"

"Look, Draig, I was just having a little fun," Eris stuttered. Hating herself for demonstrating such weakness. She couldn't look away from Draig's eyes, which burned even brighter as he leaned in toward her. "Really, I didn't mean to ..."

"I know what you did, Eris," Draig said oh so softly, the timbre of his voice chilling her to the bone.

Eris gulped. "Like I said, Draig, I only brought your father to the Dragon Vault because mom wanted me to. That's the only reason ..."

"And was it mom who told you to steal *The Book of Whispers* from the Dragon Vault?"

Eris' eyes bulged even more, her shock complete. She had planned that job to perfection. No one could have figured it out. "How did you ..."

Draig didn't let his sister complete her question. "Fafnir wants to see you, Eris. He'd do almost anything to see you, in fact. And you know how he can be when someone steals an item from the Dragon Vault."

"Fafnir knows?" Her voice broke when she asked the question, her initial concern becoming something more akin to fear.

"Do you remember what he did when Felix snatched the Shield of Achilles?"

Eris didn't reply, simply nodding at the memory. It wasn't a good one.

Felix had asked Fafnir if he could borrow the artifact so that he could perform a test on the metal. Fafnir had refused because Felix didn't have permission from the Queen. Felix had taken the artifact anyway.

No one really knew what happened when Fafnir caught up to Felix. Nevertheless, Felix was never quite the same afterward. Jumping at shadows. Having nightmares. A trace of fear always in the back of his eyes. Worried that Fafnir might decide to come after him again and finish what he started.

"I suggest you find Fafnir and apologize. Don't wait for him to find you. You know how he is."

"But if I do that ..."

"It will be worse if you wait, Eris," Draig explained. "He will go easier on you if you demonstrate the courage to face him."

"That's all well and good," Eris protested, "but I don't have the book to return to him. With it still missing, he's not going to be very understanding."

"You have nothing to fear in that regard. Much to my father's chagrin, I returned the book for you."

Eris smiled then, beginning to think that what her brother was suggesting just might work. Although she was still unwilling to commit to it. "I'll think about it." She should have assumed that he had gotten his hands on the artifact.

"Do more than think," Draig suggested. "The longer you wait, the angrier Fafnir will be."

Eris nodded, then slid along the barrier behind her until she was free of Draig. "My job is done here. I'm going to head home. Anything you want me to tell mom?"

Draig answered in a tone that was more bite than bark. "Tell her that my decisions are my own. She doesn't need to make them for me."

Eris chuckled. "I will tell her word for word, but it's your funeral."

Eris walked toward the circle carved into the floor. She stopped and turned back when Draig called to her.

"Here is what you were looking for."

Eris scrunched up her brow in confusion until she saw what he held in his hand, the book materializing out of a series of distorting waves that reminded her of the heat rising off a desert highway.

"How did you know?" Her eyes sparkled in delight, temporarily forgetting her problem with Fafnir.

"It's what you were searching for, isn't it? *The Song of the Sirens*?" He flipped the book to her.

Eris snatched it deftly out of the air. "Yes, but how did you ..."

"We all have our secrets, Eris, you know that," Draig replied mysteriously.

Eris realized that there was little point in pushing her brother for a more in-depth explanation. Because he was right. He had given her the book she was looking for.

Since her mother had forced her to make this trip, Eris was hoping to do a little shopping while she was here. But she couldn't find the volume, and she had no clue as to how to get past Draig's barrier.

"I'll return it when I'm done."

"Don't make promises you can't keep," he said with a playful smile as she stepped into the circle. "Eris?"

"Yes, brother dear?" Her usual smirk once again gracing her wily countenance.

"Do you agree with mom? Do you think that I've been hiding away?"

Going against character, Eris gave serious consideration to her brother's question before replying. Usually, she spoke from the cuff, trying to infuse her dissatisfaction with the world whenever she could. But not now.

"I can understand why you needed to step away. If I had been in your position, I would have done the same." Eris didn't use the word *hide* as their mother did. She knew that her brother never hid from anything. Doing so was antithetical to his very being. "After everything your father required of you, all that you had to do that no other Teg should have to do, I can understand. But when mom sent me here to talk to you ..."

Eris hesitated, needing a few seconds to gather her thoughts. "I could tell that mom was worried when she told me to come here. Why, I don't know. But I don't think she would send me here unless there was a good reason to do so."

"What would that be?" Draig asked, wishing as soon as the words left his mouth that he hadn't. Not wanting to deal with another sarcastic response from his sister. Surprised when she once again went against her own nature.

"I don't know," Eris replied in a sad tone. "I do know that whether you like it or not, the Teg need you. And not just the Teg in Kraken Cove."

"I don't know," Eris replied in a sad tone. "I do know that whether you like it or not, the Teg need you. And not just the Teg in Kraken Cove."

2

ONE ANGRY MOTHER

Mordred stared at his reflection in the floor-to-ceiling window, a cell phone stuck to his ear. He stood in his living room, which extended across most of the ground floor of his mansion and allowed him to admire his back lawn. Framed by two tree-lined paths, the grass ran for more than a hundred yards before it fell off the cliffs, the Long Island Sound just beyond.

His lawn was perfectly manicured, just like he was. His three-piece suit fit neatly on his lean, muscular body. His wavy dark hair was cut just so. His goatee was meticulously trimmed.

However, rather than being pleased by his appearance, instead he grimaced, then looked away. The anger that was never far from the surface threatening to break through.

He looked just like his father.

His mother liked to remind him of that whenever she felt the need to put him on edge, thereby keeping him in his place.

He hated when she did that. Because he hated his father.

He was looking forward to the day when he could examine his image in the mirror and know with absolute certainty that it was his reflection and his alone.

He would no longer see his father. He would only see himself.

The new King Teg.

And, as an added bonus, there would be no doubt that his father had passed to the Spirit World.

A day that he hoped would be coming sooner rather than later.

"We talked about this, Senator," Mordred growled, a grumble of displeasure creeping into his voice.

Just then he felt a hand on his shoulder, the image of a beautiful young woman wearing a tight skirt appearing next to his in the window. She whispered into his ear, her voice sultry and sending a shiver of pleasure down his spine.

"Are we leaving soon, honey? We're already late for our reservation."

He cupped the cell phone to his shoulder to ensure that his private conversation remained private. "In a few minutes, Candy. Why don't you sit over there so I can finish this up."

"Please honey, can't we go now? I'm starving. If you want to have a little fun later, I need to eat."

"In a few minutes," Mordred repeated, a much harder edge to his voice. "Sit. Down."

Her hand slipped off his shoulder when she stepped back, her eyes widening, a spark of fear in the back of her baby blues. She knew what Mordred was capable of if she pushed too hard, and she didn't want to be responsible for getting him angry with her again.

She could live with a bruise or two. But the pain that he could inflict upon her without leaving a mark? She couldn't deal with that agony. Not again.

Besides, she had promised him that she had learned her lesson. She didn't want to force his hand.

Mordred returned to his conversation, forgetting about Candy.

"Senator, we talked about this before. Too many times before."

Mordred's chin dropped to his chest. Was the concept of loyalty completely dead in this day and age? Was a man's word no longer good? Just something to be flung about and adhered to so long as that person's purpose was served?

"Senator ..."

The man wouldn't stop talking. He actually had the nerve to argue with him.

Mordred would have been amused if not for the fact that he was irritated and moving quickly toward enraged. In part because he was hungry and wanted to get to the restaurant just like Candy did. Even more so because it seemed that the good and honorable Senator had forgotten his place in Mordred's world.

"Senator ..."

Mordred lifted his chin from his chest, his expression hard, knowing that it would carry over into his voice. He didn't have time for this.

"Enough, Senator!" Mordred roared into his phone, gaining instant silence on the other end. "This isn't a discussion. We don't decide jointly what we are going to do. I decide what I'm going to do, and you do what I tell you to do. Are we clear about that?"

Mordred barely had time to take a breath before he heard what he wanted to hear in his ear.

"Good. Now let me be clear so that there is no misunderstanding. You will get that bill out of committee and onto the floor for a vote within two weeks. Do you understand? Two weeks and I expect it to be on the floor. Then, once that's done, and the President has signed it – and have no fear that she will sign it – the Department of Defense will bid it out and Dread Industries will win the contract. Because you will make sure that happens." He bit off his last few words so that there was no confusion. "Am. I. Clear?"

Mordred pulled the phone from his ear, not needing to listen to the series of less-than-heartfelt promises mixed in with apologies that spewed from a private office on Capitol Hill.

"Good. I'm glad to hear that we're on the same page again, Senator." Mordred tilted his head down, forcing himself to exercise what little patience that he still had left, allowing the Senator to remind them both of his loyalty.

He felt a hand on his shoulder again, shrugging it off, not bothering to look into the window. Candy should know better.

She wasn't going to like what happened once he was done with this call. Her being hungry was going to be the least of her concerns.

"Fine, Senator. I understand. And I want to make sure that you understand that not only will the contributions to your campaign dry up if this bill doesn't become law, but those pictures I showed you just a few weeks ago will be shared with the press as well as a few other pieces of information that I'm sure you'd prefer to keep swept under the rug."

Mordred gave the Senator a few seconds to splutter out several more apologies and confirm that he understood what was expected of him.

"As I said, I'm glad to hear that we're back on the same page, Senator. Let's make sure we stay there. For your sake more than mine."

The hand dropped back onto Mordred's shoulder, applying a bit more pressure. He ignored it this time.

He was about to offer one more reminder to the Senator when the grip tightened painfully, digging into his joint. He was spun around so fast that his phone slipped from his fingers and flew through the air, smashing into the glass wall and clattering to the floor.

The anger that flared in his dark eyes faded in a flash, replaced by a hint of fear.

"Mother, I'm sorry. I didn't know it was you. I didn't know that you were here."

Mordred didn't understand how it was possible that she had gotten into his house without his knowledge. Especially with the wards he had set around his private living quarters. Not even she should be able to sneak through without Mordred being made aware.

Besides, separate from the magical measures he put in place, he had given his Paladins explicit instructions to always give him warning when his mother appeared. She had a habit of popping in and out of his life whenever she wanted, and he had grown tired of it.

She was wearing a black gown. A diamond almost as large as her fist hung from her necklace.

Probably going to another one of her endless galas.

For just a heartbeat, he considered asking her how she had made it into his home unannounced. He discarded the idea quickly. She would never tell him. She would simply give him that condescending look of hers that annoyed him so much and say, "There are things that you will never know or understand. Things that you will never be able to do that I can. Best to remember that."

Still angry, he had no desire to be embarrassed as well.

Yet he couldn't let it go. How had she done it?

After the recent break-in, the item that he had worked so hard and paid so much to gain stolen from him, he had enhanced his security to an almost ridiculous level. To the point where even the Keeper of the Dragon Vault would be jealous.

The Teg who had installed his new system had promised that no other Warlock or Witch, Sorceress or Sorcerer, could do as he had done. Guaranteeing that anyone touched by the

Grym wouldn't be able to set foot on his property without his knowledge.

Mordred should have gotten a pulse of warning in the back of his brain as soon as his mother set foot on his estate. But nothing at all.

And his mother was one of the strongest practitioners of the Grym among all the Teg. The strongest if you asked her.

He'd be having more than just a conversation with the Teg who had done the work for him. Mordred was going to enjoy that experience, because he was going to ensure that the Warlock didn't.

"If I wanted you to know that I was here, Morry, I would have rung the doorbell."

"Mordred, mother." He pushed the words through gritted teeth. "Not Morry."

"Of course, Morry."

He closed his eyes and took a deep breath, working hard to keep himself calm. Getting angry with his mother was never a good idea. He had learned that through hard experience, many of the scars from previous encounters, physical and otherwise, never having faded.

"Where's Candy, mother? We were supposed to go out this evening."

"I sent her away, of course. To have her here demonstrates weakness, Morry, and as I've told you so many times before, you can never appear weak. Never. If you have any kind of attachments, your enemies can use them against you."

"Mother, I ..."

"We've had this conversation before, Morry," his mother growled, her lustrous dark hair braided intricately down her back, a few strands left free to frame her ageless face. She smiled easily, but there was barely a hint of warmth in her curled lips as she walked over to the cart set against the wall and poured herself a drink. She avoided the alcohol, selecting a ginger ale with ice instead. "If you're going to be taken seriously, you need to find the right woman and settle down. A strong woman who can watch over your fortunes. Who can ensure that no one can sneak up and stab you in the back, either literally or figuratively. Your future depends on it."

"Mother, I know that ..."

His mother ran right over him. "We've talked about this I don't know how many times, Morry, and I'd really like to stop having the same conversation. It's beyond tedious. It's almost as if you're deliberately disobeying me. You have to stop spending time with these nitwit floozies."

"Mother, Candace has a doctorate in financial arbitrage and risk management from ..."

"That doesn't matter," Morgase replied, her eyes sparking with anger at having to share this lesson again. "She's not of the Teg. You can't rule the Teg if you don't have a woman of the Teg by your side."

"When I rule the Teg, I'll do whatever I damn well please," Mordred wanted to shout at the top of his lungs. Instead, he kept that to himself, offering his mother a reluctant nod of acceptance. He had made the mistake of arguing with his mother one too many times on this subject. He would not do so again.

"As you say, mother. Now to what do I owe the pleasure of your company?" He wanted to get to the business that had brought her there. The sooner they resolved it, the sooner she'd be gone.

"The artifact was supposed to be in my hands by now, Morry. It's not." She turned to face him. Her expression hard as stone. "Why not?"

Mordred hesitated several times, trying to figure out what to say. Searching for some way to escape the brunt of her anger. Yet under Morgase's flinty gaze, he felt like a little boy again. And he hated himself for it.

"Out with it, Morry. You're wasting my time. What happened?"

"There have been a few unexpected complications that we've had to work through," Mordred offered, still not understanding how she could so easily sense when he had bad news. "That's all. It happens on occasion, and I'll deal with those complications just as I have in the past."

"What do you mean by complications?" Morgase asked, her blazing eyes narrowing, her already sharp tone somehow becoming even sharper.

Mordred didn't want to, but he had to. Never able to stand against his mother when she was in such a mood. She was on the cusp of using the Grym against him. So claiming a small victory for his discretion, he gave his mother the abbreviated version of what occurred after the artifact came into his possession.

"We've been double crossed by your hand-picked thief?" Morgase murmured, her voice becoming brittle. "Is that what you're telling me?"

"It seems so," Mordred replied in what he hoped was a placating tone. "But have no fear, I can handle this. It's simply a brief delay."

"Can you?" his mother scoffed. "Really? Because right now, how you've handled this has put all that we've strived for at risk. We signed a contract in blood with the Daemon King. We promised that we would free him from the potential constraints offered by the artifact and in return he promised that he would free us from the burden of your father. We need that item. I didn't waste a year and millions of dollars just so you could lose the artifact as soon as we gained possession of it."

"I remember quite well all that we did, mother." He tried to incorporate a hard edge into his voice, but to his ears he sounded whiny more than anything else. His mother's look of disdain confirmed that she agreed with him. "I was there.

Remember? I've been leading this effort from the very beginning."

Morgase slapped him hard across the face. What frightened Mordred wasn't the blow. Rather, it was the deadly calm in his mother's voice when she spoke next. "Now is not the time for your flippant humor, Morry. The Daemon King does not make deals with the Teg frequently, and when he does, he always takes them seriously. Lethally so."

"Yes, but mother, even if we can meet the terms of the deal, he'll still be stuck in his prison. There's no way ..."

Morgase slapped her son again, a deadness seeping into her voice as she watched him rub his cheek, the marks of her fingers highlighted by an angry red. "I didn't raise you to be a fool, Morry. Even if the Daemon King remains in his prison, he can still send his servants to do as he wills. And the first thing he'll have them do is us. Not until we've used the artifact against him will we be able to stop worrying about that."

"You can't be ..." Morry took a quick step back, lifting his hands as a way of apology, desperate to avoid another slap. "I'm not playing the fool, mother, I swear it. I just don't understand why you're so worried about the Daemon King. Next to father, you're the most powerful of all the Teg. Why should we fear that blowhard and his servants? If they come against us before we use the artifact, we can handle them. I have no doubt about that."

"You really are a fool." Morgase shook her head in disbelief. "Have you learned nothing that I've taught you?"

"Mother, please, you need to understand ..."

"You need to understand a few things, Morry," Morgase cut in, "as it seems that I've missed some key parts of your education. You need to realize that I'm actually more powerful than your father."

"I'm not disputing that, mother," Mordred protested. "That's why I'm saying that we have little to fear from the Daemon King."

Morgase stared at her son, then she shook her head in dismay. "All that I have done for you, yet you still don't understand."

"Understand what?" Mordred demanded.

"You still don't see what is staring you right in the face."

"Mother, what are you talking about?" Mordred was lost. He had no clue what his mother was implying.

"As you said, Morry," Morgase began, speaking slowly, clearly, so that there was no confusion, "I am the strongest Teg. Stronger than your father in the Grym. Stronger than Merlin. No one can stand against me in that regard. And as I was explaining before you interrupted me, your father is simply luckier than I am. He has the right friends. They've made sure that he's kept the throne while we've been stuck on the sidelines."

"Yes, mother, I know. That's what ..."

"Silence!" Morgase hissed, Mordred shutting his mouth immediately, not having seen his mother this angry in quite some time. Not wanting to be the one to bear the brunt of her fury. Some very uncomfortable memories rising up within him. "This is not a conversation, Morry. It has never been a conversation between us, even though you seem to think differently. I am the strongest Teg. You work for me. Do you understand?"

Mordred's first instinct was to deny his mother's claim. He didn't want to admit the truth. But he couldn't ignore it.

She was right. He served her. He would continue to serve her. Until he became more powerful than her. Then he would put his mother in her place. Then he would rule the Teg as they should be ruled.

"Yes, mother," he replied quietly, trying to add some tiny hint of obsequiousness to his voice, which proved difficult for him. He would give his mother her victory now, believing that not too long in the future he would enjoy his victory over her. Over all the Teg, in fact.

"Good," Morgase replied in a more even tone, mollified for the time being. "Now as I was saying, unlike your father, I look at the world with my eyes open. I see the world for what it is and not what I want it to be. That's why we are almost in the position to do what we have been seeking to do for the last three centuries."

"I understand, mother, truly I do. Have no concern about …"

"If you understood, Morry, then you wouldn't have lost the artifact that I contracted to have stolen!" Morgase shouted in a rage, her son taking another involuntary step back, his face turning pale. Remembering the many times while he was growing up that he was in the exact same situation as this one. Always dreading when it would happen again, his mother blaming him for their struggles.

"I'm sorry, mother. Truly. But I will make this right. I will." He spat out the words as fast as he could, hoping that they would ease his mother's temper.

"Listen to what I'm about to tell you, Morry, and listen well. The Daemon King is not of this world. He exercises a power that we cannot. He exercises a power that in his hands is stronger than the Grym. Until we control him, we do not control his power. Until we control his power, he is a threat. Do you understand?"

"Yes, mother."

"Yes, mother, what?" Morgase demanded.

Mordred forced himself not to growl in anger, seeking to keep a strong hold over his boiling emotions. Even now, his mother sought to control him. Just as she sought to control everything.

His first instinct was to lash out. But he had learned that doing so came at a high cost and would only prove detrimental to his future. Mordred took a deep breath. Now was not the time to challenge her. He knew that. Not yet.

"Yes, mother, I understand," he answered with as much meekness as he could manage, which wasn't very much.

She nodded, apparently satisfied by his response. "Am I afraid of the Daemon King? No. But I am wary of him. I suggest you be wary of him as well. Until we control him, we control nothing at all."

Morgase turned away from her son then and stepped up to the window, looking out at the freshly cut grass. She could see a storm settling over the compound, the Paladins walking the grounds having slipped on their rain gear. The wind was beginning to pick up, the sky darkening.

It was only appropriate, she believed. There was a storm brewing inside as well.

"Do you know where the thief who has betrayed us is?"

"I have a good idea, mother."

"And you're taking the appropriate measures to retrieve her?"

"I am," Mordred confirmed with a sharp nod. "We will have her shortly."

"Along with the artifact?"

"Of course, mother. Both her and the artifact. Have no fear in that regard."

She nodded. "You have until the end of the day tomorrow, Morry. If the artifact and the thief aren't in our hands by the end of the day tomorrow, I will take over. I will correct your mistake ... just as I have so many times in the past." There was a resignation and disappointment in her voice that hung heavily between them.

Before her son could offer even the hint of an argument, Morgase turned away from him and walked out of the room, making for the door at her back that was so familiar to her from her time living in a castle in Wales. Old wood wrapped in steel.

The protective sigils carved into the surface flashing to life when she passed through.

Yet all that was of little interest to her. Her mind on other matters.

Morgase had done a deal with the one being she normally wouldn't. But she had little choice.

It was the only way to get what she wanted. Only with the Daemon King's help could she have acquired the artifact in the first place.

If she could push the deal over the finish line, then turn it in the direction that the Daemon King was not expecting, she'd finally gain the revenge that she so desperately desired. Her brother having much to answer for. But if she failed to meet the terms of the contract and do what she needed to do ...

She didn't want to think about that. She believed that she could hold her own against the Daemon King, but she really didn't have any desire to find out.

And the only way to avoid that confrontation was to regain control over the thief and the artifact as quickly as possible.

Otherwise, the Daemon King would be the least of her worries.

Word would spread quickly among the Teg that *The Book of Whispers* was back in the world for the first time in centuries.

Many of her competitors wouldn't hesitate to claim it for themselves. If for no other reason than to turn the power contained within that ancient artifact against her.

3

AN UNLUCKY BREAK

"A winery?" Gregor demanded. "We're infiltrating a winery? You can't be serious. I thought our target was in prison." He huffed in disappointment. "I was hoping that we'd at least have to breach a wall. Maybe blow something up. This is no fun at all."

Gregor and a squad of Knights hiked along the path, avoiding the creepers and prickers that reached for them. Out of habit, they stayed close to the trees at the top of the ridge so that they wouldn't be visible to anyone who might be looking up from below.

Their leather armor had been modified with the Grym so that it blended into their surroundings, whether the forest at their backs or a cityscape. For all intents and purposes, they were invisible unless a watcher knew exactly where they were and what to look for.

"Keep your voice down," ordered Jonas. He and his ten Knights of the Round might be well camouflaged, but voices tended to carry atop ridges. He had no desire to be discovered because of a novice mistake.

"I'm just saying," Gregor continued in a much quieter tone that was close to a whisper, "a winery? Really?"

"What did you expect?" Jonas murmured, pushing out of the way a long vine that hung down from a tree growing close to the ridge line.

"Certainly not this," Gregor grumbled. From where he was marching along the crag, every so often he glimpsed the fields upon fields of grapevines running up the slope that began at the base of the ridge and ended close to a large home made of steel and glass. Several barns and warehouses were just off to the west within easy walking distance of the mansion.

Peaceful. Bucolic. Idyllic, even.

And where one of their most dangerous enemies had been forced to take up residence.

"A Supermax prison," Gregor murmured. "A mine, maybe, with a cell three miles down. Or a steel tube runed with the Grym dropped into the Mariana Trench. But not this."

Jonas shrugged. He didn't want to waste his time arguing with Gregor. Because much like all the other Knights with them, he had thought much the same as the disenchanted Gregor. He just didn't feel the need to give voice to all that ran through his mind.

Somehow the Fallen Knight had bested the Daemon King more than a decade before. And somehow the Fallen Knight had imprisoned him.

But why a winery of all places?

It didn't make sense.

Jonas sensed the Grym surrounding the large estate, the shield of energy that was only visible to those of the Tylwyth Teg.

Admittedly, the barrier served its purpose just as effectively as would any of the other options Gregor had mentioned, the Daemon King restricted to the property that extended several acres around the knoll in all directions.

Even so, it was a strange solution. And Jonas couldn't fault Gregor or the other Knights for questioning it.

He understood why Draig had not destroyed the Daemon King when he had the chance. The politics and realities involved that stayed his hand.

No one could fault him.

Draig finishing the job when he had the Daemon King under his blade would have caused more problems than it would have solved and led to a period of unrest among the Teg that was best avoided. That had been avoided thankfully.

Still, this was the solution?

Locking away one of the greatest threats to the Tylwyth Teg at a winery that also had a large open-sided barn near the lake on the other side of the hill that on the weekends was used to host bands and other entertainment while food trucks rolled in? The Daemon King couldn't leave but others could enter the property?

It seemed more a vacation for the Master of the Abyss than a prison term.

It didn't make any sense to Jonas, and he didn't like it when the facts didn't make sense.

Of course, did all that really matter? He had been given an assignment, and he would complete that assignment just as he had completed all the others given to him ever since he joined the Knights of the Round three decades before.

"I just don't understand," Gregor grumbled again, shaking his head in disbelief.

"When the Fallen Knight defeated the Daemon King, he granted leniency," Jonas said, hoping that a brief explanation would stop Gregor from asking more questions and get him to focus on their assignment. "Instead of imprisoning the Daemon King in some other place like those that you suggested, Draig locked him away here. From what I understand, it was the best decision that the Fallen Knight could make at the time."

"But a winery?" Gregor whined again. "King Arthur actually agreed to it?"

Jonas closed his eyes for just a moment as they trod along the path, pinching the bridge of his nose between his thumb and forefinger. He was losing patience with Gregor. He was a good Knight. He had served well for almost ten years. But sometimes, as he was doing now, Gregor didn't know when to keep his mouth shut and just concentrate on the task at hand.

"King Arthur said as much," Jonas explained in a weary tone, "although from what I heard he didn't have much of a choice."

"Didn't have a choice?" Gregor scoffed. "The King Teg always has a choice."

"Not this time. The Fallen Knight did the deal with the Daemon King and Merlin ratified it before King Arthur could stop them. Rather than spending his sentence in the deepest hole in Tartarus, just as he deserves, the Daemon King gets to spend it here instead."

"From where he could continue to cause problems for the rest of us," Gregor muttered.

"From where he is continuing to cause problems for the rest of us," Jonas clarified. "Otherwise, we wouldn't be here."

Although Jonas actually was more than pleased that this was the setting for his current assignment. Better this than some dreary cavern three miles below ground.

Scout the Daemon King's property and identify points of infiltration.

Simple.

No muss. No fuss.

Once that was done, Jonas would develop a strategy for when the Knights came back in force.

"If the Daemon King is locked away, why are we wasting time doing this?"

"Because we follow orders, Gregor. It's as simple as that."

"I understand that, Jonas, have no fear. And I understand as well that the Daemon King is still doing business from what looks to me more like home detention rather than a prison cell. But why make a play for him now? He hasn't bothered anyone since the Fallen Knight took him off the board. From what I understand, for the most part he's left us alone ever since Draig put him here."

"Gregor, how long have we known each other?" Jonas asked with a weary sigh.

The narrow game trail they were following along the edge of the wood was wider here, becoming more of a path as they entered a copse that would keep them out of sight for the next quarter mile before they curled around the far edge of the cliff and headed down, approaching the winery from the west.

When King Arthur had given Jonas and his squad this charge, he hadn't been able to provide much detail about the property. What magical wards and other defenses were in place. How many guards there were. How many points of ingress and egress. He couldn't really tell them anything at all.

That lack of intelligence had worried Jonas, and for good reason. In the past when he had been sent out on a mission, he had been briefed thoroughly. But for this, he knew virtually nothing. Not even Merlin could provide any useful details beyond the bare minimum.

Not only strange. Also alarming.

Maybe that's why King Arthur was so interested in learning more about the property that served as the Daemon King's prison. He didn't know all that he needed to know in order to put his larger plan in motion.

Although Jonas did know that he was getting tired of

Gregor's unending questions and complaints. If he didn't shut up soon, Jonas would shut the Knight up himself.

"Ever since I became a Knight."

"And what was one of the first lessons I taught you?"

"To always put on a clean pair of underwear before a mission because you didn't know how long it would take and you wanted to avoid chafing. I did that this morning, so no worries there." Gregor's grin, which set Jonas' temper to a simmer, was both one of pride and good humor, having little doubt that his response would get under his commander's skin despite its truthful nature.

"That, yes, although it's not relevant to our current conversation," Jonas replied with a hiss of exasperation. "The first thing I told you when you joined my squad."

"When given a mission, do the mission. Never question it."

Jonas nodded and continued quickly, worried about what else Gregor might decide to spout if he was given the chance. "Excellent. Now stop asking questions. King Arthur sent us here to scout the prison. He sent us here to prepare the way so that the Knights of the Round could come in force and eliminate the Daemon King once and for all. So that's what we do."

"You think King Arthur is ready to do that?" Gregor wondered.

Jonas shrugged. He couldn't really answer that question. It wasn't like the King Teg confided in him. Still, he had his suspicions. "The Daemons don't want to be in their world. They want to be in ours. They want to take over ours. Destroy the Daemon King and the Daemons will no longer be able to leave the Daemon Realm until a new King is selected and gains the power necessary to send them out into our world and the many others where they can wreak their havoc. It could take centuries for that to happen. That helps us now. It wouldn't have ten years ago when Draig fought the Daemon King. Thus, the change in strategy."

"I understand all that, Jonas. You don't need to sound all high and mighty."

"I was simply explaining so that you would stop asking questions," Jonas replied through clenched teeth, his patience at the breaking point.

Gregor didn't seem to notice his commander's rising irritation. Either that or he didn't seem to care. "You believe all the PR crap they're feeding us about what the Daemons want?"

Rather than berating Gregor, Jonas snorted out a laugh. "You actually expect me to answer that considering who we work for?" He shook his head in mock amusement, failing to notice how some of the shadows in among the trees that lined the path were moving in opposition to the leaves that obeyed the wind that blew south to north. "In the last few months, King Arthur has done everything short of declaring war on the Daemons. Why? I don't know. Does he have good cause? I don't know. And I don't care. As you said, when given a mission, do the mission. Never question it."

"Yes, but Jonas ..." Gregor began, wanting to continue to argue with his commander.

"Whether the Daemons actually want to take over the Teg world or it's just a ploy that's part of a larger strategy isn't relevant," Jonas cut in, seeking to prevent Gregor from going off on another tangent. "Whether we're being fed the truth or the truth as King Arthur wants us to know it doesn't matter. What the King Teg wants, the King Teg gets. And it's clear that he wants the Daemons gone. For good. Now stop asking questions and concentrate on the mission."

Jonas halted abruptly, almost running into Horatio's broad back, the Knight walking a few yards in front of them stopping. Rather than cursing at Horatio, he cursed himself for being a fool.

The other Knights, who had been doing their best to ignore his conversation with Gregor, noticed it well before he did.

They had turned outward in response, forming a small circle with Jonas and Gregor in the center.

They weren't alone in the wood. They never had been. They just hadn't noticed until now.

But what could it be?

Guards this far from the property? He didn't think there were guards, as Draig's magical barrier was enough to contain the Daemon King.

Jonas didn't have long to ponder those and the many other questions that ran through his mind. Several large shadows detached themselves from the trees, a few even dropping down from the branches above.

When those shadows materialized in the dim light that illuminated the trail, Jonas' eyes widened in shock, a trickle of cold sweat running down his spine.

He reached for the sword on his back, pulling it free from the scabbard, all the Knights with him doing the same.

"There's no need for that," growled the Daemon who stood opposite him. "We are not here to harm you. If we were, you and your Knights already would be dead."

Even Horatio's large form couldn't block Jonas from seeing the creature. At least as best as he could, because the Daemon and its ilk blended extremely well into their surroundings. Just as they were designed to do.

The Knights of the Round were quite familiar with Daemons, having come up against these creatures a great many times in the past.

That only stood to reason.

King Arthur butted heads with the Daemon King frequently, the Master of the Abyss a constant annoyance. A threat to his rule if Arthur let down his guard. Just as Jonas and the Knights had done then, never thinking that these creatures could take them by surprise.

The weaker Daemons were made of spirit, not yet having

earned the gift of substance that only could be bestowed upon them by their master. To survive and serve the Daemon King when these lowest of the Daemons came into the Natural World from theirs, they had to claim a human body.

Alive or dead these creatures rarely cared. Male or female didn't matter either.

These lesser Daemons simply needed the flesh so that they could move through the Natural World as they needed to. The only real limitation if they chose someone who died was how badly decomposed the body was.

The Arch Daemons were stronger. They had their own bodies, having earned the trust and the good will of the Daemon King. They could appear as humans. As animals. A mix between the two, such as a centaur or a shifter. Or they could take some other monstrous shape.

The only limitation was that Arch Daemons could not change their shape once they selected it. To do that, they had to return to the Daemon Realm.

That was tied to the fact that they could leave their home plane for only so long.

How quickly they needed to return depended on their strength. The tremendous energy required to enter and then remain in other worlds weakened all Daemons.

Therefore, they had no choice but to return to their own. To do otherwise put their very existence at risk.

Once back in the Abyss, they would need time to recuperate. To take in the sustenance that only could be obtained in the Daemon Realm. Then, once they had regained their power, they could decide what form to assume when next they left their own world on another task for their master.

These creatures who had slipped out from the shadows of the forest and surrounded the Knights without them even realizing it clearly were the more powerful Arch Daemons.

The five had taken the same form.

Many Knights of the Round believed it was their most lethal form.

Claws.

The hunters of the Daemon King.

Manlike creatures that were covered in greyish black scales who stood seven feet tall if not a head more. Small fangs hung over their lips, and their noses were broad and wide, almost as if they had been punched in the face one too many times. Their eyes were a deep black that appeared to glow. And spikes ran down their shoulders to their forearms, their claws larger than catchers' mitts. Thus, their name.

And, perhaps most worrisome for the Knights, a natural armor shielded their chests, arms, and thighs, which meant that it would be that much more difficult for them to cause injury with their swords. Even with their steel infused with the Grym, cutting through an Arch Daemon's hardened flesh would be a challenge, taking several strikes in the same place to breach it.

"Why should I believe you?" Jonas asked.

The Claw considered his question. The Arch Daemon understood why the Knight was hesitant to take him at his word. Knights and Daemons had been enemies since the Knights came into existence more than a thousand years before. If their positions were reversed, he would be just as skeptical.

"You shouldn't," the Claw replied, shrugging his broad, spiked shoulders. "I assume that because of your grey hair you have served as a Knight for a long time."

"I have," Jonas confirmed.

Jonas' mind worked furiously for a solution to his dilemma. Twelve Knights against five Claws?

Not good odds.

For the Knights.

The Knights were excellent warriors. Few other Teg could match them when blades were drawn.

But against this many Arch Daemons?

They would be lucky if any of them survived.

"Then you know that I and my brethren have no love for you or your companions."

"The feeling is mutual."

The Claw actually smiled at that, if it could be called a smile. The creature's sharp teeth, perfect for ripping into flesh, were revealed for just a heartbeat.

"But you also know that I and my brethren obey our master. And our master does not wish for us to draw blood. He wishes for us to take you to him."

"You want to take us to the Daemon King?" Jonas asked, not quite believing what he was hearing.

"Yes, that is what our master has charged us with," the Claw confirmed.

"Why?"

"We do not question our master, Knight. We simply do as he commands."

Jonas nodded, lips pursed as he did . It seemed that the Daemon King and Arthur Pendragon were the same in that respect. They both required unquestioned loyalty.

And perhaps this was the fix that he was looking for with respect to their dilemma. Perhaps he could get his squad out of this mess without any or all of them dying.

But he would need to handle matters delicately. Because he had little cause to place much faith in a Daemon's promises.

Jonas' concerns in that respect proved unnecessary, as Gregor took his ability to decide their next step out of his hands.

"Die, Daemon scum!" the Knight shouted. His sword raised above his shoulder, Gregor was poised to slash down with his glowing steel as he charged toward the Claw just a few yards to his front.

When Gregor attacked, all of the Knights followed. Listening to their instincts. Not thinking.

Jonas had no choice but to join them, although he did so with a deep foreboding tightening his chest.

He knew how this skirmish was going to end.

The Knights fought well. Although they met with little success. Their Grym-touched blades did nothing more than chip off a few pieces of armored flesh from the Claws the few times that they actually struck their adversaries, and even then it was more luck than skill.

The Claws were too fast. They used the shadows around them too well. There, then not. Appearing and disappearing on a whim. Evading ...

Jonas' mouth opened in surprise while he swung his steel in a wide arc, seeking to slice across a Claw's throat.

His blade missed by a hair, yet that was all the Claw needed. Sensing his momentary vulnerability as he left himself open to an attack, Jonas believed that he was about to die.

Shockingly, instead of punching his daggerlike fist into his chest, the Claw held back. Shouldering into Jonas and knocking him backward instead.

His Knights were fighting to kill.

The Claws weren't.

At least not at the beginning of the clash.

Not until their restraint left them, which happened only a few heartbeats later, the Daemons' natural instincts becoming too strong for them to resist.

Once that happened, the clash ended swiftly, one Knight after another dying a painful death, the Claws' razor-sharp digits colored in blood.

Gregor first, his head removed from his shoulders. Horatio next, much of his chest missing thanks to a Claw ripping through his ribs. Then all the others. None of his men lasting for more than a few seconds.

Until only Jonas remained.

His Knights dead all around him, he gave in to his own impulses. He knew that he stood no chance against a Claw, much less five, so he did something that he never expected that he would.

He ran.

Scrambling off the trail and into the wood, Jonas allowed his fear to guide him. His terror taking control. Leading him to he didn't know where, only caring that it took him away from the Claws.

Jonas skidded to a stop when he broke free from the trees, the edge of the cliff just a foot away from him, the large vineyard stretching out below and the mansion shining brightly in the waning sunlight.

The sounds of pursuit drawing closer, Jonas turned to face the Claws who sprinted out of the shadows. They skidded to a stop right in front of him, only a few yards away, the space along the ledge narrow and tight.

Gulping in fear, Jonas took a step backward, bringing his sword up, preparing to defend himself from the Claw who was reaching toward him.

"Stop, Knight," hissed the Daemon who had spoken to him before all hell broke loose. "We did not want this. We did not want to fight. Come with us now. Our master waits. You need not die."

But despite the Claw's remarkable speed and agility, he was too late.

As he pivoted around, Jonas' back foot slipped off the edge of the cliff. His balance lost, instead of reaching for the claw the Daemon offered to prevent him from falling, Jonas tried to swing his steel one more time.

Jonas sliced through nothing but air. Before he even

thought to scream, he was dead, a broken bag of bones on the rocky ground far below.

The Claw looked down in puzzlement, not understanding why the Knight persisted with his efforts despite the perilous nature of his circumstances. Nevertheless, he couldn't say that he was saddened by the Knight's death or those of his companions.

He was disappointed, however. And he was worried. "The Daemon King will not be happy."

"We didn't do anything," the Claw standing next to him said. "The Knights started this clash. We were just defending ourselves. Trying to disarm them until it became too much."

"That doesn't matter. We failed. Our master wanted to talk with Pendragon's Knights. That was all. And now he can't."

"He will understand," the other Claw said, although the Daemon didn't sound like he believed his own words.

"There are a dozen dead Knights on the fringe of our master's property. That's all the incentive that the King Teg needs. Arthur will say whatever he must to get what he wants. And it will be as the Knight said. Pendragon wants to destroy us. We have given him the reason to do so."

The other Claw had no response to that, the terrifying creature seeming to deflate as the reality struck him. "You're right, the Daemon King will not be happy."

4

PISSING MATCH

"Are you sure about this Raik?"

The biker, whose denim and leather strained at the seams, his immense size and bulging muscles bringing to mind a WWE wrestler, gave his pack member a snort of disgust and a condescending lift of one eyebrow. Although that last was difficult to make out.

His hair, a tangled mess that more resembled a rat's nest, and his long, thick beard that extended almost to his belt, hid most of his face. Except for his golden eyes, which burned with a manic energy.

"Lost your balls, Dolph? I didn't expect that from you."

The Renegade walking next to Raik scowled, not appreciating the insult. He did no more than that, however. Biting his tongue just as he always did.

Raik led the pack. Dolph did not want to challenge him for supremacy. He didn't even want to be perceived as challenging Raik for control of the pack.

He had seen what happened the two other times one of their pack had done so. Or rather when one of them had of his own volition and the other had been goaded into it by Raik, who wanted to make a point. Both challengers had looked like nothing more than a side of beef when Raik was done with them. Something that Dolph wanted to avoid.

No, he hadn't lost his balls. Dolph just exercised more common sense than all of the other Renegades.

"No, Raik," Dolph replied in as even a tone as he could manage. He worked hard to control his natural aggressiveness, a challenge for him despite his desire to stay on Raik's good side. "Just concerned, that's all."

He, Raik, and two other Renegades, Hubie and Harold, had driven their motorcycles into Kraken Cove, parking by the town green. As soon as they pushed themselves up from their seats, the few people out this early in the morning, the sun just beginning to rise in the east, had disappeared.

Only the bakery had its lights on, but it was still too early to open the doors.

As Dolph took in Kraken Cove, it felt like he had ridden into a ghost town. No, that wasn't quite right. It felt like he had arrived right before the gunfight that was always the pivotal scene in all those old Westerns he liked to watch.

Quiet. Still. Anticipatory. A hint of menace in the air.

"There's no need to worry, Dolph. Pull your panties out of your crack and grow a pair."

Dolph growled softly, his golden eyes flashing. He could hold back his temper for only so long. Even with his alpha.

Raik laughed softly as he swept his gaze around the town square. "Good, there's the Dolph I know." Then he sniffed the air. "Do you smell her?"

Dolph's eyes narrowed. "You want to be seen?"

"I do."

"Why? Why not just hunt like we usually do?"

"Because time is of the essence. The gal paying us said as much. We have until the end of the week. That's it."

Dolph nodded in understanding. If they didn't take her,

they wouldn't get paid. And the Teg paying them might feel the need to make an example of their failure to complete the contract. Raik wanted to avoid that, having no desire to bear the brunt of her anger.

"Are you sure that this is the best way to go about things? Standing out here for everyone to see us? We could have come into town like we did before. Without anyone knowing."

"They knew."

"They knew? How did they know?"

"You can sense it just as well as I can," Raik said, disappointed in his second. "Instead of arguing with me, pay attention."

Dolph frowned, but he did as his pack leader suggested. "The Grym."

"Of course the Grym," Raik growled. "We knew that before. That's what the Witch used to slow us down when we almost took her yesterday."

"Yes, but that ..."

"Stop arguing, Dolph, and take a sniff."

Dolph did as his boss ordered. His eyes widened. "I can't remember the last time the Power of the Ancients has felt so strong."

"That's because it's never felt this strong in one place," Raik corrected.

"The entire town. You mean to say we've wandered into a secret enclave of Teg?"

Raik shook his head. "No, we didn't wander in. We came here not giving a damn who lives here. That will give them pause."

"It might make them angry as well."

"And if it does, all the better." Raik spun around in a slow circle. "Do you smell her?"

Dolph took another sniff. "No, I don't."

"Someone is hiding her," Raik nodded knowingly. Not surprised.

"Then maybe coming here wasn't such a good idea, Raik. If there's a Teg here who's strong enough to hide her, then we might get more trouble than we want."

"I'm right, your balls have shriveled up inside you." Raik barked out a laugh. "Your voice going to change, Dolph? Rise a few octaves finally?"

Another low growl escaped from deep within Dolph's throat. He cut it off as soon as he realized what he was doing. Dolph would have ripped off the head of anyone who had just insulted him in such a way. Anyone other than Raik.

Maintaining an iron grip on his temper so that he didn't do anything rash, Dolph tried again. "I'm just worried that our coming into town will spook her." He motioned toward the buildings to their front. A bakery. A bookstore. A bar. "We know she's here. Why not hunt a bit more before showing ourselves? She can't hide here forever. We have until the end of the week. That still gives us plenty of time to locate her."

"Because I want to spook her, Dolph. I want her to run."

Dolph's brow furrowed as he thought about that. Then he began to understand. "You don't just want her. You want a fight."

Raik grinned maliciously, only his bright white teeth visible through his unkempt whiskers. "After what happened to Derrick and the others, yes, I do. Revenge is best served with a claw across the throat."

His voice contained a barely restrained hunger for vengeance. The Renegades ran the East Coast. They had a reputation to maintain.

If they didn't, some other pack would find the courage to challenge them.

Raik had little doubt that he and his crew could withstand any rivals, but it would waste time and resources that could be better used elsewhere. Especially since he had lost a good number of his pack just yesterday thanks to Derrick's incompetence. It would take time to rebuild his numbers. And that was time they might not have if they displayed any weakness.

Dolph's eyes brightened, a small smile curling his lips. "You want more than the girl." He nodded as understanding finally dawned. "You want the one who helped her. You want the Lightkeeper."

"I always knew you weren't as stupid as you looked," Raik growled.

Dolph ignored the slight. "You think only four of us can take him after what Lucius told us?"

Raik snorted in disgust, then spit a large glob of phlegm onto the sidewalk. "Guess I was wrong. Guess your balls haven't dropped after all."

"I'm just saying, Raik, from what Lucius said, it sounded like ..."

"Look what the wet dog dragged in."

The melodic voice caught the four bikers by surprise, Dolph never finishing his thought.

Raik and his brothers turned slowly, somewhat surprised to discover who had insulted them.

Standing in the middle of the deserted road was an older woman with frizzy hair that stuck out in all directions. She was wearing a multicolored robe that was hard to look at for more than just a few seconds, the pattern disorienting, all the while running her right hand through the thick fur of a monstrously large St. Bernard that was almost as tall as she was.

"Who the hell are you?" growled Raik.

"Who the hell are you?" demanded the woman. Her eyes sparked with a power that put all four bikers on edge, their hackles rising.

"You're a Witch," hissed Raik.

"I am *not* a Witch," snorted the woman, clearly offended by the remark. "I'm much worse."

Her statement led to a brief silence that was broken when Raik began laughing loudly. Dolph, Hubie, and Harold followed along, although they really weren't sure why they did.

Dolph in particular, the woman squaring up to them making him distinctly uncomfortable. The dog even more so, which he found strange and even more disconcerting, because few of the Teg could put him on edge.

Maybe it was because Dolph sensed the power radiating from the strangely dressed woman. Moreover, taking a good look at that dog, and how its eyes flashed, he got the distinct impression that there was more to that animal than met the eye. Much more. And he wasn't sure that he wanted to find out what that might be.

"I asked you your name," Raik said, taking a few threatening steps toward the woman. "I'll have it."

He stopped when the dog growled and placed himself in front of her.

"No reason to get excited, Pinkie," the woman said, speaking to the dog as she patted his flank a few times. "He's just trying to be polite, but his manners are lacking. He was never housebroken." Then she tsked. "Although you're right, darling. I can understand why you don't like him. He and his litter do need baths." The woman turned her focus to Raik then, her eyes glowing a deep purple. "My name's Peggy Rose, puppy."

Raik's eyes widened for a heartbeat, narrowing just as swiftly. Dangerously so. "Did you call me puppy?"

Peggy Rose appeared confused. "I'm sorry, puppy, but do I need to speak louder? I thought I was quite clear. Riding that hog damage your hearing? Or are you always this dense?"

Raik stared at the woman, not quite sure what to do. He hadn't faced a situation such as this one for quite some time.

Someone openly testing his authority. Questioning his dominance. "You dare to challenge me, woman?"

Peggy Rose snorted then laughed softly. "I don't dare anything. I do, puppy. I called you a puppy because you are a puppy. You're huffing and puffing like you're the Big Bad Wolf and you're going to blow all the houses down. I'm sure such a one-dimensional, lazy approach has worked for you in the past, because I know you're not stupid. But here it won't work for you ... *puppy.*"

The woman's voice deepened, hinting at a hidden power. "Because you have not yet realized, although the mongrel behind you has – I can tell by the look in his eyes, that slight touch of fear -- that there are bigger, badder, and tougher Teg than you. Several of them right here in Kraken Cove. Including me."

"You?" Raik snorted in disbelief, not sure what to make of the look of complete confidence that the woman was giving him. "Really? You seek a duel?"

Peggy Rose let out a deep laugh that was incongruous with her slight frame. "Me? No, puppy."

"I didn't think so," Raik snorted again, louder this time, having no doubt that she would back down when push came to shove.

"You'd be a waste of my time," Peggy Rose continued. "However, the fellows behind you wouldn't mind having a go. They're quite eager, in fact. They relish any chance to dish out a good beating before they sit down for breakfast."

Raik spun around swiftly, Dolph, Hubie, and Harold already facing off against this new threat. He was shocked to find standing right behind them three men with long blonde almost white hair slicked back off their scalps and beards running halfway down their chests all of the same design. What appeared to be a snake biting its own tail. Although he couldn't tell for sure. Some of the ends burnt off.

"How did you ..."

Dolph never got the chance to finish, Peggy Rose cutting him off. "Oh, how I love a good, old-fashioned pissing contest." Pinkie barked his agreement. "This is going to be fun."

"Who the hell are you?" demanded Raik.

"We are the Three Little Bears," the blonde behemoth in the center replied, his voice soft, almost a whisper, but clearly heard by everyone caught up in the encounter. He and his brothers liked the name that Cerridwen had bestowed upon them. They thought it was funny, and they needed funny after all that had led them to Kraken Cove.

"What are you talking about?" Raik asked, now thoroughly confused. "Three Little Bears?"

"I am Ragnar," the man in the center explained, shaking his head in disgust. It was so difficult to find worthy contestants these days. Except for Draig. None of them wanted to go up against Draig again. But these four stinking dogs? This could be fun. A good way to start the morning. "These are my brothers, Urs and Thorsen."

"Wonderful. Now why are you bastards ..."

"Perhaps less talking and more thinking, puppy," Ragnar said, interrupting Raik. He enjoyed the term that Peggy Rose had employed. Derogatory. Just as he wanted. Also appropriate in his opinion. "Use your senses, wolfman."

Reluctantly taking the giant's advice to heart, the response from the Renegades was immediate. They moved a few paces away from one another, gaining room to maneuver. Their golden eyes flashed brightly as they curled their large hands into fists. But they didn't shift. Not yet.

"Berserkers," Raik growled.

"Well done, wolfman. You are not as stupid as you look."

"You dare to insult me, bear?" Raik snarled, a deep rumble emanating from his chest. His teeth appeared to be longer.

Sharper. The shift was calling to him. Demanding that his true self emerge. Still, he held it in check.

The Three Berserkers sensed the struggle within the biker, knowing what could happen. But it had little effect upon them.

They stood there calmly. Completely at their ease. Waiting patiently. They didn't even reach for the three-foot-long metal bars that were strapped to their right thighs.

"I will not waste my time having the same conversation you just did with Peggy Rose," Ragnar replied in a deadly quiet voice. "And she's right. You and the rest of your litter stink. Have you never heard of a shower?"

Urs spoke then in Norwegian, the sides of his mouth curling into a mocking smile.

Raik and the other Renegades didn't understand what he was saying. Although the loud laughter that emanated a few seconds later from the two brothers told them all that they needed to know.

They were being insulted. Again.

These three Berserkers would learn soon enough the danger of treating him without the respect he deserved.

"Tread lightly, bear," Raik growled. He stepped in closer to Ragnar. So close that only a few inches separated them. "I've lost what little patience I had when I rode into this town."

"Am I'm supposed to be afraid because of that ... *puppy*?" Ragnar smiled, pleased at how his emphasis on the last word caused an involuntary tic under his challenger's left eye.

"You should be afraid, Berserker. Very afraid."

Ragnar's brow furrowed. "Is this how it is with your kind?"

"Is this how what is with my kind?" Once again, Raik was confused, finding this entire encounter unsettling because it wasn't following the pattern that he was used to.

Threat. Fight. Severe injury or death. Never his own, of course.

Yet this?

This felt like he was playing a game, and he didn't understand the rules, which meant that he couldn't win.

"You try to threaten but it sounds more like a plea for help." Ragnar's ice blue eyes flashed with amusement, gaining the reaction that he wanted from Raik.

When this engagement came to an end, he would thank Peggy Rose for asking him and his brothers to walk with her this morning. He had not anticipated this opportunity so soon after coming to Kraken Cove, and he was very much enjoying himself.

The biker growled even more deeply, his golden eyes gleaming brightly, filled with an almost unquenchable rage. Almost. "I will have your head on a spit, Berserker. I promise you that."

"Promises, promises, puppy. Don't make a promise that you can't keep, and this one, puppy, you will not be able to keep."

"You son of a ..."

Ragnar closed the distance between them in a flash, his nose touching Raik's. "Challenge me, puppy." The Berserker smiled, clearly savoring the confrontation. Clearly wanting to take the next step.

He rarely lost a combat. In fact, he never had until he had come up against Draig. Now, having tasted defeat, he felt the need to prove his talents once again. This wolfman would give him that chance.

"Challenge me, puppy," Ragnar goaded, "and you will get a chance to make good on your promise. But I make you this promise, puppy. If you play the fool and give in to your urges, I will taste your blood. Have no doubt of that. Because the bear will always kill the wolf. Always."

Raik's shoulders bunched together.

His muscles tensed.

He bent his knees slightly, preparing to launch himself at the Berserker.

His smile became a hungry leer as he contemplated what he was about to do.

He had not ridden into Kraken Cove with the intention of killing. He just wanted to flush the rabbit.

If he could force her to flee the town, then his task would be much easier. That would have to wait, however.

He had another task to complete first. He needed to demonstrate his dominance. He needed to demonstrate that there was no Teg who could stand against him and live.

His natural instincts becoming more prevalent in his decision making, he sensed another alpha standing nose to nose with him.

Raik knew how to handle a situation such as this one, because there was only one way. The way that he preferred.

"Wow. Just ... wow." Peggy Rose stood right next to Ragnar and Raik, clapping her hands together softly. She had slipped through the very large men facing off against one another with barely a sound, their focus so intent on one another that none of them even realized that she was there until she spoke. "The testosterone. I could probably smell it from a mile away. In fact, it's so bad, I'm afraid that I'm going to gag."

Her words broke the rising tension that had been just a hair away from leading the Berserkers and the Renegades down the path to violence.

That and Pinkie.

The overlarge St. Bernard was walking slowly around the small gathering of men much like how a shark circled around its prey before striking. Although the dog had eyes only for the Renegades.

Pinkie's slow stroll caught the attention of Dolph and then Hubie and Harold as well. Watching intently, they did a double take. Every other heartbeat, the dog's shape shimmered and changed.

They realized then that the woman's dog was a shifter just like they were. Not liking what they saw when the animal flickered, they took several steps back, leaving Raik to face off against the one named Ragnar.

"Raik, it's a ..."

"I know what it is, Dolph," Raik hissed through gritted teeth, his eyes still locked onto the Berserker. "I do not fear that creature."

"You might not be afraid," Peggy Rose said in a voice filled with doubt, "but I don't think that you're stupid. I suggest you and your friends say good-bye to Kraken Cove. Pinkie hasn't eaten yet this morning. You don't want to see what he's like when he gets hungry. He'll take a bite out of anything, even if it's sour and rancid."

"We are not done, Berserker," Raik said a few seconds later, finally stepping back a few feet. His movement broke for good the tension that had draped itself over the face-off.

Ragnar smiled in a way that offered a promise. "We *are* done, puppy. You have shown your true self. I know who you are."

"You have no idea who I am," Raik countered sharply.

"I know who you are, puppy, and I get the feeling that we will not meet again. Because your end will come at the hands of someone else. You will bite off more than you can chew, and you will choke on your own arrogance."

Before Raik could lunge at the Berserker, Dolph grabbed Raik by his arm. He allowed Dolph to pull him toward their motorcycles. Hubie and Harold already were seated and revving their engines.

"This isn't over," Raik shouted as he sat down and started his bike, giving a kick to the clutch and revving the engine. "You'll be seeing me again. Sooner than you'd like."

"I'll probably smell you before I see you," Peggy Rose replied, scrunching up her nose to make her point. "Take a shower ... if you know how, you mangy ..."

Peggy Rose frowned. The last of her words were lost in noise and exhaust as the Renegades gunned their engines and then sped down Market Street. She found that disappointing, because she wasn't done with what she thought would have been an excellent and very appropriate insult.

She'd save it for the next time she saw the Were. If she did. She had a feeling that Ragnar was correct.

"Thank you, Ragnar. I appreciate your and your brothers' help."

"It was nothing, although we would not have complained if we had the chance to test ourselves against those mongrels."

"I have no doubt that you would have done quite well," she offered, patting him gently on the arm. "Were you ever going to join us?"

Cerridwen stepped out from the shadows that obscured the side entrance to Tia's Bakes. "If you needed me, yes, but it seemed like you and the Three Little Bears had everything under control."

"For now," Peggy Rose murmured.

"They'll continue to be a problem," Cerridwen agreed.

"Until they get what they want," Peggy Rose confirmed.

"Or who," Cerridwen added. She was still wearing her apron, having just taken a batch of Draig's cranberry scones, gluten free of course, out of the oven. She needed to do that before joining the fun, not wanting them to burn before the morning rush.

Peggy Rose nodded. "I need to speak with Draig. Is he still at the lighthouse?"

"No, he got in early this morning. He's still at the bookstore."

Peggy Rose lifted an eyebrow. "Why do you sound so angry about that?"

"Because his sister was with him."

"Crap." Peggy Rose shook her head. What had started out as such a lovely morning was turning into a very trying day. "That's never a good thing."

5

BAD DECISIONS

"What am I supposed to do about Draig?"

Arthur Pendragon brushed his dark, wavy hair out of his eyes with a large, callused hand. He was dressed like a venture capitalist. Expensive suit. Open collar shirt. A hand-made watch carved from a tree that used to grow near Stonehenge.

However, he was anything but.

He stood in front of the ceiling-high window in his office on the top floor of the building he owned through Excalibur Capital. A private hedge fund. So private that there was only one investor.

Central Park spread out before him, the zoo just a few blocks to the north. With the sun shining brightly and not a cloud in the sky, it looked like it was going to be a beautiful day in New York City. That fact was completely lost on him.

"Why do you have to do anything about Draig?" Merlin frowned when he looked down at the sleeve of his cardigan sweater. He ran a finger over the coffee stain. Still wet. Merlin wiggled his fingers. A wispy white mist drifted out and burned away the coffee, leaving no sign of his clumsiness.

That's what he got for rushing around this morning, trying to gather as much information as he could, yet not knowing what information he needed to put the pieces of the puzzle together before they bit him in the ass.

And they were going to bite him in the ass. Of that he had no doubt.

He had been studying all the bits and bytes that had been coming in from his many and various sources and still he didn't have a clear perspective of all that was going on. That worried him.

There was a scheme in play.

He was sure of it.

Yet what it could be?

And who was at the center of it?

The only thing that he knew for certain was that all wasn't right among the Tylwyth Teg. He needed to figure out the cause before the undercurrent of concern that rippled through him shifted to fear and then perhaps into something worse.

"He lied to me," grumbled Arthur. "Can you believe that?"

"Of course I can believe it," Merlin chided. "You killed him."

"I did, you're right. And apparently I failed when I thought that I had succeeded."

"Thankfully you did." Merlin shrugged. "Besides, you were lucky."

"What do you mean I was lucky?" The man who had pulled Excalibur from the stone whipped around, his eyes blazing with fury at what he perceived to be an insult. Nothing he did ever resulted from luck.

Merlin's mild expression changed in an instant upon taking in Arthur's furious countenance. The Sorcerer's eyes flashed dangerously, his brow furrowing.

Even so, he was able to keep his agitation out of his voice. Getting into an argument with Arthur now would only prolong his time away from what he really needed to be doing.

Nevertheless, he refused to sugarcoat the truth. Arthur needed to understand that he wasn't omnipotent. He never had been no matter what he might tell himself and others.

"Draig held back during the combat."

"He did no such thing," protested Arthur. "I had him. I killed him. Or at least I would have if he hadn't tricked me."

"You had him because he let you have him. He wanted you to try to kill him. That was all part of his ruse."

"There is no way in all the hells that he ..."

"Arthur, please," Merlin said in a placating tone. "You know it just as well as I do. He could have killed you if he wanted to, but he didn't. Many times in fact during your duel. No one else might have seen it, but I did."

"He was never in a position to do any harm to me. I took the fight to him."

"Again, because he let you," Merlin replied, his expression sympathetic. He understood how hard it was for the prideful Arthur to acknowledge a harsh truth. "He was biding his time. He was using the combat to get what he wanted."

"He wanted me dead."

"If he wanted you dead, you would be dead," Merlin said in a tone that brooked no argument, his voice rising, his eyes burning, his wispy white hair sticking up as if he had stuck a finger in an electrical outlet. Patience was not one of his virtues. Not when someone didn't want to listen to him. "You know it just as well as I do. Now can we move on to a more important topic?"

"Say what you want, Merlin, I don't believe you." Arthur's expression shifted to a cunning that always worried the Sorcerer. Never a good sign because little good ever resulted from it. "I still need to do something about him."

"Why? He's not bothering anyone. He's just trying to live his life. Better just to leave him alone."

"Not bothering anyone?" Arthur growled. "After what he

did to me at the Dragon Vault? After what we lost because of him?"

Merlin shrugged, allowing some of his anger to fade away now that it appeared as if Arthur had calmed down somewhat. "Maybe it's best that the artifact is back in the Dragon Vault and that we don't have it."

"Best that we don't have it?" Arthur demanded, not quite believing what he was hearing. "Are you serious? *The Book of Whispers* was our chance to finally gain the victory we have been seeking for a thousand years. Ever since I took the Teg throne, in fact."

Merlin chose not to antagonize Arthur any further by clarifying that the victory he desired was his own. He was wasting enough time as it was this morning and getting into a pissing match wouldn't help.

"Do you not think that this conflict has gone on for too long?" Merlin asked in as mild a tone as he could manage. "Neither of you have the strength to defeat the other. That's been proven time and again."

"That was the whole point of the book, Merlin!" Arthur raged. "With that artifact finally in hand, I could have won our war once and for all. With Morgase out of the picture, I would have had one less threat to worry about."

"Morgase is not the threat you need to worry about," Merlin countered. "At least not now."

Arthur ignored or didn't hear what Merlin said, his thoughts focused on how he might still be able to gain the artifact that would give him the ability to subjugate any Teg and use the Power of the Ancients that they could call upon as if that power was his own. Enslaving them, true, but for the good of all the Teg. And he was the Teg, after all.

"Perhaps I should reach out to Eris again," Arthur mused. She had stolen *The Book of Whispers* from the Dragon Vault. If she could acquire it once, why not a second time?

Merlin didn't respond right away, not quite sure what he wanted to say. The desperation he saw in the King Teg's eyes disturbed him. It was becoming much too common.

"Eris is fickle at the best of times," the Sorcerer argued. Worried. Wondering if he would be reaching the point with Arthur that he dreaded sooner rather than later. "Besides, I wonder if perhaps she took the job initially for a reason other than the one she gave you."

That pulled Arthur from his depression and anger and his need to find some other way to acquire the artifact. "What are you talking about?"

"Perhaps Eris didn't accept your offer," Merlin suggested. "Perhaps she was directed to take it."

"By whom?"

"You know who, Arthur. Only one person could order Eris to do something."

Arthur thought about Merlin's theory. Unfortunately, the more he did, the more it made sense. "Why would she do that?"

"You'd have to ask her."

Arthur barked out a laugh. "Thank you, but no. She was quite clear about what she would do when she saw me again. I have enough problems as it is."

"Your first wise decision this morning," Merlin said with a slightly sarcastic nod that Arthur missed entirely, his mind back on what had been eating at him ever since his confrontation with his son in the Dragon Vault.

"This wouldn't be an issue if not for Draig," Arthur stated coldly. "If he had stayed dead, we would have the artifact that we need. I would have the power that I need. I, the Teg, would have nothing to fear."

"Do you really mean that?"

"Mean what?" Arthur asked, slightly confused.

"That it would have been better for Draig to stay dead," Merlin clarified, his expression strangely ambivalent although he was feeling anything but on the inside. Merlin had not wanted to meet with Arthur this morning, and the longer this dialogue continued, the more disheartened Merlin became. Seeing aspects of the man he had served for centuries that he had no desire to see. The man who had changed more than Merlin could have possibly imagined since the Sorcerer had met him when he was just a boy. "I take that to mean that it would have been better for you if your son actually was dead."

Arthur didn't answer, his face a thundercloud. Merlin understood why. He didn't want to incriminate himself.

"We have more to worry about than Draig, Arthur."

"Really," the King Teg scoffed. "More to worry about than the fact that my son has stolen Excalibur from me. That he keeps from me the one tool that could ensure the Teg's survival against our enemies. Besides all that, what else do I need to worry about?"

Merlin pursed his lips, not yet ready to respond. Then he shook his head slowly and sighed. Arthur had twisted in his own mind how he had lost his sword. Now Draig's sword. Just as Arthur was doing in so many other ways. Crafting his own reality and believing that because he was the King Teg it was *the* reality. That only his perspective was the one true perspective.

Draig hadn't taken Excalibur from his father. He never could have. The ancient weapon would never have allowed it. Rather, the sword had decided that a change was needed. That the son was more worthy than the father.

That had stung Arthur deeply. More than stung, actually. It was like an open wound that could never be healed, and that festering wound was poisoning Arthur.

"You sent Jonas and his squad to the Daemon King's prison."

"I did," Arthur confirmed. "He was charged with scouting our enemy's current residence."

"Jonas and all his Knights are dead," Merlin explained in a quiet voice.

"All of them?" Arthur asked, shocked.

"All of them," Merlin confirmed with a sad nod.

"How do you know?"

Merlin provided a brief explanation of what he had learned. "Why did you send them to scout the Daemon King's prison without telling me?"

"You had other matters to deal with," Arthur answered with a shrug. "Besides, it was supposed to be a simple job. Scout the surrounding territory. No more than that."

"No more than that? You sent them so that you could go after the Daemon King. That was their purpose. To find a way in. You believe that the Daemon King is vulnerable and you wanted to make a play for him."

"Why shouldn't I?" Arthur demanded, as if his decision to send the Knights to their deaths was a simple matter that required no further discussion. "They were tasked with that assignment when I believed that I was going to have *The Book of Whispers* in my possession. With that artifact, Morgase and the Daemon King would be eliminated as threats. For good. All for the benefit of the Teg."

Merlin nodded, though not in agreement. He could tell that Arthur was lying, or at least not telling him everything. "Is that so?"

"It is," Arthur said with a growing confidence, almost as if he was convincing himself of that fact the more he thought about it. "And now there's a debt to be paid. In blood."

"I would suggest that you wait before deciding to make good on that debt," Merlin stated calmly, even as his eyes blazed fiercely.

"You want me to do nothing?" Arthur was more than shocked. He was livid. "Daemons killed a squad of my Knights. That grievous act cannot be allowed to go unpunished."

"I know that," Merlin replied evenly, "and it will be. I am simply asking that instead you think before you act."

"You're suggesting that I go off half-cocked," Arthur said, his voice revealing his rising irritation. "You would dare to insult me?"

"I'm not suggesting anything, Arthur. Those were your words, not mine."

Arthur's expression turned shrewd in a flash. "Why do I put up with you, Merlin?"

"Because without me you never would have become what you are. That and the fact that everything you have now, everything that we've created, would fall apart around you if I wasn't here." Merlin spoke plainly, not a hint of arrogance in his tone. For him, he was simply stating a fact. No more than that.

"You really believe that?" Arthur chuckled softly, seemingly amused, although his dark eyes that burned brightly suggested otherwise. "Even after all that *I* have accomplished? Without *me*, the Teg might not even exist anymore. Without *me*, we had little chance of standing against our enemies. But we did. Because of *me*."

Merlin ignored Arthur's bragging. Apparently, the King Teg had forgotten that all that he accomplished had been the result of hard work and a high price paid, often in blood, pain, and sorrow, by so many others. And at the top of that list would be the son who Arthur wanted to remain dead.

"I know what you've done, Arthur," Merlin replied with absolute certainty. "Remember, I was by your side the entire time. As were so many others. Many of whom are no longer with us because they believed in you. They believed in the world that we were seeking to create. They gave their lives because of the future you offered. Willingly. Don't sully that sacrifice by giving full reign to your worst tendencies."

"The world that *I* was seeking to create," Arthur clarified, biting off the words. "*My* world."

Merlin smiled less than pleasantly then. Clearly, any argument he offered would fall on deaf ears. "If you'd like me to go, if you don't think that I can be of any further use to you, I'm sure that I can find something else to do. You need only say the word."

Arthur stared at Merlin before he smiled knowingly. "There will come a time when I will ask you to go, Merlin. Not now, however. I still have work for you." Besides, Arthur had no doubt that if he did leave Merlin's first visit would be to Draig. The Sorcerer and his son had been close ever since Draig was a child, Merlin taking on the responsibility of training him in the use of the Grym.

"Why do you want me to delay with respect to the Daemon King?" Arthur asked, shifting the topic.

"Williamsburg."

"Williamsburg?"

Merlin explained what had happened, as well as some of his suspicions as to why the Daemons challenged Draig.

"You want me to wait because of that confrontation?"

"I do," Merlin confirmed. "Let the Daemon King play his hand for a little while longer. Allow him to reveal more fully what he has in mind. There is little that he can do to us. And once we sniff out his plan, we can respond accordingly. Based on the facts, not supposition."

"I have a squad of dead Knights, Merlin. They deserve justice. I cannot allow that attack to go unanswered." Arthur grimaced and shook his head, not liking his advisor's proposal. "To do so would make me appear weak. And if I appear weak, then all the Teg appear weak. It will only incite the Daemon King all the more."

"You won't allow the attack to go unanswered, Arthur," Merlin explained. "You just won't respond right away. You will do so at a time of your choosing when the Daemon King will least expect it. Once we get a better sense of what he has in mind."

"Why would I accept what you're suggesting, Merlin?"

"You already know why, Arthur. You just don't like the reason. That's why you're drawing this out instead of making the decision that you know you need to make."

"Why were the Daemons in Williamsburg?" Arthur prodded.

"You already know that."

Arthur nodded. He did know. "Did the Daemons find what they were seeking in Williamsburg?"

"I don't believe so."

"Why not?"

"You already know the answer to that as well." Merlin sighed wearily. Arthur was testing him in a way that little else had since his duel with Morgase several hundred years before. However, at least with Morgase, the combat was energizing and got Merlin's blood flowing. This conversation was simply tedious.

"You're being more difficult than usual, Merlin," Arthur hinted, shaking his head in frustration as he began to pace in front of the window. "Why? We must deal with the Daemon King. He is the threat. He is also the opportunity."

"Are you sure about that, Arthur?"

Merlin's comment stopped Arthur in his tracks, the King of the Teg giving his friend and mentor a quizzical expression before he turned away and began pacing again, hands clasped behind his back. "Say what you mean, Merlin. I'm losing patience."

Merlin smiled, although not in a kind way. He was becoming increasingly irritated, and he needed to hide it. Otherwise, he would lose the chance that Arthur finally had given him.

"Arthur, I understand why you want to focus the Knights on

the Daemon King and his Horde, particularly after what happened to Jonas and his squad. However, I think there's more going on here than just that. I don't think the Daemon King is our primary concern."

"Not our primary concern?" Arthur scoffed. "Really? And why would you think that?"

"Because I believe that there is another player seeking to pull our strings. In fact, I get the feeling that this other player already is pulling our strings."

Arthur continued walking in front of the window, head down, pondering Merlin's words. "Do you have any proof?"

"Hard evidence? No."

"And that doesn't bother you?"

"Of course it bothers me," Merlin confirmed. "That's why I'm raising this issue with you now. We've faced situations such as this before. The last involving Draig when he played an essential role in halting the last ploy that was designed to usurp your throne. In the last thousand years, it's happened what, eight times? Ten maybe? I've lost track."

"What's your point, Merlin?"

"Every time it's happened in the past, Arthur, a threat to the Teg such as this one, I've always been able to sniff it out. Always. I would find bits and pieces and then threads. And then I'd follow the threads to the source. Every time. But now, just as in the past, I can see the bits and pieces. I can see the threads. But I can't follow them. A dead end every time I try to pull on them. The threads always come loose."

Arthur chuckled softly. "Maybe you're just seeing ghosts, Merlin. Maybe what you think is there, really isn't."

Merlin's eyes blazed furiously. "I don't appreciate your ridicule, Arthur. We don't have the time for this."

"Merlin, I'm not ridiculing you. I'm just wondering if you're pulling at threads that aren't there. Maybe that's why you're meeting with so little success."

Before saying something that he would regret, Merlin stopped himself. He took a deep breath, seeking the calm that wouldn't come. Despite the challenge, he was able to speak evenly, hiding the anger that was boiling within him.

"Perhaps I am, Arthur. Perhaps you're correct." Merlin shrugged. "But what if I'm right? What if there's another player we can't identify seeking to usurp the throne and gain control of the Teg? What if the Daemon King and Morgase are simply distractions?" Merlin nodded, then said in a much too reasonable tone, "I could be wrong, you're right. But what if I'm not? Are you willing to take that risk?"

Arthur stopped once again, turning toward the glass and staring out at the park, deep in thought. He had paid for his throne in blood, sweat, and tears, his and those loyal to him. Merlin was correct in that regard.

And the price paid had been worth it. With his Knights of the Round, he had brought stability to the Teg. Eliminating the turmoil that had plagued their world since well before he had pulled the sword from the stone.

What would happen if all of that came apart? What would happen if he and his Knights became embroiled in a fight that wasn't the real fight? In a fight that they couldn't win?

Chaos.

He couldn't have chaos.

He hated chaos.

Arthur preferred order.

He needed order.

It was a part of his DNA.

Observing him based on the reflection in the window, Merlin watched all the thoughts that played across Arthur's face. Just as he believed they would. Because though Arthur had allowed his arrogance to grow, he still had a sharp mind. He couldn't have survived for so long otherwise.

Many chafed at Arthur's heavy-handed approach. Many of

the Teg thought that he exercised a power that was undeserved and unnecessary.

But none of the Teg would deny that Arthur had done well for them. That his Knights had brought an order to their magical world that had been lacking before and was sorely needed.

Most of the Teg had no desire to return to that time, so they would forgive Arthur his hubris and his many trespasses to ensure the peace.

And Arthur would do whatever was required to ensure that his legacy, the world that he created, remained intact. Whole. Protected. No matter what.

"I will think on what you've suggested, Merlin."

"Arthur, please ..."

"I will think on it, Merlin," Arthur repeated, his voice harder this time.

"Just don't take too long," Merlin muttered, the Sorcerer turning to go. He needed to find more threads to pull. One of them would lead him where he needed to go. Assuming that he had the time to follow it.

"Merlin, before you leave, tell me about Kraken Cove."

"Kraken Cove?" Merlin had only been able to take a few steps before Arthur's request froze him in place. "Why Kraken Cove?"

"Because I have learned that's where my son has been hiding all this time."

Arthur's voice was deathly quiet. That worried Merlin, among all the other worries that rose up within him now that Arthur had dug out a piece of information that he had worked to keep hidden for more than a decade.

"You believe I know much about this town?"

"I do, Merlin."

Merlin shook his head in dismay. After all that they had just discussed, back to this? Arthur felt the need to focus on what was the least of his many worries.

Merlin had hoped to keep Draig's location a secret. And now he had to wonder what else Arthur might know that he shouldn't. What he might decide to do that he shouldn't.

The future had looked so bright when Arthur assumed the rule of the Teg.

And that future had been bright.

For a time.

Now, however?

Now that world was changing.

Not necessarily for the bad. Change was to be expected over the centuries. But not necessarily for the good, either.

Because just as always happened, Arthur's weakness was twisting the Teg world. Moving it in a direction that Merlin had never anticipated. And he hadn't decided yet what needed to be done because of it. How much of a correction was required.

Arthur was no longer the man that he once had been. But there was little that Merlin could do about that now.

"From what I understand, Draig lives there with some of the Teg he has helped over the years," Merlin explained, keeping any emotion out of his voice. "They have done nothing to impede our efforts. They have done nothing that we need to worry about. Nevertheless, I can look into the town in greater depth if you like."

"Hasn't impeded our efforts? Except for Draig taking *The Book of Whispers*," Arthur said so quietly that Merlin had to strain to hear him.

"Except that," Merlin conceded, unable to deny it. "Although I have no doubt that his decision wasn't made out of spite for you."

Arthur laughed then, although it wasn't a warm emotion. "You believe he took the artifact that was to be mine because he still feels a responsibility to the Teg?"

"I do."

"He left *my* world when he allowed me to think that he was dead!"

"Arthur, I understand that you're angry with him. But Draig could prove useful if …"

"Enough, Merlin. Enough." Arthur sighed, turning away from the window. "Leave me. Now. We will talk again if you are able to pull on some of those threads of yours and provide greater clarity as to this threat you're speaking of."

Merlin pursed his lips, then nodded, turning and walking out of Arthur's office with a strong step. He had gotten more from Arthur than he anticipated. He would leave his worries for a later time.

Arthur watched Merlin go, a welcome silence falling. He didn't believe Merlin. But he couldn't take the risk of disbelieving him either.

Until Merlin presented the necessary evidence, however, he would continue to rule the Teg as he had done for so long.

After all, he was a man of action. He was not going to wait. Especially since Merlin had demonstrated little interest in providing him with what he wanted. What he needed.

Arthur had learned very quickly that Merlin only shared what information he wanted to share or believed that he needed to share. No more than that.

If Arthur wanted to find out what his son was up to in Kraken Cove, there was a simple solution.

6

CHANGE IN PLANS

The scythe swept through the air in a blur, the steel meeting barely any resistance before it came to a stop against the leg of the short, brawny man wearing dungarees, work boots, and a cowboy hat. He didn't notice the blood dripping from the blade and staining the denim.

Reaching out with his free hand, he pulled free the long body of the rattlesnake that had been sunning itself among the grapevines. He dropped the still twitching carcass in the grass. A scavenger would find it later that evening. Likely a welcome meal.

His vintner had warned him that this would happen. That the snakes would come out of their burrows along the base of the ridge and seek the sun in the valley on the cooler days, many of them preferring to wrap themselves around the lines that held the growing grapes.

Not long after he had learned of this scourge, he had grown tired of dealing with the serpents. Without fail, on days like this, he would find two or three snakes atop the posts and curled in among the vines.

Now, he was wondering if there was some way that he could

make use of the fact that these little beasties infested his fields at certain times during the year.

Something that would be good for business.

Snake juice?

He shook his head at what he knew was a poor effort. Not very creative on his part. Who would buy a product sold as snake juice?

Certainly not the humans who were so enamored of his wines.

Although perhaps a different segment of the market and with a different name.

He would talk to Sharon. The head of his marketing department never flinched when he brought crazy ideas to her. She listened and then figured out how to make lemonade out of lemons.

"Stop lurking, Whisper. I've been waiting for you."

"Yes, Master. Very impressive with the snake. I couldn't have done better myself."

"Thank you for the compliment, Whisper, but it won't work," said the Daemon King. "What bad news do you have for me?" When he turned around, he lifted his head. His face was in shadows, and not just because of his hat, while his eyes burned as if they were crafted from the fires of Hell. "You've taken another skin."

"Yes, Master. I have." The Daemon appeared in the form of a young woman dressed as if she were about to go out on a jog, her dark hair in a ponytail.

"And I'm assuming that you took this new body in a way that her disappearance can't be traced back to us?" The Daemon King's eyes burned even brighter. Life was hard enough without making foolish and unnecessary mistakes that only served to increase the level of difficulty. Yet these last few years his Daemons seemed to be excelling at exactly that.

"Of course, Master," Whisper replied. She grinned, pleased with herself. "I did as you taught me."

"Good." The Daemon Lord turned away and began walking again through the rows of growing grapes, Whisper falling in beside him.

His fingers played across the handle of his scythe, fiery eyes always on the move, hunting for another rattlesnake.

When he first arrived here and began to rebuild what had been a poorly producing vineyard, he viewed the serpents as vermin. Over time, the rattlesnakes had become a type of sport for him. Childish, he knew. Nevertheless, he was always pleased with himself when he decapitated a snake in a single swing without harming any of his precious grapes.

Despite his incarceration, his skill with a blade remained. Besides, he had to have his fun when he could.

Admittedly, when he took ownership of the winery and Draig put in place the wards that prevented him from leaving without his permission, the Daemon King had been dreadfully bored.

His Daemons could come and go as they pleased.

He couldn't. And he ruled the Daemon Realm. He was the Master of the Abyss.

He had been angry because of that. Murderously so. With himself for allowing himself to be taken. With Draig for being the one to defeat him and put him in this prison.

Yet despite that, he had kept his word even though he had given it while Draig held the blazing steel of Excalibur against his throat.

The Daemon King had promised that he would do nothing to harm the Tylwyth Teg. Furthermore, he would ensure that his Daemons followed that stricture. If a conflict arose, his servants would not fight unless it was a matter of self-defense.

That last both the Daemon King and Draig knew was a bit

of a stretch. Daemons were naturally aggressive, and they had certain needs that had to be met.

Even so, they were willing to take that risk because it served both their purposes. And in the time that the Daemon King had been imprisoned at his winery, it had paid off. The conflicts between Daemon and Teg were few and far between.

As a result, strangely and entirely unexpectedly, the Daemon King had found some peace for the first time in millennia. His enemies could not get to him here. At least not easily. So, with fewer worries, he had turned his attention to other pursuits.

He had never thought that he would be good at turning grapes into wine, but he was, and what had begun as a hobby had become a thriving business.

Under his multinational company Daemon Brew – he was already well ensconced in the craft beer and hard cider market – he had formed a subsidiary, Hellas Wine. In just a few years, he had become the ninth largest producer in the world. If all continued as planned, he would be the top producer by the end of the next decade.

However, even with his business success, that didn't mean threats besides Arthur and his Knights didn't remain. Threats that he thought had died long ago. Thus, the reason he had called his best assassin to his side.

"Whisper, I have a job for you."

"Of course, Master."

He smiled. The Daemon King knew that Whisper wasn't going to enjoy what he was about to require of her. "I need you to visit the Mad Sorceress."

"The Mad Sorceress?" A hint of concern radiated from the Daemon. "You know our history?"

"I do, Whisper."

"She took one of the skins I used to wear. I liked that skin quite a lot. It had served me well."

"I know, Whisper." He remained patient with his servant. Whisper was never difficult. She just liked to talk things out first, which was fine with him since he still had several more rows of ripening grapes to patrol.

"She said that she would do the same again, Master, if I ever dared to approach her."

"I remember you telling me that, Whisper."

She was quiet for a time. Thinking. "This must be done?"

"It must." He nodded patiently, giving Whisper the time she needed. "And you are the one who must do it."

The Daemon King sliced with his scythe, the steel singing through the air. Once again meeting a momentary resistance before completing its arc.

"Well done, Master."

"Thank you, Whisper."

The Daemon King used the curl of his scythe to lift the fat body of the rattlesnake from its perch on the line, dropping it into the grass right beside the head. He smiled. The snake's jaws snapped closed and then opened once again.

The snake was dead, its brain just hadn't realized it yet. Still, a threat to those susceptible to the serpent's poison, which he wasn't.

"The Mad Sorceress is close to the Fallen Knight, Master."

"She is, Whisper." He knew that it wouldn't take her long to figure out why he was asking her to do this. "That's why I need you to speak with her. And speak only. If she attacks, rather than fight, I want you to run."

Whisper nodded. Although, clearly, she wasn't listening to the last of what the Daemon King had said. Her mind was working through the larger scenario, understanding now why her Master wanted to connect with the warden of his prison.

"Can we trust him, Master? He destroyed many of our brethren. He almost destroyed you."

"He did, you're right. The Fallen Knight could have

destroyed me. He had me under his blade. But he didn't. That's why I need you to get a message to the Mad Sorceress."

"But can we trust him, Master? After what happened in Williamsburg?"

The Daemon King didn't hesitate to respond. "We can, Whisper. He's the only Teg I would trust." He looked over at her, making sure that she was paying attention to what he said next. "Just don't make the same mistake they did. They were supposed to talk to him. Instead, they attacked him. Draig did what was required of him as a result. If you do what I require of you, the Mad Sorceress will not be a problem."

"Of course, Master. It will be as you desire."

The Daemon King knew that it would be. Whisper was one of his most trusted servants. She would follow his instructions to the letter. "Just remember that we want a conversation and not a war."

"Yes, Master."

"Now tell me what you don't want to tell me."

Whisper had hoped that her Master might forget that she was there as well for a reason other than the one for which he had requested her presence. But she wasn't surprised that he hadn't. He never forgot anything. "Ajarra asked that I tell you."

"Tell me what, Whisper?"

"The Knights, Master."

The Daemon King wiped away her concern with the scythe in his hand. "They were prowling around the border of my prison? That's of little concern. It happens from time to time. Probably just to check the integrity of their former brother's work. Ajarra is well aware of that."

"Yes, Master, but there is more."

"Tell me," the Daemon King ordered as he spun around to face her faster than was humanly possible, his eyes blazing with predatory fury. Ajarra only would ask Whisper to speak with him if she was the bearer of bad tidings.

"A squad of Knights was about to hike down into the valley."

"To do what? They usually stay atop the ridge."

"We don't know for certain, Master. We would have to ask them."

"Are you seeking to irritate me, Whisper?" The Daemon King's voice was soft, deceptively so. "Why hasn't Ajarra done just that? In fact, that's what she was supposed to do. I sensed the Knights as they approached and told her exactly where to find them."

"Yes, Master. Ajarra and her Daemons found them."

"What did the Knights say, Whisper?"

Whisper's face twisted into a worried frown. "Perhaps you would like to speak with Ajarra about that, Master."

"I am speaking with you, Whisper. Tell me. Without any further delay."

"Ajarra could not speak with the Knights, Master."

The Daemon King shook his head as he began to lose patience, scraping the tip of the scythe up and down his cheek. Whisper could not take her eyes from the bloody streak he left there. "What did Ajarra do, Whisper?"

"Ajarra told me to tell you ..."

"Ajarra should have told me herself." His voice was grim.

"Yes, Master."

"When we are done here, you will tell her to come see me. She must be brave all the time, not just in battle."

"Yes, Master. I will tell her."

"Now what is Ajarra's excuse?"

"Ajarra said that she and her Daemons had no choice. They tried to talk to the commander of the Knights. She told him that you had requested their presence. But one of the other Knights attacked."

"Let me guess. Ajarra and her Daemons defended themselves and in so doing they killed all the Knights."

Whisper hesitated before replying, then realized that there was no good reason to tell her Master anything other than the truth. Ajarra had put her in a bad position by asking her to relate all this to the Daemon King.

Whisper knew that Ajarra was only delaying what was going to happen to her because of her failure. And she agreed with her Master. You needed to demonstrate courage all the time, not just in battle. Even when it meant the possibility of your Master sending you back to the Daemon Realm.

"Yes, Master. All except for one."

The Daemon King nodded. So not all was lost. "Good. Then have this Knight brought to me."

"Ajarra can't, Master."

"Why not?" demanded the Daemon King. He pinched the bridge of his nose with his thumb and forefinger, trying to stave off the migraine that was coming on.

"The Knight is dead."

"The Knight is dead," the Daemon King repeated. He should have assumed as much. "Ajarra killed him?" If so, when he sent her back to the Daemon Realm he would leave her there for eternity.

"No, Master. The Knight slipped off the cliff. Ajarra tried to rescue him, but he refused her assistance. He fell to his death rather than taking the hand she offered him."

The Knight was a fool. Better to accept the assistance proffered.

He could only imagine how many Knights had died unnecessarily because of that overdeveloped sense of honor Arthur Pendragon instilled within them.

The Daemon King stopped, ignoring the snake he had identified just off to his right that was sleeping atop a post. He wanted to kill something. And not with the scythe. Even so, the rattlesnake didn't deserve his current ire.

"Let me get this right," he said when he finally had his fiery temper under control. "Because of what happened in Williamsburg, the Fallen Knight likely wants my head. And now, because of Ajarra's ineptitude, his father will be seeking it as well?"

"Yes, Master," Whisper confirmed with a reluctant shrug.

There was really nothing else that she could say. If the Daemon King chose to send her back to the Abyss, there was nothing that she could do to prevent it. She had known the risk of accepting Ajarra's commission. Yet Whisper had accepted it anyway, because she was never afraid, no matter the possible consequences.

"Thank you for telling me all that, Whisper. I know that you didn't want to."

"Yes, Master. You're right. I didn't."

"Please find Ajarra and tell her that I want to speak with her. I'll have what I want you to say to the Mad Sorceress ready when you return."

Whisper nodded and jogged off, seeking to get away from her Master before he changed his mind.

A good instinct on her part, the Daemon King believed. Because he really wanted to kill someone. Anyone would do, in fact. But he couldn't give in to that desire. Not yet.

The Daemon King continued his stroll down the row of grape vines, no longer caring if there were any more rattlesnakes hiding within his crop.

He didn't want to deal with headaches such as these. He shouldn't have to deal with them.

Nevertheless, he had no choice. He couldn't allow his enemies to obtain *The Book of Whispers*. If they acquired that artifact and used it against him ...

That was a possibility that he had little desire to contemplate. Because he was powerless against the bearer of that book.

After thinking about what Whisper related to him, he decided that his current strategy remained sound.

And he was right that he couldn't expect his spawn to do the delicate work that would be required as a part of that strategy. Ajarra had just proven that.

He would need an ally if he was to have any chance of success.

One ally, in particular.

Especially since Arthur had decided to make a play for him. At the worst possible time, of course.

Unless ...

The Daemon King nodded to himself as he began to realize what Arthur had in mind.

That was the only possible reason a squad of Knights would have refused to parlay with Ajarra.

His worry increasing, he wondered if he should reach out to the King Teg and offer a blood price for the Knights he lost. As a way of apologizing. Perhaps doing so would buy him some time.

He dismissed the idea almost as soon as it popped into his head.

Arthur would not be appeased. He would never be appeased.

The King Teg wanted to destroy him. Or, the King Teg ...

The Daemon King stopped, certain now of the scheme that he believed was in play. It seemed that more than one enemy was coming for him. And Arthur was the least of his worries.

Having reached that conclusion, one key question remained.

Was the Fallen Knight another enemy that he needed to concern himself with as well?

Because Whisper had asked a good question.

Could he trust the Fallen Knight?

Yes, he could, the Daemon King decided after a lengthy

deliberation. Even though he hated the Fallen Knight, with a vengeance, that was one truth that he could not deny.

The Fallen Knight had sent an untold number of his spawn back to the Daemon Realm. He had destroyed five of his Daemons less than a week ago, but those five had overstepped.

He couldn't blame the Fallen Knight for what he had done. In his position, he would have done much the same.

Even though he knew all that, should he take the risk?

Following this course could come back to blow up in his face, that was true. Then again, considering who his real adversary likely was, it was better to take that risk than not.

He did not trust Arthur or any of his Knights.

He did trust Draig.

The Fallen Knight had kept his word. Time and time again.

The Daemon King shook his head more in resignation than anger.

He was tired of all this crap. That's why he had bought the winery and asked the Fallen Knight to imprison him here after he lost their combat, knowing that the Fallen Knight – actually hoping, not knowing, and still grateful for the largesse granted to him – would be more merciful than his father.

Still, he had responsibilities to meet. He couldn't avoid them.

He would send Whisper to the Mad Sorceress and hope that she would have better luck than Ajarra did.

7

A HARD DECISION

"You are a strange Knight."

Draig didn't turn around at the comment, instead continuing to knead the dough he had been working on for the last few minutes. This would be the last of the batch. Then he could move on to the rolls that he would need later in the day.

After speaking with his sister earlier that morning, he retreated to the kitchen. He wanted some time to think. And for him, this was the best way to do that if he couldn't walk the perimeter of his island and enjoy the rhythm and color of the ocean.

He had decided on Challah bread to start. Although he knew that wasn't the only decision that he needed to make before he left his bakery.

In his mind, he could envision the maze that extended out before him. One with perils at every turn.

He wasn't yet sure which of the several paths to take. Much less whether he should even enter the maze.

He knew what would happen if he did, however.

What it could cost him.

Also what it could cost him if he didn't.

"Why do you say that Ragnar?"

The Berserker and his brothers had been drawn to Tia's Bakes by the wonderful smells wafting out onto the town green. Only he had walked into the back after asking Cerridwen for permission to do so.

Urs and Thorsen sat at the counter. Cerridwen was more than happy to fill them up with fresh coffee and all the pastries they wanted in recompense for their facing off against the Renegades.

"I know who you are. I know what you have done. I know what you can do. But I have never known a Knight who can do what you're doing now."

Draig smiled at that. He checked the oven's temperature before putting the last loaf of dough onto the baking sheet. With the warm temperature in the kitchen, he didn't feel the need to use the proving drawers.

"Not all Knights have the skills that I have," Draig replied with a wink. He wiped the flour on his hands onto his apron, then crossed his arms and leaned back against the sink counter.

"You speak the truth." Ragnar nodded toward the rising dough. Then in a hesitant voice, asked, "Do you think I might be able to learn this skill?"

Draig lifted an eyebrow, never expecting that question. "You would like to learn how to bake?"

The giant of a man appeared embarrassed at first. He crushed that emotion quickly. Almost as if he was preparing for a combat, putting on a hard face that likely would have frightened anyone else who saw it, except for Draig. "I would."

Draig nodded. "We start at five every morning. If I'm not here, Cerridwen will be. We'll both teach you."

Ragnar smiled broadly. The first smile, in fact, that Draig had seen from the Berserker. It wasn't a warm expression, and because of that more startling than anything else. Even so,

Draig was pleased to glimpse it, as it didn't last long. Replaced by a grim seriousness.

"You honor me, Fallen Knight. Thank you."

"It's the least I can do for you, Ragnar. Here barely more than a day and already you're protecting Kraken Cove and its residents. Thank you. By doing that, you honor me."

Ragnar's pale skin turned a bright shade of red. Clearly, he was not comfortable receiving praise, or perhaps he wasn't used to it. The giant shrugged, not knowing what to say. Finally, he mumbled, "We are here to serve."

"After this morning's excitement, I've got a job that needs doing that I think is right up your and your brothers' alley. Are you three up for it? It might require more than just a little intimidation."

Ragnar stood a little straighter, his eyes flashing with excitement and purpose. "We can do whatever you require of us. The Witch healed us."

"I wouldn't call Cerridwen a Witch, Ragnar," Draig warned. "She can be touchy about certain matters, and that's one of them. She's more powerful. She's a Sorceress."

"My apologies," he replied quickly, "I did not know. Cerridwen healed us. We are grateful. We seek nothing more than to serve. We are in your debt."

Draig pushed himself off the counter and placed his hands on the table that was still covered in streaks and splotches of flour. His reddish orange eyes burned a little brighter. "Guard against the Knights. Do not let them pass."

Ragnar's expression turned to stone. "It will be as you command, Lord Dragon. They will not pass."

Without another word, he shouldered the door out of his way and motioned for his brothers to follow him out into the street. They were quick to do so, although not without making sure that they took the last of their lemon and blueberry muffins with them.

"Busy morning," said Peggy Rose, who walked into the kitchen when Ragnar left. "The Three Little Bears you adopted are already proving their worth."

"Do you actually call them that?"

"Of course, I do," she replied, pulling out a stool from beneath the table with her foot and plopping down onto it. "They seem to like it. Whether amused or pleased or both ..." She shrugged. "I can't say."

"Do you think doing that is helping?"

"I do," she replied. "They're still uncomfortable, which only makes sense. They've broken a contract. As you know, that's something that Berserkers rarely if ever do. Moreover, they've decided to trust a dead man."

"I don't know how to take that," Draig said in a slightly offended tone.

"You enjoyed being dead," Peggy Rose challenged with a snort and a shrug.

"I did, you're right."

"Then stop being difficult," she ordered. "The Three Little Bears have left the only world they have ever known, and, despite your usually abrasive personality, they have decided to join our world and link their fortunes to yours."

"A big step."

"You've got that right," Peggy Rose agreed. "They'll loosen up once they've been here for a little while. Cerridwen and I will make sure of that."

"Actually, it's already beginning. Ragnar wants to learn how to bake."

"Does he?" Peggy Rose nodded, thinking about that. "The Berserker Baker. I like the sound of that. It makes me think of one of those wrestlers you see on television."

"A successor to Andre the Giant perhaps?" Draig suggested.

"I wouldn't put it past him."

"Ragnar might like that," Draig mused. "Now tell me about

what happened this morning. Cerridwen said that we had more Renegades making their presence known."

"If three Berserkers weren't enough to keep those unwashed dogs under control, Pinkie was there to keep them on the straight and narrow." Peggy Rose then gave Draig a succinct account of the confrontation that had taken place not long after the sun had risen right in front of the bakery.

"The Weres are going to continue to be a problem."

"They are," Peggy Rose agreed, "but we knew that. There's only one way they'll give up the hunt."

"That's not an option," Draig replied, his voice hardening.

"I'm not making a suggestion, Draig, I'm just stating a fact."

"After what happened on the island, I didn't expect that they would be so direct as to come into town. It feels like a challenge."

"They wanted to make a point."

"And they made it. But I think there was more to it than that."

"Pressed for time?" wondered Peggy Rose.

"That would be my guess. Whoever is pulling the strings is getting anxious."

"Which means those beasties are as well. You can use that."

"I can, you're right."

"And how did it go?" Peggy Rose asked, a gleam in her eye, having faith that Draig would do what was necessary with respect to the Werewolves.

"How did what go?" Draig replied in a distracted tone, his focus still on how he might want to handle the Renegades.

"Your illicit meeting with Riga?"

Draig's eyes narrowed. "There was nothing illicit about it."

"Come now," Peggy Rose prodded. "You and your former lover on the beach. Alone. The sun coming up."

Draig ignored what she was implying. "How could you have possibly even known that she visited?"

"I have my ways," Peggy Rose replied, injecting as much mystery into her voice as she possibly could.

"Really," Draig said, his tone hinting at his disbelief. "Are you stalking me again?"

"No more than I need to." Peggy Rose gave him the broad grin that never failed to make him smile as well.

"You're impossible, you know that?"

"I do know that, and it helps to keep things interesting. Besides, I know Riga. She's very possessive about the Teg she cares about."

"I'm well aware of that fact."

"Have you two decided to make another go of it? I know someone who might like the sound of that."

Draig blocked off that avenue of thought in a flash. "No, we both know that wouldn't end well for either of us."

"But you two still like to spend time together?" Peggy Rose prodded. "That's progress, at least."

"We're not trying to kill each other if that's what you mean."

"That's exactly what I mean."

"Enough about Riga," Draig said, not wanting Peggy Rose to dig into his private life any more than she already had. "We need to talk about Melissa."

"You still don't know what to do about her?" Peggy Rose asked, a hint of surprise in her tone.

"Why do you say it like that?"

Peggy Rose shrugged. "It's just unlike you."

"How so?"

"When situations such as this have come up in the past, usually you managed them in a very decisive manner that involved a good deal of blood."

It was Draig's turn to shrug. "I'm not that Teg anymore."

"The decisive one or the bloody one?"

"The latter."

"You say that even after what you did to that pack of Were-wolves when they came ashore at Raptor Bay?"

Draig lifted a hand to say that there was very little that he could do about that. "I didn't really have much of a choice. And, in all honesty, Seamus and the pups did most of the work."

"The pups? That's what you're calling those monsters?"

"Just because they don't like you ..."

"I don't care about whether they like me. I care that they are fickle creatures at best and they ..."

"Can we get back to the topic at hand, Peggy Rose? We're going down a rabbit hole." He gave her a broad grin. "See, decisive."

"You really can be infuriating, you know that?" she growled.

"I do."

"If you want to talk about this, then let's talk about it." Peggy Rose leaned her forearms on the table. "When you first came to Kraken Cove, you would have eliminated Melissa without a second thought."

"I wouldn't have killed her. At least not unless I had no other option."

"I'm not saying that you would. I am saying that you would have hustled her out of town as quickly as you could."

"But I'm not," Draig nodded.

"You're not."

"And you'd like to know why."

"Did I mention how infuriating you can be?" Peggy Rose spit out.

"You did, and you're right. Under other circumstances, she already would be gone." Draig leaned down so that there was only a foot between them. Their eyes level. "But these are unique circumstances."

"Would you care to explain?"

"I get the sense that Melissa is just one piece in a much larger game."

"No shit, Sherlock. You're going to have to do better than that."

Draig smiled thinly, then crinkled an eyebrow. "Not enough sleep last night? Usually, you're not this cranky in the morning."

"I slept fine, smartass. I'm testy because I had to face down four very large Weres this morning and then deal with you. It's not even nine and it's already been a trying day."

"Fair enough," Draig admitted. "If I'm right that there's more going on here than just a hunt for the book, then Melissa is the easiest way to get the answers we need. I'm flying blind. I don't have all the information that I require to navigate whatever this complicated situation might be. She can help me do that."

Peggy Rose pushed herself off the table and leaned back. "Forget what I said about you not being decisive." She nodded her head, impressed. "You want to use her as bait."

"That's the direction toward which I was leaning." He pushed himself off the table, then walked over to the oven, checking the temperature one more time. Pulling open the door, he placed the eight loaves on the racks, closed the door, then set the timer. "The Renegades know that Melissa is still alive. They also believe that she still has the book. That means they don't work for my father."

"And if you stay close to Melissa, the Weres will come for you. Then you can confirm who is behind this. And perhaps have a little fun as well."

"Exactly what I had in mind."

"Devious," Peggy Rose confirmed. "I never should have doubted you."

"Still, that might not give us all that we need. *The Book of Whispers* is a part of what's going on. Likely the catalyst. However, there's more to this larger strategy than meets the eye."

"You don't think it's just another gambit by either Arthur or Morgase or both to get the better of the other?"

"If it was that and only that, I'd let them try to kill each other without a second thought."

And if it was just that, it certainly would have made his life easier. But he knew in his bones that whatever was going on was more than just his father and his aunt rekindling their age-old feud.

There was a larger conspiracy in play. He was certain. If he was going to get some answers, he needed to start pulling on some threads, just as Merlin had taught him when he first began his service as a Knight.

Besides, he couldn't think of any other way but one to navigate the maze that he saw spreading out before him. Definitely a risk based on what happened earlier that morning in town as well as the encounter on his island.

Nevertheless, a calculated risk. He couldn't ask for any more than that.

Peggy Rose gave Draig a knowing look. "You're right. You can't send her off yet, not without knowing all that's in play. Not knowing if she's playing a larger role than we can see. Not knowing who all the other players are." That left only one option in her mind. "The Druid?"

Draig nodded. "The Druid." She might be able to help him see what he was missing. And, visiting her would serve another purpose as well.

"Before that, can you do me a favor?" asked Peggy Rose.

"What's that?"

"I need you to speak with someone."

"Who?"

"Someone I think you should talk to."

"Why are you being so cryptic?"

"Because I can be infuriating as well when I put my mind to it."

"Funny." Although Draig didn't sound amused.

"I do my best," she replied with a pleased smile.

"Why do you seem worried?"

"Because this isn't someone you want to speak with. But you need to."

"It might have to wait."

"As long as it doesn't wait for too long."

Draig nodded. Peggy Rose wouldn't make a request like that unless it was necessary. "When?"

"I'll set it up and let you know."

8

FINALLY AN AGREEMENT

His eyes flashing with a burst of fire, Draig took hold of the Grym.

The door was slightly ajar.

He had climbed the steps to the attic in Hestia's inn and stopped right in front of Melissa's room.

Usually, he wouldn't have been worried. Now, however, understanding who was interested in taking her ...

Draig had to assume the worst.

Placing a few fingers on the door, he pushed it open slowly on silent hinges. Stepping through, he ran his keen gaze over the attic suite.

The sheets and blankets on the bed were tangled into a large ball. Her clothes were strewn about. A cluttered pile of books lay by the couch fronting the bay window.

Nothing untoward.

The only thing Draig could confirm was that Melissa was a mess. Literally. Perhaps even figuratively.

"What in all the hells are you doing in here?"

Draig shifted his gaze to the left before he heard the words, sensing the movement beforehand, his hand grasping his shillelagh in a tighter grip.

Melissa walked out of the bathroom wearing jeans and her bra, though not her top. She seemed to have forgotten that last critical item as she squared up to him.

"Do you usually barge into a woman's room without knocking?"

Draig fought hard to hide his smile. He gave her a lift of his eyebrows and a slight nod. But she wasn't finished with him.

"Have you no respect for my privacy?"

Recognizing that she was just beginning to pick up a head of steam, Draig cut her off before she could get going. "I'm sorry. When I came up, the door was ajar. I was worried."

What Melissa was going to say next ended up caught in her throat. "Oh." She nodded. "That I can understand."

Draig motioned toward the bathroom door. "Hestia left you some extra towels and I assume she didn't close the door all the way. My apologies. I wouldn't have come in if I had known."

"So, you were worried about me?" she teased, already having forgiven the intrusion.

"Before we continue this conversation, can you do something for me?"

"What's that?" Melissa replied with a sparkle in her eyes. For a reason she had no desire to acknowledge, she was pleased that he was concerned about her.

"Could you put on a shirt please?"

Melissa's eyes bulged, her face turning a bright red. Actually not just her face when she realized what she was wearing ... and what she wasn't.

She turned around quickly and grabbed the closest t-shirt at hand from the crumpled pile of clothes on the floor, pulling it over her head. She didn't face Draig again until she was fully clothed, splotches of red still coloring her cheeks and her chest.

"I was just getting dressed when you interrupted me."

"Again, my apologies," Draig murmured. "It wasn't my intention to catch you like this."

"Likely story," Melissa challenged, that spark of amusement still in the back of her eyes. "Why are you here so early anyway?"

Draig ignored her question, instead walking toward the window. He studied the alignment of the gnomes.

Melissa stepped up next to him. "They've shifted their positioning again." She shook her head. "I don't understand it. Every time I look at them, they're in a different configuration."

"They're not just garden gnomes."

Draig's comment earned a questioning glance from Melissa. "Not just garden gnomes?"

"They've moved again?" Draig asked, wanting to confirm. "Since the last time you looked at them."

Melissa's brow furrowed. "Yes. They're never in the same position. Does Hestia move them around? I would have sensed her using the Grym to do that, but I haven't."

"She doesn't need to. The garden gnomes are alive."

"Are you for real?" wondered Melissa. "What do you mean they're alive? They can't be alive."

"Well, you're right," Draig agreed, correcting himself. "They're not alive so much as they've come back to life."

"Come back to life? Garden gnomes? You feeling all right this morning, Axel?"

"Draig," he corrected in a quiet voice, the brief clench of his jaw suggesting that he wasn't pleased that she had called him by his first name. "Only Merlin and a few other Teg call me Axel. Not even my father."

"Sorry, I just thought that our friendship had grown to the point where I could call you that."

Melissa offered him an expression of innocence that he knew was just a mask. She was poking at him, wanting to see how he would react. Under other circumstances he probably wouldn't have been bothered by her need to test the boundaries between them. But he wasn't in the mood.

Therefore, he ignored her apology, understanding that it was just an attempt on her part to put him on edge, which likely meant that she wanted something from him.

"Hestia is skilled in more than just the Grym," Draig explained.

Melissa closed her eyes and took a deep breath. It seemed that he was just as good at getting under her skin as she was at getting under his. "I haven't been awake for very long, but you're already testing my patience. Just spit it out."

Draig smiled. Crusty in the morning. Good to know. Although it could have something to do with him seeing more of her than he should have.

"Necromancy. She contracts with the spirits of the dead to keep watch over the inn. To do that, she links their spirits to the garden gnomes. That's one of the reasons that Safe Haven is a safe haven. Think of the gnomes as an early warning system. They sense the Grym as well as a host of other energies and essences that signify potential threats."

Melissa nodded. That made sense. It was also quite impressive. Very few of the Teg had the capacity to speak with the dead. It was a rare and thus highly valued skill.

"What about all the Teg living in town? That doesn't set off any false alarms for the gnomes?"

"No. Hestia teaches them what to look for and what they can ignore."

"Have they sensed something?"

Draig followed Melissa's gaze out the window. There were always gnomes looking in all directions, Hestia ensuring that every avenue of approach to the sanctuary she had created was under surveillance.

However, the bulk of the spirit-infused statues were pointed toward the west and the forest that began on the other side of the road.

"Yes, they have."

"What do you think it could be?"

"I think you already know the answer to that," Draig replied quietly.

"The Werewolves."

"The Werewolves," Draig confirmed. "We need to have a conversation."

Melissa continued to stare out the window a few seconds more before peeking at Draig out of the corner of her eye. She sighed, then sat down on the couch. "Thank you for at least waiting until I was fully dressed."

Draig held in check what he wanted to say. He could see her small smile. She was trying to get another rise out of him. So he got right down to business, refusing to allow her to delay or distract any longer.

"After what happened in the Dragon Vault, Arthur Pendragon believes that you're dead."

"Thank you for that." She was quite pleased by the success of his ruse as it helped to reduce some of the pressure weighing down upon her. Even so, she didn't believe that her relief would last forever.

"However, your other employer still thinks that you're alive."

"My other employer?" Melissa couldn't stop herself from gulping even as her eyes widened. "Why would you think that I have another employer?"

"I don't think that you have another employer. I know that you do."

Melissa nodded, unable to bear his fiery eyes and hard expression for more than just a few seconds. She leaned back into the couch, arms across her chest. "You sound very confident of yourself, Draig. Almost arrogant."

"Take it as you like," he replied, shifting his position so that his sharp gaze locked onto hers. "I can see the truth in your eyes."

Melissa's initial reaction was to dispute his statement and claim her innocence. Staring into those reddish orange flames, she realized that it would do her little good.

"I didn't want to work for her," she muttered, sinking deeper into the back of the couch.

"Few Teg ever do," Draig acknowledged. "She has something on you."

Melissa ripped her eyes away from his after a great deal of effort then closed them, leaning the back of her head against the soft fabric. "She does."

"Is it something that I can help you with?"

Melissa shook her head slowly from side to side. He knew that she was working both sides of the street, yet instead of getting angry he offered his help instead. She had yet to figure him out, and she wasn't certain that she ever would. In fact, she wasn't sure that she wanted to. "No, you can't."

"I'm sorry."

Melissa opened her mouth to reply, then closed it just as quickly. She was having a difficult time making sense of Draig.

The Dragon.

Arthur Pendragon's most skilled assassin.

She knew what he had done. She also believed that she had a sense of who he really was thanks in part to her spending some time with him, the stories that her mother had told her about him helping to complete the picture.

He was ruthlessly efficient. One of the most powerful of the Teg. Also one of the most feared. A target on his back and he didn't care.

A straight shooter, he fought for what he believed was right. He had the guts to challenge his father, the King Teg. And he was compassionate even when doing so made his life more difficult.

A contradiction in many ways. And in others ...

What you saw was what you got.

And more often than not, Melissa liked what she saw.

"What gave it away?"

"The Werewolves who are still lurking around town."

"They're still here?" Melissa closed her eyes for a moment, clenching her hands into fists to keep them from shaking. She should have assumed as much. That would certainly explain the garden gnomes.

"Peggy Rose had a little talk with them this morning."

"Peggy Rose?"

"A friend of mine. I'm sure you'll meet her eventually."

"I will?" Melissa was a little worried about that, not missing the slightly amused tone in his voice. As if he was looking forward to that engagement in large part because he wouldn't be playing a primary role.

"Yes, she wanted to speak with you. Peggy Rose has never liked Morgase, and they've had a few spats over the centuries."

"She doesn't trust me." Melissa wasn't a fool. She doubted that it would be an entirely friendly encounter.

"Why should she?" Draig didn't see any point in trying to sugarcoat the depths of Melissa's problems. "The Renegades work primarily for Morgase. She knows that you're still alive. She wants you or the book or both. Probably both."

"And I've brought all this to your doorstep," Melissa murmured. "I'm sorry. That wasn't my intention. I just came here because I thought I might be able to find some leverage that I could use to extricate myself from all this."

"And how's that working for you so far?"

Melissa snorted out a soft laugh even though she didn't want to. "Not very well."

"Do you understand exactly what *The Book of Whispers* can do? What could happen if it falls into the wrong hands?"

"That doesn't matter," Melissa replied, sidestepping his questions, "because it won't happen. You returned it to the Dragon Vault."

"I did, but that's beside the point. You believe that your mother sent you here to find some way to slip out from between Arthur and Morgase."

"She did," Melissa confirmed.

"Did you ever think that perhaps she sent you here not so much for that but rather because I was here?" He asked the question quietly, although with a conviction that she couldn't ignore.

Melissa stared at Draig. She wasn't frightened by his fiery gaze this time. Rather, she was intrigued by it.

At first, she thought to offer a mild insult, playing off of what could be taken as his veiled hubris. She didn't, instead thinking about what he said.

Her eyes crinkled when she finally smiled. She had been played, although not by Arthur or Morgase.

This was so like her mother. Guiding her. Putting her where she wanted Melissa to be without Melissa even knowing it.

Draig was right. Her mother wanted her here because he was here.

She should have been annoyed. Furious, in fact. Since her mother did this to her all too frequently.

But now, she was more grateful than anything else.

Draig had already proven his value with respect to her mother's subterfuge several times over.

If not for Draig, Melissa would be dead or captured, and which of those two was worse considering who was after her, she really couldn't say and she didn't want to think about.

"I was going to say that you are incredibly stuck up," Melissa began, "but I can't. Because you're right."

"Painful to admit, isn't it?" Draig prodded with a wink and a grin.

"You have no idea," she grumbled.

"I hope you realize that I'm trying to help you."

"I do," Melissa replied.

"And you do realize that it's very hard to help you when you're not being completely honest with me?"

"Not being completely honest?" Melissa adopted an expression of innocence, even infusing her tone with a faint hint of pique at such an unsubstantiated charge. "Why would you say that?"

Draig didn't bother to reply, simply staring at her. It wasn't long before she cracked.

"All right, yes. I have been keeping some things from you. But even if I told you, it wouldn't have mattered. It wouldn't have prevented what happened."

"Maybe not," Draig agreed. "Even so, it would have made things easier knowing that you were working for both my father and my aunt."

"Yes, I was working for them. I think we've confirmed that many times over. And you knew that already. As soon as you sensed the Werewolves." Draig offered her a nod to confirm her suspicion. Yet she still felt the need to defend herself. "But the point needs to be made that I wasn't working for them by choice."

Draig's gaze hardened, his eyes flashing dangerously. He heard the lie.

"All right, all right." Melissa pushed herself up from the couch and leaned her head against the window frame. The gnomes remained in the same positions they had been in when she sat down. Whether that was good or bad she didn't know. "I chose to work for your father. With Morgase, I didn't have a choice."

"And that makes me wonder."

"Makes you wonder about what?" Melissa turned to face him.

"What else you might be hiding from me."

Melissa shifted, placing her back against the wall. Draig hadn't moved. He hadn't done anything. Even his eyes didn't burn any brighter.

Yet she sensed how the ambience in the room had changed in a flash. A sense of menace radiated from Draig. He the hunter and she the prey.

"There is nothing else," she replied in a very quiet voice. "Nothing at all."

Draig didn't say anything. He simply kept his fiery eyes locked onto hers.

Feeling the pressure intensifying, she gulped. She really needed a drink. And not water.

"You can stare at me all you want, I have nothing else to share with you that would be of use."

Draig didn't reply for a time, not letting her go. Finally, he nodded, pushed himself up from the couch, and walked toward the door. "When you're ready to tell me all that's going on, let me know. Although by then it might be too late for you."

"Wait, where are you going?"

Draig had his hand on the doorknob and was already turning it. "There's more going on here than just Arthur and Morgase playing their usual games with you caught in the middle. If you can't tell me what's going on, or you won't, then I need to go elsewhere for my answers."

"I told you what I know," Melissa said in an indignantly defensive tone. "Are you accusing me of lying?"

Draig pulled open the door. "No, I'm accusing you of only giving me part of the truth."

"That is completely unfair," Melissa protested, her voice rising, hoping that her anger might buttress her claim of innocence. "I cannot believe that you would ... wait, stop."

Draig was already out in the hallway, the door closing behind him. She hustled across the room and caught the frame with her hand before it shut. "Would you please just wait? A few seconds, no more."

"Those seconds are already gone," he replied as he headed toward the staircase.

"Stop. Stop! Please!"

Draig didn't turn to face her until he reached the first landing.

"I told you everything I know," she pleaded. "You have to believe me."

Draig gave Melissa a sad smile. "Why? I have no cause to trust you."

He walked down a few more steps.

"All right, all right," Melissa continued in a pleading tone. "Yes, there is more going on. I just don't know what it is. That's why I didn't share it with you."

"You're going to have to do better than that," he prompted over his shoulder as he continued down the staircase.

"The Daemon King."

Draig stood balanced on the top step of the next landing upon hearing that. After what happened in Williamsburg, it made sense. "What about the Daemon King?"

"Right before your father gave me the job I was waiting in the foyer to his office. I heard him speaking with one of his Knights. I didn't catch it all, but I did hear that. Something about the Daemon King and a winery."

Draig stared at her as he began to fit the pieces together. However, the only piece that he was having a problem with was her.

Melissa was worried. That much was obvious. And with good cause.

Morgase and Arthur were powerful enemies to have. And

he didn't get the sense that she knew more about the Daemon King than she already had revealed.

Yet despite that, he still didn't think that Melissa was telling him everything. And he didn't think that he was going to get it out of her now.

"Thank you for that." Giving her a nod, he began to make his way down the stairs again.

"Where are you going?" Melissa called from the railing.

"To get some answers."

"I'm coming with you." She reached back and pulled her door closed before trotting down the stairs after him.

"Why would you want to do that? It's better if you stay here. Safer."

"Because I brought this problem to you. I shouldn't leave this all on you."

"Very admirable of you," Draig said, a strong dose of doubt in his voice.

"What? You don't believe me?"

"Not entirely, no."

"You really are a pain in the ass," she grumbled as she caught up to him on the next landing.

"I've been called worse," Draig confirmed.

"I bet you have." She reached out with her hand and grasped his arm, stopping him. She almost let go when she saw his eyes flash in warning. "You're right, I want to come with you not just because of the reason I gave you. I want some answers as well."

"And a way to get out from between Morgase and Arthur."

"That also," Melissa admitted. "But wouldn't you if you were in my position?"

Draig stared into her eyes. He saw the truth there. He saw as well that she was still hiding something.

That was all right with him. For now.

He had expected as much.

Melissa was very good at deception. But so was he. With her concerned about herself, she wouldn't see all that was really happening.

"Come on," Draig said.

He continued down the stairs, Melissa right behind him.

"Where are we going?"

"To see the Druid."

"Don't you mean to see the Wizard?" Melissa asked, a slight smile in her voice.

He didn't bother to reply, just giving her a disappointed look over his shoulder.

"What? You don't remember *The Wizard of Oz*? The yellow brick road?" She caught up to him quickly. "It was a funny comment."

"You might want to restrain yourself when we visit with her. The Druid hated that movie."

Melissa chuckled, understanding coming swiftly. "You tried the same joke on her, didn't you?"

"I did. It didn't go over well."

When they reached the bottom of the stairs, Melissa nodded to the backpack that Draig picked up from where he had left it against the counter. "What's in the bag?"

"You know because of the gnomes what's likely waiting for us in the woods?"

Melissa gulped again, not bothering to reply. Just nodding.

She had hoped that the Druid lived down the street. Apparently not.

"Peggy Rose gave me some goodies that should help if they get too close."

"Wonderful. Just wonderful," Melissa grumbled. "What have I gotten myself into?"

Draig held the door for her as they walked out of the Safe Haven. "What? You thought this was going to be easy?"

"I should have known better. Nothing is ever easy with you."

"No truer words have ever been spoken about Draig." Hestia stood at the bottom of the stairs. She was wearing a broad-brimmed hat and gardening gloves, several clipped roses in one hand, shears in the other. "He's been this way ever since he was a child."

"Not helping, Hestia," Draig said. Even though he was displeased by her comment, he bent down and gave Hestia a kiss on her cheek before striding down the walkway.

Melissa offered Hestia a shrug and then scampered after him.

"Give my best to Riga," Hestia called after him.

Draig didn't bother to turn around, although Melissa saw that Hestia's request made him bristle.

"Who's Riga?" Melissa asked when she caught up to him on the street.

"Who's who?"

He was distracted. The gnomes had moved again.

Still facing toward the west. Still focused on the forest, which reached out from Kraken Cove to the mountains that beckoned to him just a few miles away.

Yet their positioning had changed ever so slightly. Most of them now were focused on the southwest.

Taking hold of the Grym as they continued to make their way into town, Draig extended his senses in that direction.

The gnomes had moved for a good reason. He should have assumed that this would happen.

Regardless, there was nothing he could do about it now. And he was prepared if it proved necessary. When it proved necessary, he corrected.

"Riga?" prodded Melissa, realizing that Draig had disappeared for a few seconds. "Who is Riga?"

"Riga is the Morrigan."

Draig said it so matter-of-factly that it took Melissa a

moment to comprehend what that actually meant. "The Morrigan? The real Morrigan?"

"Yes, the real Morrigan. There is only one, and she's a piece of work." Draig stepped off the curb and crossed the street as they drew closer to the town green, Melissa right on his heels.

"The Celtic Goddess of War?"

"Among other things. Yes."

"Why did she come here?"

"Well, she didn't really come here."

"You mean to Kraken Cove?"

"Correct."

"Then where did you see her?"

"She visited me at the lighthouse."

Melissa threw up her hands. "Why do you insist on being so difficult? You couldn't just tell me that instead of making me work for it?"

"I need to have a little fun when I can, don't I?"

"Sometimes I don't know whether to hit you or ..."

Melissa stopped herself before she completed that sentence. When she glanced to the side, hoping that he wouldn't see the movement, she caught Draig's grin. That set her face on fire.

"Fine. We'll do this your way." Melissa continued with her questions. "Why did the Morrigan visit you at the lighthouse?"

"We needed to have a talk."

"You needed to have a talk with the Celtic Goddess of Death?"

"You know your mythology."

"I do. I also know that mythology is poorly named. Because in our world, the realm of the Teg, it's not myths. It's all too real."

"Another point in your favor."

"Are you trying to aggravate me?"

"No more than usual."

"You really are a ..."

"Pain in the ass," Draig finished for her. "Yes, you've made that abundantly clear."

Melissa took a deep breath, attempting to release some of her irritation. "Why would the Morrigan visit with you?"

"Nothing that's of concern to you," Draig replied in a deceptively calm voice. "She's a friend."

"A friend," Melissa repeated, giving him a knowing look that he ignored. "The Morrigan, a goddess who can bring dead warriors back to life, is your friend?"

"She is," Draig confirmed.

As they approached Tia's Bakes, she offered him a sly glance. "She's more than just a friend, isn't she?"

"You really like to ask a lot of questions, don't you?" Draig retorted, trying to turn the tables on her.

"It's the only way to learn anything," she replied with a shrug and an overly pleased grin.

"And yet you do your best not to answer questions when they're put to you."

"One of my failings, I'll give you that," Melissa admitted. She shook her head as if she was trying to solve an unsolvable problem. "What are you?"

"What do you mean?"

"You're a friend," Melissa said, wrapping the words in air quotes, "of the Morrigan. For the luck of the Teg. Really? The Goddess of Death?"

"I am what I am and that's all that I am," he replied as he reached for the door to the bakery and held it open for her.

"A Popeye reference? Seriously? At a time like this?"

9

THE THREE BROTHERS

"You said that we were going to see the Druid."

Arms crossed, Melissa was in the kitchen at the back of the bakery, Draig staring intently at the oven timer.

"We are," he confirmed.

"Then what are we doing here?" It was warm in Tia's Bakes, understandably so, and she already had drunk three black coffees to wash down three chocolate scones. Worse, a fourth pastry was calling her name.

"A gift to pave the way."

Melissa shook her head, not quite understanding what he meant. He had been all hustle and bustle when they left the Safe Haven. Now, he leaned back casually against the counter, arms crossed as well, seemingly not a care in the world.

"How much longer?"

Draig didn't bother to reply, instead nodding at the timer.

Eight minutes.

If she stayed here any longer, she'd be on her sixth scone. "I'll wait for you outside. I need some fresh air."

Draig nodded. "Just don't go too far. We've got to get going."

Melissa nodded, lips pursed, pleased that she was able to

contain her irritation. If they needed to get going, then why was he baking? This was ridiculous.

It wasn't until after she pushed her way through the swinging door and then out through the shop and onto Main Street that she thought about what he said.

Was it just an innocuous statement? Don't go too far because they were going to leave soon? Or was there more to it than that? A hint of concern perhaps? A warning?

Grumbling to herself, she walked across the street and stepped up into the white gazebo centered on the town green. She leaned her hands on the railing as she stared at the edge of the cliff and then the ocean beyond.

Such a wonderful sight.

It was quiet here in Kraken Cove. Peaceful.

A beautiful oceanside town.

She liked it.

Even with the Werewolves prowling along the border, she felt safe here.

Assuming that she could get out from under all the problems weighing her down, was this the kind of place where she could stay for a while? Maybe even think about staying for more than just a little while?

She wasn't sure. Although there was a distinctive attraction that hinted she might want to …

"Good morning, Miss Gorgonella. I hope we're not disturbing you."

Melissa turned slowly. The voice was quite polite. Even so, there was an underlying chord of peril that struck an immediate nerve within her.

Her eyes widened, goosebumps running down both her arms.

Two men stood in the gazebo with her. They blocked her only exit unless she jumped the railing at her back.

Ready for that if it came to it, she took the next few heartbeats to study her two unwanted visitors.

They were dressed exactly alike. Cleanly pressed grey suits with perfect creases. Starched white shirts and thin black ties. Fedoras that reminded her of what businessmen wore in the 1950s.

"I don't believe we've met although I've seen you in the bookshop and then by Renzetti's," Melissa said in a pleasant tone.

One of the men nodded, giving her a smile that was anything but warm. "That's very impressive Miss Gorgonella. Most of the Teg we visit don't see us until we allow them to."

"Allow them to?"

"Yes, one of our unique abilities," the other identical twin replied. "It's quite useful for the work we do."

"And what work would that be?" Melissa asked. She was afraid of what the answer was going to be.

"Finding Teg who don't want to be found."

"Then you're looking in the wrong place, because as you can see, I'm right here," Melissa quipped. She even managed to offer a slight laugh, although it died quickly in the back of her throat.

The two men displayed not a single emotion between them. Their expressions were perfectly the same, and that scared her in a way that nothing else ever had.

"Yes, you are," one of the identical twins agreed.

"You've led us on quite a chase," the other continued.

"Chase?" wondered Melissa. "I don't know if I'd call it that."

The two men nodded as one, apparently willing to concede the point.

"Be that as it may," the man standing to her left said, "please give us the item and we will be on our way."

"No harm will come to you," the other added. "So long as you relinquish the item."

"I'm sorry, but I don't know what you're talking about."

Melissa attempted to incorporate a real lack of understanding in her voice. She got the feeling that she failed miserably based on their expressions ... or rather the lack thereof. A rare occurrence for her. Then again, she had never met Teg like these before.

"Miss Gorgonella ..." the man on her left started. She cut him off.

"I really don't know what you're talking about. I just came here for a few days of vacation. That's all. I'm sorry I can't help you."

"Please, Miss Gorgonella," the man to her right said. "There's really no need for this. Return the item to us, and we will be on our way."

Melissa shrugged and then smiled, trying to make them think that she wasn't flighty so much as a little ditzy. "I'm sorry, but I really don't know what you're referring to."

Both men sighed at the same time, their reactions flawlessly synchronized. "Please, Miss Gorgonella. We know you're lying. We know it was in your possession. We can sense the residue."

"We just want the artifact," said the other. "We are not here for you. We are here for what you possess. There is no need to make this situation more difficult than it needs to be."

Melissa started to respond, then stopped herself. She looked in both directions without moving her head, not wanting to give her intentions away.

If she didn't trip leaping over the railing, she might be able to get to the path along the cliff before these two caught up to her. Then she could create a barrier with the Grym as she did when the Werewolves were after her – a much larger one this time -- and she doubted that in their suits and polished dress shoes they'd be able to scale the cliff with the agility her previous pursuers demonstrated.

"Miss Gorgonella, it won't work," said the man standing to her left.

"We are more than we appear to be. You will not make it to the cliff walk before we catch you. It is not a good decision on your part."

"How could you possibly know ..." Melissa stopped talking, realizing that she was only implicating herself. She pushed herself off the railing and stood with her back straight even as she bent her knees. They might be right, but she wasn't going to make it easy for them. "I'm sorry, gentlemen, but I don't know what you're talking about."

A brief silence followed. The two men weren't irritated by Melissa's obstinance. Rather, they appeared to be more resigned than anything else.

The identical twins once again reacted in concert, shaking their heads from side to side, their shoulders slumping slightly. They both had been hoping that this would be an easy job. A simple grab. No snatching involved. Because they were tired of the violence, worn down by it.

Yet once again what was supposed to be an easy job was playing out just like all the others. They were disappointed because now they had little choice regarding what they would need to do next. They were hired with a very specific set of instructions.

"Please, Miss Gorgonella, one last time. We have no desire to hurt you. We are making a very simple request. Meet it, and we will leave you in peace and whole."

"Why would you hurt me?" Melissa asked, playing for time. "I'm telling you the truth."

All the other options that came to mind for extricating herself from this pair clearly bad ones, she reached for the Grym, the Power of the Ancients flowing through her.

She stepped back immediately, her lower back hitting the rail. The two men sensed what she was doing, and they had responded instinctively. Moving a few feet away from one another, billy clubs that gleamed dimly appeared in their right hands.

"Who are you?" demanded Melissa, a shiver of fear running through her.

She sensed the Grym within both of them. They had the same level of strength. And, much to her displeasure, they were stronger than she was. That didn't bode well.

"Who we are doesn't matter, Miss Gorgonella," one of the men said. "What matters is that we are here now."

"Please, Miss Gorgonella, this does not need to end badly. We know you have it. If you hand it over, there will be no need for us to take drastic measures."

"We would prefer not to, Miss Gorgonella," the other said.

"Tom. Harry. I didn't expect to see you here."

The two men turned, although neither revealed the surprise that shot through them.

They recognized the voice. How could they not?

Besides, he was the only Teg who could sneak up on them.

"We didn't expect to see you here, Draig," Tom said.

"We didn't expect to see you anywhere," Harry added, "since you're supposed to be dead."

"Although we had our doubts," Tom continued, "as did several other Teg."

"They're still looking for you," Harry explained apologetically. "We heard that they needed to see your body before they were willing to believe that you had passed over."

"I'm not surprised," Draig replied amiably. "The usual culprits?"

"A good assumption," Tom confirmed. "It seems that some of the Teg really don't like you."

"Strange, don't you think, since I'm so likable."

Tom and Harry both smiled in unison, the first real emotion that either one had displayed since they approached Melissa.

"Would you mind keeping this to yourselves? My father knows for certain that I've returned from the dead. Not everyone else does yet."

"If your father knows, everyone will know soon enough if they don't already."

"True, but whatever additional delay I could have would give me the time I need to be ready for what likely happens next."

Tom and Harry both nodded immediately. "Of course, it's the least we can do," Tom confirmed.

"Thank you."

With Draig engaging the two men, Melissa stepped around them on silent feet and trotted down the steps, not coming to a stop until she was right next to Draig. Actually a few steps behind him. Why wasn't she surprised that Draig knew these two?

Tom and Harry both nodded again, pleased to be of assistance.

"May I ask why you're here?" Harry asked.

"It's my home. This is where I came upon my death."

Tom and Harry smiled again.

"It seems like a lovely town," Tom said.

"It is," Draig confirmed. "I wouldn't be here otherwise."

"And your presence explains why so many Teg live here as well," Harry said.

"What can I say? I'm likable."

Tom and Harry broke out into loud laughs, the synchronicity between the two unsettling Melissa.

"We'd love to continue to catch up," Harry said, "but if you don't mind, we came here for Miss Gorgonella. She has something that we must acquire before we can leave."

"I hope you understand," Tom said.

Draig nodded. "I do, and I'm sorry to get in your way." He caught out of the corner of his eye the pleading look Melissa gave him. He smiled. This would be an easy way to get her out of his hair, if he hadn't decided that he couldn't allow that. Not yet. "However, I require Miss Gorgonella's assistance on a matter of immediate importance."

"And we can talk again once your matter has been resolved?" Harry asked, neither he nor Tom needing to hear any more than that.

"We can," Draig confirmed.

Tom and Harry looked at one another for the most fleeting of moments, then nodded.

"Of course," Tom said. "We'll catch up with Miss Gorgonella when your work with her is done." No one missed the intention behind his words.

"Thank you for your flexibility," Draig replied, giving them both a nod of respect. "Are orange and cranberry muffins still your favorite?"

"They are," the brothers replied in unison.

"Then please stop by my bakery." Draig nodded over his shoulder. "Cerridwen just pulled a batch out of the oven. I'm sure that she'd love to see you. It's been too long."

"Thank you." Tom replied. "That is very kind of you."

"It's nothing," Draig said, waving them over to Tia's Bakes. "Standard rules?"

"Standard rules," Harry confirmed.

"My business with Miss Gorgonella might take a few days. You said you liked the town. Why not stay here while you're waiting. Get a real feel for Kraken Cove."

"That's very kind of you," Tom replied. Both brothers smiled. Clearly, they appreciated the offer.

"If you need a place to stay, I'd suggest the Safe Haven at the far end of the street. Ask for Hestia and tell her I sent you."

Melissa's eyes almost bulged out of their sockets upon hearing that. She was staying there. How could he make them an offer like that?

"We will go there after we visit your bakery. Thank you, Draig. It is good to see that some of the Teg still hold to the old ways."

Draig gave them both another nod of respect as they walked past him.

Melissa remained silent until Tom and Harry walked into Tia's Bakes. "You heard what they wanted from me, yet you treat them like old friends? You even suggest that they stay at the same place where I am? What were you thinking?"

"You said you didn't need my help," Draig replied with a shrug. "Besides, like you said, they're old friends ... of a sort."

Melissa had no response for him other than anger, her face just as red as it had been when she realized she was standing in front of Draig wearing only her bra. Nevertheless, she stopped herself from offering him the scathing rejoinder that might prevent the help that she did indeed need from him.

"You are such a pain in the ass," she muttered.

"Again, not the first time I've heard that."

Realizing that allowing her anger to rule her wouldn't do either of them any good, she tamped it down as best as she could.

"Who were they? They gave me the willies. And they sensed when I took hold of the Grym. Most Teg can't do that."

"They aren't most Teg," Draig replied. Turning away, his backpack across his shoulders, he headed for the trail along the cliff. Melissa had to trot after him to catch up. "They're the Three Brothers."

"The Three Brothers?" That didn't make any sense to Melissa. "There were only two. Where is the third? Hiding somewhere?"

"No, he's dead," Draig replied. Reaching the path, he increased his pace, making for the trail head at the southern end of the coast and demonstrating no interest in explaining any further.

"What?" She hadn't expected remorse from him, but she had expected … something more than what he gave her.

"The third brother. Dick. He's dead."

"But then why …" Melissa shook her head, beginning to think that asking the question that had just come to mind would be a waste of time.

"Strange that they're here for you, don't you think?" Draig pondered.

"Me?"

"You."

"That's really not all that strange, now is it? Not after the conversation we just had."

"It wouldn't be if not for the fact that they're not working for my father or my aunt on this job."

"How do you know that?" She infused her voice with curiosity rather than concern. At least she hoped she did.

"I have my ways."

"You really can be …"

"A pain in the ass, I know." Draig chuckled softly. "Both Arthur and Morgase cheated the Three Brothers. They won't work for either one."

Melissa frowned. "Then why would they be here for me?"

"You tell me. And don't tell me it's the Daemon King who hired them. The Three Brothers wouldn't work for him either."

"I wasn't going to say that."

"But you're not going to tell me."

"I can't tell you what I don't know."

Draig offered Melissa a raised eyebrow and a frown of disappointment. Melissa averted her gaze, not wanting to see it. She didn't like how she felt, yet she could do nothing about it.

"Who were those two? Really?" she asked, trying to move away from what for her was an exceedingly uncomfortable topic.

"The Three Brothers?"

Draig pushed out of the way the steel gate that extended across the path. Allowing Melissa to pass, they stepped onto the trail that would take them through the woods to the mountains beyond.

"Who else would I be talking about?" she sniped.

"The Three Brothers handle very specialized jobs," Draig explained. "Jobs that most other Teg can't handle. They're very efficient, they complete their task to the letter of their assignment, and they never fail."

"That's wonderful to hear," Melissa groused, not liking that one bit.

"You asked," Draig replied. It wasn't long before they were walking in a strange twilight, the heavy canopy above only allowing a few stray rays of the sun to break through. "A word to the wise?"

Melissa nodded.

"If The Three Brothers are here for you, the Teg who's looking for you has a great deal of power, influence, and wealth. You might need some help."

"I don't need any help," Melissa growled, even though she grasped that she really did.

"If you say so," Draig nodded, although obviously he didn't believe her.

Rather than offering him the sharp reply that was on the tip of her tongue, she asked him a question instead. "What else can you tell me about The Three Brothers?"

"Quite a lot actually."

Draig continued along the trail at a steady pace, Melissa right beside him. After a few hundred more yards, she couldn't contain herself any longer. "And?"

"I'll tell you later if we have time."

"Why not now?" Melissa demanded.

"Because of what's in the woods with us. Or did you forget about them?"

Melissa's cheeks colored red for the third time that morning. He was right, and she had forgotten. The Three Brothers could wait. They had to deal with a more immediate challenge.

"No, I didn't," Melissa lied. "Just one more question?"

"Could I even stop you if I wanted to?" Draig asked.

Melissa smiled, appreciating his humor even though it was at her expense. "What are the standard rules?"

"Few Teg follow them now. They're complicated and there are a lot of them," Draig replied, hoping to put off her interest.

"Humor me."

Draig sighed, realizing that it would be better to answer her so that he could focus on what he had no doubt would be coming their way. "I welcomed them to the town. I granted them the gift of hospitality. They are now my guests. I will treat them as such. And they, in turn, will not seek to complete their assignment until we are done with what we're doing now. An agreement of sorts."

"Then they'll take me when we're done with the Druid. How does that help me?"

"You said you didn't need my help," Draig explained with as much innocence as he could manage, which wasn't much.

"Draig ..."

"Once we return to town, we will meet with The Three Brothers and work out the details of what happens next. It's all very civilized."

"And what if The Three Brothers ignore the standard rules?"

"They won't," Draig replied with a confidence that Melissa couldn't ignore.

"How do you know?"

"I trust them."

"You trust them? They were hired to kidnap me if I couldn't give them the item they wanted."

"That may be so, but The Three Brothers keep their word."

"They may have in the past. How do you know they still will? How do you know they won't break it?"

"They won't." Draig's tone suggested that Melissa was aggravating him. She didn't care.

"But if they do?" she pressed.

Draig gave her a smile then shrugged. "You said you could take care of yourself."

For just a heartbeat, Melissa stared at him, not knowing what to say. But then she did.

"You're insufferable."

"I've been told that many times before as well."

10

THE BEARS VS. THE KNIGHTS

"You can't be serious? You're leaving us here?"

Gaheris opened the side door to the Mercedes camper van. He hopped out while still holding the handle. Five Knights of the Round stared back at him, Kaleb the most startled.

"Set up a perimeter and keep an eye out. I'll be back by tomorrow morning at the latest."

It was late afternoon, the sun just beginning to dip in the sky. Gaheris had pulled off Route One onto a fire road a mile outside Kraken Cove. Finding a small glade shaded by a thick forest canopy, he turned the vehicle around so that it was pointing back the way they had come before cutting the ignition.

An ingrained habit. Be ready to move. Always.

"We came here because we were supposed to accompany you into the town," Kaleb protested. Displeased by Gaheris' decision, his narrow eyes sank deeper into their sockets, his brow knitting together. "We were supposed to confront the Fallen Knight."

"No, you weren't," Gaheris clarified. "I was supposed to talk to Draig. That's it. Arthur sent you as backup. If I have need of you. And right now, I don't."

"That may be ..." Kaleb admitted reluctantly. Gaheris didn't give him the chance to complete his protest.

"If I have need of you, I'll give you a call. Until I do, stay here. Set up a perimeter and be ready."

Gaheris tugged on the side door, slamming it shut.

Kaleb stuck his head out the window, not yet willing to give up. "We came here for the Fallen Knight!"

Gaheris whipped back around. He hadn't brought his sword with him, leaving it in the van. He trusted Draig, but not all the Teg living in the town, so best that he didn't antagonize them if he could avoid it.

He wouldn't enter Kraken Cove unarmed, however. Instead of bearing the steel blade gifted to him when he first joined the Knights of the Round, he carried two daggers. One sheathed along his thigh, the other in a scabbard at the small of his back.

As he gave Kaleb a cold stare, he would have liked nothing more than to use those daggers on his fellow Knight.

Why Arthur had saddled him with Kaleb and his squad, he didn't know. Although he could guess. It came down to trust, or rather the lack thereof.

But that had nothing to do with his current desire to truss Kaleb up like a slaughtered pig and hang him from a tree branch.

If Kaleb wasn't snoring loudly during the drive up the coast from New York City, he was talking loudly. Telling his friends what he thought about the Fallen Knight. What he would do to Draig when he came face to face with him.

The man was a fool. He had joined the Knights of the Round after Draig died. Or rather was said to have died.

Kaleb and the Knights in his squad had no clue as to what Draig was capable of. The power he could bring to bear. What he did to those who dared to challenge him.

Gaheris did.

Therefore, although Gaheris would enjoy watching Draig put Kaleb in his place – kick his ass in reality, that thought making him smile -- he had no intention of allowing Kaleb and his men into Kraken Cove because he had even less desire to deal with the unnecessary problems and resulting repercussions he was certain these Knights would cause.

"You came here because you were ordered to," Gaheris stated in an emotionless voice. "I lead. Set up a perimeter and keep an eye out."

"This is my chance, Gaheris," Kaleb almost pleaded, his voice whinier than usual. "You can't take it away from me."

"Chance for what?" Gaheris turned his back and began walking down the wide trail toward the road.

"To make a name for myself in the Knights," Kaleb explained quickly. "For all of us to do that. Whoever defeats the Fallen Knight becomes a legend."

"You think that you have what it takes to challenge the Fallen Knight?" Gaheris scoffed over his shoulder as he continued on his way.

"I know I do."

"Then not only are you a fool, Kaleb, but you're also delusional. If you draw steel on Draig, he'll kill you in a heartbeat."

With that, Gaheris disappeared among the shadows, Kaleb and the other Knights losing sight of him in the gloom.

"Gaheris, what the hell are we supposed to do tonight if you're not back?" Kaleb yelled.

"You're in a camper van," Gaheris replied mockingly from farther down the road. "I'm sure you'll figure it out."

Silence descended, Kaleb slinking back down into the passenger seat. He stared out the windshield, not quite believing that Gaheris left him behind.

How could that crusty bastard do this to him? How could he

not understand why challenging the Fallen Knight was so important to him? Why it was necessary?

The Knight who killed Axel Draig would be honored before all others in the Round. He would get his pick of assignments. He would be on the fast track to advance within the ranks.

And his name would never be forgotten.

The Fallen Knight was said to be the greatest warrior to ever serve Arthur Pendragon. Vanquishing him would give Kaleb that title and the honor associated with it.

Yet Gaheris had taken that opportunity away from him.

Kaleb spun his chair around swiftly. His four friends stared at him, having stayed quiet during the exchange.

"Can you believe this?" he demanded.

The other Knights didn't seem all that angry or disappointed about being left in the van. In fact, they seemed more than satisfied with their fate. That made Kaleb even angrier.

"He just left us here. Does he not know who we are?"

"Gaheris knows what he's doing, Kaleb." Jacque, a Knight who needed two seats because of how broad he was, sat hunched over in the back of the van so that his head didn't hit the ceiling. "He's been a Knight for a long time. In fact, no one really knows how long he has served."

"Jacque is right," Hernan added with a nod. "Besides, Gaheris is in charge of this mission. What he says goes. You know the penalty for disobedience."

"Jacque is right that Gaheris has served a long time in the Knights," Kaleb agreed. "But so what? That doesn't mean he's right. It just means that he's old."

"He's still our commanding officer." Tory sat next to Hernan. He shrugged his shoulders. "Even if we wanted to go into town, which I really don't, what are we supposed to do?"

Ricardo nodded, agreeing with what Tory said. He didn't talk much. He had lost his tongue to a Daemon not long after he joined the Knights, and he tried to avoid drawing attention to that fact.

"That might be," Kaleb agreed, realizing that just being angry wasn't going to get him what he wanted. "Gaheris leads. However, that doesn't mean Gaheris is right."

"Kaleb, we all understand what you want," Tory said, speaking for all of them, "and although none of us have any real desire to go up against the Fallen Knight like you do, you need to let this go. Gaheris gave us an order. Our job is to do as he commanded."

"Gaheris is a has-been, Tory. You know it just as well as I do. The old fool should have retired long ago."

"Kaleb, be careful what you say," Jacque warned. "I've seen Gaheris in the practice ring. He doesn't look old to me when he's got a sword in his hand."

"I can take him," Kaleb snorted.

"I don't know about that ..." Hernan began. Kaleb cut him off.

"He can't do this to us," Kaleb stated with more force. "It isn't right."

"Right or wrong doesn't matter," Jacque shrugged. "He just did, and we follow his orders."

"Did you know Gaheris and Draig are friends?" Kaleb asked, hoping a different tack might make his friends more amenable to what he wanted them to do.

"Were friends," Hernan corrected. "From what I understand, Draig will kill him on sight. So Gaheris going into town by himself ... all I can say is that he's got some guts."

"Then we should be there, don't you think?" Kaleb prompted. "He could use our help."

"Are you truly as stupid as you seem to be?" Hernan leaned forward in his seat and placed his forearms on his knees. "You don't care about Gaheris."

"I do care about him. He's a fellow Knight."

"I'm not buying it," Hernan continued, the other Knights nodding in agreement. "Why do you want to take on the Fallen Knight? The man is legendary. He began training as a killer when he was still in the crib. Killing you, killing any of us for that matter, would offer him little challenge. I doubt he'd even break a sweat."

"That's a load of crap," Kaleb replied. "He's just a man. He can be killed just like almost every other Teg."

"He was dead and now he's not," Jacque murmured quietly. "He survived a combat with King Arthur. I don't know anyone else who can say the same."

"Exactly," Kaleb said, sensing an opportunity. "The Fallen Knight got lucky. It's that simple. It's the only explanation."

"If you believe that then you are truly a fool," Hernan stated with absolute certainty.

"So, you want to stay here by the van while Gaheris goes off in search of the man we could make our names off of?" Kaleb refused to admit defeat.

"You haven't figured that out yet, Kaleb?" Tory asked with a heavy dose of sarcasm. "Gaheris gave us an order. We follow his orders."

"Look, you don't have to do what I want to do," Kaleb tried again, finally settling on an approach that he believed might work. "Perhaps we just need to look at this in a different way."

"What way would that be?" Jacque scoffed.

"Gaheris told us to set up a perimeter."

"He did," Hernan confirmed.

"And we will," Kaleb said. "I'll just extend it a little bit farther than we might usually."

Jacque shook his head, not surprised by Kaleb attempting to push the boundaries. He had known him for almost ten years. They had been recruited to the Knights of the Round in the same class. And if he had learned nothing else about Kaleb, it was that in the end Kaleb would do what he thought was best for himself. Always and without a second thought.

"You're going to extend our perimeter to the edge of town."

Kaleb smiled now that he had pinpointed the solution to his problem. "I won't go into town. I promise. I just want to take a peek. That's all."

The Knights crammed into the van stared at Kaleb. They should have assumed that this was going to happen. Because it had happened before. Kaleb doing what Kaleb wanted to do.

Jacque shook his head from side to side. He didn't have the energy to continue the argument. "Fine. Do what you want. Can we just get out of this van? Tory let one go and I can't breathe."

"That wasn't me," he protested. "Ricardo ate those beans when we stopped for lunch."

Ricardo didn't bother to defend himself. Instead, he reached for the handle and pulled open the van's side door. He hopped out quickly, because Jacque was right. The stench was awful.

The other Knights hustled out after him.

"Ricardo, you need to stop eating ..." Kaleb's words ended abruptly. He scowled. "Who the hell are you?"

Three very large men who looked like they just stepped out of a documentary on the Vikings of old stood across from Kaleb and his friends. They were even bigger than Jacque, and that was a rare accomplishment.

"Who we are doesn't matter," the blonde, bearded giant standing in the middle of the trio replied in a deep voice that rumbled like thunder. "Why we are here does."

"I disagree," Kaleb said. He took a step toward the three, seeking to exert the authority ingrained within him as a Knight. "Answer me. Who are you?"

Kaleb's question was met with silence. The trio of giants stared at the Knights. They clearly were unconcerned that the

Knights' steel blades infused with the Grym were waiting for them just over their shoulders.

Hernan and Tory took a half step back toward the van. Jacque and Ricardo wanted to do the same. Instead, they managed to plant their feet into the ground.

The Knights had fought all manner of Teg and monsters, yet these three radiated a coiled aggression and competence that made them nervous.

"We are the Three Little Bears," the giant in the middle replied. Then he laughed. A deep laugh. His two companions joined him.

The Knights looked from one to the other, not knowing how to reply. They didn't understand the joke. And that only made them more nervous.

Who were The Three Little Bears? Kaleb and his squad wondered. And why were they called that? Because they certainly weren't little, and they certainly hadn't walked out of a children's story. More concerning, what were they doing here?

"And we are Knights of the Round," Kaleb said with as much authority as he could manage once the three giants had stopped laughing.

"Yes, we are aware that you are Knights," the giant in the middle confirmed with a nod.

"Then you know that you stand no chance against us. Leave. Now. We have better things to do than to show you exactly what happens to difficult Teg."

The three giants stared at the Knights, their blue eyes frigid, although there also appeared to be flecks of amusement in the back. Those flecks turned into another round of laughter.

"You find this funny?" Kaleb demanded in a harsh tone. "You laugh at Knights of the Round?"

"We do laugh," the giant in the middle confirmed.

Kaleb's face turned a bright red, unable to ignore the insult.

"Kaleb, take a breath, man," Jacque whispered to him.

"There's something off about these three. We need to be careful."

Kaleb ignored his friend's advice, instead allowing his anger to take hold. He was a Knight of the Round! One of the best! Soon to be *the* best! He would not be treated in this way.

"If I draw my sword," Kaleb said in a very quiet rasp that resembled Clint Eastwood's in the *Dirty Harry* movies, his favorite films while growing up, "you will die. Do not insult me again."

"We do not insult you, Knight," the giant explained. "I simply answered your question."

"You laughed at me," Kaleb growled.

"We laughed because what you said was funny. If you viewed it differently, then the blame lies with you."

Kaleb reached over his shoulder and pulled his sword free from its scabbard. "You insulted me. I don't like to be insulted."

The giant's eyes narrowed. "Be careful little man. You don't want to make us angry."

In a flash, glowing three-foot steel bars inscribed with runes appeared in the right hand of each giant.

"Kaleb, don't do it," Jacque warned in another whisper. He and the other Knights were shifting nervously from one foot to the other. Every few seconds glancing at the camper to confirm that it was still there. Gaheris had left the van pointing back down the road for a reason. It might be time to make use of his good planning. "You don't need to do this. These three ..."

"What are you?" Kaleb asked, ignoring Jacque. "Are you costume players? Are you dressing up early as Thor for Halloween? Is that it?"

The giant in the center shook his head in dissatisfaction. "Thor prefers a hammer, not a steel rod as we do. And I would never try to be him for All Hallow's Eve. He's a bit full of himself. He doesn't deserve the attention that he receives and he certainly doesn't need more."

"Thor prefers a hammer? Are you a fool? Did you not recognize my challenge…"

Kaleb never had the chance to complete his insult. Because just a heartbeat later, he was lying on the ground, a large, angry red welt forming on his forehead.

Jacque and the others, stunned by how fast the three giants moved, tried to pull their swords. They didn't stand a chance.

The fight, if it could even be called a fight, was over in seconds.

Five Knights lying in the leaves and dirt. Three unconscious. Two moaning and well on their way to joining their friends.

"Hold, Urs," Ragnar ordered. His brother knelt over one of the wounded Knights, about to bring his steel down atop the man's head. "Draig said no killing. Not yet."

Urs nodded. "My apologies, brother. I lost myself for a moment."

"It is nothing," Ragnar replied. He grasped the ankles of two of the men and started to pull them toward the van where Thorsen waited with lengths of rope he had pulled from his backpack. "Let's take care of these Knights so we can be done with them."

"That was all that the Dragon requested of us?" Urs asked as he grabbed the legs of one of the Knights and dragged him across the ground, not minding when every few feet the Knight knocked his head on a rock.

"No, the Dragon says that these Knights are the least of our concerns. He wishes us to hunt."

"For what?" Urs asked, his interest piqued.

"Wolf … and perhaps something worse."

11

I FOUND MY THRILL

"Where are we going?"

For the last several hours Melissa and Draig had hiked along the trail, which had become gradually more difficult as they headed away from Kraken Cove and entered Schoodic Forest. The sylvan hills soon would give way to the base of the mountain range that now was less than a mile away.

If that wasn't bad enough from Melissa's perspective, the trail was narrowing and becoming rougher. Roots and rocks were getting in their way more frequently and there were several sections that had been washed out by the rain of the last few weeks.

She was grateful that Draig stopped frequently. Melissa had not yet reclaimed the level of fitness that had been so essential to her success before ... well, she didn't want to dwell on that bad memory so she locked it away.

She was even more grateful that when Draig searched around them with the Grym, he had yet to find anything that gave him cause for concern.

"To see the Druid," he replied as he led her up a much

steeper incline, the peaks toward which they were hiking visible every so often through breaks in the fall foliage.

"I know who we're going to see." The irritation plain in her voice was only exacerbated by the fact that she felt like she was slipping backward two steps for every step she took, more crawling than walking up this section of the trail. "You're having way too much fun at my expense."

Draig smiled, which she caught out of the corner of her eye right before her foot slipped out from beneath her. Her hands went down toward the ground instinctively.

"Crap," she grumbled, flicking the mud off her fingers and having no doubt that Draig's smile had just gotten a little bit wider.

Having no desire to see that smile as he gave her a hand getting out of the mud, and certain as well that she would fall on her face if she didn't look where she was going, she kept her focus on the path.

"Sorry, I couldn't resist."

"I didn't know that there were many Druids left."

"There aren't," Draig confirmed. He climbed to the top of a large rock that had rolled down from the heights above and blocked the trail, then crouched down. He offered Melissa his hand and helped her over the obstacle. "Leya is one of the few still alive."

"Leya?"

"Leya Coeden."

"Has she always been here?"

"No. She visited not long after I came to Kraken Cove and after a few weeks she decided not to leave."

"Why did she come here?"

"The same reason most of the Teg do."

"Are you always so obtuse?" Thanks to the difficulties she was experiencing on their hike, her vexation was very close to the surface. Draig's reticence only aggravating her that much more.

Before she could offer another sharp comment, Melissa almost fell back down the slope, her foot slipping on a root. Draig caught her under the arm just in time.

Once Melissa was back on her feet, Draig offered her more of an explanation, recognizing that he needed to be more expansive if he was to avoid an argument. "The Romans, after their invasion of Gaul, worked hard to eradicate the Druids. Emperors Claudius and Tiberius in the first century played a particularly crucial role in that effort. That persecution continued in Britain."

"Why did the Romans go after the Druids in the first place?" She didn't understand the reasoning. She didn't know much about the Druids, but she doubted that they could have been much of a threat in the ancient world to a military power such as Rome.

"In order to justify their actions, the Romans said that it was because of horrific Druidic practices, such as human sacrifice and some other nasty stuff. Some of the claims were legitimate, most were made up."

"Human sacrifice?" Melissa wondered. "Do we have to worry about that now?"

Draig chuckled. Reaching back, he took Melissa's hand and helped her join him on a small ledge that offered them the chance to rest before they began the final leg of their climb up the switch-backing trail that would take them onto the mountain that rose before them.

"With Leya, no we don't. Today's Druids no longer engage in those practices."

"The Romans were trying to impose their form of civilization on an uncivilized world?"

"That was their primary excuse."

"Excuse? How so?"

"The Romans, Julius Caesar in particular, weren't just interested in eliminating the Druids. They also sought to enslave them."

"Enslave them?" Melissa had never heard that, although she would be the first to admit that she didn't pay as much attention as she should have when she was in school. "I don't know my ancient history as well as I should, but I don't recall learning that the Romans, much less Caesar, wanted to enslave the Druids."

"A little-known fact lost to history," Draig explained as he headed up the trail, Melissa right next to him even as her aching muscles protested.

"Why would Caesar want to enslave them?"

"For their power, of course," Draig replied. "The Roman Empire was expanding. The Druids were perceived as a threat, but also as an opportunity. Caesar and many of the emperors to follow, particularly Claudius and Tiberius, sought to enslave the Druids so that they could use their power for their own ends. Ultimately, those emperors wanted to conquer the world, and they believed that the power the Druids could call upon could help them do that."

"That all makes a terrible kind of sense," Melissa murmured. "Yet if Leya came here, you're suggesting that she's still being hunted."

"On occasion, she and the other remaining Druids are. Therefore, best that they stay hidden." Draig stopped when they reached the next ledge. After searching around them with the Grym, he frowned.

"Do we need to worry?" she asked as they continued up the mountainside, Melissa staying with him despite the burn in her thighs.

"Not yet."

Melissa nodded, assuming that it was only a matter of time

before their hike became a chase. "Then who's hunting the Druids now?"

"Julius Caesar, of course," Draig replied as if it was the most obvious answer in the world.

"Julius Caesar?" snorted Melissa. "How could Julius Caesar still be hunting the Druids? Brutus and a bunch of senators killed him."

"Did they?" Draig asked with a lift of his eyebrows.

"Yes, in the Curia of Pompey in Rome. On the Ides of March. I do remember that at least."

"Who do you think wrote that history?"

"There were several accounts ..." Melissa stopped herself. "Wait, you're telling me that isn't what happened? That there's another version of events?"

"There's always another version of events. Sometimes many. You've heard the saying to the victor go the spoils?"

"Of course."

"There's another saying that's just as important. History is written by the victors."

"Then who wrote the story about Caesar's assassination?"

"Caesar."

"Caesar? There's no way that he could still be ..." Melissa lifted her hands to stop Draig from saying what he was going to say, needing to come to grips with what he was telling her in his very obtuse way. "You're saying that Caesar, who could have ruled Rome and exercised the full power of the Roman Empire, faked his own death rather than do that?"

"He did."

"Why would he do that? The man lived for power. That's all he wanted, and it was right there for the taking."

"Think about it," Draig suggested.

She ignored what she took to be another of his exasperating responses. "How do you know this?"

"He told me."

"He told you?" Melissa couldn't believe what she was hearing. "Julius Caesar is alive and well?"

"And among the Teg," Draig confirmed.

Reaching the next ledge, they stopped. Melissa waited until Draig completed his search with the Grym.

"Julius Caesar is still alive. I'm supposed to believe that?"

"Yes, he's now of the Teg."

"And he's still hunting the Druids?"

"When he can, yes, among his many other interests. He stole as much of the Grym from the Druids as he could, but much to his regret he discovered that even he has limitations."

"Skipping over how Julius Caesar learned to harness the Grym by stealing it from the Druids – we'll talk about that later when we have more time – why would he continue to hunt the Druids if he could take nothing more from them?"

"He has a vendetta against the Druids."

"Why?"

"Because he fears that if he could do what he did to obtain the Grym, someone else could."

Melissa thought about that as they started their way up the trail again. It made all too much sense in a sick kind of way. "He doesn't like competition."

"He really doesn't," Draig confirmed.

"Then why give up being the Emperor of Rome? He would have been the most powerful man of his time."

"In his part of the world," Draig corrected. "We don't want to forget that there were the Chinese. The Atlantans."

"The Atlantans? You can't be serious?"

"All too serious because they are a serious people. But we'll talk about them another time." Draig offered Melissa his hand, then continued his explanation once they climbed over the roots and rocks that had washed over the trail. "My point is that men such as Caesar exercise power, become a part of history in the process, but they also die. The ultimate insult in many respects."

"Caesar didn't want to die," Melissa said, beginning to understand his primary motivation.

"He did not. Caesar wanted power just as you said, he still does, but even more he wanted to live. More living, more power. A simple calculation. With the Druids, he saw an opportunity to gain both since many of the Teg have the capacity to live for centuries if not millennia. That being the primary factor in his decision making, he weighed the power that he could exercise as the Roman Emperor against that which he believed that he could employ by stealing the Grym from the Druids. It proved to be an easy choice for him."

"So to gain the power that he wanted, a power that exceeded that of Ancient Rome, and to ensure that he could live to enjoy it ..."

"He began to enslave the Druids, taking from them the power that they themselves needed to survive. To ensure his power over the centuries, he learned how to harness the Druids' potency for his own ends."

"Much like a vampire," Melissa suggested.

"Very much so," Draig agreed, "draining the Grym from those he caught."

"And he's still hunting them because ..."

"He's learned again that he has certain limitations. He's not really of the Teg, he just joined the Teg for a time. And that time will eventually come to an end."

"He needs the power of the Druids to extend his lifespan."

"Exactly so," Draig confirmed. "However, by killing the Druids to obtain the Grym, he's created the means for his own death."

"There are only so many Druids left, which means that he's close to eliminating his primary tool for maintaining his own power."

"Quite the conundrum for him," Draig nodded. "If he can find a Druid, he'll take the Grym from them, but in so doing knowing as well that time is short. He's seeking another way to do as he began to do more than two thousand years ago. However, he hasn't enjoyed much success."

"I don't feel sorry for him."

"Neither do I."

"I don't want to believe what you're telling me," Melissa murmured, shaking her head in disgust, "but it makes too much sense."

"Caesar isn't unique," Draig explained. "Lord Acton, a British historian, stated that 'Power tends to corrupt and absolute power corrupts absolutely.'"

"I'm familiar with that saying."

"Julius Caesar is the perfect example. He ruled Rome. He had more power than any other man in the ancient world. Yet that wasn't enough for him."

"That's why he wanted the Druids."

"Yes, because the Druids could threaten his power and also lead him on a path to more power." Draig shook his head, a deep sadness seeping into his voice. "The Druids that he enslaved gave him that power against their will and it cost them their lives."

Melissa was quiet for a few heartbeats, thinking. "If Caesar didn't believe that being the Roman Emperor gave him the power that he wanted, then what could ever satisfy his greed?"

"You know the answer to that," Draig prompted.

This time, Melissa wasn't irritated with him, instead appreciating his nudge. "I'm surprised Caesar hasn't been more of a problem for your father."

"He has been from time to time. He's never had the strength to challenge the King Teg directly. He's only cut at the edges. He's also on occasion worked with my father when their interests are aligned."

"How so?"

"Eliminating the competition."

"And your father never sent you after him?"

"He thought about it but decided that doing so would give Caesar more standing than he deserved. He's always viewed Caesar as an upstart."

"Ironic, don't you think," Melissa said, "considering how your father came to power."

"Ironic indeed," Draig agreed. "My father decided on a different course of action that he knew would be just as effective, perhaps even more so, than going after Caesar directly."

Melissa's eyes widened, and not because of the view that she glimpsed as they broke through the tree line briefly, the Atlantic Ocean gleaming brightly off to the east. "He wanted to check Caesar's power, and since he decided not to send you after Caesar himself ..."

"He sent me after the Druids," Draig confirmed with a nod.

"That is more than just cold-blooded. And to decide to do that to his own people." Melissa struggled to wrap her mind around such callousness and self-interest.

Draig stopped suddenly, Melissa walking past him a few feet before she realized. She assumed that he was using the Grym because his eyes flashed dangerously when he looked to the south.

"Anything to worry about?" she asked quietly. She wasn't sure if she was ready for what she knew she couldn't avoid for much longer.

"Not yet," he replied. "But soon."

"Just as with my mother, you didn't follow your father's orders," Melissa said as they continued along the path. Just one more ledge and then it was a straight shot to the plateau above them. From there, they could continue deeper into the mountains.

"I didn't, no."

"You saved them." She didn't sound surprised. She did sound slightly impressed.

"I did."

"Can I ask you a personal question?"

"When have you ever hesitated to ask me a personal question?" Draig wondered drily.

Melissa smiled. "Good point." She stopped for a few seconds. "That's where we're going?" She pointed toward the mountain just a few miles to their front that rose at the western end of the plateau upon which they now stood.

"Yes, it's not much compared to the Rockies, but a good climb for the East Coast. Blueberry Hill. About four thousand feet."

"Why that name?"

"Because of all the blueberries that grow there. We actually get our blueberries from Leya for Tia's Bakes. And it's because of Leya that the mountain has another name."

Draig continued down the trail, Melissa staying with him as they left the ridge and disappeared into the shadows of the forest. It was quieter here, the only sound to be heard the whistle of the wind through the leaves.

The undergrowth was denser as well. Large ferns spread out along a forest floor covered by a latticework of roots. Leaves that were bigger than a serving platter littered the ground as the trees prepared for winter, moss covering the bark in a thick layer and long vines trailing down from the branches. So much so that she had to duck under or swipe the creepers out of the way with her hand every other step.

Every so often, she glimpsed small rises in the ground off to the left and right. She didn't know what they could be, although they reminded her of burial mounds.

A shiver ran through her body at that thought. There was a presence to this wood that she couldn't quite comprehend. It was like they were walking through a primordial forest several thousand years old. The trees exuding a serenity and gravitas she had never experienced before.

"Were you going to share?" Melissa prodded.

"Druid's Peak," he replied.

"That makes sense," she murmured. "From what I recall, and now I can understand why after your explanation of what the Romans, and particularly Caesar, sought from them, Druids are difficult to find."

"You can only find a Druid if a Druid wants you to find them," Draig confirmed.

"Then how are we going to locate your friend atop Druid's Peak?"

"Because there's more to Druid's Peak than what you see now."

"The larger mountain is hidden?"

"That's the best way to describe it."

"Much like a magical illusion?"

"Correct," Draig said. "That's why only those Teg Leya wants to visit with can find her. Few among the Teg can compete with her ability in the Grym."

"Then how do we find her? Or rather how do we reach the point where she finds us?"

"The trail we're on now continues past the mountain and links to several others. One of those paths will lead us to the Druid and her home atop the Druid's Peak."

After the Dragon Door and then the Dragon Vault, Melissa didn't bother to ask for any more details, not wanting to get bogged down because she knew Draig wouldn't offer her much more than he already had. "And you can find this trail?"

Draig nodded as he swept his gaze from right to left and then back again. He looked over his shoulder. Then he began his search once more. Other than the wind rustling the monstrous leaves and setting the vines swaying, he didn't see anything that should worry him. But he didn't need to see the Weres to know that the Renegades were hunting them.

"Yes, I can find the path. Druids and those with the Sight can."

"But I'm assuming that only helps us so much."

"Digging for information even though you already know it," Draig accused, although he said it with a smile.

"Just confirming what little I know."

"Fair enough," he replied. "Those with the Sight can find the path, but that doesn't mean that we can get past the magical illusion that hides the Druid's Peak. Not without Leya's permission."

"And if we tried to enter without her permission?"

"Then we would meet a very painful end ... if Leya is in a good mood."

"And if she isn't?"

"If she isn't, which is often the case, then a long and painful end."

"Leya has a mean streak?"

"She does," Draig confirmed in a tone that suggested that was a good thing. "Step carefully. Druids have become more reclusive over the centuries. And for good reason. Leya rarely leaves the mountain, and when she does, she tends not to leave the forest. She prefers to avoid the Teg unless she can't, and she only allows a few people to visit with her."

"The Sight," Melissa repeated, assuming that Draig was one of those people with that unique skill. "My mother mentioned that power when I was younger, but she didn't tell me much about it."

"It's not something that can be learned," Draig explained. "You're born with it."

"Is that how Druids become Druids?" she wondered.

"In part, yes. Those Teg with the Sight often become Druids. Or did before the Romans."

"But not you?"

"No, not me. Although it's much less common, those with the Sight don't always become Druids. Besides, my father had other plans for me."

"Back to the personal question that's been bothering me."

"That's all you seem to have," Draig said good-naturedly. "Questions."

"It's the only way to learn anything," explained Melissa. "Why did you decide to go against your father? Why did you rescue the Druids? Why did you rescue my mother?"

"An answer to all that would take more time than we have."

Melissa refused to allow him to escape so easily. "Give me the CliffsNotes version."

"You keep telling me that I can be a pain in the ass," Draig grumbled, "but you really ..."

Melissa laughed. It was a good laugh. A deep laugh. It helped to release some of the tension that she was experiencing.

She didn't know why she enjoyed engaging with Draig in what she viewed as a duel of wits, but she couldn't deny the truth of how their encounters made her feel. "Yes, I know, I'm a pain in the ass as well. My mother and sisters would be more than happy to agree with you."

Draig laughed softly, using that time to decide what he wanted to say.

"My father wasn't the man I thought he was."

Melissa waited for more. After they had hiked another hundred yards, she realized that he had nothing else to offer. "That's all you're going to say? Really? On such a salient topic?"

"You really can be ..."

"A pain in the ass," Melissa finished for him. She smiled, though not completely. She didn't laugh because she could tell that he was holding back. "We just went through all that." She nudged him in the shoulder with hers. "You're not getting out of this so easily. Tell me. There has to be more to it than that."

"Look, I really don't ..."

"You went against King Pendragon, Draig. The strongest of the Teg. Your own father. I can't think of a single Teg who would do what you did." Melissa shook her head, still trying to make sense of the risk he had taken. "What you did requires a mix of courage and stupidity. Likely more of the latter than the former. You ..."

"All right. I'll tell you if you promise to stop badgering me."

As they continued beneath the trees, Melissa glanced at him from the side, staring into his reddish orange eyes for a few heartbeats. "I promise, so long as it's the truth."

"The truth? That's a very subjective term."

"For your father, perhaps. Not for you."

He had to admit that she had him there. "My father wasn't the man I thought he was."

"You already said that."

Draig ignored her. "And when I came to that realization, I grasped as well that I wasn't the man that I wanted to be. Because of him in some small part. Because of me to a much greater degree. I made the mistake of allowing him to mold me into what he wanted me to be."

"A moment of epiphany?" Melissa asked, though without the humor that Draig anticipated.

"When I was younger, I worshipped my father. I saw all that he did for the Teg. I believed that everything he did, all the sacrifices that he made, were for the Teg. The Teg always came first in whatever decision he made and action he took." Draig shook his head slowly from side to side, angry at his father, more so at himself. "And I got to help him do that. Or so I believed."

Melissa allowed Draig to dwell within his thoughts, the

gloom of the wood darkening as they entered the mountain's shadow.

"And then, I discovered that I wasn't important to him. At least not as his son." He smiled, although there was little warmth in the gesture. His father had played him for a fool. "Rather, I was important to him as a tool. Nothing more. When I recognized that, I recognized as well that my father didn't think of the Teg first. He thought of himself first. Because he equated himself as being the Teg. What he needed was most important, no matter the cost, because what he needed was what the Teg needed. At least that's how he looks at the world."

"A harsh lesson to learn," Melissa said in a very quiet, sad voice.

"You have no idea."

Melissa considered what Draig told her. Thanks to the tension visible in his expression, she had no doubt that he held back a great deal of his reasoning, only offering her what he was comfortable sharing. "Many of the Teg placed in your position ... they wouldn't have done what you did. They wouldn't have saved the Teg they were sent to kill. They would have simply kept on with their work, not having the guts to challenge the King Teg."

Draig's eyes flashed then, so brightly that for just a heartbeat a sphere of light lit the gloom around them. The emotions he usually kept locked away rising to the surface. "I couldn't save them all."

The bone-deep sadness that Melissa heard in his voice almost broke her heart. She desperately wanted to learn the cause.

She understood, however, that trying to press him on that topic now would be useless. Seeking to distract him, she returned to a Teg that she was still curious about.

"How was it that you met Caesar?"

Draig didn't respond right away, still lost in his thoughts. For a time, Melissa didn't think that he would answer.

"Caesar approached me," he said after taking a deep breath, his severe expression easing as he did so.

"He approached you?" She was more than surprised. She was astounded. "Even though you are the King Teg's son?"

Draig nodded. "It made sense if you think about it the right way. Julius was raised on Roman politics. Patricide, fratricide, all of that was a part of the game. Roman rulers often had to worry more about their family members seeking to depose them than the so-called barbarians pushing at the boundary of the empire."

"He wanted you to kill your father."

"He did," Draig confirmed. "He made several promises as well as to what I would gain if I did the job for him."

"You didn't kill him for making the offer? Why not?"

"I thought about it. Although my killing him certainly would have been justified, if for no other reason than the fact that Julius Caesar is a pompous jackass who walks around as if he's the very center of the world, I didn't. You're right."

"A good reason to get rid of him, I'll give you that."

"Instead, I accepted his offer."

"You accepted ..."

"I accepted so that I could learn who among the Teg was working with him. Julius didn't have the power at the time to take control of the Teg if I did as he asked, so I assumed there was someone guiding him from the shadows."

"And there was?"

"There was. And I almost got her. Almost." Draig shook his head ruefully.

"Why didn't you?"

"That's a story for another time. Follow me."

"This is the path?"

"It is," Draig confirmed without an ounce of doubt as he stepped between two massive ferns.

When Melissa followed him, she found herself on a trail that was scarcely large enough for a deer. If you didn't know what to look for, there was no way that anyone could have found the path.

"This will take us where we need to go?"

Draig nodded, although he didn't bother to turn around. "It will. Then Leya can decide if she wants to meet with us."

Draig stopped abruptly, losing himself to the Grym.

"They're close, aren't they?" Melissa asked, her nerves coming through in her voice.

"Not too close, but they are getting closer." Draig pulled the backpack from his shoulders, then began to rummage through it.

When he found what he wanted, he pulled the drawstring closed and slipped the backpack over his shoulders again.

"What are those?"

He had turned toward her, revealing a dozen small, metallic mechanisms that resembled dragonflies. "They're going to give us some more time. Place your hand atop mine."

Curious about what Draig was going to do, Melissa did as he said without asking a single question. A rarity for her.

Draig offered her an explanation, appreciating her restraint. "Peggy Rose made these for me." Thin streams of the Grym spun out from his fingertips, swirling around the dragonflies, then around her hand.

"That's great ... but what are they?"

"Magical tags of a sort." He released his hold on the Grym. "I've infused them with our scents."

Melissa nodded in understanding and smiled broadly. "You're going to give the Weres so many trails to follow that they won't be able to follow us."

"That's the goal. It should work, at least for a time." Draig threw the dragonflies into the air, the devices buzzing above their heads for a few circles before shooting off in every direction but the one that they were going. "Werewolves track by scent, the strongest by magical scent. Because they can move so rapidly, they'll figure out the ruse sooner rather than later. When they do, they'll come back to the last place they smelled us and then begin the hunt anew."

"How much time have you bought us?"

"I can't say," Draig shrugged. "Hopefully enough."

"And if we haven't earned enough time to get to the Druid?"

Draig shrugged. "Why worry about something that hasn't yet come to pass?"

"Because we have a pack of Werewolves on our heels," Melissa said with more force than she intended. She forgave herself, because she had no desire to experience another chase as she had when the Weres hunted her through the streets of Kraken Cove.

"Wait here," Draig said.

He stepped off the trail, Melissa losing sight of him as he slipped in between the ferns, vines, and other undergrowth that made hiking through this wood so difficult.

"Draig!" she called in a harsh whisper.

Why would he leave her like this and not explain what he was doing?

Because that's what Draig did, her annoyance at his lack of communication the only thing that was keeping her fear from gaining control over her.

She thought about following him but decided against that tactic immediately.

Melissa would never find him. All she could do was stay where she was and hope that he returned.

As the seconds turned into a minute, and then that minute into five more, her fears threatened to take hold. She stood there as if she were rooted to the ground, afraid to move even just a step.

Every shifting shadow, every sound -- although there was little more than leaf scraping against leaf thanks to the touch of the wind -- drew her focus.

Where in all the hells had Draig gone?

A snap a hundred feet to her right, somewhere beyond the ferns, made her flinch.

Taking hold of the Grym, she waited. Fearing the worst.

She gasped, jumping off the ground more than a foot when a large squirrel shot across the deer trail just a few feet in front of her.

She didn't know if she should be thankful or angry, her rapidly beating heart finally beginning to settle.

She decided to be thankful. But then a howl echoed through the wood, the chilling sound freezing her blood.

Somewhere off to the west. How far, she couldn't tell. She had little experience in the wild, being a city girl at heart.

Then another howl, this one answering the first, off to the east.

The Weres were tracking them. Narrowing their search.

Maybe Draig's dragonflies didn't work as well as he had hoped.

That fear consuming her, she wondered when Draig would be back.

Her eyes widened when she realized that might not be the right question to ask. Would Draig even bother to come back?

She was the cause of his current problems. It would be much easier for him just to take her out into the woods and leave her here for the Werewolves to find her.

No more Melissa, no more problem.

Life returns to normal in Kraken Cove.

Draig would no longer need to deal with her.

No, Draig wouldn't do that to her. Right?

He wouldn't. She was sure of it.

Especially not after all that he had done for her. Why make the effort when he could have left her for the Weres the first time? No one would have known that she was missing if they had kidnapped her from the lighthouse.

"You're right," Draig said from right behind her. "I wouldn't." He gave her a smile and stepped past her. "Although I will admit that the thought did cross my mind. More than once in truth."

"The thought of ..." Melissa forgot the Werewolves for just a second, stunned by his admission. Both because he seemed to be able to read her mind and that he had even considered leaving her to her fate in the first place. "How could you possibly know what I was thinking?" With the Weres closing in on them, she knew now wasn't the time to discuss this. Nevertheless, she couldn't help herself.

"I could see the look on your face," he replied. "It was easy to interpret."

Melissa nodded, but then she frowned. How could he see her face? He was behind her when he came out from between the overgrown ferns.

She was about to ask him just that when another howl ripped through the Schoodic Forest. It sounded much closer. Too close, in fact. "How far away?"

"Still a few miles," Draig replied. "The dragonflies are doing their work. Nevertheless, the ruse won't last forever. Come on." Draig turned and started down the path, calling over his shoulder, "We're almost where we need to be."

She hurried to catch up to him. "What were you doing?"

"Leaving a few more gifts for the Weres. If we're lucky, what I did will slow the pack down. Give us a few more minutes."

Before Melissa could ask what those gifts were, Draig disappeared, sliding between two ferns and leaving her behind.

She pushed her way after him and found herself on another trail that was no bigger than the last, the massive ferns that sought to reclaim the path scraping against them on both sides.

"What do you mean by gifts?" Melissa was just a few steps behind him, having no desire to be left behind again.

"Just a few things I learned when I was a Knight of the Round."

"With whatever you did, how long do you think we have?"

Melissa's question appeared to be quite timely. Another howl blasted through the wood. Then another. And one more. All with a greater clarity than before. That could only mean one thing.

Then another howl followed a few seconds later, but this one was cut short by a shriek of pain. Her gaze drawn toward the noise, Melissa almost ran into Draig's broad back.

He stood there on the trail, searching around them with the Grym. When he was done, Melissa interpreted his grunt for displeasure. Then without a word, he opened the space between two very large ferns and revealed the next path they needed to take.

"Thank you," she murmured as she stepped through. "That was your work?"

"It was," Draig replied as he walked by her. She couldn't miss the menacing, very pleased smile that twisted his lips.

She really wanted to know what he had done, if for no other reason than she was intensely curious as to his abilities with the Grym. Nevertheless, Melissa didn't push. Instead, she did something that she seldom ever did.

"I'm sorry."

Draig didn't say anything, continuing along the trail. Melissa expected the customary response. It was the right thing for him to do. Maybe he didn't hear her.

"I'm sorry," she repeated, a little louder.

"I heard you the first time."

"Then why didn't you say anything?" A touch of heat entered her voice.

"I was searching around us with the Grym. I thought you would be interested in knowing how close our pursuers were."

A sharper howl, more authoritative than the first, tore through the forest. Draig nodded, knowing what that howl was. The leader of the pack giving his Werewolves their instructions.

"How close are they?" She felt like the straight man in a comedy duo.

"Closer than we would like."

"Can you be any more specific?" Melissa's irritation was swiftly becoming anger. He had not yet responded to her apology.

"Two miles at the most. The dragonflies and the traps are the only reason they're not on our heels yet."

"How many?" Melissa could do a great many things with the Grym, yet just as it was with every Teg, there were certain skills that no matter how hard she tried she could not master. Each Teg had their own strengths and weaknesses with respect to their application of the Power of the Ancients, and despite her great skill, she had no ability to search around them as Draig was doing with such ease.

"Almost two score," he replied. "Probably a few more."

That number made sense to Draig based on the number of Renegades that he, Seamus, and the three pups had eliminated at the Raptor Bay Lighthouse. Werewolf packs tended to contain a dozen of the beasts.

Whoever led the Weres here had brought three packs with him. Overkill to take one Witch. Unless the leader of the pack believed that the Dragon and his friends were helping that Witch.

A series of howls broke the silence of the wood, one right after the other. They sounded like confirmations.

"They know where we are?" Melissa asked.

"That would be my guess," Draig confirmed.

"You never responded to my apology."

"I thought you had forgotten about that." Draig should have expected that she wouldn't let that go despite their current challenges.

"I don't forget anything." Melissa said it with a smile. She thought she heard the same in his voice, although she couldn't tell because his back was turned.

"One of your unique skills?"

"It certainly helps in my chosen profession."

"I can imagine."

Draig stopped again, Melissa catching herself this time before she ran into him. He turned slowly in a circle.

"Don't we keep going?" Melissa asked. She nodded down the narrow trail that they had been following.

Draig didn't reply right away, his gaze fixed toward the southwest on something that only he could see.

"No, we don't," he said finally.

Melissa realized that she had been holding her breath while she waited for his reply. She let it out slowly and then breathed deeply.

"They're closer?"

"No, not yet," Draig replied. "They're trying to get ahead of us. They're working their way up our southern flank. They want to surround us on the trail."

"You can see all that?"

"I can," he confirmed. "Besides, it's what I would do if the roles were reversed."

"But this is the only trail that takes us where we need to go." Melissa's worry threatened to once again become fear.

Draig gave her a smile then, although it wasn't friendly, and it wasn't directed toward her. Rather, it seemed like he relished the opportunity to test himself against a larger pack of Werewolves.

"Actually, it's not."

Draig pushed his way through the ferns. This time, however, there wasn't a trail for them to take on the other side.

To greet them, there was only a thick undergrowth of more ferns mixed in with bushes and a jungle of vines hanging down from the tree limbs.

Draig stepped past her and hiked toward the north, away from the trail they had been on.

"Where are we going?"

"The path we were taking isn't the only way to get where we need to go."

For the next few minutes, they hiked through the brush. Then Draig disappeared through another line of ferns.

Melissa picked up her pace, worried that she would lose him. Pushing her way through the gorse, she missed a step, the ground giving way beneath her.

She found herself falling. A rocky, dry streambed rising up to meet her.

She didn't have the time to scream. She could only cringe, closing her eyes, anticipating the pain to come.

She grunted in shock instead, feeling herself spinning through the air, two strong hands on her hips. When she opened her eyes again, Draig's fiery orbs greeted her.

"Careful."

"The warning doesn't help after the fact," Melissa muttered, although she didn't have the energy to put a lot of antagonism into her voice.

She stepped back from Draig, or rather he allowed her to by removing his hands. He smiled then, clearly amused by her irritation.

Rather than offer a smart response of his own, he turned

and walked down the streambed, scrambling this way and that to avoid the worst of the rocks that stuck up from the silty ground.

For just a few heartbeats, Melissa hesitated before following him. She could still remember the feel of his hands on her waist. How he ...

She gave herself a metaphorical kick in the ass. Why the hell was she thinking about Draig's very strong hands? Why was that few seconds of the entire chase stuck in her mind?

Shaking her head to snap herself out of it, she trotted after him, following much the same path that he took.

"Can I ask you a question?"

Draig didn't stop. He sensed that the Weres were cutting the distance between them. They were still focused on the path that Draig and Melissa had been on. It wouldn't be long, however, before they realized their mistake and adjusted their strategy.

It was going to be tight. Maybe too tight.

"Can I stop you?"

Melissa smiled. She was certain by the tone of his voice that he was more amused than annoyed by her request.

"No, you should know that by now."

"Ask."

"You mentioned when you were talking to The Three Brothers that you appreciated their discretion, but that it wouldn't be long before the rest of the Teg knew you were alive again."

"That's right. I did." Melissa wanted to go back to that comment? Now of all times? Draig had not a clue as to how Melissa's mind worked, and he was beginning to think that was a good thing.

"Why?"

"Why what?" Draig didn't understand what she was asking.

"Why are you concerned about coming back to life? You're still one of strongest of the Teg. Few of us can challenge you and expect to come out whole on the other side."

"That may be," Draig replied. "But some still can. Why fight if you don't have to?"

"You think they will?" Melissa didn't know all the Teg who might want Draig dead, but she assumed there were quite a lot because of the work that he had done for his father. "They'll give in to their desire for vengeance even while knowing the risk?"

"Vengeance or greed," Draig clarified. "Some of the Teg will think that they will work their way into Arthur's good graces if they bring him my head."

"Good point," Melissa admitted.

"I've been dead for a while," he continued. "It's going to be a bit of a shock for some. But, yes, I have no doubt that some of the Teg who want me dead will come after me."

"And that's why you want The Three Brothers to keep your rebirth under wraps?"

"Not so much for me," he explained. "More for the Teg who trust me and depend on me."

Melissa nodded, understanding his concern now. He wasn't worried about himself. Rather, he was worried about the Teg living in Kraken Cove.

The Teg he had helped escape from his father.

Teg like her mother.

If Draig's enemies couldn't kill him directly, they might try to get to him through the people he cared about. The people who relied on him.

"Do you think it will come to that?"

"I hope not." Draig squeezed between two large rocks that came up to his shoulders, the boulders so large that they touched the banks of the streambed. He could only imagine how ferocious the water flow was at this partial dike during the rainy season.

"But you're still worried."

"I know the Teg who want to kill me. I know what they're capable of and what they're willing to do. So, I'm more than just a little worried."

He waited for her to squeeze between the boulders. When she did, he continued toward the north, the streambed beginning a slow curl to the west.

"Tom and Harry giving me a little extra time to prepare for what I expect will come my way, assuming that we both survive the next few hours, could mean the difference between life and death for some of my friends."

"I really am sorry," Melissa offered, and she meant it. "This was never my intention. I didn't even know you were living in Kraken Cove."

She felt terrible. She had come to the town with the goal of extricating herself from the mess in which she had found herself. Yet it seemed that Melissa only had succeeded in catching Draig in her web and in the process put what he had created in Kraken Cove at risk.

"I know," he replied softly. "It wasn't your fault. It just happened."

Although Draig didn't entirely believe that. He didn't believe in happenstance.

Medusa had sent Melissa to Kraken Cove for a specific purpose, though Draig had little doubt that there was more to it than that.

He had little doubt as well that there might be someone standing behind Medusa who had a hand in making that suggestion.

The howl that blasted through the forest and died away quickly with a sharp whimper broke Draig from his train of thought. He smiled ever so slightly. He had heard the agony in the shriek.

Good. A few more minutes gained if they were lucky.

Melissa followed in silence, waiting for another howl. Nothing yet. "I really am sorry. My goal wasn't to reveal where you were. I didn't even know that you were alive. I just wanted to find the primer and be gone."

"I know," Draig replied softly. "That's just the way of it sometimes. Unintended consequences and all that."

"It's a tough spot that I put you in. I understand that."

He shrugged. "It was bound to happen. I just didn't realize it would happen so soon. I've enjoyed living in Kraken Cove ... and not having to worry about someone trying to stab me in the back."

Melissa didn't want to say it, but she felt that she needed to. She needed to acknowledge the truth. "Thank you."

"For what?" Draig asked. She had spoken so softly that he barely heard her.

"Helping me."

"I thought you didn't need my help," he said, laughing softly.

"Really? You're going to be difficult now?" Melissa spoke sharply, although it was hard to miss the amusement laced in. "I'm trying to be nice, Werewolves are trying to pick up our scent, and you're going to be a pain ..."

Draig held his hands up over his shoulders, seeking peace. "You're right, I'm sorry. A bad habit on my part. Pushing when I don't need to."

"Just to be clear," Melissa said, "I do appreciate your help. However, you need to understand that I am not a damsel in distress. Far from it." She was almost growling when she said it. "So you can get that stupid trope out of your mind. I don't need your help. I'm allowing it because it makes my life easier. Clear?"

"Crystal," Draig replied, fighting hard not to laugh. He felt that if he did, it would ruin the moment for Melissa. And she deserved it.

Another howl broke the quiet of the wood. And then several more.

Draig shook his head in disappointment.

"Let's pick up the pace," he urged. "If we need to fight, this isn't the place to do it."

12

THE HUNT

Wiping his catcher's mitt of a paw across his whiskered face, then scratching at the unkempt reddish-brown beard that ran all the way down to his cowboy belt, he couldn't quite believe what he was looking at.

He had never seen the like. And he had seen quite a lot. Much of it his own doing.

Raik growled loudly. The rat's nest that was his hair bristled. His nerves sparking.

He tried to stay focused. His rising anger making that difficult.

He was about to shift.

He wanted to shift.

He craved the power that he could only achieve in his true form.

Relying on the strength of his iron will, he kept himself in check.

Not yet.

But soon.

Soon he would let himself go.

"Did anyone see what happened?"

Luca stood before him. Part of him, anyway.

His pack brother had been cut in two at the waist.

Luca's bottom half remained erect, feet firmly planted into the ground, still caught in a magical trap, a dim white glow marking the bounds of the snare. His upper half lay face down just a few feet away.

Raik had to give Luca credit. He had gone down fighting. At least as well as he could expect to since he was battling a power against which he was powerless.

Luca had been smart. Snared in his human form, to break free he tried to shift.

Probably believing that the massive strength and speed he gained by taking his lycanthropic form would give him the extra boost he needed to escape the trap.

It wasn't enough.

His body had begun the shift, but he was too slow. The Grym too fast and too potent.

That certainly said something about who had set the trap. It revealed a strength and skill that only a few among the Teg could master.

An experienced Were could assume their more natural form in less than a second. This snare completed its grisly task in just a heartbeat.

Based on the remains, Raik assumed a scythe made of the Grym cut through Luca before he could complete the shift. And not a drop of blood spilled.

The magical blade that sliced through Luca cauterized the wounds at the same time it killed him. The smoking flesh and charred bone confirmed that conclusion.

Impressive work. Raik would be the first to admit that.

In fact, just as impressive as the last trap he examined.

Jamaal had been so focused on the scent he had been following, so ravenous to catch their prey, that he hadn't paid enough attention to his surroundings.

Never thinking that he might be the prey instead.

Raik had followed the same game trail as Jamaal, but he stopped just in time, catching sight of what waited for him only a few yards to his front. Jamaal's impetuousness saving Raik's life.

Jamaal had sprinted between two trees. When Jamaal exited the tight space, his body continued for several yards before collapsing in the dirt and leaves, his head rolling to a stop farther along the trail.

Raik examined that space with a keen eye. It was difficult to make out. He had only glimpsed it when a stray ray of sunlight found its way through the smothering foliage.

The chord of energy strung between the trees was thinner than a hair and only visible when the light struck it a certain way. Set at the perfect height as well.

After losing two more of his pack, Raik should have been angrier than he was.

But he wasn't.

Instead, he was excited.

Finally, he had a worthy adversary and a hunt that merited his effort.

"No," several of his brothers, all as big as NFL linebackers, rumbled.

A few bowed their heads. Not in acknowledgment of their dead comrade. Rather hoping to avoid the tirade they expected from their leader, because Raik never handled any type of setback well.

Raik nodded, expecting as much, his eyes never leaving Luca's remains. Definitely not the work of the Witch. Nor were those bloody dragonflies his pack chased all over the forest.

Now that had been clever work. And his brothers had fallen for it like a pack of dogs chasing after a bone.

Sad.

Very, very sad.

His brothers had been fooled so easily, and Luca and Jamaal paid for their folly with their lives.

Normally, after a mistake such as this, he would have beaten a few of his brothers just to make a point.

He would have enjoyed offering that reminder. It was an excellent way to release some of his stress.

He didn't, however.

That would have to wait until after he and his Renegades gained what they were after.

Because he had the scent.

The real scent.

With barely a thought, Raik assumed his true shape. Growing twice as large as he already was, his clothes disappeared, replaced by a coat of thick reddish fur. His shoulders broadened and became more muscular. His arms and legs elongated, claws replacing his fingers and toes. His face lengthened into a snout with razor-sharp teeth.

When he pulled his golden eyes away from Luca and turned around, his Weres waited for him. All of them transformed into lycanthropes. All of them ready to finish the hunt and avenge their dead brothers.

"We end this now!" Raik roared. "Bring me the head of the Fallen Knight!"

DRAIG AND MELISSA sprinted along the streambed.

It wasn't easy. They kept their eyes down most of the time, watching their footing because of all the rocks and branches that littered the uneven ground.

Sensing that Melissa was tiring, Draig skidded to a stop. Reaching out his free hand, he grabbed her arm and brought her to a halt before she dropped to her knees.

"Don't get a lot of exercise?"

He meant it less as a joke and more as a way to keep her focused. A little anger often could provide a much-needed second breath.

"Not this kind of exercise," Melissa wheezed.

She didn't have the wind to take issue with his comment, and she could only blame herself.

Where she was now resulted from her decision to take the job that she scarcely had any time to prepare for. She had spent a week in the gym and little time on the treadmill.

While she was swimming toward the shore on that fateful night that had dropped her right into the center of this mess, she had known that she wasn't ready for what might be demanded of her physically.

Although she certainly hadn't anticipated being chased through a forest by a pack of Werewolves.

For just a heartbeat, Draig considered continuing along the streambed a little bit farther. After a quick study of Melissa, who was still struggling for breath, he threw out the idea.

They were close enough.

He thought.

He hoped.

And, if not, it was going to be one hell of a fight.

Using the Grym, Draig searched around them.

It didn't take long.

The Werewolves were coming faster now.

Making right for them.

The utility of the dragonflies and his traps had come to an end.

The law of diminishing returns.

He had expected as much. He could play off the Weres' instinctive aggression only for so long.

Still, his tricks courtesy of Peggy Rose and his traps taught to him by Gaheris had served their purpose, giving them the extra time they needed to get closer to their final destination.

Draig smiled as he watched the pack approach, sensing an opportunity as the scene played out in the back of his mind.

They all had shifted.

All of them twice the size of prehistoric dire wolves.

All of them angry.

All of them hungry.

And a couple of the more rabid Weres were a dozen or so yards ahead of their brothers.

Good.

He could use that.

"How far?" Melissa wheezed, no longer gasping, finally beginning to regain her wind.

She was bent over at the waist, hands on her knees, taking a series of deep breaths. She pushed herself up, moving her hands to her hips. She needed to be vertical and expand her lungs, otherwise she was going to puke.

"Five hundred yards. Not long now."

"Do we run?"

"There's no point," Draig replied. "Fighting them here is as good as fighting them anywhere else in this streambed."

Melissa nodded. His decision made sense. Besides, she was tired of running.

"How many again?"

"Three dozen. Probably a few more." Draig said it in a way that suggested he wasn't all that concerned by that number.

Melissa certainly was. Even after observing his skill with that sword of his on the beach in front of Raptor Bay Lighthouse.

They could put up a good fight. Of that she had no doubt.

But she knew as well that there was only one possible result against so many determined and deadly opponents.

Not wanting to think about that, she decided to ask a question that had been on her mind ever since she had met the baker who turned out to be so much more than just that.

"Why does everyone call you Draig?"

Draig frowned, not expecting the question, although he knew why she asked it. He shrugged. "Why not?"

"It's your last name."

"It is."

"Why don't you use your first name? Why not Axel?"

Draig didn't really have an answer for her. "It's just the way it is. Almost everyone but Merlin called me Draig when I was a child, and it stayed that way as I got older. After I became who I became, it seemed more appropriate."

Melissa nodded. Not too far off in the distance she heard the first of what soon became a chorus of howls.

She ignored them. She would deal with her fear when the time came. Not before. Just as her mother had taught her.

With that goal in mind, she threw another question at Draig. "Was your father a fan of Guns and Roses?"

"Who?"

She stared at him in shock. "You've got to be kidding me. You don't know who Axl Rose is?"

Draig laughed, his reddish orange eyes brightening. "Of course I do. I'm not entirely culturally inept. Besides, he's not what he seems."

"Not what he seems? What do you mean by that? Wait. You've met him?"

"That's a story for another time."

"You always say that as soon as you've piqued my interest," she complained.

"Are you ready?" Draig asked. His eyes glowed with a greater intensity.

"Ready."

Draig nodded. Melissa nodded in turn, working hard not to gulp. "Good, because it's time for the fun to begin."

He turned away from Melissa, facing in the direction from which they had come.

Draig smiled when the two Werewolves dashed between the ferns and jumped down into the streambed.

Only fifty yards away and closing fast, their clawed feet tore up the dirt and rock.

The Werewolves howled in anticipation as they caught sight of their prey. Jaws open. Strings of spittle flying from their sharp fangs.

"Draig," Melissa called.

He was just standing there, and she didn't understand why.

She had taken hold of the Grym, ready to go down with guns blazing. Understanding that taking on a Werewolf was no easy task. Much less three dozen.

They were determined. Cunning. Vicious. Lightning fast.

Why wasn't Draig doing anything? He didn't seem to care that the Werewolves were eating up the ground between them at a blood-chilling pace.

Blackthorn shillelagh in his right hand just as it always was. But in his left, he was flicking between his fingers what appeared to be a smooth oval rock.

What was he going to do?

Play the role of David?

He didn't have a sling. Was he just going to throw it at them?

What could he possibly do with one small rock against two very angry, very hungry Werewolves?

"Axel!" Melissa screamed, desperate to get his attention.

Before she finished her shout, the Weres no more than fifteen yards away from him, Draig tossed the rock into the air rather than at the charging beasts.

Melissa watched in amazement, the rock shimmering a white so bright when it reached its zenith that it lost its shape, veils of energy streaking down to the ground and forming a dome thirty yards in diameter.

Draig had trapped the pair of charging Weres.

With them.

THE TWO WEREWOLVES ignored the dome of energy that sprang up around them.

They didn't know what it was or what it could do.

They didn't care.

They had gotten past this trap without being harmed, unlike their less fortunate brothers.

Best of all, their prey stood right before them.

Waiting like the fools they were.

Not fleeing like they should.

The Weres needed to take the Witch. That would be easy enough. They knew how to fight a Witch even if she was strong in the Grym.

So the Witch could wait.

They would start with the Fallen Knight.

They would take his head as Raik demanded, and they would enjoy every second of the kill. Vengeance for those lost to the pack.

Draig read all that in their bloodthirsty expressions. He had seen much the same many times before, having fought more Weres than he could recall.

Their anger and desire didn't bother him in the least. Rather, it pleased him.

Once again, he had separated a few of the Weres from their pack and put them right where he wanted them by playing on their overdeveloped sense of aggressiveness.

He was pleased as well that the last toy Peggy Rose had made for him worked perfectly. With her unique application of the Grym, just as he requested she had crafted a protective dome that took shape the instant he triggered the item. Though taking into account the beasts that shared the space with him, perhaps kennel was the better term.

"Indestructible," she had said. "Unless you know how to destroy it."

But it was too early in the game to think about doing that.

The pair came right at him, ignoring Melissa.

Draig's grim visage curled into a momentary smile.

The Weres were making his job easier. So much the better for him.

At the very last second, right before the Werewolf that was just a few feet in front of the other one dug his razor-sharp claws into Draig's chest, he pivoted out of the way and trailed his leg behind him.

He caught the Were in the lead across the back of his knees, the lycanthrope grunting in surprise as his claws went to the rough ground in an attempt to cushion his fall.

The second Werewolf was forced to change course. Hurdling his struggling brother, who was crawling more than sprinting as he tried to keep his balance, the second Werewolf skidded to a stop.

The first Werewolf scrabbled across the streambed, thinking that he had succeeded. He discovered quickly that he faced another challenge.

He had run out of space.

The lycanthrope crashed headfirst into the magical barrier with a resounding smack. Snout punched up against the shimmering energy, he remained in place for a few heartbeats before sliding down to the ground. If not unconscious, close to it.

Draig had hoped that the Werewolf might break his neck. No such luck and not surprising. As he had learned, these beasts could absorb more punishment than most other Teg.

At least the Were was dazed. Groaning. Not yet trying to rise or shake his head to clear it of the fog that had descended.

He would have finished the beast when he was down, but Draig didn't have the time.

The other Were was turning toward him.

As Draig shifted his positioning to face off against the Werewolf, he had a chance to glance beyond the protective dome.

The rest of the pack stood just on the other side of the thin, glowing shield. A few pounded in frustration on the surface. Most simply stood there growling, making their displeasure known. Flexing their claws. Waiting for their chance. Assuming that the barrier could remain in place for only so long.

And they were right about that last, which meant that Draig needed to keep the proceedings moving along.

He locked eyes with the towering lycanthrope standing in the center of the flea-ridden pack.

The beast was staring back at him. Not growling. Not howling. Rather intent. Patient. Unconcerned by the unexpected change of events. Knowing that the course of those events would change again. And when they did that he would be ready.

The leader of the Renegades and a familiar face.

Raik.

Draig should have killed the evil bastard long ago, but he never had the chance.

Now he did, and he was grateful for the opportunity.

Eliminating a good number of the Renegades and having a go at one of the most brutal Weres in the Teg world? This was going to be more fun than he had anticipated.

Giving Raik a confident nod that was more a promise than a greeting, Draig ducked and stepped to the side.

The Were who had slid to a stop before slamming against the barrier streaked by him. His claw, swiping for the back of Draig's neck, missed by no more than a hair.

But a hair was more than enough for Draig to take advantage of the mistake.

Thrown off balance by the power of his swing, Draig used his momentum against the Were.

With a quick flick of his boot, he tangled the monster's clawed feet.

Unable to stop himself in time, the Were crashed to the ground in a small cloud of dirt and grit, not coming to a stop until he slammed his maw against a spiky rock that stuck out several feet from the dry streambed.

Draig smiled when he heard the hard smack, but he didn't see it. He adjusted his positioning, returning his focus to the groggy Were.

Melissa remained off to the side, staying well away from the beast. Draig sensed her hold on the Grym, but she made no move against the Were. Yet.

She seemed to be a bit shocked that so much had happened so quickly. Draig had taken down both Weres in no more than a few seconds.

To buy a little more time with the Were making his first attempt to regain his bearings, Draig took a few quick steps and kicked with a bone-jarring strength.

His boot crunched into the groggy Were's groin, earning a low groan of pain. The beast sliding back down the barrier and clutching his aching midsection.

Sensing the movement behind him, Draig spun back around, the blackthorn shillelagh revealing its true self. Excalibur shining brightly in his hand.

The Were who had swiped at him and missed was back on his feet. The beast, about to lunge at him, stopped abruptly. Realizing that he had been found out.

The Werewolf glared at Draig. Growling softly. His tongue licking at the blood where several of his sharp teeth had been before he smashed his snout against the rock.

The lost teeth were just an inconvenience. They would grow back within the hour.

Weres healed quickly from even the worst injuries. Because of that unique characteristic, it took a great deal to kill them. And there were only a few ways to ensure that they didn't rise again.

"You dare to stand against me, Fallen Knight?" the Were rasped.

The Renegade seemed intent on keeping Draig in place, perhaps hoping that his injured brother would rejoin the hunt.

Draig didn't mind. The break served his purposes for a time.

"Kill him, Dudley!" several of his brothers urged from the other side of the barrier.

"Finish him!"

"Rip out his heart!"

Creative as always Draig thought as he allowed those and the other cries and curses coming from the pack to wash over him.

Just to be certain, Draig glanced quickly over his shoulder. Nothing had changed.

Melissa remained in place, watching his confrontation while at the same time keeping a wary eye on the ball-broken Were who was still on the ground, moaning and holding onto his nether region.

"Dudley?" Draig asked, realizing he had a few extra seconds. "Really?"

"You make fun of me?" Dudley roared. "I will feast on you before you die."

Draig shook his head, slightly amused that it had been so easy. "No, I'm not making fun of you. I'm just surprised. I've met a lot of Werewolves over the years, but never one named Dudley."

The Were's glare intensified, his golden eyes shining brightly. Then he lifted his maw and howled, releasing some of the fury that was threatening to overpower his reason. "You will pay for your insolence, Fallen Knight. I promise you that."

"Prove it, Dudley," Draig said in a deadly quiet voice. "I'm right here. Prove that you can kill me."

Dudley took a step forward at Draig's instigation, desperate to make good on his promises. Yet he hesitated again, ignoring the shouts and howls from his brethren urging him forward.

This wasn't the type of fight that Dudley was used to. Because of that, he wasn't sure how to handle it. Especially with two of his brothers dead and another injured just a few yards to his left.

Dudley was more comfortable with the hunt. Chasing his prey. Killing his prey before they even realized that he was after them.

How this hunt was coming to a close differed from all the others he had participated in.

This wasn't a hunt.

This was a combat.

Against a man who thrived during a combat.

Dudley sought to change the dynamics if he could upon reaching that conclusion.

"Do you not have the courage to fight me without your sword, Fallen Knight?"

Dudley had seen the look that had passed behind Draig's eyes. There was a confidence there that surprised him and not a single ounce of fear. That's what had given Dudley pause.

"I think not, Dudley. I don't have claws like you do. I need to have a little bite as well."

Dudley glared at Draig for a few seconds more, his brothers' cries for him to attack surging over him. Pushing him to take action. Demanding that he draw blood.

With that chorus behind the Were, Draig knew that it would only take a gentle nudge to get Dudley moving in the direction that he wanted. "Are you a coward, Dudley? Are you afraid of the Fallen Knight?"

Dudley shot forward in a blur, right claw swiping for Draig's throat and catching nothing but air, his prey not there.

Draig had pivoted and taken a step back. And rather than using his sword, he punched Dudley hard in the kidney, earning a grunt of shocked pain for his effort.

Draig wasn't done. Before Dudley could come back at him, he kicked out with his boot, finding the crunch of Dudley's shin breaking and the resulting howl very satisfying.

Despite the terrible pain, Dudley swept his claw behind him in a broad arc.

He hoped to take Draig by surprise. Across the face. The throat. The shoulder. Anywhere that would force back Dudley's much-too-skilled adversary.

It didn't work.

Draig wasn't where Dudley expected him to be. He ducked Dudley's swing and took a few steps back, the Were's motion bringing him face to face with Draig.

Dudley's golden eyes widened and flashed in bewilderment. Draig's shining steel blade slicing through the air in a blur was the last thing the Were saw.

Just as happened with Jamaal when he ran through the energized cord, Dudley's broken body collapsed to the ground. His head, eyes wide with shock, rolling across the dry streambed until it hit the glowing barrier.

Coming to a stop right in front of Raik.

Draig gave the leader of the Renegades a sharp look and then a nod when their eyes met again, hinting at what was to come when they met in combat.

Draig didn't permit the challenge to last long. He turned swiftly, prepared to finish the other Were, sensing the beast finally pushing himself back up off the ground.

Draig realized that he wasn't fast enough.

Not because he couldn't get to the Were in time.

Rather, because Melissa had gotten to him first.

She had worked through her fear, attacking the Were from his blind side when she realized that the beast was going to rejoin the fight.

A dagger made of the Grym punched between his lower ribs did the trick.

The Were staggered a step before he dropped down to one knee. Pressing a claw against the wound, there was little that he could do. The trickle of blood swiftly became a steady flow.

The beast sagged, then keeled over, head smacking the ground before rolling onto his side and offering a feeble groan as he bled out. The weapon crafted from the Grym prevented the wound from closing just as would have been the case if silver had been used.

Draig nodded his thanks to Melissa, who still appeared to be a bit dazed. He knew she was a good thief. And though he could tell that this wasn't the kind of work that she liked to do, clearly she did it well.

"Thank you."

He left her where she was standing and walked over first to the Were who had lost his head and then to the one Melissa killed. He studied their right arms, because it was always the right arm.

He had always suspected this, but he hadn't known for sure until just now.

There were more than a hundred Werewolf packs in the world. Each with a distinctive brand for their members.

A Were earned his or her brand when they were accepted into the pack.

These two lycanthropes had a brand that identified them as Renegades. But beneath that brand there was another that had been burned off, a few remnants visible beneath the new mark.

Each of these Weres had belonged to other packs. Until they were expelled.

He could only imagine what transgressions had pushed this pair to join a pack led by Raik.

"What are you doing?" Melissa asked.

Seeing the Weres staring hungrily at her through the shimmering barrier, she was ready for them to make their escape. Assuming that they could make their escape. As it was looking now, she wasn't very confident of gaining that opportunity.

She stood just above Draig's shoulder. Magical dagger still in hand.

Ready to be anywhere else but there.

"Just learning something new," he replied with an almost irritating calm.

"Do I even want to know?"

"Likely not at this moment." Draig pushed himself back to his feet.

"Draig ..."

Excalibur in hand, he ignored Melissa and strode toward the barrier. The shimmering energy wasn't shimmering as brightly as it had been when Draig first set it in place.

Every so often it flashed now. The shield losing its strength. And Raik knew it.

"You will be mine soon, Fallen Knight," Raik growled from just a foot away, the energy that separated them fading swiftly.

"Promises, promises," Draig replied casually, ignoring the lethal looks directed toward him by the Weres crowding around their leader.

They all wanted a piece of him. And they might get their chance. Just not yet.

"I keep my promises, Fallen Knight." He ran his golden eyes over the barrier. It flashed again. "It is only a matter of time. You can hide from me for only so long. I will always find you, no matter what rock you decide to burrow under."

Draig's eyes narrowed, then he nodded. "I have no intention of hiding from you, Raik. Have no fear of that." He smiled then, although it was as far from a friendly smile as it could be. "The next time we meet it will be your head on the ground rather than Dudley's."

Having nothing else to say and cognizant that time was short, Draig turned on his heel and strode back to Melissa. She could sense what was happening just as well as Raik could.

"How much time do we have?"

"Another minute or so," Draig replied. The barrier flashed again. Then it faded in color to a dim yellow before snapping back in place. He shrugged, obviously unconcerned. "Maybe less."

"What are we going to do?"

"Have a little fun," Draig answered, although his brightly glowing eyes weren't smiling.

He turned away from Melissa, then spoke over his shoulder. "You might want to close your eyes."

Draig didn't wait to see if Melissa listened to him. He was already kneeling down swiftly, slamming the hilt of his sword onto a large, flat rock that rose a few feet above the dry streambed.

A massive explosion of light erupted, the blast of energy that followed destroying the remnants of the barrier and throwing back the massed Weres.

RAIK PUSHED himself up from the ground.

Carefully.

He feared that if he moved too quickly, he would fall back down.

His unkempt fur was singed, actually burned in a few places, charred flesh revealed beneath.

His vision was blurry. His eyes were watering. His ears were ringing, blocking out all the other sounds he should be hearing.

He stood in place, waiting for the dust to clear, waiting for his head to clear, before he even considered taking a step.

But he didn't need to move to get a better look at what waited for him.

Dudley and Lester's bodies were gone. All that remained were two piles of ash.

Gone as well were the Fallen Knight and the Witch.

How his foe accomplished that, he didn't know.

Raik lifted his snout toward the branches above him and howled in rage.

The Fallen Knight controlled a power that few could challenge. Yet, Raik never knew that he was capable of disappearing like a Las Vegas magician.

Shaking in fury, Raik sniffed the air.

He couldn't locate either the Fallen Knight or the Witch.

He wasn't worried, however.

He would. Once the dust, dirt, and debris settled, he would find them.

He would hunt them no matter where they went, because this wasn't just a job now. This was personal.

The Fallen Knight and the Witch could run for as long as they wanted, but they would never escape him.

He started stumbling more than walking around the streambed, pulling up the Weres yet to regain their feet.

A few couldn't, the blast too much for them.

He didn't know how many could continue the hunt.

He did know that the hunt wasn't over.

Not until he had the Fallen Knight's head in his claws.

13

THE DRUID

"What in all the hells did you do?" Melissa couldn't figure out how Draig had gotten them out of what to her had looked like an inescapable trap of their own making.

"With the dome?" Draig asked, not certain as to what she was referring. "Peggy Rose helped me out with the structure of …"

"Not with the dome." Melissa cut him off. She was irritated. She was confused. In large part because a great many things happened around Draig that she didn't understand. And she hated that. "How did you get us away from the Weres? Did the blast do that? Take us somewhere else on the mountain?"

Draig smashing the hilt of his sword against the stone had blinded her. After that, all she could remember was a massive rush of wind that threatened to knock her over.

When she opened her eyes again, she was still standing in the streambed. However, the Renegades were nowhere to be seen.

Draig nodded. He understood her disorientation. It had been much the same for him the first time he tried what had whisked them away from their hunters.

"The blast was just a distraction. If it removed a few more of the Weres then all the better for us."

He reached for the Grym, searching around them quickly.

They were safe for the moment.

"Draig ..." Melissa urged, what little patience she had left fading rapidly, her eyes narrowing in anger. Whatever he had done, it felt as if she had been broken apart and then put back together. Thankfully as she was supposed to be. Although she still felt slightly sick to her stomach.

"Think of what I did as similar to what happens when you walk through the Dragon Door."

"You mean you open the door and after you step through you're wherever you want to be?"

"Yes, just on a much smaller scale and with a much smaller range."

"Then where is the Dragon Door?" she demanded. "I didn't see one."

"I didn't use the Dragon Door," he replied. "Think of it more like we slipped through a portal."

Melissa stared at Draig, not quite sure how to interpret what he was saying. "You can do that? Seriously?"

"Do what?"

"You folded time?" Her expression suggested not just astonishment, but also a good dose of respect and a pinch of fear.

Draig shook his head, one of her eyebrows rising in question.

"I didn't fold time," he explained. "I simply applied the same principles upon which the Dragon Door functions. I folded space."

"You folded space?" Her voice couldn't hide her disbelief. Although after what she had just experienced, she wasn't in a position to challenge him. "What are you? You basically Star Trekked us out of there."

Draig smiled then offered her the Vulcan sign with his right hand, his blackthorn shillelagh in his left. "One of my favorite shows."

"Mine too," she admitted reluctantly as she continued to wrap her brain around what she had just learned. "That's all you can tell me? How do you even do that? Folding space is just a theory. How do you actually make that happen?"

"I can tell you more later."

"Why not now?" she demanded. She was tired of his incomplete answers. He didn't hesitate to give her the truth, just never the entire truth. And that nagged at her. All the while choosing to ignore her own hypocrisy.

"Because when I folded space, I was only able to take us a few miles away from where we were. I have no doubt that Raik and his pack will be after us again as soon as they're back on their feet." He then motioned with his hand. "And because we're here."

Melissa had allowed herself to become so consumed by what Draig had done to effectuate their escape that she had yet to examine their surroundings. That and the fact that she needed a few minutes to settle herself so that the urge to puke didn't overwhelm her if she moved.

Her eyes widened as she slowly spun around. "We've entered the Druid's domain?"

"We have," Draig replied with a smile. "Leya has granted us entry."

He always liked visiting here. It filled him with a peace that he couldn't attain anywhere else.

Perhaps most impressive, just like nature, the world that Leya Coeden had crafted atop the Druid's Peak was ever-changing, always growing, always adapting, always moving in a new direction.

The direction that nature chose, Leya just helping to guide it.

The massive ferns, trees wrapped with vines, and heavy

underbrush that grew just a few miles below them on the mountain were gone. As Melissa took in her new surroundings, it reminded her of Muir Woods, the old-growth redwood forest in Northern California.

Her mother had taken her there with her sisters likely hoping that the calm and serenity of the towering trees would wash off on her and her siblings. Settle them down for a few hours and give her mother a little peace and quiet.

It hadn't, unfortunately. At least not with respect to her sisters. As they wandered among the trees, they were just as annoying as they always were.

There were some differences here atop the Druid's Peak, however. A great many, in fact.

A series of paths led out of the streambed and in among the trees, those trails curling up the slope.

Flowering bushes and vines formed intricate designs along the paths that made her slightly dizzy if she looked at them for too long. There were also arches made of rose bushes, thorns mixed together with flowers of almost every imaginable color, extending over the trail.

Off to the side, long grass was mixed in with wildflowers that grew in some pattern that she couldn't discern. Yet for some reason she didn't understand, the pattern put her immediately at peace despite the terrifying struggles that had led her there.

"I can't believe what I'm seeing," Melissa whispered. "This is absolutely incredible."

She jumped a few inches off the ground when she heard a soft voice right by her ear.

"Impressive, isn't it? Some of my best work."

Melissa turned quickly, stumbling back a few feet, her heart beating faster than it should. Before she could utter the expletive that was on the very tip of her tongue, Draig cut in.

"Melissa, I have the pleasure of introducing you to Leya Coeden, warden of Druid's Peak."

Melissa gasped out a breath, then she forced a smile, her nerves still on edge. "I'm sorry, I didn't realize you were even there."

"It happens all the time," Leya replied. "My apologies for taking you by surprise."

Although Melissa could tell from her tone that the Druid really wasn't sorry. More like she enjoyed it. As if she were testing Melissa to see how she would react.

That thought led Melissa to the question she wanted to ask. "How do you do that? Move so quietly?" Melissa gave the woman an appraising look. "You're not folding time, are you?" She said the last while nodding to Draig, a dry smile twisting her lips.

"No, dear," Leya replied, chuckling softly. "Nothing so extravagant as that. He was showing off again, I take it?"

"Just doing what was necessary," Draig claimed.

"Of course you were," Leya replied, her tone revealing her disbelief. "Draig has many talents. In fact, sometimes I think he has more talents than he deserves."

"My mother says much the same," he sighed.

Melissa gave Draig a curious look. He had never spoken of his mother. And unlike his father, who clearly was not on his good side, and that an understatement if ever there was one, his voice carried a warmth while speaking of his mother that she had never heard before.

"That's because your mother is a smart woman," Leya said, then murmured just beneath her breath, "a dangerous one as well."

As Draig spoke with Leya about the Weres who had hounded them during their hike up the mountain, Melissa took the available time to study the Druid.

When Draig first told her that she would be visiting a

Druid, the vision that came to mind was quite out of place by at least five or six centuries. She had imagined Leya wearing brown and green robes and perhaps even a crown of flowers while walking around in her bare feet.

Definitely a misconception on her part, because that wasn't the case at all.

The best that Melissa could do in describing the Druid was crunchy. She looked like any other person who loved to hike. It was almost as if she had outfitted herself at Orvis or REI, her feet in what appeared to be a comfortable pair of Birkenstocks.

And as she listened to the brief conversation, Melissa picked out the Druid's quick wit. Leya enjoyed teasing Draig, and it didn't seem to bother him. That suggested to Melissa that they had been friends for a long time.

Yet there was an anomaly to Leya as well. Because Melissa could tell that how Leya presented herself didn't reveal who she truly was.

Melissa sensed the tremendous power within her. There was as well an ancientness that radiated from her. As if she had existed in the world for thousands of years, even though she didn't appear to be very old. No older than Melissa herself, in fact.

"Don't try to figure it out, my dear. I'm a study in contradictions."

"I'm sorry, what?" Melissa asked. Her cheeks flushed red when she realized that she had been found out.

Leya smiled warmly. "People have been trying to figure me out for a long time. It's not worth the effort."

"I wasn't trying to ..." Melissa began to protest. Leya ran right over her.

"Just remember one thing, dear." Leya's eyes flashed dangerously, her brow darkening.

"What's that?" Melissa murmured in a voice softer than she would have preferred.

"You don't want to get on my bad side." Leya spoke quietly but with an authority that sent a shiver down Melissa's spine.

And then, turning her attention back to Draig, the Druid's expression changed just as swiftly as it had formed.

"Did you draw blood?"

"I couldn't help it," Draig shrugged.

"They probably wouldn't have given up on you regardless."

"You're right about that." He nodded toward Melissa. "That's the job for them right there."

"That may be, but you're on their list now. They won't stop hunting you."

"A blood debt," Draig nodded. To Melissa, he didn't appear to be concerned by that fact.

"Exactly so," Leya agreed. "Come on." She turned and started walking up one of the paths to the left that would take them below a natural trellis formed of rosebushes sprouting yellow, white, and red. "The Weres can't get through my illusion, but the beasts can still hunt along the periphery. Better that we keep them confused for a little while longer, and a little more distance from them will help us do just that."

"DID YOU MAKE THESE TODAY?" Leya asked, a broad smile revealing her pleasure and several crumbs. She wiped a touch of frosting from her lip with her finger as she took another bite from one of the cinnamon rolls Draig had brought for her.

"Just this morning," Draig replied.

He wasn't eating one himself, wanting to make sure that Leya had some leftovers.

Instead, he sat back on one of the rocking chairs placed on the front porch of Leya's A-framed cottage.

Melissa still couldn't quite believe the construction. Leya's home appeared to be an intricately carved and crafted cabin.

But it wasn't. It was more than that. So much more.

She had studied the walls carefully. There were no seams. No cracks.

It appeared to her as if the Druid had carved the cottage out of a single tree, the design and ornamentation incorporated simply for the aesthetics.

"Just as good as your last batch," Leya confirmed with a happy nod. She relished her next bite.

"I aim to please," he replied modestly.

Draig's eyes were closed. However, Melissa didn't think that he was relaxing. She had no doubt that he was deep in thought.

About the Weres?

She didn't think so.

From the hardness of his expression, it appeared as if he was preparing himself for a combat, getting his mind right so that his body would follow, the Weres the least of his concerns. Yet if that was the case, what could be more important than the gang of Werewolves hunting them?

"When you want something."

Draig opened his eyes then and gave Leya a wolfish smile. It didn't affect her in the least as she continued to lick the frosting from her fingers before wiping them with a napkin. "You know me too well."

Melissa watched the exchange with a great deal of interest. There was a lot more going on in this conversation than just what was being said.

And she was having a hard time figuring out Leya. At that moment, she appeared to be a happy young woman and not the one who had offered her a veiled threat before they turned up the path that led to her home.

Leya chuckled softly. "Sometimes I think I do, you're right, but it's too late now."

Draig's smile broadened. "Would you do it all again?"

"I would," she replied without a second thought.

Melissa scrunched up her brow. More than just a little curious. Another mystery for her to solve.

There was history between Draig and the Druid. What could it be? And could it affect why they were there?

Melissa shook her head from side to side ever so slightly. She would think about that later. She was still trying to get a grip on how Draig had gotten them into the Druid's domain.

Folding space? Really?

She couldn't quite believe it. Star Trek, indeed.

She was going to make Draig show her how he did it. She might not be able to accomplish the maneuver herself, but she needed to understand how he did it. Some of the principles might be applicable to her regular line of work.

"And how is your journey going?"

Draig didn't reply immediately to Leya's question. Instead, his expression turned slightly sad. Almost wistful. "Slower than I would like."

Leya nodded, not surprised. "It always is. But you're on your journey. That's the most important thing. You are on your journey." She reached over and patted Draig on the knee when she said the last.

"I'm sorry," Melissa interrupted, no longer able to contain her curiosity even though she felt as if she were intruding on a private conversation. "Journey? I'm a little lost."

"I'm sorry, dear. We're being rude."

"I'm just trying to understand," Melissa clarified. Because of Leya's youthful appearance, her choice of terminology, *dear*, a term she usually associated with her grandmother, was a bit jarring. "That's all."

"Of course you are, dear," Leya agreed. "Just as we all are. The world around us. Ourselves." Leya gave Melissa a pointed look that she couldn't ignore. "It is so much easier to hate than learn or seek a new perspective. Wouldn't you agree?"

Draig stared at Leya for quite some time, his hard expression having returned. He knew that Leya's question wasn't directed toward Melissa. "It can be, yes."

For just a second, Melissa thought that Draig was going to offer a different reply. One that was a bit less diplomatic as he seemed to be a little agitated.

"Do you still believe that the journey you've selected is the right one?"

Draig's eyes flashed. "I do," he responded softly. "This is my journey now. This is the one that I must follow to the end. No matter where it leads me."

Leya nodded with satisfaction upon hearing that. Pleased. Also relieved. "The spark is strong within you, Draig. Keep it so."

"The spark?" Melissa asked, a quizzical expression clouding her features.

She still felt as if Draig and Leya were engaging in a conversation in which she had no role to play. One in which the Druid was testing Draig. One that they had conducted several times before.

And she doubted that if they explained what they were actually talking about that she would understand much of it. But she did want to comprehend some of it. Because at the moment she felt as if she were in the middle of a personal growth retreat. Not as a participant, but as a spectator. And that was an uncomfortable place to be.

"Yes, the spark," Leya nodded, taking pleasure in the word. "An ancient term. One that has power for those of us who believe."

"What is the spark?"

"The spark is knowledge," Leya explained. "Or understanding. Comprehension. Whatever you want to call it. Of yourself and, just as important, how you fit in the larger world."

"A self-awareness in a sense?"

"Exactly, dear. That's an excellent way to put it." Leya leaned in, her eyes catching Melissa's. From where Melissa sat, it appeared as if her mesmerizing orbs flashed different colors, one after another, never settling on one hue for more than a heartbeat. "When I first met Draig ... he was lost."

"I didn't know it then," Draig added.

"He did not," Leya confirmed.

"Many of the Teg would still say that I am lost," Draig offered, his dry wit making an appearance.

"And many of them would be correct if you continue to be a pain in my ass," Leya countered in a harder tone, not appreciating his interruption.

"I'm sorry about him." Melissa gave the Druid a sad smile. "He's like this much too frequently. I assume it's a defense mechanism."

Leya nodded in agreement, a small smile curling her lips. "I believe you're correct, dear. Perhaps compensating for ..."

"Hey, now," Draig interrupted. "I'm not in the mood for a therapy session."

"Nor do we have the time for that," Leya agreed. "It would take much too long. Returning to the track that Draig tried to throw us off, when I first met our mutual friend, he was lost." Leya shrugged and lifted her eyebrows to the sky. "It only made sense, after all. What was required of him had made him so. The key variable, though, was that unlike those who could have and most likely would have continued to drift down into the blackness that was pulling at them, he chose to fight against the pull."

"It wasn't easy," he admitted.

"Nor should it be," Leya offered. "If it was easy, then what you did wouldn't have mattered as much as it did."

"So that was Draig's journey?" Melissa asked, trying to understand. "Draig breaking free from his father?" She assumed that had to be what the Druid was talking about.

"Only in part," Leya confirmed. "Draig began his journey

before he chose to leave his father. When he began to question. When he began to see the world and his place in it through a new lens."

"And that was the spark?"

Leya nodded, clearly pleased with Melissa's question. "Yes, that's when I first saw the spark in Draig." She leaned back into her chair. "It has been a long journey for him to reach this point, and it will be a longer journey still, because he still has far to go."

"A never-ending journey," Draig grumbled, although that finding didn't appear to upset him.

"Maybe so," Leya admitted, "although certainly a worthwhile one. Wouldn't you agree?" Leya's eyes suggested that she expected only one answer from him.

"I do," Draig replied with a sincerity that was usually lacking when he was put under pressure.

"That's the only reason that I came here," Leya said as she reached across and patted Draig warmly on the knee. "That was the only reason that I trusted him."

"And hopefully your trust was warranted." Melissa was curious. In large part for her own sake, because she had been forced to place her trust in Draig as well.

"It was indeed," Leya confirmed.

"You said that the spark is knowledge. Comprehension. Seeing more of the world than just your small part of it."

"I did."

"Then how do you know when you have the spark?"

Leya studied Melissa for a time, recognizing a desperation there. A need. Yet she sensed as well that Melissa didn't quite know what she needed.

The Druid nodded, seeing what was there and what was lacking. Much like Draig. Distinct as well.

Melissa was lost.

She needed to find her journey.

If she had the courage to do so.

The question was, would she?

Not everyone did. Not everyone had the capacity. Not everyone had the desire. Not everyone had the courage.

Because there always was a price to be paid for taking the risk of beginning a new journey. For going beyond what you are and trying to become more than just that.

"You'll know it when you see it," Leya replied cryptically. "Have no fear of that." She leaned in toward Melissa, her eyes flashing much as they had when she issued her warning in the streambed. "What you need to worry about is whether you have the daring, the fearlessness, to follow your spark when you find it."

Melissa couldn't pull her gaze away from the Druid's, and she tried, because staring into those multicolored orbs -- searching, questioning, challenging – was more than just a little uncomfortable. It was almost painful.

"Enough with the discussion on esoteric topics," Draig said, his words breaking the Druid's hold on Melissa. She sat back in her chair feeling slightly dazed and a little beat up.

"Quite right," Leya agreed, giving Melissa a nod before shifting her focus back to Draig. Apparently, she had obtained from Melissa what she wanted, although Melissa had no clue as to what that might be. "You came here for a reason. Not just with respect to the Werewolves hunting you. And not just because of the trouble that Melissa has brought to Kraken Cove."

"That wasn't my intention," Melissa protested quietly. "I didn't want that to happen."

Draig ignored her. Melissa was only a part of what he had been thinking about. The catalyst, perhaps, yet still just a piece of the larger puzzle that really worried him. "There's something in play that's touching the Teg ..."

"There always is," Leya agreed.

"Yes, you're right, but it's different this time, and I can't figure out what it is," Draig replied, his voice thoughtful. "It feels different as well."

"Different how?" Leya prodded.

"In some ways, it feels like the schemes that we've faced since my father took power."

"The struggle for position. Perhaps even for succession?"

"Yes, that," Draig confirmed. "But that's normal among the Teg, is it not? Stability is not our strong suit. In fact, it's almost as if the desire for stability goes against our very nature."

"I won't disagree with you. But there's more to it?"

"There is," Draig confirmed with a distracted nod as he continued to think about Leya's question. "Whatever it is, it feels ancient. Almost forgotten. It's like the door to a crypt that has been closed for millennia has been reopened and has allowed an evil back into our world."

"That's very descriptive," Leya prodded, "as well as a bit concerning."

Draig nodded as he tried to refine his explanation. "It feels the same as some of the previous maneuvers among the Teg, the struggle for power and position as you suggested, but there's a strangeness to it all."

"How so?"

"From what I can piece together, it's not just the normal players."

"A wizard working from behind the curtains?" suggested Leya.

Draig nodded again. "Yes, exactly that."

"But you don't know who it might be. And you want to determine if your intuition is correct?"

"Can intuition really be correct?" asked Melissa. She held up her hands in her own defense, shrinking back from the sharp looks that Draig and Leya both gave her. "I'm not challenging you, I'm just asking. There's an inexactness to intuition, at least in my own experience. Just as often wrong as right."

"In your experience," Leya agreed, "but not in others'. Draig's intuition tends to be spot on. Best that he follow it."

"Sorry, I was just saying ..."

Leya turned away from Melissa again, once more focused on Draig, her attention always short and intense. "And beyond that?"

"I don't know," Draig admitted reluctantly. "All I know is that I need to figure it out, because whatever it is that's happening among the Teg, or perhaps even to the Teg, whatever might be coming or maybe even is already here, I have no doubt that it has bigger implications than all the crap that usually runs through our world."

"You know what will be required of you to find your answer?" Leya spoke in a solemn tone.

"I do," Draig replied. He pushed himself up from his rocking chair and strode to the end of the porch, leaning on the railing. He didn't really see the trails that led down the steep slope and the accompanying kaleidoscope of color. The peace that he wanted, that he craved, when he walked within Leya's wood, was nowhere to be found. "I don't have a choice, Leya. It must be done."

Leya nodded sadly. She knew that he was going to make this decision. How could he not? And there was little point in trying to convince him otherwise.

"Needing to do good just as always," Leya said softly. "Still on the journey. Always on the journey. That is good. For your sake. For ours as well."

"Needing to do right," Draig corrected as he bowed his head and took a deep breath.

"Is there a difference?" Leya challenged.

"Sometimes there is," he murmured. "All too often, in fact."

Leya stared at Draig's back for a time, then the Druid

smiled warmly. "I wish you would visit more, Draig. I always enjoy our conversations. Even when they make my entire body shiver."

"I got the sense that you didn't like a lot of visitors. Even me."

"True," she admitted. "I do not like visitors all that often. But you're a different matter entirely. I enjoy watching you grow. I enjoy watching as the world shapes itself around you. As you become more a part of the world. That last is important. Critical. For you and the Teg."

"I think you're giving me too much credit, Leya."

"I don't think that I'm giving you enough."

"What exactly is Draig going to do?" Melissa interrupted.

Once again, Melissa struggled to keep track of the conversation. She didn't understand most of what they were discussing, and that irritated her to no end. Because she knew that what they were talking about was important and was connected to her in some way.

"There are always rumblings among the Teg," Draig explained. He turned around and leaned back against the railing, crossing his arms. "Unrest. Always. If there weren't, I'd be worried."

"You're saying there's more to it than just that?" Melissa asked.

"I am," Draig confirmed. "The tremors are usually caused by two of the Teg you're most familiar with."

"Arthur and Morgase." Melissa was grateful that Draig didn't tell Leya why she was familiar with two of the most powerful of all the Teg.

"Exactly so. But this time it's different. It feels different anyway. And as Leya has suggested, when I follow my intuition, it tends to play out as I expect."

"You believe that there's a third player involved?" A touch of anxiety struck Melissa, fearing that the conversation was about to become a confrontation.

"I do. That's where the signs are pointing." Draig smiled, although it wasn't a warm one. "Arthur and Morgase have been so focused on their conflict that they tend to ignore what doesn't involve them directly. Or rather what they can't imagine might involve them. That could work against them now."

"I really wouldn't mind seeing one or both of them go," muttered Leya, "especially after your father sent you to eliminate me and my brothers and sisters."

"I understand why you say that," Draig said in a calm voice, "but I know that you understand as well what could happen if one or both of them are removed."

"Chaos," grumbled Leya, who clearly wasn't pleased at having to admit that. "You know, sometimes I think a little chaos might be preferred to the constant machinations of that pair."

"When can we go?" Draig asked.

"Soon," Leya replied. "Dusk will be upon us within the hour."

"Go where?" Melissa asked. Lost once more. Also grateful that Draig had chosen not to push her harder.

"To a place where Draig can find the answers that he's looking for," Leya replied. "We go to the Circle." She pushed herself up from her chair and started cleaning up the remains of her snack. "I just hope that Draig survives. The last time he was in the Circle, it didn't go as well as I had hoped that it would."

14

WORRY AND FEAR

As soon as the last rays of light touched the western horizon, Leya led Draig and Melissa farther up the peak on a trail that started right behind her cottage. It would have been difficult for a mountain goat. Thankfully, they didn't have very far to go.

A quarter mile at most.

Melissa was grateful for that as she struggled up the rocky slope. Yet despite the challenge, she didn't flag.

The top of the mountain called to her, her curiosity pushing her forward. When Melissa asked the Druid why streams and flashes of color that resembled the Northern Lights appeared without rhyme or reason just above the crest, Leya looked back over her shoulder with a mysterious smile as she continued to climb, giving her no more than that and a cryptic reply.

"There are places in this world that are not just our world."

Melissa had no clue as to what to expect when she first set foot atop the Druid's Peak, and she certainly wasn't prepared for what greeted her.

Despite night having fallen, the surrounding mountains lost in darkness, an otherworldly glow bathed the summit. The light radiated out from the center of the two-story stone monoliths that brought to mind Stonehenge.

The Circle.

When they first arrived, a gentle breeze swept across the summit. Ruffling her hair. Cooling the sweat on her brow.

She and Leya stopped where the trail met the crest. The Druid grasping her arm and holding her in place, a shake of her head warning Melissa that this was as far as they would go.

Draig continued along the path that led down a gentle slope, not stopping until he stood in front of the entrance to the ring of stone, the space between the monoliths just large enough for him to squeeze through.

The instant he did, the breeze shifted into a gusty blow that forced Melissa and Leya to shield their eyes. The blasts buffeting them. Pushing at them. Tugging at them.

The mountain's response hinted to Melissa that they weren't wanted there. That they were being warned. That if they went any further, the wind would stop them.

Yet even with the blasts of air knocking into her, forcing her to dig her running shoes into the rocky soil, demanding that she turn away and turn back, Melissa couldn't pull her eyes away from Draig.

He didn't move for several minutes, seemingly impervious to the wind. It made her think of the expression on his face that she didn't think she was meant to see when they were talking with Leya back at her cabin. The one that suggested that he was preparing himself to enter the Colosseum like a gladiator of old.

Was that what he was doing now?

Preparing himself for a fight?

Was that why he was waiting?

Perhaps, but she had no way of knowing.

Time was short. Draig had been clear about that.

Still he hesitated.

This seemed very unlike him. She hadn't known Draig for very long, but she did know that when he decided to do something, he did it. He didn't wait.

Insufferably decisive from her perspective.

Melissa needed to know what he was doing. She only gained a step before Leya's strong grip on her arm tightened. At the same time a blast of air threatened to knock her off balance, forcing her to step back next to the Druid.

As soon as she did, the wind calmed. Just enough to remind her that she had no place here atop the Druid's Peak.

"You can't." Leya's eyes remained fixed on Draig as well.

"Why not?"

"One may enter the Circle," Leya intoned. "Only one may leave."

"Why? This isn't a cage fight."

Leya finally glanced at her, offering her a brief smile at her reference, but only for a second. Her concern for Draig was plain in her eyes. "A Circle is a sacred place. A place of energy. Of life. Of death. Of substance. Of shadow."

"Yes, but why only ..."

"A place where much good has been accomplished," Leya murmured, "and a place where much evil has been done in the name of what is right."

"That's all well and good," Melissa said, once again having a hard time following what the Druid was telling her. "But what does that have to ..."

"Patience, girl," Leya snapped. Her eyes locked onto Melissa's, holding her gaze and freezing her in place. "You seem to think that the world revolves around you. It does not."

Melissa was about to protest the Druid's charge, the woman sounding like her mother. Rather than offering one of the trite responses that she had shot out so frequently when she was a rebellious teenager, wisely she kept her mouth shut.

Leya's eyes had shifted again. Returning to the kaleidoscope of color that both amazed and terrified her.

A warning. It was at that moment that Melissa realized just how dangerous the Druid was.

"The world moves as it will, and upon it there are those who can affect its turning."

"Draig is one of those," Melissa said, beginning to understand.

Leya offered Melissa a brief nod. "He is. And because he is, when he enters a sacred place such as a Circle, his unique traits mix with the power that already resides there. Intensifying that energy. Strengthening it. Turning it into something else entirely. Making it wilder. Giving it life."

"You make it sound like he's a catalyst."

Leya smiled thinly at Melissa's suggestion. "In a way, he is. Yet he is so much more than that." She released her hold on Melissa, certain that the Witch would stay with her. "You can see it now."

Melissa shifted her gaze back to the Circle, following Leya's nod in that direction. The Druid was right. She could see it.

The wind had picked up again, the gusts threatening to knock her from her feet if she didn't lean into the battering blasts. The light radiating from the Circle had grown brighter, so much so that she could only look at it indirectly, needing to tilt her head and shield her eyes with her hand.

Because of the intense brilliance, Draig appeared to be no more than a dim figure standing at the edge of the radiance. She tilted her head a little more, trying to hear above the shriek of the wind.

"What is that?" she yelled to Leya.

It sounded as if someone was talking to her.

Barely above a whisper. No, that wasn't quite right. More than one whisper teased her. More than one voice. Many more voices. Hundreds. Maybe thousands.

But she couldn't make out any of it. The whispered words all merging into one. A constant, teasing, annoying buzz in her ears that she couldn't escape.

"What you hear are the voices of the dead. They welcome Draig. They invite him into the Circle. He must decide if he will accept their invitation."

"The voices of the dead?" Melissa found that hard to believe. "How is that ..."

"Even possible?" Leya shook her head in mild disappointment. "You are of the Teg, Witch. You should know that in our world, there is a very fine line between the possible and that which is not. Draig is a catalyst of sorts, just as you said. At times, he can mold the world around him rather than the other way around. He can bring the separate together in ways that others cannot. Should not. He does so now."

"What exactly is he doing?"

"I can tell you no more than I have. What he does is not for us to know. Only him."

Melissa bit back the sharp reply on the tip of her tongue. She was getting tired of the Druid's answers. Or rather answers that really weren't answers. Responses that only led to more questions. So she tried a different approach. "Why is he doing it?"

"He seeks answers."

"Yes, but from whom?" Melissa asked through gritted teeth, tiring of the exercise.

"From the dead, of course. For the dead see all. They hear all. They remember all. They can tell all. If they desire to."

"Draig is going to speak to the dead to learn more about the threat that the Teg face?"

"He will," Leya confirmed. "If he chooses to do so."

"He's done this before?"

"He has."

"And he's gained the information that he needed?"

"He has," Leya confirmed.

Melissa's expression shifted to one of slight disbelief. She knew that there was a great deal that the Teg could do with the Grym, the Power of the Ancients giving them unique skills and abilities. Yet she knew as well that there were limits. And she believed that this was one of them.

For just a second, she feared that she had been caught in a scam. Just like the séance she had attended with her friends as part of a bachelorette party, Madame Esmeralda telling them all their futures. When the supposed psychic had gotten to her, she had said nothing about a Dragon, which Melissa now believed should have been top of mind if the woman had known what she was doing.

"He can speak to the dead?" Melissa asked in a questioning tone.

Despite all that Melissa was watching, all that she was hearing, all of it making her think that she had walked right into the middle of a horror film, she was having a hard time grasping this reality. Because from what she knew, this should have been impossible.

"A pity." Leya gave Melissa a sad look, shaking her head ever so slightly. "You were not raised among us."

"How could you possibly know that?" Melissa demanded, bristling at the statement.

Melissa bent down, a blast of wind streaking out from the Circle and almost catching her by surprise. For a heartbeat, she worried that she was going to lose her footing. That she was about to go tumbling back down the trail since she was on the very edge.

But she didn't. She steadied herself with a hand to the grass, and when the gust receded, she stood once more. Leya released her grip from around her elbow, and when she did Melissa nodded in thanks to the Druid.

"How I know does not matter. What matters is that I do

know. Perhaps most important, I know why your mother did what she did."

"There is no way that you could know …"

"She did the right thing," Leya continued, offering a nod of approval. "But her desire to protect you and your sisters cost you as well. You do not know all that you should know, all that you need to know, to be of the Teg. So instead of questioning, listen. Learn. Believe."

Leya's voice wasn't demanding. Rather it was firm. And it did as the Druid wanted.

Melissa frowned but nodded. Acquiescing to Leya's requirement that masqueraded as a request.

"Druidic Circles offer those few with a very rare ability the chance to use them as a tool. They are amplifiers of a sort. They come to life when one of the Teg with the strength and ability to employ them enters."

Leya nodded toward the blinding light, Draig's form barely recognizable, only his edges visible. And those only faintly. "Draig has that strength and skill, because Draig is a Teg, a powerful one, a rival to his father and aunt in the Grym, in fact, perhaps even Merlin as well, but he is so much more than just a Teg."

"What do you mean more than just a Teg?"

Leya ignored Melissa's question. It wasn't hers to answer. "Every Druid has the same ability as Draig. Every Druid can make use of a Circle. None of us can do so on the scale at which Draig can."

That revelation surprised Melissa. Then again, it didn't. It seemed to be par for the course when it came to the mysterious Teg who enjoyed pretending to be a baker and a lighthouse keeper … all while carrying around Excalibur hidden in plain sight as a blackthorn shillelagh.

"Because Draig is more than just a Teg, his other nature grants him skills and talents that few others can master much less dream of. We do not have time to discuss all that he can do. Nevertheless, he will do now what he has done before in search of the truth. He will rip the veil."

"Rip the veil?" Melissa didn't understand what Leya was talking about.

"Yes, that is why the voices of the dead are calling to him. Why we can hear them, if only as whispers, their essences, their consciousnesses, drifting beyond the Circle."

"The dead can reach beyond the Circle?" That thought chilled Melissa to the bone, the sharp burst of wind that struck her just then making her shiver.

"No, so long as the stones stand and the Circle remains whole, the dead cannot reach us. But we can hear them. Best just to ignore them."

"So long as the stones stand the Circle remains whole?" That comment caught Melissa's attention. "What happens if the Circle is no longer whole?" Melissa didn't know exactly what that meant, but she could guess.

"Best not to think about that," Leya replied, offering Melissa a smile and nod of assurance. "Draig has done this before. He will rip the veil so that while he is in the Circle, our world and the Spirit World will become one. Then he can talk to those he needs to."

"You're being serious?" Melissa didn't know what to say, still having a hard time accepting what was happening and what was about to happen. Nevertheless, she felt the need to say something, even though she thought that she sounded the fool as soon as her words left her lips.

"I understand that this is difficult." Leya didn't offer Melissa the harsh words or glare that she anticipated. "It was for me as well when Draig first did this."

"Druids don't do this?"

Leya shook her head emphatically. "Druids are about life.

We are not about death. Draig is unique. He is both life and death."

Melissa ducked down against another blast of wind, trying to wrap her mind around what the Druid was telling her. *He is both life and death.* Ominous.

She was beginning to think that she had been a fool to follow her mother's advice and come to Kraken Cove. Her mother knew what was waiting for her here, and not just the artifact that she required. Yet she still sent her right into the claws of the Dragon?

Why would she do this?

Why would she want her to be so close to the Dragon?

There was an obvious answer to her questions. Protection. Just as Draig had done for her mother, he could do for Melissa as well. They had talked about that. However, there seemed to be more to it than just that.

Her mother had liked to say that the simplest explanation often was the best explanation.

Good advice. But not always the right advice.

Melissa shivered again. The air was colder now. Becoming frigid in seconds. When she breathed out, her breath frosted in front of her.

"It's happening?" Melissa's voice cracked, her astonishment plain.

"It is," Leya replied.

The light radiating from the Circle had dimmed just enough for her to glimpse Draig's shape with greater clarity as he advanced beyond the monoliths. As soon as he stepped onto the circular tile set in the very center, a stream of power blasted into the sky much like a spotlight, the beam turning night into day before it spread out in all directions, unfolding itself into a dome of energy that settled atop the stones and then crept into the spaces between them.

"What is that?"

Leya closed her eyes before replying, just beneath her breath offering Draig an ancient prayer of protection while he was caught between two worlds.

"The dome protects us and will remain so long as Draig remains in the Circle and draws breath."

"And if Draig doesn't draw breath?"

Leya ignored the Witch's question again. She didn't want to waste her time answering a query to which Melissa already knew the answer.

"Within the Circle, our world and the Spirit World are now one." As if to prove Leya's point, the blinding radiance surrounding the ring of stone reduced itself to a dim glow. Even so, they could not see beyond that shimmering shadowy barrier, long streaks of white and black energy swirling across the surface like thousands upon thousands of snakes had nested upon it. "Draig seeks what he seeks."

"And if he doesn't?" Melissa repeated with a harder edge.

"He will," Leya said softly. "He has to."

Melissa studied the Druid, still not quite sure what to make of all that was occurring atop Druid's Peak. She had witnessed some unique experiences among the Teg. But nothing like this.

"And if he does not?" Melissa didn't like asking the question, because she believed she already knew the answer. Nevertheless, she couldn't stop herself from asking again.

"Then he enters the Spirit World, and he stays there."

"He dies?"

"In a way," Leya replied, "and in a way he does not."

Melissa almost growled, her irritation threatening to get the better of her. The Druid's half-answers and insinuations were wearing on her. "Can't you just give me a straight answer?"

Rather than being angry, Leya smiled, commiserating with Melissa. Having gone through this herself, she knew how hard it was. "I cannot explain it any better than that, because I don't know how to. I cannot do what Draig can do, therefore I cannot experience what he is experiencing within the Circle. All I know is that Draig shouldn't be doing this. His odds were poor to begin with and the more time he spends in the Circle, the more his odds will worsen."

"If his odds of success are poor, why didn't you stop him?"

Leya chuckled softly at that. She turned her eyes up to the tapestry of stars shining above her. With the radiance of the dome having softened, and the wind having died down to a gentle breeze, it had turned into a beautiful evening.

If not for the fact that one of Leya's oldest and dearest friends was risking his life again for a people who rarely had any use for him.

Brave?

Foolish?

Probably both.

But that was Draig, was it not?

Identifying what needed to be done. Then doing it.

No matter the cost to himself.

All because his father had deceived him.

"You can't stop Draig. No one can stop Draig. He is a force of nature in and of himself. To try to do so ... you will only be swept away."

Melissa thought about what the Druid said. She was not in a position to argue with her.

She glanced at the Circle shrouded in power, the streaks of black and white energy now solid and having created a dizzying design atop that barrier's surface.

She couldn't see what he was doing, and that was probably for the best.

Draig had decided that this was necessary. That he needed to do this.

If that was the case, why did she feel responsible for the position in which he had placed himself?

A small voice in the back of her head told her that she was

the cause of the risk that he was taking. He had said that she was only a part of the larger scheme that he needed to figure out. Still, if she had …

As she considered her current circumstances, Melissa sighed both in resignation and disappointment. It was too late now. What was done was done.

"Why are Draig's odds poor?"

Leya didn't reply immediately. Her gaze returned to the Circle, her eyes narrowing. She sensed the shift in power that had just occurred beyond the barrier of swirling black and white that now resembled a frozen game of Tetris.

Yet there was nothing that she could do about it. There was nothing that she could do to assist Draig.

He was on his own. Just as he usually preferred to be.

"Draig has entered the Circle several times before."

"And he's come out again." Melissa's frown of worry curled into a small smile. "He can do so now."

"We can hope," Leya replied, "but we must be realistic as well."

"How so?"

"Within the Circle, with the two worlds meshing into one, Draig now exists both in our world and in the Spirit World. That places a strain on him. A pull. And not in the right direction."

"What happens if the strain becomes too much for him?" Melissa had a sense of what the answer might be, but she still felt the need to ask the question.

"It will rip him apart. That is how he will lose himself to the Spirit World."

Leya took a deep breath and then let it out slowly. The tension was already building within her.

She didn't bother to tell Melissa that the longer Draig spent within the Rip in the Veil, the more likely that he would be ripped apart as well. Even with someone of his strength and power, only so much could be expected.

"As I said," the Druid continued, "he has done this before. That is why the spirits are so anxious to see him once again. Because the more he does it, the closer he gets to the Spirit World ..."

"And the more likely that he loses himself entirely," Melissa finished for the Druid.

"Exactly so," Leya confirmed.

"And he's still doing this?" Melissa shook her head in confusion.

The more time she spent with Draig, the less she understood him. She hated that, because usually she could read people with ease. Understanding their motivations and desires. Making use of all that in her work.

But Draig?

For the most part, he was nothing more than an enigma. Just when she thought that she had him figured out, he surprised her. Every time. And usually at great risk to himself.

Leya gave Melissa a sad smile. "He is. As I said, Draig must do good. It's much like a penance for him. Even when he argues it is only necessary, he must do good. Despite the cost. Necessary or not, good is good."

"There is nothing we can do for him?" Melissa asked, seeking one more time to offer what assistance that she could.

"There is not," Leya replied with a deep sadness. "At least not at this moment."

"What do you mean?" Leya's tone set an alarm bell ringing in the back of Melissa's head.

"Assuming that Draig does not remain within the Spirit World, you need to tell him."

Melissa almost choked on her spit, her words difficult to come by for several seconds.

"Tell Draig what?" she gasped when she could speak again.

"You must tell Draig all," Leya warned, her multicolored

eyes flashing with a power that made Melissa take a step back. "He cannot help you otherwise. You must tell him all."

"I do not need his help," Melissa protested.

"If you did not need his help, you would not be here now. You would not have come to Kraken Cove to begin with."

"I did not come to Kraken Cove to ..."

Leya cut her off. "You have not told him all that you are involved in. If you do not, you will both pay a steep price. Not just you. That is not fair to Draig. He continues to pay for his mistakes. He should not have to pay for the mistakes of others."

"What I do is my business. It has no bearing on what's happening here. It has no bearing on Draig."

"Does it not?" Leya challenged. She sounded less than convinced.

"Why do you think I even want his help?" Melissa lifted her arms and put them back down to her sides quickly.

"You are fooling yourself, Witch."

"I am not ..."

"Please, Melissa." Leya had never called her by her first name. Doing so now stopped the Witch cold. "You need to tell Draig all. He cannot help you if you don't." She motioned toward the Circle and the energy that was slithering across the surface again. She should have been pleased that Draig had succeeded, at least in part. The slithering white and black told her that Draig had finished the incantation and ripped the veil, the strands of white and black competing against one another with greater vigor now. "Draig is in there, risking his life, because of a threat to the Teg. A threat of which you know more than you are revealing. You need to tell him."

"I did not come here for Draig's help. I came here ..."

"If you didn't come here for Draig's assistance, then why would you stay if not for his assistance?"

"I didn't ..." Melissa stopped herself.

Why did she stay?

True, the Weres were hunting her since Morgase was still after her. But Arthur thought she was dead. At least for a little while longer. That gave her time with which she could work. And she had escaped worse than Weres before.

She preferred to be on her own. To exercise full control over her life.

Making good decisions. Making just as many bad decisions. And when she made bad decisions, finding some way to work her way out from under them.

Without anyone's assistance.

"You may not have come here to Kraken Cove because of Draig, but you stay here because of him. If you argue otherwise, you are only fooling yourself."

Before Melissa could reply, a shriek that sounded like a thousand banshees screaming in unison erupted from the Circle. Then the silence of the graveyard descended.

More remarkable, the streaks of slithering black and white stopped again, hardening into what resembled a grey stone.

Solid. Unmovable. Indestructible.

The hair on Melissa's arms stood on end, as did the curly locks atop her head. If she could look at herself in the mirror, she assumed that she resembled a female version of Albert Einstein. She felt like she had been caught out in an electrical storm.

"It begins," Leya intoned.

"What do we do?" Melissa asked. She looked quickly at the Druid, seeing that the charged air was affecting her in the same way as it was her.

"We wait," she replied softly, "and we hope that Draig returns to us. That he does not lose himself to the spirits. Because no matter how much many of the Teg might like that result that is a loss that the Teg would not survive."

15

RIP IN THE VEIL

The instant that Draig stepped between the stone monoliths and into the Circle, he worried that he was making a mistake.

The energy radiating from the ancient ruin tugged at him.

Called to him.

Wanted him.

Needed him.

And just as much as that energy desired him, he desired that energy.

The power sizzled across his body.

Invigorating him.

Pricking at his skin.

Teasing him.

Testing him.

Making promises of what could be ... if only he let go.

If only he joined with the power that tempted him so.

It was those promises that concerned him.

If he weakened, if he listened to those promises, he would gain exactly what he wanted.

And that's what frightened him.

That's what sent an icy chill straight to his heart.

Because those promises came with a price.

He knew what would happen.

The promises would be kept, and he would be lost.

That would be the cost.

Steeling himself, Draig advanced deeper within the Circle. His blackthorn shillelagh clacked on the time-worn stones beneath his feet that were set in a swirling pattern that resembled a comet, the tail along the outer edges of the Circle.

He focused on that sound. The clacking. Using that to stay in the world. To not give in to the demands of the power that so desperately wanted to help him. That so desperately wanted him.

He ignored the surge of light that blasted into the sky. He didn't watch it unfold and trickle down into a dome.

Locking him away from his world.

He had seen it all before.

Several times.

He didn't need to see it again.

It was only a distraction.

And he couldn't afford any distractions now.

He kept his eyes fixed on his goal even as he reveled in the warmth and radiance that played across him.

Even as the voices churning around him gained in volume.

Whispering into his ear.

Goading.

Threatening.

Begging.

Promising.

Pleading.

Teasing.

Sometimes he could make out a few of the words. Even a fragment of a sentence.

But no more than that.

There were too many voices.

Too many questions.

Too many demands.

Too many desires.

All of it merging into an unceasing stream of noise that made his ears ring.

He could give in.

He could surrender to the cacophony.

He could listen to the spirits.

A small part of him wanted to.

The teeth in the back of his jaw were beginning to ache as the static increased in volume.

Becoming more insistent.

More desperate.

Until that's all he could hear.

The murmurings.

The demands.

The needs.

The cravings.

He could give in. The desire to do so surging within him.

It would be so simple.

So easy.

To do as the voices wanted.

To give the spirits what they needed.

The urge to surrender was almost too much to bear.

Painful.

Excruciating.

Pleasurable.

If he gave in, then it would all be over.

He would no longer feel as he did.

He would no longer be who he was.

He would be ... no more.

And all that he had done would disappear into the shadows with him.

The good.

The bad.

All gone.

Even his memories.

He would be free.

That's what the voices promised him.

And that's exactly what would happen.

The voices never lied.

They couldn't lie.

But the voices never spoke of the price that needed to be paid to achieve the promised freedom.

The price that he would have to pay.

The price that he didn't want to pay.

Gritting his teeth against the pressure and pain building within his skull, Draig stopped in front of the cromlech set in the very center of the Circle.

He placed his palm against the smooth, cool stone altar that rose to just above his waist.

The thousands of voices in his head intensified.

Pushing.

Prodding.

Poking.

Promising.

Sensing his weakness.

Sensing their opportunity.

Seeking to push him over the edge.

Seeking to push him into the madness that would set him free.

"Enough," Draig whispered in a strangled voice, at the same time releasing a small thread of the Grym into the cromlech.

The effect was immediate.

The surge of energy shot down from the stone altar and into the ground, that blast of power revealing the runes carved into the stones upon which he stood, flashing a bright white, following the pattern and shooting to the very edge of the Circle and then into the stone monoliths guarding the sacred place.

The blinding power that Draig released pulsed for several seconds, bathing him in a new light.

Cleansing him.

Sweeping away the voices.

Clearing his head.

Returning the sanity to which he had been holding onto by just his fingernails.

Unlocking his reason.

And then, mercifully, there was silence.

A quiet so deep, so profound, that Draig took several seconds to savor it.

Holding his breath.

Not wanting to make a sound himself.

Not wanting to let go of the moment.

Needing the peace and the calm.

Knowing that he could hold onto it for only so long.

When he breathed again, the world returned to him.

The silence remained, although not so deep.

The faint crackle of the energy, black and white threads playing across the dome, audible as a faint buzz in the back of his head.

Still, much better that than the voices.

The promises.

The demands.

The threats.

All tempting in their own way.

All lethal for the same reason.

A reason that Draig had no desire to contemplate.

He stepped back from the cromlech, feeling like himself again.

Whole.

Rational.

At peace ... or as close to being at peace as he could be.

He knew who he was again.

He knew what he had done.

He knew what he had to do.

He smiled ruefully.

Even though he had known what was going to happen when he entered the Circle, it had been a close thing. He had almost tipped over the edge to be lost in the darkness forever.

But he hadn't.

He was grateful that he had the strength to withstand the assault long enough to quiet the voices.

To quiet the dead.

Now he savored the silence.

Caught in a purgatory of his own making.

He remembered the last time he stood within a Circle.

Why he had taken that risk.

He had been visiting his mother and her family.

His family as well.

Although it didn't always feel that way.

He had been struggling with so many challenges then.

Searching for answers to questions he didn't know how to ask.

Questions he didn't know that he needed to ask.

His mother had warned him not to enter the Circle.

It was too dangerous.

He was too dangerous.

He had ignored her.

And his arrogance, his need, had almost cost him his life.

But it had saved him as well.

From himself.

What he had learned had revealed the path that he needed to take.

It had confirmed as well that he could not make amends for all that he had done. All that had been required of him.

But he could try.

That he had to try.

Otherwise, the price that he would pay would be worse than that demanded by the dead.

He almost hadn't exited the Circle then.

When he discovered the truth about himself.

When he discovered his own weakness.

It was almost too much for him.

It had almost broken him.

But it hadn't.

Instead, it made him stronger.

It hardened his purpose.

It made him who he was today.

When he walked into that Circle, he had been the Fallen Knight.

When he exited, he was the Dragon.

Tired of wandering through his memories and understanding that he could only remain within the Circle for so long before his resistance weakened, the spirits lurking just at the edge of his consciousness, he set his blackthorn shillelagh in front of him, both hands resting on the knob.

In a flash, the staff took its true form.

Excalibur.

The sharp point firmly grounded in the stone, his hands grasping the hilt, Draig closed his eyes and called upon not only the Grym, but also the Power of the Draca that resided deep within him. A power gifted to him by his mother.

A burst of light erupted from the shining steel and sped across the runic floor of the Circle, racing up the stone monoliths and then shooting back toward the cromlech and setting the stone aglow.

He didn't look.

He couldn't look.

He focused on his task.

Eyes still closed.

Breathing evenly.

Sending more and more energy surging through the Circle. The threads of black and white that were slithering across the dome stopping. Hardening.

The power centered on the cromlech, the flat, horizontal capstone gleaming brighter than the sun.

There wasn't a crack.

It was more subtle than that.

It was the sound made when a piece of paper was torn in half.

A rip.

In the Veil.

Draig opened his eyes, watching as the tear in reality that began just above the altar revealed a shadowy glint. A wispy grey mist flowed through the opening, expanding slowly at first, and then faster and faster.

The flashing of the runic stones continued, although their intensity dimmed when the smoky threads touched them, the colors of Draig's world becoming less vibrant.

When the process was complete and the two worlds were one, the world of the Teg and the world of Spirit sharing the Circle, Draig felt as if he had stepped into a black-and-white movie.

He released the power he had been sending into Excalibur, using the sword as a focal point for the spell he had worked.

And then he waited.

Knowing what was coming next.

Girding himself for it.

A dim figure appeared at the edge of his vision. And then another. And one more.

Flashes, no more.

There, then not.

But still recognizable.

Still frightening.

Still heartbreaking.

Spirits of the dead joining him in the Circle.

Spirits he knew.

Spirits of the Teg he had lost.

Spirits of the Teg he had killed.

All calling to him, the buzz beginning in his ears again.

The same demands.

The same desires.

The same promises.

He ignored them all.

He refused to allow them purchase within his consciousness.

"Enough," he whispered.

The crescendo of noise in the back of his brain died away.

Silence again.

He savored it. But only for a heartbeat.

"Do you seek to join us?"

The raspy voice sent a shiver down Draig's spine.

He ignored the feeling and turned slowly.

The reason that he had entered the Circle and ripped the Veil had arrived.

A tall figure draped in wispy black robes stood before him. Cowl up, hiding his face. Although the deep black eyes hidden within flashed every time a spark of light struck them.

The figure resembled the Grim Reaper without the scythe.

But this figure was much worse than the collector of souls.

And much more powerful.

"Not yet," Draig replied.

A silence settled between them. Neither moved. Both waiting.

The cowled figure hovered a few inches off the ground.

Draig stood ready, Excalibur in his hands, never quite sure what was going to happen when he entered the Spirit World.

"Good," the shadowy shape replied. "You're more trouble than you're worth."

The floating apparition's robes began to swirl, spinning faster and faster, a whirlwind of black that gradually transformed.

The cowl disappearing.

The robes as well.

Replaced by a tall man wearing a sharply pressed black suit. A starched white shirt with an open collar. Shiny black shoes that gleamed brightly.

He was handsome. Too handsome in Draig's opinion. Long black hair swept back over his shoulders. A strong jaw.

It was as if a model had stepped out from the pages of a fashion magazine.

But still a sense of malevolence radiated from the man, centered in his glowing black eyes that every so often sparked a fiery red.

A predator.

Although not in the way that most would think.

Which was why Draig, though relaxed, ran his fingers over the hilt of his sword.

He had visited Bile three times before.

And three times before the Celtic God of the Dead had allowed him to return to the Natural World and the Teg.

Each time with more reluctance than the last.

In consequence, there was nothing to guarantee that the Lord of Spirits would allow it a fourth time despite what he might say.

"You don't seem surprised to see me."

Bile smiled, his teeth a white so bright that they mimicked the intensity of the blast of energy that had first radiated out from the cromlech.

"You can't surprise me anymore, Draig." Bile smiled as he said it. Although his smile never reached his eyes. "Not after all that you've done before."

Bile's eyes never changed. Haunting. Searching. Hunting.

Seeing all, Draig believed. At least when it came to what happened in the world he ruled. Because all the spirits spoke to him. All the time. Telling him what they had seen. Telling him their secrets. Telling him whatever he wanted to know. And Bile liked to know everything there was to know.

"Why is that?" Draig asked the question with as much insouciance as he could muster, which wasn't much.

"Because no one else of the Teg has ever visited so often," Bile replied. "You're like the crazy cousin who arrives unannounced, stays for a few days, and then when he leaves, I have to spend the next month cleaning up the mess he's left behind."

Draig smiled, certainly not in a position to deny the claim.

Bile was dangerous. In his world, his rules. And although most of those rules were sacrosanct, in place for eons, there were some that changed. When it suited Bile's purposes.

And although where they were within the Circle wasn't entirely Bile's Spirit World, Draig still needed to be careful.

He didn't want to push his luck.

He and Bile got along.

So long as their interests were aligned.

"I'm sorry about that," Draig said. "It's never my intention to cause you grief."

"It never is, I know," Bile murmured. "It's just so exhausting." He shook his head as if he were speaking with an unruly younger brother. "But that's just the way it is with you. You're like a bull in a China shop. And if that wasn't bad enough, you're also pulling everyone behind you, whether intentionally or not changing the world around you."

"That's never my intention," Draig protested mildly, his

heart not really into offering much of a defense. Because in many ways, Bile's description was right on target.

"Of that I have no doubt." Bile smiled then. A real smile. His eyes actually warming for a heartbeat. "That's why I like you. You make the world interesting, and that's always fun to watch. Although I do prefer that you do what you do in any world but mine."

"Thanks ... I guess."

"Oh, it's definitely a compliment," Bile confirmed. "Unfortunately, those same characteristics of yours that I so enjoy observing create a challenge for me."

"What would that be?"

"I don't know what to do with you."

"How so?" Draig wasn't certain if he should be even more worried than he already was.

"You should be here with me in the Spirit World. Dead many times over. Your goose should have been cooked centuries ago, yet you still stand among the living. You're the only Teg to ever escape me."

"Healthy living," Draig suggested, a quirk of a smile curling his lips.

Bile snorted then laughed, a melodic tone much in keeping with his current appearance.

Draig had never heard Bile emit such a sound before, and it put him on edge, because he knew what Bile was capable of. What the god had done and would not hesitate to do again in the future if it served his interests.

"That's rich," he said when he was done with his fun. "Although I suspect there's more to it than that." He nodded toward the sword. "Excalibur certainly helps. Your heritage as well that you try so hard to keep hidden."

"I won't deny it."

"And there's the challenge," Bile said with a sharp shake of his head. "You should be here, in the Spirit World, obeying me, but you're not."

"I'm sorry that I'm putting you out."

Bile snorted out another laugh. He had always enjoyed Draig's humor. "On the contrary, you're helping me."

"I don't understand."

"Nor should you," said Bile. "In truth, right now, I don't want you. Not yet."

Draig's eyes narrowed. Bile was many things, and first among them was that he was possessive. He wanted what belonged to him, and woe to any who stood in his way. When it was time to die, he put his hook into you and never let you go. Unless you had a role to play for him.

"I don't know if I should be pleased to hear that or disappointed."

Bile laughed again just as he had done before. The mellifluous tone seemingly incongruous for all that Draig knew about the God of the Dead.

"This is why I enjoy our conversations so much, Draig. Everyone else I talk to is always afraid. Worried about what I'm going to do to them. Whether I'm going to sentence them to a thousand years of torture. Place them in a pit of darkness that has no end. Take the Prometheus route and chain them to a ledge, an eagle cutting out the liver every day only for it to grow back overnight and the same terrible punishment to occur the next day and the next."

Bile shook his head, still smiling, clearly relishing those possible fates as he thought of them. "Yet despite all that I am, you speak to me as an equal. You're not afraid. I like that. And it worries me."

"Why would it worry you?"

"Because you will end up here with me eventually, and I don't know what to do with you when you do. I don't yet know what fate you deserve. And even here, your ability to twist the world around you will affect my world as well. That will make my rule of the spirits more difficult than it already is. I'm not ready for that."

"Then perhaps we can put it off for a little while longer." Draig offered his suggestion with a calm that was truly impressive, even as his insides churned.

Bile studied Draig, his brow furrowing, lips pursed. Judging. Measuring. Deciding.

"Fair enough," he said with a smile that wasn't really a smile. "Have no fear, I'll find a solution to our little dilemma when the time is right. Although I doubt that you will be pleased when I figure out what to do with you."

"I assumed as much long ago," Draig replied, having expected no less.

"No doubt you did," Bile said with a nod. "Now on to business. But before that, be aware that when it's time for you to go, any resistance you face isn't coming from me. It's a result of you coming here so frequently. Every time you visit my world, a little bit more of your spirit is cut away, staying here. You'll need to deal with that when we're done."

"I understand."

"Good, now let's get to it," he said, rubbing his manicured hands together. "I have some punishments to mete out, and I can't wait."

Drag hesitated, just for a moment. It was only natural after all.

"You have my word," Bile said solemnly. He gave Draig a nod to buttress his statement. "I will not hold you here. Only you can do that this time."

Draig nodded, appreciating the promise. Draig knew Bile to be driven. Volatile. Vindictive. Vicious. Vengeful.

Treacherous, he was not. He kept his word. Always.

Another reason he and Bile often saw eye to eye.

Draig stepped forward until no more than a foot separated them.

"You do understand the risk that you take by doing this?" Bile wouldn't have bothered to ask the question of anyone else. Because there was no one else like Draig.

Draig sighed and nodded. "It needs to be done."

Bile snorted at that, then shook his head sadly from side to side. "You say that every time. Do you hate yourself so much that you don't care what happens to you?"

Draig didn't reply immediately, thinking about what Bile said.

He didn't hate himself.

Not anymore.

Nevertheless, he still had a great deal to pay for. Taking a risk such as he was doing now helped to ease the guilt that plagued him.

He would still be hunted. He would still be hated. But at least he could ease his conscience just a tiny bit. Perhaps offer another payment for the misdeeds that haunted him.

Draig shook his head. "I'm the only one who can do this. That's why I'm doing it."

"Right," Bile replied softly. "Just as always."

Then he reached out a hand. The instant Bile's fingers touched Draig's forehead, the world around Draig disappeared.

16

LOST IN MEMORIES

Draig thought of himself as hovering above the earth, even though he still stood within the Circle and he understood that the scene playing out just below him was a memory.

His memory.

It felt like it had happened just yesterday.

Draig glided gracefully around the practice ring, short sword gripped tightly in his right hand, arm extended, blunted tip sticking out in front of him at shoulder height.

His opponent was bigger than he was. Broader. Mostly muscles. And he had a great deal more experience.

Kieran.

The self-proclaimed king of the training ground.

Three years older than Draig. Just like all the other children cheering from the other side of the waist-high stream of energy that circled the practice space and prevented the onlookers from interfering with the combat.

The youths, all wearing scratched leather armor, all holding short swords in their hands, cheered for Kieran.

Not because they liked Kieran.

Rather because they hated Draig.

He was too young.

He was too inexperienced.

He wasn't ready.

He was different. His strange eyes just the tip of the iceberg.

He shouldn't be there with them.

He was only there because his father wanted him there. They were certain of that. And what Draig's father wanted, he got.

Kieran sauntered clockwise around the circle, moving in time with Draig.

The much larger boy didn't appear to be concerned about his opponent. Not in the least.

No one had ever beaten him in the practice ring. No one ever would.

Certain of that truth, Kieran kept his practice sword in front of him, although not with the diligence that Draig displayed.

Confident in his victory, Kieran wanted to put on a show.

Kieran took three more steps before he feinted a lunge, then stepped back, laughing as Draig slid back a few feet to evade the attack that didn't materialize.

The boys and girls laughed with Kieran. Offering Draig a steady stream of taunts.

Draig was sure that they were all thinking the same thing when he began to circle the ring again. Tracking Kieran. Searching for an opening.

He was weak.

He was a coward.

He didn't stand and fight.

He didn't have what it takes to be there.

He shouldn't be there.

He wasn't one of them.

But he knew as well that they were all quite pleased that he was the one in the ring. Not them.

Kieran bullied everyone. But he didn't bully them when he was bullying Draig. Therefore, they would enjoy and make the most of their temporary position of power for as long as they could.

Before their small world that encompassed the barracks and the training center returned to the way it usually was.

"What's the matter, little one?" Kieran taunted. "Afraid of me?"

Draig didn't reply. He kept moving. Sword held at the ready just as he had been taught. His eyes never leaving Kieran as he hunted for the chance that he wanted.

Keiran feinted another lunge.

This time, Draig didn't step away. He held his ground.

With a sharp, economical motion, he knocked Kieran's blade away and stepped farther to the side, not allowing the larger boy to continue with his attack without opening his left side to a counterstroke from Draig.

Recognizing the danger, Kieran halted his advance faster than he wanted to, then stumbled backward. He was surprised by Draig's tactic. He had expected that the smaller boy would seek to escape him.

Uncomfortable at the thought that Draig might not be afraid of him like all the other Knights in training were, he tried to hide his unease with a little bluster.

"It seems that the little mouse has some bite," he laughed. His friends lining the ring laughed with him. "Yet there is little that he will be able to do with such small teeth."

Draig didn't say a word. He was barely even breathing.

Cool. Calm. Composed. Hyper-focused. Seeing, hearing, sensing everything around him with a greater clarity.

He kept his gaze on Kieran. Studying him. Beginning to discern the pattern of his movements.

The jeers and taunts that his classmates offered Draig from beyond the border of the practice ring had no effect on him.

He was used to it.

He had been the target of their animosity as soon as he had begun his training, which had been several years sooner than anyone else since the inception of the Knights of the Round.

For his father, an honor.

For those also seeking to become Knights of the Round, a slight that they felt the need to correct whenever they could.

Draig had been confused about all of it at first.

He didn't understand why the boys and girls who should have been his friends hated him so.

Merlin had explained it to him. After that, Draig realized that there was nothing that he could do about the situation in which he found himself. Nothing except seek to excel. To be better than his many adversaries.

Because that's what they were. Adversaries. They weren't classmates.

Not to make a point or to get back at them in any way, but rather to ensure that he protected himself. Understanding that once he demonstrated any success that the taunts and hard looks would become something more if he didn't stand up for himself.

He had experienced it several times already. His fellow trainees seeking to take their frustrations out on him.

After the last encounter, only a few days old, his supposed comrades in arms needed to build back up their courage and forget what happened the last time they had grown bold in making their displeasure and disgust with him known.

Several of the larger boys had tried to impress upon Draig their opinion that he didn't belong there.

Ganging up on him. Planning on giving him a beating. Wanting to remind him of where he stood with them.

That hadn't gone well ... for the Knights in training.

And because of that and their several other failures, now they hated him even more. Finally having acknowledged what would happen if they went after him again with anything more than words.

Words that could be painful.

That often played through his mind when he tried to sleep at night and he was so exhausted that he couldn't even dream.

Still, only words.

Words that Draig had learned to block out.

Kieran lunged again, this time getting in close to Draig. The larger boy assumed that Draig would skip out of the way, just as he always did.

To counter that, Kieran attempted to employ his strength and shoulder Draig out of the way. If he could knock Draig to the ground, his work would be done. He would win the combat and at the same time he would have exerted his dominance once again. He would strengthen his position among the other recruits and ensure he was still the top prospect.

A thought that he relished. That made his small eyes glower with an undisguised envy mixed with hatred. Those same eyes soon gripped by a sudden fear.

Kieran's strategy was a good one against most any other opponent.

Not against Draig, however.

Draig was too fast. Not only sliding away from Kieran's lunge, but also gaining the space that he needed to avoid the real attack.

When Kieran tried to use his shoulder, Draig was already past him.

Kieran couldn't stop himself in time. Draig trailing his leg behind him didn't help, catching Kieran's foot and sending the large boy tumbling hard across the ground and smacking his head against the barrier that circled the ring.

Rather than attack Kieran while he struggled to regain his senses, Draig stood ten feet away. Waiting for Kieran to come at him again. Knowing that his adversary had no choice but to do so.

Kieran couldn't afford to lose this practice combat. If he did, he would lose his standing with his peers. And that was a reality that a bully like him simply couldn't permit.

"You will never be one of us," Keiran snarled when he pushed himself back to his feet. "You never can be! You're a mongrel! No better than a dog, Draig! No better than a dog! Although pup more likely."

His rage mixed with the shouts and screams of those watching driving him forward, Kieran rushed toward Draig, staggering a bit, the knock to his head affecting his balance.

Draig didn't move, feet dug into the ground. Eyes narrowed. Recognizing that the moment was almost upon him.

Right before Kieran's practice sword smashed against the top of his head, Draig ducked and rolled, sweeping Kieran's feet out from under him.

Kieran fell heavily to the ground, face first, eating the dirt, the breath knocked out of him.

Before he could even think about trying to take the breath that would not come, Draig slammed a knee into his back, making it even harder for Kieran to regain the air that he was so desperate to taste.

And when he finally did, gasping, yearning to fill his lungs, Kieran realized that he was done.

The mouse had beaten him.

Draig continued to dig his knee into his back, holding him in place, the tip of his blunt sword pressed against the back of his neck.

Kieran was dead.

"Well done," grumbled Gaheris.

The Knight responsible for that day's training stepped into the ring, the energy circling it disappearing in a flash.

With Gaheris approaching, Draig pushed himself off of Kieran and stepped back.

The larger boy gulped at the air like a fish out of water, finally filling his lungs.

Gaheris swept his eyes over the silent Knights in training who stood fixed in place. Unable to comprehend what they had just witnessed. Not quite believing that David had vanquished Goliath.

"You see now that size does not matter in a combat," Gaheris said in a quiet but commanding voice. "All that matters in a combat is skill and applying what you have learned in the way that you have been taught. Yet even with all that, perhaps most important," the Knight said, glancing at Kieran briefly, distaste and disappointment flashing across his face for just an instant, "focus and control are a must. Never underestimate your opponent. Never place yourself in a position where your emotion rules your reason. If you do, just like Kieran, you die."

Gaheris waited a few seconds, his hard eyes sweeping over the assembled recruits. Hoping that at least some of the them learned from what they had just observed and some of what he had just said stuck with them. Although he had his doubts.

He was less than impressed with this current class of Knights. Except for one.

"Dismissed."

The Knights in training dispersed quickly, several staring at Draig as they walked away. Seemingly looking at him in a new light. But only a few.

"You're still a mongrel," grumbled Kieran as he stepped out of the circle and stumbled after his friends. "Still no better than a dog."

Draig's eyes flashed. Gaheris was right. Giving in to your emotion usually ensured a poor result. Now, though, he really wanted to do just that. The need to continue administering the lesson he had been giving Kieran growing within him.

He had gone no more than a step after the larger boy, practice sword still in hand, when a strong hand gripped his shoulder from behind, holding him in place.

"I know what you want to do, but you can't."

Draig closed his eyes in frustration before turning around to face Gaheris. "Why not?"

"You are not like them."

"That's what Kieran said."

Gaheris nodded, then stated in a very calm voice, "He's right."

The composure of the older Knight helped to calm Draig, the rage within him no longer a boil. Now just a simmer.

"I don't like being different, but there's nothing that I can do about it. I'm not just of the Teg."

"You're not," Gaheris agreed, "and is that really a bad thing? Just because they make fun of you? You really want to be like Kieran and his friends?"

Draig thought about that. For a moment, he was going to answer yes. Then he shook his head no. The truth too much for him to ignore.

"Being different is a good thing," Gaheris explained, willing with his eyes and his tone for Draig to listen. Hoping that the lesson he was offering now would stick with Draig, because it was an important one. He would need it in the future. "Why be like everyone else? Besides, their words can't hurt you. Their lack of understanding can't hurt you. They act as they do because you're different. Because they don't understand you."

"They're afraid of me," Draig murmured, comprehension dawning.

Gaheris nodded. "They are, and that is their failing. It does not have to be yours. You are of the Teg, but you are something more as well. They cannot take that away from you unless you allow them to. Don't let them."

With that, the memory faded. Draig drifting in a silent pitch black until a white light far off in the distance appeared and drew closer. Brighter than a star, it beckoned to him.

ANOTHER MEMORY. Just like the last one. Crystal clear. As if he was reliving the experience.

Hands on his knees, Draig gasped for air, sweat pouring down his brow, hair matted to his head.

The thin air made it hard to breathe, the race that he had run for the past hour not making it any easier.

He stood on a ledge that crested the almost vertical slope of snow and ice that he had just climbed. In any direction he turned there was nothing to see except for craggy, snowcapped peaks, the bright sun forcing him to shield his eyes from the glare.

He would have enjoyed taking in the view for a few minutes more, but he could catch his breath for only so long.

The hunt continued, and he was still the prey.

The creatures had begun the chase several miles below.

Up and down steep inclines, one slip ensuring his death. Over, under, even through snow that could be packed down hard or crumbled into a sinkhole at the slightest touch, the threat of being buried alive all too real. Through caverns and gullies carved by the wind, rain, and ice that appeared more bluish than clear.

His mother had warned him that this winter the Yetis were ranging farther from their territory higher up in the peaks.

Seeking food.

Of course, he had only listened to her with half an ear, never suspecting that he would run across a fist of the beasts.

Coming very close to being their next meal. Of course, that remained a distinct possibility, the odds of that improving with every step he took.

Because the Yetis were still after him.

Draig's breath caught when he glimpsed a whisper of movement on the slope a few hundred yards below him.

It had been barely anything at all.

A soft rustle.

Maybe just the wind brushing across the snow.

For just a moment, he thought that he might be mistaken.

That it was just the wind stirring up a few loose flakes.

A quick search with the Grym told him otherwise.

Another flash, less than a hundred yards below the crest.

They were closing on him.

Faster than he would have liked.

He couldn't see the creatures clearly.

He wouldn't unless they chose to reveal themselves.

His pursuers' natural camouflage allowed them to blend in perfectly with their wintry environment, so trying to locate them without the Grym was a waste of time.

Draig turned on a dime and sprinted up the goat trail behind him, seeking the cut in the mountain that he had spied just a few hundred yards above.

He should have assumed as much.

Yetis were relentless when they caught the scent of their next meal.

And this pack apparently had decided that it would be him.

In fact, he was still alive only because of a quirk of luck.

He had been climbing a sheer cliff covered in ice, relying on the steel picks in his boots and his ice axes to reach the top.

He was almost to the crown, glad that the climb was about to come to an end, when he sensed that he wasn't alone.

But for the life of him, Draig couldn't understand why he believed that.

Looking back over each shoulder and then up and down, he hadn't seen anything to confirm the feeling that was growing stronger within him.

That would confirm the prickle of concern that felt like an icicle punched into the back of his neck.

Still, he paid attention to the feeling.

His sense of approaching danger was never wrong.

About to drive the axe in his right hand into the ice so that he could conclude his climb, at the very last instant he raised it in front of his face instead.

Just in time.

The Yeti's sharp claw scratched across the steel haft rather than digging into his neck.

Draig glimpsed the beast's reflection in the ice, adjusting his positioning in response.

He was amazed that the creature had gotten so close to him. He wouldn't even have been aware of the threat if not for that lucky look.

Hanging from an ice shelf, a monster trying to kill him, Draig gave in to the instincts that had served him so well when he trained in the practice ring.

Ripping his right boot free from the ice, he turned his body and kicked to the side.

Earning a shriek of rage when the steel pick that extended out for several inches from the toe slid into the Yeti's fur-covered flesh, Draig sought to take advantage of the beast's surprise, swinging with the axe in his right hand.

He caught the Yeti at the same time that the creature was swiping at him again.

The Yeti's momentum aided Draig, who needed to do little more than hold his weapon in place.

Unable to halt his motion, the creature drove the palm of his claw onto the long blade of the axe, the tip poking through the back of his hand.

The Yeti reared back with a loud hiss, tearing his claw free with a sickening squelch. The beast's movement was so violent that he lost his grip and slid down the ice shelf, his only being able to use one claw making it difficult for him to arrest his fall.

Draig didn't wait to see what happened to his attacker.

He had barely listened to his mother when she warned of these creatures infringing on Draca land.

But he did recall a key point.

As some believed because of false histories, Yetis were not solitary creatures.

And they never hunted alone.

Reaching the top of the ice shelf through sheer force of will, he sensed the other Yetis on the cliff.

No more than a few minutes behind him.

He didn't stay and fight.

Instead, he ran.

As fast as he could.

Leading the Yetis on a wild chase.

Hoping that he lost them.

Believing that he might have a handful of times.

Always disappointed though not surprised when he realized that his efforts failed.

That the Yetis continued to keep pace with him.

Almost as if they were enjoying the hunt, and they were in no rush to reach the conclusion because that conclusion already was assured.

Yetis never failed on a hunt.

From the ice sheet where he was first attacked he ran for miles through the mountains, finally stopping atop the ledge after another arduous climb, and now sprinting between the two large rocks that appeared to be sentinels if you looked at them the right way.

Past the two guardians, he raced into the crevice beyond that was barely wide enough for him. So tight, at times, that he needed to turn sideways to make his way through.

He might have found exactly what he was looking for.

The Yetis were twice as large as he was. They couldn't follow him here.

Draig cursed himself for a fool when a shadow flashed above him. And then another. Followed by one more.

The Yetis didn't need to follow him in the crevice.

The Yetis climbed better than he did.

They were staying with him along the rim. Probably enjoying his attempt to escape, which in the end proved useless.

Because his race had come to an end.

When he burst out of the crevice and skidded to a stop, he stood on another ledge that was barely larger than the practice ring he had trained in at the barracks on his father's estate.

Looking behind him and then up, he took a few steps closer to the edge at his back, a drop of a few thousand feet greeting him.

He had hoped for a gentle slope.

He would have been satisfied with a steep slope.

Any kind of slope, in fact, that would allow him to try his luck on the mountain rather than against the Yetis who stood on the ridge above him.

But it wasn't to be.

He had run his race.

He considered the long dagger strapped to his thigh. A gift from Gaheris.

He left it there, deciding to use the ice axes that had served him well so far.

He pulled those tools that would now serve as his weapons from where they were hooked to his belt behind his back.

Then he waited.

There was no point in running now.

He'd never make it back into the crevice.

He was cornered with nowhere to go.

Except through his hunters.

Glancing up to the top of the ridge, he didn't get a good look at the Yetis with the sun in his eyes, only gaining a sense of their immense size.

The fist of Yetis, including the one he had wounded on the ice wall, jumped down the thirty-foot drop to the ledge. Finally, with the black rock of the mountain at their backs, Draig had a chance to study his hunters.

The Yetis did, indeed, closely resemble gorillas, although they were not just twice as big. They were three times larger and they were covered in a thick white fur that appeared to be almost translucent based on how they moved.

That made sense to Draig. That was why he didn't see the Yeti who tried to kill him on the ice shelf until the very last second.

Snow and ice, these creatures blended in flawlessly with both.

Their claws were perfectly suited to their needs as well, a big factor in their unique ability to climb. Their fingers and toes were almost a foot long and appeared to be as sharp as his axes. Another reason they were such lethal adversaries.

Draig was tired.

He was angry.

He didn't like being hunted.

And he was done.

He refused to run anymore even if he was given the chance.

As a result, his initial thought was to attack despite facing five formidable opponents.

Better to die moving forward, Gaheris had liked to say, rather than moving backward.

But against five Yetis?

Probably not the best path that he could choose.

So he decided on a different approach.

He couldn't fight five Yetis at one time.

Therefore, he needed to ensure that didn't happen for as long as he could.

Reaching for the Grym, he shot a streak of energy toward the three Yetis standing to his right.

The creatures ducked, just as Draig hoped they would. But they didn't escape the blast that struck the rocks behind them, shards of stone and boulders breaking free and slamming into the trio from behind.

Draig ignored the three beasts knocked to the ground and sprinted toward the two Yetis to his left.

He jolted them into motion when he slid feet first on his back across the frozen surface right between one of the Yeti's legs, slashing with the axe in his left hand and cutting across the creature's calf all the way to the bone.

The wounded Yeti reached for him, but the beast, hobbling on one leg, was too slow.

Draig dodged his swipe, the creature's claw missing by no more than the hair on his head, and shifted his attention to the other Yeti.

Draig swung with the axe in his right hand, aiming for the creature's knee.

The Yeti was fast.

But not fast enough to avoid the attack entirely.

Draig struck a glancing blow along the top of the Yeti's knee. It was still enough to earn a hiss of pain from the beast, the wound small but deep, cutting to the bone.

Before the pair of Yetis could come at him at the same time, he sent a blast of the Grym right between the two beasts, knocking them backward against the rockface.

Then he was racing toward the Yetis to his right who were pushing their way out of the rubble after his initial use of the Grym.

Draig danced and glided across the icy surface.

Almost always attacking.

Rarely needing to defend himself.

Combining the use of his ice axes with the Grym.

Never getting in a killing blow.

But, just as importantly, never allowing the Yetis to get in a killing blow either.

Despite the dire nature of his circumstances, which he assumed would worsen over time, he lost himself in the combat.

He reveled in the movement, the snap decisions he made with barely a thought. His instincts and training guiding him.

Here, on the ledge, his death all but certain, he could let go in a way that he normally couldn't when he visited with his mother.

He could lose himself in the combat.

He could be the person he was.

He could be himself.

He could forget the usually veiled though sometimes open animosity that ran as an undercurrent beneath all his interactions when he stayed with his mother here in the mountains.

Many of his mother's people looked down on him.

They didn't perceive him as a Draca.

Rather, they saw him as an oddity. Perhaps even a mistake.

What they didn't say more painful than what they did say, Draig reading it in their eyes.

He didn't belong there.

He was a half-breed.

A mongrel, just like Kieran had said a few years before.

He wasn't one of them.

He would never be one of them.

He would always be less than them.

It was hard for him not to believe that himself.

For the first fifteen years of his life, he had never met his mother.

Not until last summer.

His father thought that it would be a good idea. His mother had been asking about him. Wanting to spend time with him.

Even though she had left him in his father's care not long after he was born.

At least that's what his father had told him.

It didn't make sense to him. Why the interest after fifteen years?

But there was little that he could do.

Draig assumed that his father had acceded to his mother's request, even argued for it when Draig hesitated, because his father wanted him out of his hair for a few months.

Draig had acquiesced reluctantly.

It was very hard to say no to his father.

In fact, no one said no to his father.

Last summer, his first here in the mountains, had been painful for him. Difficult didn't even begin to describe it.

He was an outsider.

And his mother's family, his family, had made it perfectly clear that they wanted nothing to do with him.

After that experience, he had hoped that he wouldn't have to come back this year.

But here he was.

Back in the mountains his mother ruled.

And to avoid the stares, the hard looks, and the words offered that meant something completely different from what was said, he spent as much time as he could away from his mother's home in the peaks.

He enjoyed his daily wanderings, until today, of course.

And at least during this visit his mother was spending more time with him. Curious about him. Asking questions. Listening to his answers. Even telling him a little bit about herself.

Last summer she didn't seem to know what to do with him. He assumed that she was wondering why she even wanted him there. Whether she had made a mistake.

He pushed those thoughts from his mind in a flash.

Sensing the movement at his back, Draig pivoted and rolled, slipping out of the grasp of the Yeti that had snuck behind him. The creature trying to seize him in a bear hug and crush the life out of him.

For the beast's effort, Draig drove the long spike of his axe through the Yeti's clawed foot as he tumbled past.

When Draig was back on his feet, he realized that he was exactly where he had been when the combat started.

Herded to the very edge of the crest.

Nowhere to go but for the long vertical drop beneath him.

The five Yetis arrayed against him.

Clearly angry.

Definitely frustrated.

Hungry as well.

They growled. They snorted in fury. They dug their clawed feet into the rock. A few beat their chests with their powerful arms and howled.

Even so, they didn't rush toward him as he thought they would.

He had bloodied each one, the red streaks on their fur confirming his success.

A small victory.

Draig still faced terrible odds.

He resigned himself to his fate, knowing that he could put it off only for so long.

Yet despite the terrible nature of his situation, he refused to go down without a fight.

He refused to be easy meat for these Yetis.

He would prove that he was worthy of being the son of the Queen of the Draca.

Standing there with the axes in his hand, he allowed his rage to rule him.

A white-hot heat filled him.

As it did, the world around him began to look different, a reddish-orange haze coloring his vision.

He could sense the Grym surging within him. But mixing with it was another power.

A stronger power.

One that he had never experienced before.

One that he didn't even know resided within him.

With nothing to lose, he allowed that power to take him.

To consume him.

To scour him clean.

To build him anew.

To make him who he truly was supposed to be.

For just a split-second, he felt as if he was leaving his body.

Transforming.

Becoming a new entity.

A more potent entity.

It felt as if he was taking on a new shape.

A monstrous shape that he could see in his mind's eye.

The reddish-orange haze overwhelming him, remaking him, strengthening him, Draig crouched down swiftly, slamming his ice axes into the frozen ground.

As soon as the sharp tips struck, a blast of energy erupted from him, a blinding flash of light shooting out in all directions.

The energy he released scorched the stone, streaks of black marring the frozen surface.

The shockwave reverberated throughout the mountains.

The ledge that he stood on shook dangerously. Swaying. Crumbling at the edges. Threatening to slide off the rockface, though somehow the crag maintained its grip on the mountain.

When Draig stood, he was himself again.

Although his eyes remained as they were, coloring the world around him a reddish orange.

The power that surged through his blood, setting it afire, hidden deep within and locked away until that moment, filled him with a confidence and competence he had never experienced before.

Once released, he would never be able to contain that power again.

He savored that knowledge, even more the sensation surging through his body.

He felt ... whole.

He felt as if he was truly who he was meant to be.

And he had no doubt that because of this new discovery about himself, he could more than manage five Yetis.

The Yetis were back on their clawed feet after being knocked to the ground by the blast.

They stood against him again. Although they were no longer growling, gnashing their teeth, or beating their chests.

Instead, the beasts stared at him. Studying him. More curious than afraid.

He hadn't expected behavior such as this from them.

He was ready, nonetheless.

Yet instead of rushing toward him, the Yetis turned away and climbed the rockface at their backs, disappearing over the ridge.

All except for one.

The Yeti nodded to Draig before following his brethren, disappearing as soon as he topped the ridge.

"They respect you."

The soft voice came from behind him. When he turned, his mother stood there on the very tip of the ledge.

"You were here the whole time?"

She stepped closer to him, placing a hand on his shoulder. When he flinched just a hair, she pulled back.

She understood his hesitation. They were still new to one another. She was trying to become a part of his life. She didn't really know how to do that, but she did know that she couldn't rush it. Patience, a trait that she often lacked, was key.

"No, I just saw the end of the fight. What you did to demonstrate your dominance." Her eyes swept over him, making sure that he hadn't received any wounds beyond some scratches and a few bruises.

Draig couldn't be sure, but he thought that his mother might be proud of him.

"I don't know any Draca who have stood down a fist of Yeti and survived," his mother said.

Definitely impressed, he decided. "I was just doing what was necessary."

"You didn't kill them," his mother continued. "You could have. You had the right to do so."

Draig nodded. "That doesn't mean it was the right thing to do."

"Do you always do the right thing?" his mother asked. There wasn't a hint of sarcasm in her voice.

Draig smiled then. "Do you?" It was a challenge.

His mother's smile broadened, though she didn't take up the gauntlet he had thrown at her feet. "Come on. It's time for dinner. We have much to talk about."

"Can we eat first? I'm starving."

His mother chuckled softly. "We can eat first." Just like every other teenager in the world. Always hungry.

"And perhaps some of those cinnamon rolls you made for dessert?"

"For dessert," she agreed with a nod. "Not before."

"Fair enough," Draig agreed.

"Good, because after dinner we need to talk."

"About what?"

"You."

"Me?"

"You, and who you truly are. What you can truly do."

DRAIG ENTERED the inky black once more, the experience jarring after where his mind had been just moments before. Yet as soon as the calm of the void settled over him, the flash of light appeared in the distance, streaking toward him, ripping him free from the solitude and emptiness.

A third memory. This one just as vivid as the first two.

He swept his gaze over the large room in which he stood.

It was a comfortable space. A hodgepodge of carpets covered the floor. Just as many were fixed to the walls, offering an additional warmth. Lanterns hung from chains bolted into the ceiling. Long tables covered in a variety of equipment that brought to mind a chemistry lab were set against the walls on both sides, leaving the center of the room free.

Draig stood on a large circular mat.

A sparring mat.

Something with which he was quite familiar.

He knew where he was. He had been here before. A long time ago.

He wasn't in a room.

He was in a large cavern. He couldn't see it, but he could hear the gentle rush of a waterfall not very far away that sent a soothing sound throughout the vast space.

Draig advanced deeper within the cave, the waterfall becoming louder with each step he took.

He stopped at the rug blocking his way at the very back, the waterfall just beyond.

Using the Grym, he searched around him. Needing to make sure.

Although fairly certain about what he was going to find, he

didn't want to deal with any surprises on what should be a straightforward job.

His father had sent him to deal with a Teg charged with stealing magical artifacts and potions from the stockpile kept by the Knights of the Round. A simple task compared to some of the other assignments the King Teg had given him in recent months.

Draig wanted to complete this piece of business and get out of here.

For some reason that he couldn't understand, what he was doing just didn't feel right. Still, that wouldn't stop him from doing his job.

Because that's all it was to him. A job.

Reaching over his shoulder with his right hand, he slid the sword free from the scabbard across his back. With his left, he pulled the rug to the side and stepped into a slightly smaller chamber, the waterfall visible at the very back.

Rugs covered the stone floor here as well. More tables ran along the length of the wall. And to his left, working at one of the tables with his back turned, was the reason Draig had spent the last two days hunting in the Adirondacks. The large man sat on a stool hunched over a workspace filled with tubes, beakers, Bunsen burners, and boiling liquids that was set up in a manner that likely would have made Rube Goldberg proud.

"Did you really think that you were going to escape me, Russell?"

Russell looked up quickly and spun around on his stool, startled, almost falling out of his seat.

"I was kind of hoping," the bearded giant rumbled. He pushed himself up and stepped away from the table, taking one quick look at the apparatus to ensure that all was working as it should be, before he focused his full attention on Draig. "I didn't know that what I did rose to a level that required the Dragon to hunt me down."

Draig shrugged ever so slightly. "You caught me between jobs."

Although Russell's comment continued to play on Draig's mind, because it was an astute one. His father had given him this assignment himself. He only did that when he believed it was critically important. And his father had been very strict with his instructions, the result that he wanted quite clear.

Draig hadn't questioned his father about any of that, even though he didn't quite understand why he was being sent after a Teg who had stolen a few items. Usually, his father gave him the more challenging assignments. Not something like this. A squad of Knights could have done just as well, although perhaps not have found Russell as fast as he did.

"I guess I'm lucky that way," Russell murmured.

"I guess so," Draig agreed.

Russell studied Draig. He needed a few seconds to think because he was afraid. Because just as every other Teg knew, when the King Teg sent the Dragon after you, there was only one possible result.

Nevertheless, Russell was close to completing what he was working on, and that needed to be his priority. Not his imminent death.

"I know how this is going to end," Russell said with an impressive calm. "I was wondering if you might give me a few minutes to finish what I was doing before we get to that?"

Draig smiled, not expecting the request. He did think about it, although not for very long.

His father had told him that in the hands of a skilled Teg the potions and artifacts Russell had stolen could be used to compel others. To control them. To make them do as the Teg desired.

Anything at all.

Even kill themselves.

Draig couldn't take that risk. "I'm sorry, Russell, but I can't."

"I thought as much," Russell replied. Disappointed though not surprised. The Dragon wasn't known for his patience. He was known for the thoroughness and efficiency of his work.

With barely a rustle of movement, Russell launched himself at Draig. In the time it took for his feet to leave the ground and swipe at Draig's face, the giant shifted.

His human form disappeared.

In Russell's place sprang a massive tiger.

Draig's father hadn't told him that Russell was a Were.

He slid to the side, avoiding Russell's attack by no more than a whisker.

When the snarling tiger shot by him, Draig could have slashed across the beast's hind quarters.

But he didn't. He held back instead, driven by a doubt he didn't understand.

His hesitation certainly went against his training.

"Russell, you don't want to do this." Draig watched the massive tiger turn back toward him. Growling, sharp teeth exposed.

He needed to kill Russell just as his father had ordered and be done with it. Any delay on his part only increased the risk of his own death.

The tiger stared at Draig, the shifter's eyes glowing a fiery orange. With a roar, Russell leapt at Draig.

Draig pivoted to the side again, avoiding the claw aimed for his chest. This time he didn't allow Russell to pass by unharmed.

With an economical slash of his blade, he cut deeply across the back of the tiger's right leg.

The tiger howled in agony, tumbling along the floor, blood splashing across the carpets.

Before the Were could regain his footing, Draig was there. He held his blade to Russell's throat.

Despite his pain, Russell became absolutely still, feeling the metal cutting into his flesh.

"Shift back," Draig ordered in a remorselessly quiet voice. "Now."

The tiger hesitated, the muscles in his shoulders bunching.

"Shift back now, Russell." Draig pressed his blade a bit harder against the Were's throat. "I'm not asking again."

A few more seconds passed. Then, just as fast as the Teg turned into a massive tiger, Russell was back in his human shape. Lying across the carpet, moaning softly, reaching for the long gash across the back of his leg, a slow trickle of blood dripping down the outside of his throat courtesy of Draig's blade.

Draig removed his sword then and leaned away from his quarry. Crouching. Well balanced. Ready. Just in case. Because he always assumed the worst.

"Why didn't you kill me?" gasped Russell.

Draig didn't answer right away. "I don't know."

And that was the truth. He didn't know.

By all rights, Russell should be dead. Draig had refrained from making the final cut despite his father's order.

"I didn't do what your father said I did."

Draig stared at Russell. The Were changed his positioning just a hair so that he was on his side, left arm pushing his chest off the ground.

Draig's eyes narrowed. "You didn't steal several powerful magical items and potions from the Knights of the Round?"

"I did do that," he admitted. He smiled when he said it. "But I didn't do it for the reason that your father told you."

"What do you mean?" Draig asked. Curious. Also, a little worried. The voice in the back of his head growing more insistent, the sense that something was off about this entire hunt becoming stronger.

"I didn't take all this for me," he nodded toward the table at his back. "I only did it because I needed to. I had no choice.

There was no other way." Russell closed his eyes, hissing at the pain that radiated from his leg. His voice was a low growl when he spoke again. "Your father wouldn't give me what I needed. I asked him, but he refused."

"What are you talking ..."

Russell pushed himself up from the carpet faster than Draig thought possible. Snarling. Shifting. Hands becoming claws. Arms elongating. Body lengthening and expanding. Fur sprouting. Tail extending. Clothes fading.

The wound along the back of Russell's leg saved Draig. It hindered the transformation.

Slowed the change.

Slowed the Were.

Russell would have killed Draig if he was whole and not in pain. If he hadn't lost so much blood.

The shift took longer than usual as a result. By no more than an extra millisecond.

Yet that was all that Draig needed.

Less than a heartbeat.

Draig barely moved.

He shifted his positioning just a hair, raising his sword, point extended.

Russell gasped, then choked.

Not yet fully a tiger. Caught in between.

His leap took him right onto Draig's blade. Steel piercing his chest, the tip sticking out of his back.

Russell stared into Draig's eyes. The reddish-orange flames sad. Disappointed. Not satisfied.

Draig saw a whirlwind of emotions as Russell gasped again, a stream of blood flowing from his lips. The Were returning to his human form as he died slowly. Painfully.

Regret.

Hope.

"Please," Russell whispered, his voice becoming softer as the light left his eyes. "Please help ..."

Draig turned to his left, easing Russell down to the ground as the Were took his last breath. Once he was gone, Draig pulled his sword out of Russell's chest, wiping the blood from his blade with a cloth.

Draig knew that it was going to come to this. His father had ordered him to eliminate the Teg.

He had done it before.

More times than he cared to remember. Because he had a hard enough time sleeping now as it was.

Draig frowned.

Why did what had just happened bother him so much?

He hadn't intended to kill Russell.

Russell hadn't given him a choice, however.

Draig had reacted instinctively, Russell pushing himself onto his blade while reaching for him.

A clean kill.

Yet not so clean.

Draig pushed himself to his feet.

He should feel some emotion other than this sense that all wasn't quite as it should be, shouldn't he?

But he didn't.

He didn't feel anything at all.

This was simply another assignment.

Just like all the others.

This was no more than a task that needed to be done.

Yet it wasn't. At least not entirely.

It was more than that.

He couldn't deceive himself.

Because Draig felt ...

Sorrow.

Remorse.

He had never experienced either emotion before when sent out on a job.

Why now?

The eyes. It had to be Russell's eyes.

Why did he see hope in Russell's eyes?

Why did Russell plead with him at the end?

He wasn't pleading for himself. Draig was sure of that.

Russell knew that he was dead as soon as Draig appeared.

If he wasn't hopeful for himself, if he wasn't pleading for himself, then he was …

Draig gritted his teeth, his head beginning to hurt. Another migraine coming on.

It had become more of a problem in the last few months.

Always right after he completed a job.

And then, just as before, the small voice in the back of his head that he listened to more often than not told him that something was wrong.

With him.

He shouldn't be so callous.

So uncaring.

So … cruel.

He tried to crush the voice that had taken up residence in his head around the same time that the migraines had begun.

But he couldn't.

Nothing that he tried worked.

Every other time he had succeeded.

Every time.

Shutting up the voice.

But not this time.

Despite his best efforts, the voice stayed with him.

An annoying buzz in the back of his brain.

It was becoming more difficult to ignore, the voice growing louder after every job now.

Russell's eyes.

Why did Russell plead with him at the end?

Draig strode over to the table where Russell had been working when Draig entered the cave.

He bent down and studied the tools and equipment. The potions and substances.

Russell was making an elixir with what he assumed were the items that he had stolen.

But this didn't make sense. What Russell had taken, what he was working with, the crystals and the liquids, they were all used to heal.

Not to compel.

And that's what his father had told him.

The Were had stolen items that could compel another Teg to do whatever he wanted.

Yet none of what he was examining could do that.

Draig stood straight, cocking his head to the side.

Just off to the right, hidden in shadow.

He had heard a sound.

Faint. Just there.

He walked into the gloom, sword held at the ready.

Another rug hung from the ceiling.

He used the Grym to search ahead of him, not having any idea what was waiting for him.

Draig swept the carpet to the side and stepped into a smaller chamber, a trickle of water running down the stone wall and falling into a small pool.

He was behind the waterfall.

Several lanterns hung from the ceiling to light the space.

A woman lay on a cot placed near the pool. Sweat poured down her face, soaking the blankets that covered her.

She was shivering. Pale. Eyes closed. Mumbling deliriously. Barely breathing.

Hope.

A plea.

He knew why now.

"I had no choice."

That's what Russell had said. He didn't have a choice.

Arthur Pendragon wouldn't give him the supplies he needed to aid the ailing Teg. Russell didn't have a choice, so he had stolen them. And his father had been less than pleased by that.

Draig's expression hardened.

His father had lied to him.

As he knelt by the woman to see what he could do to help, he wondered how many times before his father had lied to him.

17

BACK IN THE PRESENT

Emerging once again from the pitch black was just as jarring for Draig as the previous two times. It felt as if he had been living in two different realities, those two realities tugging at him with equal force, creating a headache reminiscent of a spike being driven into his brain with the repetitiveness of a crew laying railroad tracks.

Thankfully, that pain eased quickly, becoming nothing more than a dull ache when he opened his eyes again.

He was back in the present, Bile standing before him.

"Do you do that on purpose?" Draig asked. Not accusing, just curious.

"Only with my friends."

Draig wanted to shake his head at what he assumed was a jest. He didn't. If he did, it would only take longer for the ache in his skull to subside. Instead, he smiled thinly. Closing his eyes, he breathed deeply.

Who knew the God of Death had a sense of humor?

"I'd hate to be one of your enemies."

The ache fading as he came back to himself, when Draig

opened his eyes, the muted glow of the Circle was a welcome sight.

"That you would," Bile agreed. "My enemies usually don't survive what you just experienced."

"I'll keep that in mind."

Bile nodded. "That is your past, Draig."

"How is that relevant to the answers I seek?"

"It reminds you of what you are made," Bile explained. "How you are made."

"And I need to know that why?"

There were a great many events and actions in his past that Draig didn't want to remember, yet he had learned that he couldn't escape what he had done. That he could never heal the pain he caused. That he could never make amends for all the mistakes he made. No matter how hard he tried.

"Because you are who you are for a reason."

"Aren't we all?" Draig countered.

Bile nodded. "In part, yes. But there is more to you than just that. You are of mixed breeding after all. That makes you unique."

Draig wasn't offended by the comment as other Teg might be, as he had been when he was younger.

After spending more time with his mother, despite the coldness and scorn offered by many of the Draca, not all treated him now as they had when he first visited.

He had grown proud of his heritage the more he learned about where he came from and the lineage of which he was a part. Two royal lines that had merged ever so briefly and then broken apart again, following distinct paths. Likely never to connect again.

He was proud of some of it anyway.

That thought brought to mind one of his lessons with Merlin when he was a teenager. The Sorcerer had assumed responsibility for Draig's education, primarily because his father didn't have the time.

Or so his father said.

Draig believed that it was really a lack of interest. Because he had learned that his father would say whatever was necessary to justify his actions, not all of those justifications true. Just as his last memory confirmed.

"Our past molds our future," Draig murmured, not realizing that he spoke out loud one of Merlin's favorite axioms.

Bile nodded, pleased. "Exactly that. But with you, Axel Draig, Axel Pendragon, Axel Draca, Fallen Knight and Dragon, the Teg of many names and none, you have a unique talent."

"What do you mean?"

"The past molds your future, that is true. But it is you who will mold the future of the Teg."

Draig pondered that statement, not quite sure that he understood what Bile was suggesting. Not quite sure that he wanted to. "That's a heavy responsibility."

"It is indeed. The question now is whether you have the strength to manage that responsibility. Those who have come before you have not."

"Those who have come before me?"

Bile ignored him. "Do you dare to see the future, Draig? It can be more painful than the past."

Draig hesitated. He had done this three times before. Entering the Circle for guidance. And each time the future had not been what he had hoped it would be.

He assumed that would be the case if he looked into the future again. Because when he peered into the future, he looked not upon certainty, but rather possibility.

Paths that were open to him.

Paths that he could take based on the choices he made.

That's what the future was, after all.

A series of choices.

A plethora of possibilities.

Certain possibilities gaining substance based on the decisions he made. Each decision offering more possibilities. Requiring that more decisions be made. A never-ending series of choices to be made.

Now, however, he had no choice.

He had come too far. Viewing the past would do little for him if he did not risk a glimpse of what might come to be.

He nodded, trying to infuse as much confidence into the motion as he could, which really wasn't very much at all.

The inky black returned the instant Bile's fingers touched his forehead.

DRAIG ROLLED TO THE SIDE, a massive scythe made of molten rock sweeping through the space where his head had been just a moment before.

He didn't have time to take his feet, the scythe sweeping back toward him with a frightening speed.

He raised Excalibur just in time, an ear-splitting clang ringing out as his shining sword blocked the fiery rock seeking to bite into his muscle and break his bone.

Draig's muscles tensed. The blood vessels in his neck bulged. Sweat dripped off his brow.

Not only from the heat of the glowing rock that pushed closer and closer to his face, but also because the effort that he was expending was doing little to help him.

He couldn't prevent the molten rock from burning into his flesh. Thin strands of lava already scalding his arms. It was only a matter of time before the scythe struck home.

"You are not as strong as you think, Dragon."

The deep, rumbling voice broke Draig's concentration for just a heartbeat. He was unwilling to take his eyes from the scythe that slowly but inexorably pushed Excalibur back toward him. He couldn't help himself, however. Draig looked up ever so briefly.

That very brief lapse didn't help his efforts.

He was losing this combat, and he didn't even know who he was fighting.

He had yet to pierce the mask of swirling black that hid his opponent so well, Draig only able to determine that the shape was that of a man half again as tall as he was. Beyond that, he had not a clue. Other than the fact that his attacker was stronger than he was and was quite skilled in the use of the scythe that dripped molten rock.

"You will die," the voice continued. "A painful death. An excruciating death. I will make it so. You deserve no less."

Draig didn't reply. He couldn't.

He could do no more than stare at the blade coming toward him, inch by inch. Only seconds away from cutting into him.

Once that happened, he was dead.

The combat would end quickly.

He felt his muscles weakening. Quivering. Shaking. The effort to hold back the scythe too much for him.

He needed to fight.

He couldn't give in.

Yet as the glowing blade maintained its steady advance toward him, continuing to fight only ensured his death.

That conclusion finally gave him an idea.

Going against all logic, Draig stopped fighting.

He allowed the force his adversary applied against his sword to push him backward, using the momentum to roll over his right shoulder and then dive to the right when the scythe slammed into the stone where he had been crouching just a moment before.

Draig dove back to the left, the scythe slamming into the

stone once again, splashes of molten rock flying through the air.

For the next few seconds, that was all that Draig knew.

Constant movement.

This way and that.

Not thinking.

Just moving.

Somehow surviving even as the glowing scythe sliced across his flesh a dozen times or more.

None of the burns debilitating.

None of them slowing him down.

All of them painful.

All of them reminding Draig of the fate that awaited him.

And then the assault finally came to an end.

Draig not understanding why, though grateful for the brief respite.

The shadowy figure stood across from Draig. Still as a statue.

"You are quite an entertaining foe, Dragon. I commend you for that. But you cannot escape me. You will never escape me."

Draig listened to his adversary's words with half an ear, more interested in the images that formed behind the murky figure.

There for just an instant, then gone just as fast as they appeared.

Two images.

Two possible paths from which he would need to choose.

Two possible conclusions.

Neither of which appealed to him.

Although the two possible futures did reveal to him who his adversary was.

"Your end is now, Dragon," the masked giant rumbled. The creature strode toward him, scythe raised behind his shoulder, the weapon already sweeping down through the air toward him.

Draig didn't move. He couldn't move. Frozen in place by the two futures that he had glimpsed.

One that he expected.

His own death.

The other ... more difficult to interpret.

"You will not be reborn, Dragon," the giant roared. "The Dragon dies with a single stroke."

Draig watched as the glowing steel swept toward his neck.

Right before the blade severed his head from his body, the inky black returned, as did the feeling of his head being split in two, although thankfully not by his adversary.

"Typhon," Draig whispered, ignoring the pain that pulsed in his head, hoping that it would subside with time.

Bile nodded. "Not the enemy I would choose to have."

"I thought he was destroyed long ago."

"He was defeated long ago," Bile clarified. "He still survives. He waits. He hides. He prepares."

"He is the cause of what stirs among the Teg?"

"You tell me," Bile replied.

Draig lifted an eyebrow. Bile's usual disinterest in the Teg seemed more forced than real this time.

Typhon was an ancient god. A terrible god. And one against which few if any could stand.

In the world of the Teg. In the Spirit World. In any world, in fact.

"Bile, I've got a splitting headache."

"Yes, but you're still alive."

Draig nodded, recalling their brief conversation before the God of the Dead sent him into the future. "For which I am grateful. But rather than leading me around, can you speak plainly please?"

"You don't need me to tell you of what I speak, Draig. You're simply being more difficult than usual."

"Bile ..."

The God of the Dead raised his hands, hoping to fend off Draig's rising temper, which was made plain by the fiery reddish orange of his eyes.

"I rule in the Spirit World. You can rule in your world. If you choose." "Rule?"

Bile shook his head in disappointment. This didn't have to be as hard as Draig was making it. Though Bile assumed it came more from Draig's lack of interest than his lack of comprehension. Bile just needed to push a little more.

Draig was brave. Determined. Loyal, often to a fault.

Yet he was blind as well.

Purposely so at that moment. At least with respect to this matter.

"Why do you think that you cannot see the result of your combat against your real nemesis?"

Draig didn't reply, the two images that he had viewed playing through his mind on a constant loop.

The first had been quite easy to understand.

Life or death.

The common result from any combat.

Two entered the ring. One left. The other didn't.

Although on this path, he was the one who didn't exit the ring.

Typhon would kill him.

One possible fate.

And after all that he had done, he could not deny that he deserved a death such as that.

The first path seemed almost certain. Death at Typhon's hand the overwhelming possibility.

Typhon was a god, after all. A primordial god with a power that exceeded his own. One of the Ancients. The Grym flowing throughout the Teg world coming from him and his brothers and sisters.

But Bile was suggesting that there was more to it than that. Another possibility.

One that frightened him even more than his own death.

"You know what the other path is, Draig. You just don't want to acknowledge it. Do not let your fear blind you."

Draig glared at Bile, hating that the god was forcing him to confront his greatest fear. What this other path would require from him. What it would give him.

The least likely path compared to the first. Although still a possibility. Slim though it might be.

He could take his father's place.

Draig could rule the Teg.

Just as Merlin had hinted at over the years.

Draig's eyes widened, understanding what such a path becoming reality truly meant.

For him.

For his father.

For all of the Teg.

This second possibility frightened him more than the possibility of Typhon separating his head from his shoulders with his scythe crafted from molten rock.

Bile laughed softly. Draig's comprehension of the two unpleasant choices that the Fates had laid before him easy to read on his face.

"You see it now, and you are right. Death is a possibility, a strong possibility, although perhaps not so terrible a fate as what would befall you if you defeated the god."

Draig couldn't help but think about what Bile said.

The Fates were playing with him now. Giving him an almost impossible choice.

Draig's greatest fear wasn't dying. There were times in his past when he would have preferred that. Welcomed it, in fact.

Seeking penance in his death for all the crimes that he believed that he had committed.

More than willing to die if it meant that his death helped to protect the Teg.

No, his greatest fear was what would be required of him if he took his father's place among the Teg.

That in so doing, he would become his father.

A man not of morals but of means.

Not of ethics but of necessity.

Driven by the need to remain in power.

Driven by the desire to ensure his place.

No matter the price to be paid by the Teg.

To become what he didn't want to become.

That's why he had left the Knights of the Round by faking his own death. That's why he had left his father's side.

Because he knew what was happening to him.

What he was becoming by doing as his father ordered.

What he would be if he didn't change his path.

Draig closed his eyes for just a heartbeat and took a deep breath. He was right back where he started.

The Fates clearly were playing with him. Thinking more on his dilemma, perhaps it wasn't as simple as that.

Were they in truth giving him an opportunity?

Were those really the only two choices that he could make?

Die at the hands of Typhon and doom the Teg?

Or, in order to defeat Typhon, become the ruler of the Teg? And in so doing doom himself to a fate that would be more terrible than death and even more destructive for the Teg?

Because he believed that he knew what the future held for the Teg if he took his father's place.

So were those the only two choices?

Could he not influence those two possible fates in some way?

"That is all that is revealed," Bile said, seemingly reading his mind, a hint of sadness in his voice.

"Are there no other options?"

Bile waited quite a while before replying. "I do not know. But know this, Axel Draig. Axel Pendragon. Axel Draca. You are one of the few who can rip the Veil and join our worlds together. You are one of the few who at least for a time can twist fate around your fingertips."

Draig nodded. He had hoped for answers upon entering the Circle.

He had gained some.

But it seemed as well that he had also stirred up even more questions and concerns.

Regardless, Draig realized he couldn't hide anymore. He needed to emerge once again into the Teg world.

Maybe then he could find some solution to this dilemma that didn't doom the Teg or himself.

"Thank you, Bile," Draig said. Not sure of all that he needed to do, but at least clear about the next few steps that he needed to take.

Bile nodded, then turned toward the cromlech, the dim glow becoming dimmer. The shadows that colored the natural world pulling back.

The merger between the Spirit World and the Teg World was breaking apart.

Before he stepped through the rip that was closing at a rapid rate, Bile turned, offering Draig a smile.

"Tread carefully, Fallen Knight. You stand on the edge of the blade. If you fall, you will never escape. Either my hold or Typhon's."

"And you don't want me in your world. Not yet."

"That I don't," Bile confirmed with a chuckle, "which is why I will let you go now without a fight."

"Thank you for that."

Bile nodded. "Do what must be done, Draig. For the sake of your world. For the sake of mine as well. Typhon belongs in neither. Best that he is sent back to Tartarus where he belongs."

"It is done," Leya said, sighing with relief.

She and Melissa watched as the dome of energy slowly retreated, the threads of black and white moving again, pulling back across the surface. The dim radiance of white that lit the Circle once more gaining dominance.

The wind died down and a deep silence descended.

They didn't have long to wait before Draig exited the Circle, walking between the two stone monoliths.

They were relieved. Worried as well because of his severe expression. As if he prepared to go to war.

"You understand what the Teg truly face?"

"I do, Leya."

"Do you understand what will be required of you if you accept this challenge?"

"I do."

"Yet still you will accept it?" Leya already knew how her friend was going to reply. Because the Draig who stood before her now was not the same Draig as the one who walked into the Circle.

"I don't have much of a choice, Leya."

"You always have a choice, Draig."

Draig's expression hardened even more, almost to the point where he was glaring at the Druid. Yet there was no reason to unleash his anger upon her. She wasn't the cause of his dilemma.

And she was right. He did have a choice.

He could choose to do nothing.

He could choose to remain in Kraken Cove and turn his back on the Teg.

And why not?

The Teg, most of them anyway, had turned their backs on him many times before.

With good reason, he admitted. And there was still a great deal that he had to make amends for.

Besides, he knew what it would cost the Teg if he didn't do what was required of him.

"No, not now," Draig replied softly. "Now there is only one choice."

Leya gave him a sad smile. "It is difficult, always feeling the need to do what you believe is right."

"The possible cost to me doesn't really matter," Draig replied. "I have much to atone for."

"One of these days you must let your guilt go."

"Just not today." Draig walked past both of them, following the path that would take them back to Leya's cottage. "We need to get going."

"The Weres?" Melissa asked.

"They remain a problem," he said over his shoulder, "but they're the least of our concerns. Something worse."

"You know the cause of the unrest?" she asked.

"I do."

"And?" Melissa asked.

"And it's exactly what I thought." He stopped then, facing them both and giving them a meaningful look. "There's only one thing to do."

"What's that?" asked Melissa.

"Destroy it before it destroys the Teg."

18

GETTING ANTSY

"I don't have time for this, mother," Mordred growled.

He paced around the boardroom with his head down and hands behind his back. Every so often, he glanced up at the large, backlit sign made of glass that was fixed to the wall.

The Orkney Foundation.

The name that his mother selected when they set up their operations in New York City never failed to amuse him.

A reminder of where she came from, she had told him once. A reminder as well as to where she never wanted to return.

"Neither do I, Mordred." Morgase studied her son as she tracked his movement across the room. "I am hosting an awards ceremony later this evening, and I need to get to the Lincoln Center within the hour."

Mordred chuckled at that, although he didn't stop his pacing. "If only the world knew who you truly were, mother."

"I could say the same of you, Mordred." Her voice remained even, under control, the only sign of her rising irritation the brief flash of anger in the back of her eyes.

"True," Mordred admitted. "But you won't, just as I won't, since our deceptions prove so useful to the both of us."

"Mordred, would you please sit down so that we can talk like adults." It wasn't a request.

Mordred ignored his mother, actually picking up the pace, knowing that his doing so would annoy her all the more.

"What did you do to Candy, mother?"

"Candy?"

Mordred snorted, though not in amusement. "You know who I'm talking about. The woman I was with the last time you visited me on Long Island."

Morgase didn't reply right away. Brow furrowing slightly. She was surprised.

Her son usually didn't care when the women he was seeing fell out of his life. Most often because of his own doing. As her son had told her many times before, there was always another conquest waiting for him just around the corner.

The mayor's daughter. A senator's wife. The head of a multinational corporation. A microbiologist focused on infectious disease. A pop star. A Tik Tok influencer.

It didn't really matter to Mordred so long as the woman met one or more of his primary requirements.

Rich. Powerful. Connected. Able to give him what he truly desired at that moment.

Love and affection were never a consideration.

"I told you before and I'll tell you again, Mordred. Your dalliances will become problematic for us if you don't adjust your criteria for selecting your next victim."

"They're not victims," Mordred scoffed. "They are assets."

"Simply a play on words, Mordred. No more than that." She said it to appease him, hoping that she could still conduct the required conversation in a civil manner. Adopting a more demanding approach might complicate matters between them in the future.

"Where is Candy, mother?" Mordred asked the question again in a deceptively calm voice. His angst couldn't be missed, however, fingers tightening their grip around one another. He was trying to control the temper that often got him into trouble, especially with his mother. But it was a struggle. He was tired, so tired, of Morgase involving herself in his affairs. "She's important to me, and not just because she's good in bed."

Morgase chuckled at that. "Not just another of your floozies?" She shook her head, partly in amusement, more in disappointment. "I've told you many times before ..."

"Which means you don't need to tell me again," Mordred cut in, his tone stronger though still respectful.

Morgase ignored the interruption, not rising to the challenge. "You will be the King of the Teg one day. Hopefully one day soon. If you want the Teg to follow you ..."

"I must limit the women I spend time with to the Teg." Mordred wanted to scream. Instead, he snapped. "You've told me that so many times it's often the only thing I hear before I go to bed at night. It gets in the way of more pleasurable pursuits."

"Good. As it should. Because it's true. The Teg will not follow you ..."

"Whether the Teg will follow me is immaterial, mother." His back turned, Mordred didn't see how Morgase's eyes flashed again in anger. She never appreciated it when anyone, including her son, treated her with disrespect, real or perceived. "When I am the King of the Teg, I will be their ruler. Their monarch. Their warlord. They will do as I say, when I say. It's as simple as that. For them, it's not a matter of following. It's a matter of obeying."

"The Teg are not so easily cowed, Mordred. You should know that by now. I may hate my brother, but I will be the first to admit that he's danced well these last thousand and more years. If he hadn't, then he would have lost his throne long ago. If you can't learn to do the same, the various powers and factions among the Teg will ..."

"Arthur Pendragon remains in power because of Merlin," Mordred snarled, unable to contain the rage that was bubbling up within him. He hated his father with a passion that could only be matched by his feelings for one other Teg.

"You simplify matters too much, Mordred. It would be good for you to study ..."

"Where is Candy, mother?" Mordred asked for a third time. His anger reduced to a simmer.

Morgase's lips pinched together. Any other person would have felt her wrath for continuing to press her. She gave her son greater leeway, though not for much longer. She was losing patience rapidly.

"Why is she so important to you?" Morgase's eyes narrowed. Clearly, there was more going on here than just her son's lustful heart.

"As I said, she was quite good in bed ..."

"Stop wasting my time, Mordred."

Mordred smirked. He enjoyed getting under Morgase's skin. Although he knew that he could push only so far. His mother was many things. She was not a fool. And certainly not as even-tempered as she was pretending to be. "When you last visited, I told you she had experience in finance and arbitrage."

Morgase remembered, nodding her head slightly. "She was helping you with one of your schemes."

Mordred smiled. "Midas has proven to be more difficult than anticipated. As you said, the Teg cannot be easily cowed, and the pressure that I've applied has had little impact upon him. He still balks at my demands."

"You're trying to apply pressure in another way."

"I was. Candy was managing the strategy for me. I need her back for that reason."

Morgase did not respond right away, her expression becoming shrewd. "I will do what I can to locate her."

"You will locate her. You know exactly where she is."

Morgase smiled again. Her son was many things. He was not a fool ... at least most of the time. "How do you know she isn't six feet underground?"

"I don't," Mordred said with a shrug. "I do know, however, that you would have done your research before you took her. You would have been curious about her and why I've kept her at my side for so long. Therefore, you wouldn't have killed her. Not yet anyway. Not until you got all the answers you wanted from her."

"What are you hoping to extract from Midas?"

"A partnership."

"He won't accede to that request no matter what you do," Morgase said with a calm certainty.

"Probably not," Mordred agreed.

Morgase chuckled. "You're trying to distract him."

"I am," Mordred admitted. "While I keep Midas focused on me, Candy is managing the scheme behind the scheme."

He continued to stride around the conference room, hands behind his back, head down.

Morgase found it strange.

She knew her son to be neurotic at times. So fixed on a matter that he could think of little else.

Clearly, he was in such a state now. His current behavior made that clear.

Even more telling, Mordred paid little attention to the view just to her left. He coveted the offices of the Orkney Foundation, situated on the eighty-fifth floor of the Empire State Building.

He wanted the space for himself. He loved the vista that he had been ignoring ever since he swept through the conference room doors.

Usually, he stood by the window, dreaming of what it would be like to enjoy this view every day. Even more, relishing the stroke to his ego, the sense of increased power and reputation, that he would attain if he could finagle the space for her foundation out from under her.

But he hadn't done anything more than stalk into the room and begin his pacing.

He was preoccupied.

And not just because Morgase had taken Candy away from him, just as she had taken so many other women away from him.

She had a good idea as to why he was in such a state, although based on past experience she assumed that it was going to take a gentle nudge before he revealed all to her.

"How much do you anticipate taking from Midas?" Morgase had never liked the man.

Not because he was greedy, or rather had been. Greed was a lever that she understood and that she could use.

No, she didn't like Midas because he made her uncomfortable.

She couldn't use his greed against him because he had changed his stripes even though she had believed thanks to hard experience that most tigers couldn't.

Rather than trying to build his fortune to fund a profligate lifestyle as had been his modus operandi when he was younger, Midas was trying to do good in the world with all the money he made.

It was sickening.

In large part because she had yet to figure out how to get Midas back under her thumb. And it sounded like her son was trying to do that now, not yet having figured out how to sink his hook into him. Or perhaps he had.

"At a minimum, five hundred million."

Morgase considered that. Mordred tended to be conservative with his estimates, so he was likely expecting to gain much more from whatever scheme he was running with the help of his financial floozy.

"Fifty percent."

Mordred snorted out a laugh. "Really, mother? You think I will cave in so easily? I don't even know if Candy is still alive."

"Sixty percent," Morgase countered. She only knew one way to negotiate.

"All right, all right," Mordred replied. He couldn't make any money at all off of Midas if he didn't have Candy, and he was unwilling to risk his mother pulling the entire operation out from under him. "Fifty percent."

"Done," Morgase replied with a coy smile. "I will have Candy back to you by midnight."

"Thank you," Mordred said, nodding in satisfaction. "Whole and unharmed. With that done, I'll take my leave so you can go to your fundraiser ..."

"Awards dinner," Morgase corrected.

"Fundraiser. Awards dinner. Does it really matter?" Curling around the corner of the table, he turned toward the doors. "I've got other business that needs to get done. I'll keep you apprised of the work that Candy is doing for me once I have her back safe and sound."

"That's why I asked you here, Mordred. Business."

The commanding coldness in Morgase's voice stopped Mordred with his hand on the door.

"Beyond you extorting me, what business would that be, mother?"

"Don't play the fool, Mordred. It's beneath you." Morgase's eyes sharpened, knowing what her tone would do to her son. She didn't have long to wait.

Mordred whipped around, his anger plain.

Her son had taken hold of the Grym, streams of energy dancing across his fingertips.

Morgase tsked. It seemed that she was wrong.

He was a fool.

"Be very careful, Mordred." Her smile became predatory. "Release the Grym. Now."

"And if I don't?"

"Then I'll spank you like the petulant child that you are." Morgase tilted her head to the side, mulling that option. "Although perhaps a stronger hand might be required rather than paddling your bottom red. A reminder of who I am and who you are, my son."

"You wouldn't dare," Mordred hissed, not quite believing what he was hearing.

"Wouldn't I?" Morgase caught the flash of concern that ran across his face. She was quite disappointed. Still, after all this time, after all the lessons she had given him, when his ire was up, he could not conceal his emotions no matter how hard he tried.

The standoff continued for a few more heartbeats. "Release the Grym, Mordred. You will not enjoy what I do to you if you don't."

Mordred huffed and puffed a little more. Then he clenched his fists, knuckles turning white, face turning red.

Despite hating himself whenever he heeded his mother, he let go of the Power of the Ancients.

If it had been anyone else other than his mother challenging him, Mordred would have let his fury rule him.

It would have been so satisfying to put the all-powerful Morgase in her place.

But he knew the truth no matter how much he hated having to admit it.

He was one of the strongest of the Teg.

He was not as strong as his mother.

"Good decision, my son," Morgase applauded, giving Mordred a nod much as she did when he was just a child and he had done something that pleased her.

Her reaction sent a hot bolt of anger shooting through him. This time, he controlled it.

Those condescending nods had been few and far between, his mother more often than not scolding him as she offered a lengthy critique and demanded that he improve himself.

As he got older, he learned that her reaction wasn't so much for him as it was for herself.

He may be her son, but he was more than that to Morgase. He was also another tool to be used in her own battles. Especially those against her brother ... and his father.

"Have a seat, Mordred. I'm tired of you wearing down my carpet."

"I'll stand," he replied, crossing his arms in front of him.

A small measure of defiance.

Morgase allowed it. She wanted him tractable. She did not want him broken.

If he was broken, he would be of little use to her.

"Tell me, Mordred."

Mordred kept his eyes down on the floor, wavy, dark hair covering his face. "I already told you."

"Don't waste my time, Mordred."

"I don't know what you mean?"

"Did we not just talk about you acting the fool?"

The challenge in her voice lifted his head. "I am not acting the fool."

Morgase snorted, though not in humor. She was getting tired of the willfulness laced into his voice. "Are you not? You offered me Midas to keep me away from the real matter between us. He is no more than a minnow in the larger strategy that is now in play."

"I did no such ..."

"Enough!" Morgase pushed herself to her feet faster than a striking scorpion, placing her hands on the conference table and leaning forward. Her eyes swirled with a power about which Mordred, caught within its grasp, could only imagine and crave.

"I did not mean to deceive you."

"So you say, Mordred, but you forget that I know you better than you know yourself."

He did speak the truth. He didn't mean to deceive her, but he couldn't help himself. It was too much a part of his nature. A trait she lay the blame for at the feet of his father.

"Truly, mother, I ..."

"Tell me." Morgase's voice was more than quiet. More than cold. It was lethal.

Mordred couldn't help himself. The fear that he had experienced so frequently as a child consumed him once again.

He hated himself for his weakness. Even more, he hated his mother.

"I spoke with Raik a few days ago. He wasn't happy."

"Why not? And why should we care?"

"He tracked the Witch to a town on the Maine coast. Kraken Cove."

"As he was paid to do. Where is she? We should have her by now as well as what she stole from you."

"I don't know," Mordred replied, dreading what was going to come next.

"What do you mean you don't know?"

Mordred's eyes widened. His mother had taken hold of the Grym, threads of energy sparking around her. Thousands upon thousands. Swirling. Spinning. Growing.

He explained as quickly as he could. "I don't know. We both agreed. You and me. It would be an easy job for the Renegades. And they've never failed us before with a snatch and grab. They tracked the Witch to the town. But Raik kept jabbering about one of his packs disappearing. That he was going to check up on them himself. He said something about the Lightkeeper, and then he ..."

"Stop." Morgase's order was quiet, though effective, Mordred halting the flow of information. "Raik said the Lightkeeper? You're certain of that?"

Mordred nodded. "Raik said that's what one of his men told him. The only one to return from the town alive."

Mordred was about to say more. His mother's raised hand stopped him.

Morgase pushed herself off the table. She turned and walked to the window that ran along the length of the conference room, crossing her arms.

As the sun began to set, she saw everything and nothing both at the same time as she stared out at the changing color of the sky.

"The Lightkeeper," she murmured to herself.

Could it be?

She thought about that question.

There could be only one answer.

Or at least only one answer so long as she had no proof to convince herself otherwise.

Why couldn't it be?

A body had never been found.

Curious back then. Now concerning.

"You haven't heard from Raik and his pack since he left for Kraken Cove?"

"I haven't," Mordred confirmed with a shake of his head.

"You've already lost three Berserkers in Kraken Cove?"

Mordred nodded, unable to say the words.

"And now an entire Werewolf pack?"

"I don't know."

"And Raik used the term the Lightkeeper."

Mordred's eyes narrowed. He had been so consumed by Midas and the money that he hoped to make that he hadn't been paying enough attention to what his henchman was telling him.

He felt as if he should be familiar with that name.

The Lightkeeper.

But why?

Thinking more deeply, he was certain that he had heard it before.

In what context though?

He gasped, his eyes widening in disbelief.

It couldn't be. Could it?

"The Lightkeeper was a term applied on occasion to ..."

"You're only realizing this now?"

Mordred stood in front of his mother in shock, the full ramifications of what she was implying striking him like a punch in the gut.

That wasn't quite right. It was more like a kick to the groin. Multiple kicks.

"How could that even be possible?" he demanded in a soft voice. "There were witnesses. There is no way that the Lightkeeper as he was so wrongly called could ..."

"Consider the players involved. Even with witnesses, of course it's possible."

Morgase chuckled softly as she thought more about her discovery. She tried to appear calm and composed, amused even. However, her emotions, roiling within her, threatened to get the better of her.

No plan ever played out as she thought it would. There was always a wrench thrown into the works.

She had assumed that would happen to what she and her son were working on now, all of it targeted toward her brother.

She had never guessed, however, that this particular wrench would be the cause of the problems they were experiencing.

He had been gone for so long.

Dead.

Buried.

No more than a memory.

That's what the witnesses had claimed.

Yet as she had just explained to her son, considering the players involved, why trust what the witnesses saw.

Thinking about who had been there, they probably saw what they were supposed to see.

Even if she was correct, however, why would the Lightkeeper return now? Why not just enjoy his death?

Was he still working for his father?

Her eyes sparked at the thought. She cursed under her breath.

If this Lightkeeper was the Teg she thought him to be, they needed to act quickly.

"Even after all this time, even though he doesn't know your hand is in this, he's making you look the fool," Morgase murmured.

Her comment was less to insult her son and more to hide her growing discomfort. Definitely not fear, she told herself. She wasn't afraid of anything.

Or anyone.

Even the Lightkeeper.

Even the man who used to be known by several other names, many of them less flattering. Some of them more terrifying.

"Why couldn't the bastard just stay dead?" Mordred growled, his rage building, finding it difficult to control as his face turned a bright red, marring his handsome visage. "Always getting in my way. Always seeking to hold me back. Always working to make me look bad."

"You have only yourself to blame for looking bad, Mordred. Blame the Lightkeeper all you want, but you must take responsibility for your actions. Your failures as well."

"How dare you ..."

Mordred made the mistake of taking hold of the Grym once again, his fury too much for him.

Before he could take another breath, he grunted in pain.

Slammed against the window, he smacked the back of his head against the glass.

He remained there. Held in place. Unable to move. Barely able to breathe. The fear that consumed him drowning out his anger.

Mordred was quite powerful and skilled in the Grym, but he couldn't hold a candle to his mother.

"We do not have time for your whining, Mordred." His mother stood in front of him, sparks of the Grym dancing across her clothes and her skin. "Find out what you can about Raik and his wolves. Midas will have to wait. We need *The Book of Whispers*. I will not lose this chance to usurp my brother. And I will not become the plaything of the Daemon King. Do you understand me?"

Mordred couldn't nod. The power holding him in place was too strong. Too unyielding.

Morgase nodded. Reading the subservience in his eyes, she released her hold on him.

Mordred slid down the window and dropped to the floor, reaching out with a hand so that he didn't fall to his knees. He would never bend the knee, even unintentionally, to anyone.

"I'll let you know what I find out," he said very quietly. He slunk out of the conference room, head down, too embarrassed and angry to meet his mother's eyes.

She didn't care. Just another emotional scar of his own making that Mordred would have to deal with.

Morgase had needed to use a strong hand with her son before. She assumed that she would need to do so again. Because if nothing else, he was predictable.

As soon as Mordred left, thoughts of her son and his latest failure faded in her mind. She stepped closer to the glass, watching as dusk transformed into night, the lights of New York City taking over.

Her plans had been moving forward so well.

Until now.

A feeling of unease settled in the pit of her stomach. One that she always listened to.

It felt like the wheels were about to fall off.

She couldn't allow that.

And the only way to ensure that didn't happen was for her to take matters into her own hands.

Since her son had failed so miserably, she couldn't take the risk of leaving what needed to be done with him.

Too much was at stake.

She reached into her pocket and pulled out her cell phone, the number she wanted on autodial.

"I need you to find someone for me."

"All right," a husky voice answered. "Do I need to kill this someone?"

"No, not unless it proves necessary."

"Now you're taking all the fun out of it."

"Can I trust you with this?" The voice at the other end of the line had never failed to complete an assignment Morgase had given her. Even so, Morgase also knew from experience that the woman, though quite skilled and efficient in her work, sometimes struggled to control her bloodier tendencies.

"Why do you ask?"

"You know why." Morgase didn't feel the need to remind her.

The silence on the other end of the line dragged on for more than a minute, Morgase demonstrating a patience that she rarely did for any other Teg.

"Where?"

"Kraken Cove."

"Why me?"
"You know why."

19

DO NO HARM

Melissa walked just a few steps behind Draig as they followed the trail that snaked away from the Druid's home. Rather than make for where they had entered Leya's domain, Draig led them through more rugged terrain on the other side of the mountain, planning to loop back around when they reached a lower elevation.

He hoped to slip by the hunting Werewolves. Although he hadn't sounded very confident about the tactic when he explained it to her.

As a result, Melissa wasn't going to hold her breath.

If she had learned anything at all during the last few days, it was that Werewolves were tenacious hunters. They always ran down their prey.

A quarter mile farther down the slope she glimpsed a brief shimmer, a flash of sunlight through the trees revealing the Druid's magical barrier that protected her domain.

Protected them.

Melissa understood that time was short. Shorter, in fact, than even Draig suspected.

Nevertheless, knowing what was waiting for them on the

other side, she wasn't looking forward to hiking back into the Schoodic Forest.

And that wasn't the only worry running through her mind. She couldn't get out of her head the brief conversation she had with Leya before she and Draig left the Druid's cottage.

Draig was outside already, using the Grym to search around them.

Melissa was about to exit Leya's comfortable home, offering her thanks, when the Druid's iron grip on her arm held her in place in the doorway, leaving her caught between the light just beyond the cabin and the shadow behind her.

Thinking back on it now, the imagery was the perfect sign if ever there was one.

"Do not hide all from Draig." The Druid had been insistent. "He cannot help you if you do."

"I'm not hiding anything from Draig," Melissa had insisted. "You have nothing to fear."

Leya had not released her hold on her, though the effort was unnecessary. Her multicolored eyes that spun wildly had kept Melissa frozen in place. "You don't understand, do you?"

"Understand what?" Melissa had tried to tug her arm loose. It hadn't worked. It was like trying to break free from a steel manacle locked around her wrist.

Leya had shaken her head, her expression one of sadness. "So smart, yet in some ways still just a novice. Your mother did you a disservice in that regard."

"I have no idea what you're talking about," Melissa had whispered fiercely, not wanting to attract Draig's attention. "I will not allow you to speak badly of my mother. You have no idea what she has done for me and my sisters. You have no idea what she ..."

"I do not insult your mother, child," Leya had cut in. "I know your mother better than you think. I know why she is important to you. Why she is important to Draig."

"What do you mean? Why is my mother important to Draig?" Melissa had sighed in frustration. "All you do is talk in riddles. You need to speak ..."

Leya had released Melissa's arm then and stepped back, nodding toward the door.

Melissa had stared at her, not quite believing that she was being released so easily. Not wanting to miss the chance, she had taken a step farther away from the shadow and out into the light.

"Remember, Melissa, your mother trusted Draig. With her life. Your life. The lives of your sisters."

"I know that," Melissa had replied in a peevish tone, still on the front porch.

"If your mother trusted Draig, then you should trust him as well."

Melissa had stopped then, the steps leading off the porch right in front of her. She had been angry. Angrier than she had been in a long time. But at what? Leya? Or herself? "As I said, Druid, you speak in riddles. It is hard to trust when there is little clarity."

Leya had nodded mysteriously, then smiled. She had remained in the doorway, framed by the sunlight that was peeking through the branches above them.

"You brought your problems to Kraken Cove not understanding the true nature of those problems. How your problems would become larger problems. And how those problems would multiply as well."

"I did not bring my problems intentionally," Melissa had argued, feeling the need to defend herself. "I did not know they would follow me. I only came here for a solution."

Leya had nodded again in that sly way of hers that only served to irritate Melissa all the more. "You knew they would, child. Your denial rings hollow. You just didn't understand how they would grow. It is much like throwing a stone into a lake and watching the resulting ripples grow bigger and bigger, expanding in all directions."

"You're talking again in that way of yours that ..."

"Listen instead of arguing against everything I say, and you might understand more."

Leya hadn't spoken sharply or raised her voice. Nevertheless, the flintiness of her tone had stolen away Melissa's breath.

"You believe that you are the only one affected by what you are doing now," Leya had continued. "You are not. What you have done has affected all the Teg. You may not have realized that when you became involved in whatever you are involved in, you may still not realize it now, but you will. I promise you that." The Druid had offered her a sad shake of her head. "You will regret, for which I give you credit. But will you be able to correct your mistake? That ... I cannot see."

"How could you ..."

"No more questions." Leya had spoken to her as if she was an unruly child. "You have brought your problems to Kraken Cove, but those problems will not end here. They will grow and multiply. They will affect all of the Teg. You had no way of knowing that, so I don't blame you. Still, I warn you now. You must look beyond your small world. You must consider all the Teg in the decisions you will need to make during the next few days. More than just your mother's life will depend on it."

Melissa had stared at the Druid, unable to take her eyes from her. Not knowing what to say. Not sure how the Druid could speak on a matter that she should know nothing about.

At a loss for words and becoming more and more uncomfortable, she had trotted down the steps two at a time. Leya's soft voice had frozen her in place before she had taken more than a few steps away from the cabin.

"Do not cause him any more pain. Draig carries it around like a weight on his shoulders. He does not need more. If he takes on too much, he will never be able to escape it."

With the barrier almost upon them and the safety of the Druid's domain soon to be in the rearview mirror, Melissa hoped that the conversation with Leya would fade away, thereby allowing her to focus on what she needed to do next.

It didn't.

It played through her head like vinyl on a record player.

How could the Druid have discovered her real motivation?

Melissa had been wracking her brain, trying to figure that out.

She couldn't.

She was at a complete loss.

She didn't know how the Druid had done it. Nevertheless, she was certain about one thing.

She had seen it in the Druid's eyes before the woman had released her from that iron grip of hers.

A threat.

A promise.

A possible result that Melissa wanted to avoid at all costs.

She didn't know if she could, however, not if she was to achieve her ultimate objective.

"You alright?" Draig asked.

Melissa stopped abruptly. Lost in thought, she had almost walked right into him. Trying to hide her unease, she gave him a winning smile. "Yes, sorry, just thinking about something. That's all."

Draig studied her for a few heartbeats. She was telling the truth. He was certain of that.

Just not all of it, which was really no different than usual.

He smiled as well, letting it go. For now. She was nervous. Clearly on edge. Likely because the barrier rose right in front of them.

"Then let's go."

He took a step forward. Her hand on his arm made him lower his foot.

"The Weres?"

"Still hunting. They won't stop hunting until they find us."

"But ..." She tried not to allow the irritation that had been pricking her nerves ever since she left the Druid's home to get the better of her.

She snorted with a mix of amusement and frustration. It seemed that breaking Draig of his habit of only revealing some and not all would take more work than she anticipated, although the irony of that thought was not lost on her.

"But they aren't where we'll be stepping through. They're no closer than a league right now."

Melissa nodded nervously, pleased to hear that.

"Besides, we won't be entirely on our own."

With a wink, he pushed his way through the magical shield, which shimmered brightly as he did so.

Taking a deep breath in a useless attempt to calm her nerves, Melissa stepped through as well, the barrier shifting, folding, stretching, as she passed through.

Who in all the hells were these three?

Her immediate reaction was to reach for the Grym.

Yet seeing Draig's friendly smile, she chose not to. Wisely, she decided, when she realized who these petite women, all with an ethereal, otherworldly beauty, were.

Faeries.

Rarely seen. So much so that many among the Teg believed that these magical folk were extinct, all of them eradicated during the Blood Wars.

Apparently not. That bit of Teg lore incorrect.

She studied the women just as keenly as they were studying her.

Pixielike faces. Short hair, each with a different color. Starting on the right, green then blue then red.

Each one carried a long bow, a quiver of arrows over a shoulder, and a long knife on both thighs. The trio wore woodland garb of browns and greens that allowed them to blend into the forest. If Melissa didn't look right at them, she found it difficult to pick them out from the background.

"It has been too long, Draig," the red-haired Fairie said.

"Too long?" Draig chuckled. "We all had dinner together the week before last."

"Still too long," the green-haired Faerie agreed.

Draig seemed more amused than anything else. "My apologies. Perhaps we could have dinner again soon."

"We will, Draig," the blue-haired Faerie who stood in the center of the trio said. "Now who is this woman?"

Melissa's eyes widened, beginning to think that she might indeed need to make use of the Grym. The Faerie's tone and flinty expression included not only a challenge, but also a warning laced with distaste and distrust.

She did not know much about Faeries other than the fact that they were quite powerful, employing a form of the Grym that was tied to the woodlands that they tended, their strength greatest when they were within their groves. And Melissa assumed that these three lived here in Schoodic Forest.

"Melissa is the reason that I visited with Leya," Draig explained calmly, apparently unconcerned by the tension radiating from the three Faeries.

"Seeking answers," the red-haired Faerie said.

"Seeking answers," Draig confirmed.

"And that is why you asked us to come here?" The blue-haired Faerie tilted her head to the side as she continued to examine Melissa. By her frown obviously not all that impressed.

"It is."

"That makes sense." The blue-haired Faerie nodded. "I can see why you are not interested in this one. Best that remains the case."

Melissa opened her mouth to reply, then closed it just as

quickly. She didn't know if she should be insulted by what the Faerie said. She did know that she didn't understand all that was going on around her, so better to leave the dialogue that seemed more a negotiation to Draig.

"Yes, she is not your type and certainly not to our taste," the red-haired Fairie agreed.

A howl drifted among the trees, sending a shiver of fear through Melissa. Not too close. Still, not far enough away to suit her.

"Shall we get down to business?" Draig asked.

The trio of Faeries nodded as one.

Draig turned. "Melissa, allow me to introduce you to three of my very good friends. I would offer you their Faerie names, but I can't."

"Why not?" Melissa was too curious to keep her mouth shut.

"Our names are very long and difficult to say," the red-haired Faerie said, "and we only share them with the Teg we know and trust. We do not know you, so we have no cause to trust you. We will keep our Faerie names close. However, we know Draig quite well."

Melissa's cheeks colored ever so slightly when the Faerie offered her a lift of her eyebrows and a knowing smile, her hint unmistakable.

"Fair enough." Melissa didn't know what else to say as her cheeks flushed even more. Was she jealous? No, that couldn't be possible. Still just her nerves. Thanks to her final encounter with the Druid.

"You can call my sister with the blue hair Gertrudis. Winnifer with the green." The two Faeries stared a challenge at Melissa that she ignored as best as she could. "You can call me Marge."

"Marge?" Melissa couldn't help herself, not expecting that to be her appellation.

"Marge," the Faeries repeated as one. "Do you have a problem with that?"

Melissa shook her head quickly. "No, of course not."

"Good." Marge, who was clearly the leader of these three, gave Melissa a hard look for a few seconds more. "Now down to business." She directed her focus to Draig. "Dinner next Sunday."

"Done, with the proviso that I'm in town. If I'm not, then dinner the next Sunday I am back in Kraken Cove."

"Agreed," confirmed Winnifer.

"And every Sunday until the solstice," added Gertrudis.

Draig didn't reply immediately, his expression suggesting that he was thinking about the additional requirement.

The seconds dragged on, another howl sounding. This one closer than the last.

Yet still Draig stood there. Not saying a word. Simply staring at the three Faeries. Melissa was about to respond for him in the affirmative to the Faeries' demand, but then he nodded.

"Done."

"Done," the three sisters replied in unison.

"We will do as you asked," Marge said. "We cannot promise you how much time you might gain. But we will do what we can. We always enjoy hunting Werewolves, but they will only fall for our tricks for so long."

"I understand," Draig said. "Any time you can earn us, I will appreciate."

"We will see you on Sunday?" Marge asked.

"Sunday," Draig confirmed with a nod and a big smile.

Giving Draig a discerning look, Melissa got the feeling that he didn't view dinner with the three Faeries as much of a burden.

In a blur, the Faeries disappeared between the trees and ferns, streaks of red, green, and blue their only sign of passage, each one moving in a different direction.

"They'll distract the Weres for as long as they can," Draig explained. "We need to get going. The sooner we are off the mountain the better."

Another howl sounded within the wood. Then a whole series, one right after the other. Some closer than others.

Melissa fell in next to Draig as he pushed his way between two ferns and jumped down into another dry streambed that had been hidden from view.

"I thought the Faeries all died in the Blood Wars."

"Many of them did."

"But not all?"

"No, not all."

Draig didn't offer her any more information than that. She sensed the sadness that had taken hold within him. She got the feeling that there was a story to tell, but now wasn't the time to push for it.

"Who are those three Faeries?"

"Friends."

"The way they were looking at you, and from what Marge said, they seem to be more than just friends." Melissa frowned. Had she allowed a touch of jealousy to seep into her voice?

"Just friends," Draig confirmed.

"I don't know," Melissa challenged, her tone carrying a faint edge of disbelief. "The way they were looking at you and then at me ... they definitely don't like me. It felt as if they viewed me as competition."

"Well, you are hard to like," Draig replied, giving her a lift of his eyebrows and a tilt of his head, "so that's not all that surprising."

She punched him in the arm as they hiked down the streambed, the slope becoming steeper. He chuckled softly when she did.

"I'm not in the mood for jokes."

Draig shrugged. "Winnifer, Gertrudis, and Marge can be a little possessive at times. That's all."

"Possessive? That's what you're calling it?"

Draig picked up his pace, forcing Melissa to trot after him. He had no desire to discuss with Melissa his relationship with the Faeries. It was complicated and not easily explained. Not after what he had done during the Blood Wars.

"Come on," he called over his shoulder. "My friends will only be able to do so much for us. The Weres will be after us sooner than we would like."

The howls were growing in intensity, each one distinct to Draig's ear, revealing just how many Weres were a part of the hunt.

Yet there was no order to their calls. No commands that Draig could discern. At least not yet.

He was certain that he had Marge, Gertrudis, and Winnifer to thank for that.

Werewolves were excellent hunters.

He would never waste his time trying to deny that fact.

What many of the Teg didn't know was that Faeries were even better hunters.

The Renegades would learn that the hard way, and that didn't bother Draig in the least. In fact, he kind of wished that he could watch the encounters that were already taking place deeper within the wood.

But he couldn't. He needed to stay focused on his larger task.

Because even with the Faeries' help, Draig was worried.

He didn't like what he sensed in the wood with them.

A large pack.

Perhaps all of the Renegades.

Formidable opponents. Angry as well after their last engagement.

Raik and his pack would want revenge.

And, despite the help provided by the Faeries, Draig had no doubt that he would have to deal with them before he and Melissa made it back to Kraken Cove.

Not liking the conclusion that he reached didn't mean that he could ignore it.

Those thoughts guiding him, rather than taking the most direct route that would lead them back to town, he decided to head more toward the west.

If he was going to fight the Weres, he wanted to do it at a place of his own choosing. Where he had a better chance of defending himself and Melissa.

Blood was going to be spilled.

That was inevitable.

He just wanted to make sure that most of that blood belonged to the Weres.

20

THE HOLLOW

"Why aren't we running?" Melissa's hands were on her knees as she sucked in as much air as she could.

She and Draig had made good time along the trails and dry streambeds that spiderwebbed down the Druid's Peak. For a time, she thought they might even make it back to Kraken Cove before the Werewolves caught up to them.

A false hope, she realized.

When they began their escape, the howls of the Weres faded behind them. She assumed because of Winnifer, Gertrudis, and Marge, the three Faeries proving their skill by delaying their pursuers.

Although not for as long as Melissa would have liked.

When she was certain that the Werewolves were back on their trail, their howls growing louder by the second, Melissa guessed that they had gained a half hour on their hunters. Maybe a few minutes more.

She and Draig certainly hadn't wasted the gift the Faeries had given them.

Nevertheless it didn't matter.

The Weres closed the distance between them at a frighteningly rapid pace.

"There's no point."

Draig stood next to her. Melissa didn't know if she was more irritated by the fact that she was hunched over, gasping for breath, and sweating profusely thanks to the last hour of effort or that the sprint down the mountainside hadn't affected Draig at all.

He wasn't winded. She couldn't see anything more than a light sheen of perspiration on his forehead. And by the glint in his eyes, he appeared to have enjoyed the exercise that had almost caused Melissa to expel what little there was in her stomach.

"What do you mean there's no point?" Melissa was less than pleased by Draig's admission. It didn't fill her with the confidence she desired and needed.

"They're seconds away." Draig shrugged, as if to say that he had expected to be in this position from the very start ... and that it didn't bother him in the least. It was almost like he was looking forward to the confrontation.

Melissa gave him a questioning look. Almost accusatory, in fact. "We're going to fight them here?"

"Yes, we are."

Melissa nodded as she pushed off her knees and stood tall before she spun around slowly, examining the battlefield that Draig had selected.

She wasn't a fighter. She was a thief. Even so, she recognized the value of the ground they stood upon.

Sheer cliffs rose at their backs and circled almost all the way around them. It was as if a titan of old had punched down into the mountain and created a hollow crafted of stone.

With the steep sides extending to a height of several hundred feet, the Weres would have a difficult time attacking them from above and behind. Particularly since the stone carried a razor-thin edge that cut into flesh at the slightest touch. Doable if the Werewolves were desperate, but not the smart move.

To Melissa's inexperienced eye, not a bad pick by Draig. A defensible location. For how long, however, she couldn't really say.

Because she understood the limitations of their environment as well.

The hollow had only one point of egress. With the howls of the Werewolves gaining intensity, she realized that the only way that they'd be able to escape their hunters, who were likely already in the crevice that led into the hollow, would be to fight their way through them.

Maybe that was why Draig appeared to be on edge, although in a good way. As if his world had gained a greater and necessary clarity because there was now only one choice to make.

A choice that he looked forward to as he stood there calmly, blackthorn shillelagh leaning against his shoulder like a baseball bat.

Melissa realized then that this was his plan all along.

To tilt the odds in their favor as much as possible understanding that a clash was inevitable.

A good strategy, she had to admit. Still, she was worried.

"Like Custer's Last Stand?"

Draig pulled his eyes away from the gap in the crag long enough to give her a wink and a resolute nod. "I hope not, but we'll see. You never know how a fight is going to play out."

"I'm glad to see that you're not overconfident."

"Far from it," Draig replied.

Then he was gone, Melissa startled by how quickly he moved, no more than a blur.

Gliding forward, Excalibur appeared between his hands, the glamour applied to the blade gone.

Draig ducked as a massive Werewolf -- blondish brown fur ragged, dirty, and streaked with blood in several places; no doubt the work of the Faeries -- sprinted into the hollow.

The Were swiped at Draig, seeking to decapitate him.

It didn't work out as the Werewolf wanted.

The beast's claw cut through the space where Draig's head had been just a heartbeat before.

Unable to halt his progress even as he dug his claws into the ground, the Werewolf howled as Draig cut across the back of both of the beast's legs and sliced his hamstrings.

Draig, having stolen the shifter's greatest advantages – speed and mobility, left the Were roaring and rolling on the ground, clutching hopelessly at his legs, while he advanced toward the gap between the cliffs.

Unlike the day before, Melissa didn't hesitate.

With the wounded Were focused entirely on Draig, staring at his back, not even deigning to notice her, Melissa slipped forward, magical dagger crafted of the Grym in her right hand.

She ended the Were's painful howls by punching her weapon into the back of his neck.

That grisly task complete, Melissa danced back to where she had been standing before. The cliffs at her back, dagger held at the ready, she watched Draig take on the next attacker.

The second Were who entered the hollow did so with greater caution, demonstrating a discipline rarely associated with creatures of his kind.

The shifter stood at the entrance, facing off against Draig. Studying his adversary.

Standing several feet taller than Draig, the Were chuckled as he stared down at the Fallen Knight. Cracking his knuckles, the Were lifted his fang-filled maw to the sky and howled. An expectation and promise of victory in the sound that reverberated off the surrounding stone.

The Were turned his gaze back toward Draig, the beast's golden eyes flashing brightly.

"You believe that you can stand against me, Fallen Knight?"

The Werewolf's voice was raspy, thick, his snout making it harder for him to speak than when he was in his human form. Though the words were understandable.

"I'm standing against you now, you flea-ridden fur bag." Draig shook his head sadly from side to side. "And I'm sorry to say it, but I really don't think you're going to give me much of a challenge. I doubt I'll even break a sweat before I kill you."

If Draig had been hoping to nudge the Were into a rage-filled rush, it didn't work. The Were held his place, nodding ever so slightly as he examined Draig and the blade in his hand.

"Why is that, Fallen Knight?"

"Because you couldn't fight your way out of a sheep pen."

The Were chuckled at the insult. "You seek to provoke me."

"Is it working?"

"No, it's not."

Draig smiled. "It was worth a try."

"Perhaps it ..."

The Were never completed what he was going to say, launching himself blindingly fast at Draig.

Five hundred pounds of muscle, tooth, and claw seeking to rip Draig apart.

Draig barely moved, pivoting back and to the right. Rather than swinging his sword, he lifted it parallel to the ground, allowing the Were's momentum to do the work for him.

The blazing steel sliced through a wrist, the claw reaching for him severed. But that wasn't the worst of it, Excalibur also biting deep into the Were's chest and neck.

Draig allowed the Were's forward progress to pull his arms backward, his sword sliding free when the Werewolf tumbled to the ground and rolled to a stop not too far away from Melissa.

The Were's head hung from a few pieces of flesh and tendon and no more than that, the creature dead before he hit the ground.

Not Draig's cleanest work, although certainly good enough.

Draig positioned himself next to Melissa. He didn't want to worry about tripping over the bodies at his back, preferring a clean space before the real fight began.

He didn't have long to wait.

A handful of Weres sprinted into the hollow, skidding to a stop when they saw what waited for them.

Growling in anger, they spread out, blocking the path that led out from the stone-wrapped battleground.

Several more Weres followed. Then even more. The Were-wolves kept coming until Melissa counted twenty-seven in all.

Fewer than she had anticipated. Draig's traps and tricks and the Faeries likely to blame for the reduction in the pack's ranks.

The last Were to enter was the largest of them all. The Were who had almost caught them before they escaped into the Druid's domain.

Raik.

The leader of the pack, eyes gleaming with a manic, almost psychotic fervor, growled deeply as he pushed his way past his brothers, not stopping until he stood no more than ten feet away from Draig.

A power play on his part.

It didn't affect Draig in the least.

He stood with his legs spread no further apart than his hips, Excalibur's point sticking into the dirt, Draig resting his hands on the top of the hilt.

"You have led us on quite a chase."

"I like to make things interesting," Draig replied, a wicked glint in his eyes.

"Yes, you do. Even enlisting the aid of Faeries to do what you cannot."

Draig ignored the veiled insult. "You failed to catch them." He wanted to confirm that, worried about his friends.

Raik's growl somehow became even deeper. He was reluctant to admit to his failure, but he did. "We will. If they are foolish enough to come at us again, they will pay for their arrogance." Raik tilted his snout. "We caught you, didn't we?"

"Did you? Or are you exactly where I want you to be?" Draig's smile broadened when he nodded at the bodies of the two Weres crumpled on the ground.

Raik didn't reply immediately, instead studying the remains of his brothers. His scowl deepening.

"You are mistaken, Fallen Knight. You are exactly where I want you to be." Raik's eyes flashed brightly. "Kill them!"

Draig hoped that he could get in a quick strike, anticipating what Raik planned to do. Seeking to create chaos by cutting down the leader of the Renegades. And he was about to.

Two steps. That was all that he needed to take.

Two steps and he could drive Excalibur through the monster's gut.

He was fast enough to do that.

But if Raik moved just a hair and Draig missed, then it would result in a longer and much more dangerous combat.

That didn't bother him. He was confident that he could offer the Were a challenge the beast had never faced before. Besides, he had fought worse foes many times before.

Yet giving in to that desire left Melissa with too many Weres to fight on her own.

Acknowledging the need for a more cautious approach, he stepped back so that he stood side by side with the Witch, Excalibur held before him as the pack of Werewolves surged toward them.

"Focus only on the Weres coming at you from the right

side," Draig ordered, sensing her fear. Her resolve as well, which he valued. "I'll take care of the rest."

Melissa nodded. She didn't have time to reply.

The Weres were clawing for them.

Melissa heeded Draig's command, shifting her footing so that she could defend against the beasts coming at them from their right side. As she had done when fighting against the Berserkers what seemed years ago but was only days, she molded a small shield over her left forearm with the Grym, keeping the magical dagger in her right hand.

The next few minutes were no more than a dream. Melissa scarcely heard the noise of the clash, the scrape of claw against shield and blade, the roars and howls, even her own screams of rage.

Her focus was so intense that her scope narrowed to the ten feet to either side of her, seeing no more than that.

Dagger sweeping through the space.

Stabbing.

Slicing.

Shield streaking through the air, never failing to catch claw or tooth, although it was a close call several times.

Placing her faith in Draig, understanding what the Fallen Knight could do, she had no idea what was happening behind her.

Knowing as well that she was the weak link in their partnership, she refused to fail. She refused to allow the Weres to get past her and at Draig's back.

To that end, Melissa kept moving.

Allowing her instincts to guide her.

Reveling in her success.

Ignoring the pain of the scratches she earned on her arms. Never anticipating that she would still be alive while battling against she didn't know how many Weres.

A hand on her shoulder shattered the void that had wrapped itself around her as soon as the battle began.

She spun quickly, dagger at the ready.

Startled, she took a step back. Breathing a sigh of relief.

Not a Were.

Draig.

A smile and a nod, as well as something else in the back of his flaming eyes.

Pride?

She couldn't be certain.

Then she noticed the silence that had fallen within the hollow. Her eyes swept from left to right.

She felt sick to her stomach. Disconcertingly pleased as well.

A third of the Weres lay on the ground. Dead or dying.

It didn't matter which. None of them would be rising again.

Draig had done the bulk of the work, a small wall of bodies arcing around the space that he had been defending.

A pair of Weres lay on the ground only a few feet away from her.

She had killed two Werewolves?

Melissa didn't remember any of it. Only concentrating on her motions. The immediate decisions that she needed to make. Her thinking fast and clear. Instinctual.

She was proud of herself. She had protected Draig's blind side, giving him a chance to reduce the number of Renegades. And she had reduced the number of Renegades as well.

"You good?" Draig asked.

Melissa waited a few seconds before nodding, needing to make sure that she wasn't about to spew on her boots. Once she was certain that she had her nervous stomach under control, she nodded.

"Yes, I'm good."

Draig nodded. "You did well."

Melissa smiled shyly, accepting the compliment. "We're still in a bind."

"We are," Draig admitted. His eyes locked onto Raik, who stood in the center of his remaining Werewolves.

The Weres appeared uncertain now. They had expected an easier fight. Even after what had happened to their brothers during the hunt. Even after this brief skirmish.

They couldn't quite wrap their minds around the fact that the Fallen Knight still had some bite after all these years.

"What are we going to do?" There was no hint of fear in her voice. Only purpose.

"We aren't going to do anything," Draig replied cryptically. He had eyes only for Raik. The alpha of the Renegades stood in front of his brothers. He was seething. Barely able to control his rage. Good. Exactly how Draig wanted him. "I am."

"What do you mean by ..."

Draig stepped a few feet in front of Melissa before she could finish asking her question.

"I claim the right of challenge."

A hush fell among the Weres gathered behind Raik.

"You would dare?" Raik growled, the monstrous Werewolf standing tall, flexing his shoulders, making himself appear bigger than he already was.

"I not only would, I do," Draig replied confidently. "I have proven that I can stand against you." He nodded toward the Werewolves lying dead at his feet.

"You are not a Were," Raik countered, ignoring the soft murmur at his back, what was left of his pack clearly not understanding his hesitancy. "The right of challenge is for a Were who seeks to displace the leader."

"The fact that I am not a Were is of little concern. I can claim the right of challenge. Not to claim leadership of the pack. But to claim your life." Draig took another step forward, his eyes narrowing, his voice quieter. More demanding. "You know this just as I do. Your brothers as well. Do you not adhere to the laws that govern all Weres? Do you throw the Covenant to the side so easily?"

"This is rarely done." Raik had entered the hollow believing that he had cornered his prey. Now, he was the one who felt cornered. "You are beneath me, Fallen Knight."

"Then you should be able to kill me with ease."

"That is not the point. That ..."

"Are you afraid, Raik?" Draig whispered, although his voice carried easily within the hollow crafted of rock, circling around the sharp stone. "Is that why you hesitate? Do I frighten you, Raik? Do you fear that you cannot stand against me?"

"I accept," Raik snarled, unable to help himself.

"WHAT IN THE name of the Ancients do you think you're doing?"

Peggy Rose reached out and grasped the Berserker's forearm. He turned back toward her. Not angry that she had stopped him. Rather, he was surprised that the woman who barely came up to his chest was so strong.

"We owe a debt to the Fallen Knight," Ragnar murmured quietly, or rather as quietly as the giant could. They hid in the crevice that led out into the hollow. None of the shifters had opposed them as they approached. The Weres were overconfident. Almost arrogant. They never considered the possibility that someone might hunt them while they were hunting the Dragon. "We have to give him aid."

"Sit your ass back down," Peggy Rose ordered in a sharp whisper. They couldn't afford to give themselves away.

Ragnar didn't move. Nor did his two brothers. Urs and Thorsen waited to see what Ragnar was going to do.

"Listen to the lady, boys." Gaheris stood on the other side of the gap, staying in the shadows. One eye on the Berserkers. The other on the drama playing out in the hollow. "She has the right of it."

Peggy Rose appreciated the Knight's support, although she didn't know if it would do her any good. She understood Ragnar's desire. It was the same as hers.

There was a time and place for everything. This was the place. Just not the correct time …yet.

She had met Gaheris as soon as he walked into town that afternoon, not wanting him to get into trouble with any of the residents. None of the Teg living in Kraken Cove had a high opinion of the Knights of the Round and a single Knight traipsing through their territory might be too tempting to resist.

She took him to her shop so that they could have a talk before he went in search of Draig. After explaining his purpose, she decided to accompany him, Pinkie at her side as always.

They had come upon the Berserkers right before they began the trek up the mountain. Upon completing the task that Draig had given them, the trio of brothers were making their way back to town when they heard the howling deeper within the wood. After their encounter on the street with the Renegades, assuming the worst, they decided to investigate.

It hadn't proven difficult to find Draig in the forest. Rather than trying to locate him – Draig having a remarkable knack for disappearing in almost any environment if he chose – they tracked the Weres instead.

"Explain," Ragnar rumbled.

"Why do you think Draig entered Schoodic Forest?" Gaheris asked with as much patience as he could manage. He had met men like Ragnar and his brothers many times before. They were definitely an asset in a fight … so long as they maintained control over their tempers.

"To visit the Druid. The Witch told us."

"I am not a Witch," Peggy Rose hissed quietly. The anger in

her voice earned a low growl from Pinkie, who took a step toward the Berserker.

Rather than being intimidated, Ragnar smiled, apparently pleased by the St. Bernard's challenge. "My apologies. If you are not a Witch, then what are you?"

"I am a Sorceress."

Ragnar lifted an eyebrow. "A Sorceress is stronger than a Witch?"

"Much stronger," Peggy Rose replied.

"What's the difference between a Sorceress and a Witch?"

"Do you really want to find out, Ragnar?" Peggy Rose's hard glare suggested that she might enjoy giving him that lesson while he wouldn't enjoy the experience in the least.

Ragnar chuckled softly, his good humor releasing the tension that had been building up among the small group. "If not to visit the Druid, why did Draig enter the forest?"

"He did come here to visit the Druid," Gaheris explained. "He came here for another reason as well."

Ragnar stared at the Knight, still trying to understand why this man loyal to Arthur Pendragon, the King Teg who wanted his own son dead, was in turn helping Arthur's son.

Peggy Rose said that he and his brothers could trust the Knight. That was all well and good. He would keep an eye on him, nonetheless.

"Draig didn't want the Werewolves to go back into town. He wanted them to follow him to a place where he could deal with them quietly."

"Well done, Ragnar," Peggy Rose said, finally releasing her iron grip on his forearm. "Brains and brawn. Quite the combination with the ladies, am I right?" Peggy Rose gave the Berserker a wink.

Ragnar's eyes widened, not knowing if the Sorceress was making a joke at his expense or suggesting something else entirely. His face coloring so quickly amused Urs and Thorsen, his brothers chuckling softly at his discomfort.

"He still requires our assistance." Ragnar sought to shift the matter back to one with which he was comfortable.

"He does," Gaheris confirmed, "but we wait."

Urs and Thorsen looked from the Knight to their brother and then back again. They listened to Ragnar. He was the oldest. He was the leader. But this Knight exercised an innate authority that was difficult to ignore.

"We cannot wait." Ragnar lifted a foot to walk out into the hollow. That's as far as he got, Gaheris' commanding look holding him in place.

"He is doing this for us."

Ragnar thought about that. Then he nodded, understanding and approving. "Do you have a plan, Knight of the Round?"

Gaheris smiled. He knelt down and picked up a stick. The Berserkers crouched next to him, Peggy Rose looking over their shoulders, as he began to sketch in the dirt.

"When the duel begins, Peggy Rose, I want you ..."

RAIK STARED AT DRAIG. Almost in a rage.

He had made a mistake. He was sure of it. He should have ignored the Fallen Knight's demand. It was within his rights to do so as the alpha of the pack.

But he hadn't.

He had heard the rumblings at his back.

If he didn't accept the Fallen Knight's challenge, his brothers would think him weak. Soft. Perhaps even vulnerable.

He could never permit that.

Better dead than weak.

That was the way of his pack.

Though he had little fear of dying this day.

He believed that he had made a mistake by permitting this farce, but he wasn't worried. At least not too worried despite the seed of doubt that was beginning to germinate in the back of his mind.

He had never lost a duel before. He certainly wouldn't lose to the Fallen Knight.

"You are lucky," Raik growled.

"To be surrounded by a pack of mangy Werewolves?" Draig replied with a hint of scorn. He sensed the Were's anger, and he was more than willing to make use of it if he could. "The smell could kill a Teg all on its own."

The Renegades had stepped back fifteen feet, then spread out in a semicircle, keeping Draig and Melissa with their backs against the crag while creating the space required for the combat.

That was fine with Draig. Just because they had him where they thought they wanted him didn't mean that they actually did.

Raik ignored Draig's insult even as his temper caused a white-hot rage to flash in front of his eyes, almost blinding him.

"To still be alive," he growled. "I did not have to accept your challenge."

"Yet you did."

"I did."

"Why?" Draig asked, although not out of curiosity. "Concerned about what your pack would think of you if you had not?"

Raik's growl deepened. It took a great deal of effort for him not to spring at his adversary right then.

"Because when I kill you, my stature will increase in my pack, among all the packs in fact, and among the Teg. When I kill you, I become the slayer of the Dragon. I become the Were who killed the son of the King Teg. I am the one who made sure that the Fallen Knight truly fell."

Draig chuckled at that, clearly amused. "I'm honored that you place so much value on me."

"You laugh at me, Fallen Knight. You dare?"

"I feel like we already had this conversation," Draig said with a straight face, although his eyes were filled with scorn. "Do we really need to have it again?"

"And now you mock me." Raik's growl threatened to become a snarl. He flexed his claws, his entire body vibrating at the thought of the combat to come.

"No more than you deserve," Draig admitted.

"Draig, what are you doing?" Melissa whispered. She stood just a few feet behind him, her eyes scanning the crowd of Weres. Draig had told her that during the combat, they would leave her alone. That if they attacked as a group, it would be after the duel. Still, she wanted to be ready. Just in case. She trusted Draig, but not the Weres. "Are you trying to provoke him?"

Draig nodded ever so slightly in response, his eyes never leaving the golden orbs of the enormous Werewolf standing against him.

"You think too much of yourself, Fallen Knight. You should have stayed dead."

"I've heard that a lot in the last few days. I'm beginning to think you're right."

"Then I shall help you on your way. And I promise you that once I am done with you, you will not rise again."

"That's very kind of you," Draig said, inclining his head.

The Fallen Knight's mocking tone once again brought that white-hot rage flashing in front of Raik's eyes. This time, he chose to surrender to it. To savor it. To use it.

"Do you have any final words?" Raik stalked toward Draig,

his snarl rumbling off the surrounding stone. "I am about to send you to the Spirit World."

"You first."

Draig glided forward so swiftly that he caught Raik by surprise. The Were never expecting him to attack first, much less with such speed.

Before Raik could even think about defending himself, Draig passed him by, slashing with his sword, the blazing steel slicing across the Were's forearm and continuing down across his thigh.

"I am the Fallen Knight for a reason, Raik," Draig said from behind the Were.

When Raik spun around to face him, Draig was already gone. Gliding down the Werewolf's other side, he slashed with Excalibur, slicing across the back of Raik's other leg and then across his ribs as he brought the blazing steel up in a tight arc.

He danced away before Raik could catch him with a hasty almost desperate backhanded swipe.

"I am the Dragon for a reason, Raik."

"You think that you are better than me!" demanded Raik. The Werewolf turned more slowly than he would have preferred, the injuries to his legs affecting his mobility. Nevertheless, his wounds would not be enough to prevent him from killing Pendragon's son. "You think that you can defeat me?"

"I know I can, Raik," Draig replied with a quiet confidence. "I wouldn't be here otherwise."

Raik's rage knowing almost no bounds, his insides churning, his mind narrowing to the single task that he had set for himself, he lifted his head to the sky and howled. The haunting, frightening tone echoed off the walls of the hollow and then the mountains to the west.

Then, with a snarl, spittle flying from his razor-sharp teeth, Raik launched himself at Draig.

Raik sought to get in close, thereby preventing Draig from using his sword.

Though the Were was fast, he wasn't faster than the Dragon.

Draig spun around and to the right, steel sweeping through the air behind him and cutting across Raik's lower back.

Raik arched in pain, turning as quickly as he could as the slow burn of this new wound radiated out into every part of his body.

"You will pay for that, Fallen Knight! I will tear your head from your shoulders and feast on your brain!"

"Prove it," Draig replied calmly, clearly not afraid. His reddish-orange eyes flashed, promising the Were a similarly painful result if he attacked again.

Raik either didn't catch the warning or he didn't care. His adrenaline and fury fueling him, his wounds refusing to heal because of the application of the Grym, he charged toward Draig on all fours, his claws digging up the dirt and rock in his way.

Draig bent at the knees, sword held out in front of him, knowing that he had to time perfectly what he had in mind.

The instant before Raik's claws sliced into his gut, Draig leapt into the air, flipping backward, turning, at the same time slashing with his steel, a long streak of red appearing along Raik's back from his shoulders to his hips.

Draig landed on his feet, facing the Were. His expression flinty. Certain.

Raik spun back around, standing tall once again, looking over his shoulder at the nasty slice that had missed his spine by less than a millimeter.

Lifting his snout to the sky, he howled again. The sound a mixture of pain and hate.

Raik's eyes shining brightly with fury, he lunged.

Draig stepped to the side.

And then again.

And again.

One more time.

Raik swiped with his claws, seeking to close with Draig. Yet always missing. Cutting through air rather than flesh.

Draig always close, but never close enough to be caught by the Were. Pivoting. Turning. Sliding.

Raik's assault continued, Draig moving around the space reserved for the duel with a remarkable grace.

To Melissa, it was much like watching a toddler tire himself out while having a tantrum. Although in this case the toddler was a quarter-ton Werewolf with a very bad temper.

And then it stopped.

Raik landing hard on his back. Teeth and spit flying through the air. His face a bloody mess.

Having grown tired of evading Raik's attack, Draig had timed his strike perfectly. Smashing the hilt of his sword across the Were's face with a power that would have made Muhammad Ali proud.

"Get ready, Raik."

"Ready for what?" Raik could barely get the words out of his bloody, damaged snout as he pushed himself back to his feet. More slowly this time. Still dazed from the blow that had sent him to the ground.

"For the end, Raik. Because it comes now."

Draig didn't bother to wait for Raik to reply. He sprinted forward, sliding across the ground and slamming into the Were's legs with his feet.

Raik was a massive Were. Twice as tall as Draig when he took his lycanthropic form.

But even a beast of his strength and size could not stay erect when struck such a blow with both of his legs leaking blood and his body working overtime to heal a half dozen other serious wounds and injuries that would not heal with their customary speed, the Grym-infused steel of Excalibur ensuring that Raik would suffer through every ounce of his agony.

Raik fell hard onto his back again, the breath knocked from him.

He never regained his feet.

The last thing Raik saw was the tip of Draig's gleaming sword piercing his throat and then his vanquisher's remorseless eyes staring down at him.

Draig wasn't even breathing hard when he pulled his bloody sword free and stepped back toward the wide-eyed Melissa.

She was stunned by not only how quickly Draig had killed the leader of the Renegades, but that he had done so without taking a wound himself.

As were the Renegades.

The Werewolves remained fixed in place, as still as statues, trying to comprehend what they had just witnessed, their eyes locked onto Raik's corpse.

Not a single Were howled in rage. There was only silence.

Not respectful. More anxious.

Draig had killed the pack's alpha so quickly and with such controlled ferocity that they were struggling to comprehend what their eyes were telling them.

"Your leader is dead," Draig said. His voice pulled their eyes toward him. "I have won the challenge. You may take Raik and go. I give you free passage back to your home territory."

The Weres pulled their gaze from Raik's body and stared at Draig. None of them moved.

The expression of the Werewolf closest to Draig changed. Golden eyes tightening. Body tensing. Growling.

Another Were mimicked the first and then one more. It wasn't long before the entire pack glared at Draig with hatred in their eyes and a deep, almost uncontrollable hunger.

Draig shook his head in disappointment. He had expected as much.

"What's the matter?" whispered Melissa. She was tracking all the Weres, searching for the one who was going to attack first.

"I gave them the chance to leave. They're not going to adhere to the Covenant."

"Covenant?" Melissa had never heard of it, although she assumed that it was critical to their current circumstances. "What does that mean?"

"That I'm going to have to kill more of them to get my point across."

According to the law of the pack, the victor of a challenge became the leader of the pack.

Draig, of course, couldn't assume that position. He wasn't a Werewolf.

However, according to the Covenant, an ancient document that governed the Teg, and particularly the relationship between the various kinds of Teg, because Draig could not assume leadership of the pack upon killing Raik in a fair combat, the Werewolves should have gathered their dead and left so that they could select another leader.

Most important, regardless of their animosity toward Draig for eliminating their alpha, according to the Covenant they should leave him alone. He had earned the right to depart unharmed. No blood to be spilled between them until after the next full moon.

But as the growls rose to an almost deafening crescendo, Draig understood that wasn't going to happen. The Weres weren't going to let him walk out of there unscathed.

They didn't care about the Covenant and what breaking it meant.

These Weres no longer adhered to the culture and strictures of their kind or the traditions and laws of all the Teg that had allowed them to survive in a semblance of peace for so long.

Draig really couldn't say that he was surprised. All of these Weres had been expelled from their original packs. They had joined the Renegades because there was nowhere else for them to go.

Rogue Werewolves tended to die quickly without the succor and protection of the pack, so they had given more than their loyalty to Raik. They had thrown away the beliefs upon which they had been raised.

They didn't care about honor or traditions.

They didn't care about the Covenant.

They only cared about revenge. About completing the job they had been given.

They wanted blood.

His blood.

Several of the Werewolves lifted their snouts to the sky, howling, gnashing their teeth as they advanced toward Draig and Melissa.

They had strength in numbers.

The Fallen Knight and the Witch might kill some of them, but they couldn't kill them all.

And they might have been right.

However, they never counted on Pinkie.

The massive hound transformed as he raced through the gap and into the hollow. Growing larger than a grizzly bear, his canines lengthened into fangs and a dozen sharp spikes appeared on his long tail.

The St. Bernard was gone.

In its place charged one of the offspring of Cerberus.

～

Pinkie's howl was louder than any offered by a Werewolf, so loud in fact that a few large pieces of jagged rock fell off the surrounding crag, causing several of the Weres to jump out of the way before they met a gruesome death.

And those were the lucky ones.

Not so the Weres targeted by Pinkie. The massive dog, claws longer than steak knives, crashed into the beasts closest to the crevice, sending a fist of them flying through the air like they were nothing more than bowling pins.

Pinkie spun around swiftly. Clearing the space around him, the spikes on his tail earned several howls of pain from the gutted Werewolves too slow to get clear.

One Were decided to be brave, thinking that he could catch the monstrous animal by surprise.

Snarling, claws extended, the Werewolf took three big strides and then leapt through the air. His eyes widened in anticipation, thinking that he had timed his attack perfectly. The dog's back was turned, his tail sweeping away from him, the back of his neck exposed for his claws and fangs.

A few quick stabs followed by a vicious bite and the Were would have his kill.

He was wrong, and it cost him his life.

A blast of energy struck the Werewolf, sizzling across his flesh and slamming him against the stone wall. He hung there for a few seconds on the jagged edges of the stone until his weight and gravity became too much for him.

The dying Were slid down the crag, the sharp rock slicing into his flesh, shredding his body into a pile of bloody meat before he crumpled to the ground at the base of the cliffs.

"Coward!" raged Peggy Rose.

The Sorceress stepped into the empty space Pinkie had crafted, protecting his back, sending blast after blast of energy toward the shocked Werewolves as her pet swiped and slashed, eviscerating any of the Weres who got too close.

The survivors of Raik's pack thought they had trapped their prey in the hollow. They were only then beginning to realize that the trap had been set for them.

They were never the predators.

They had always been the prey.

PINKIE'S ATTACK caused a mayhem that the Three Little Bears were happy to exploit.

The Werewolves either attacking or fleeing, sometimes both at the same time because of the whip-snap speed of the monstrous hound, they had no idea as to who advanced on them from behind.

Ragnar, Urs, and Thorsen sprinted out from the gap, peeling off to the left as the Knight directed so that they wouldn't get in the way of the Sorceress and her hellhound.

They had no intention of employing the steel bars holstered on their thighs.

They sought a more personal experience.

More intense.

More visceral.

Their icy blue eyes flashed right before they shifted.

They became larger. Faster. More ferocious.

Taking their primal forms.

When the Weres on that side of the hollow finally turned to face them, they didn't see three blonde giants charging into their midst.

They saw three huge, blonde bears that made the largest polar bear appear small.

The brothers used their greater size to their advantage, crashing into their opponents, taking a handful of them to the ground before the Werewolves could organize a defense.

Stunned by the attack, two Weres never rose again, a quick

swipe of a claw across a throat by Urs and then Thorsen sending them to the other side, their blood pouring out onto the dirt and rock.

A third struggled to pull himself away from the raging Berserkers. A determined effort by the Werewolf, but hopeless.

Ragnar broke the Were's back when he dug his claws into his legs and smashed his spine against the jagged rocks of the crag.

Having no avenue for escape, a Werewolf with grimy grey-black fur leapt for the kill.

With a quick swipe of his claw, Urs finished the beast, removing the Werewolf's head from his shoulders before turning his attention to the handful of Weres now back on their clawed feet and racing toward him and his brothers.

With a savage joy, the Werebears threw themselves at the smaller shifters.

Claws slashing.

Fangs snapping.

Hungry for the fight.

Hungry to assert their dominance over their hated enemies.

Gaheris was the last to join the clash.

Waiting as he should, though it was a struggle for him.

Wanting to get into the mix.

Needing to make certain that his plan was working before he did.

Because if it wasn't, he would put himself where he needed to be to ensure that they won this battle.

Much to his delight, the strategy that he put into play was achieving his desired objectives. Of course, he understood much of their success resulted from the Teg that he sent into the fight.

Gaheris had never understood how Peggy Rose had tamed that monster, although he certainly appreciated the beast's contribution. What had been a St. Bernard was an absolute terror, sending the Werewolves scurrying this way and that, ensuring that they could think of nothing else other than staying away from Pinkie's bloody maw and razor-sharp tail.

The Knight moved to the right, keeping well clear of the three Werebears, Sorceress, and Cerberus' spawn, not wanting to get caught in that bloody mix, seeking to get closer to Draig and the Witch.

Draig appeared to have matters well in hand. Any Werewolf who got too close paid a bloody and final price. While the Witch demonstrated a skill that couldn't be denied, becoming more than just a nuisance to the few Weres struggling to get past her dagger and shield.

Gaheris made use of the few seconds he had before he was noticed to dispatch two of the beasts. One with a slash across the back of the neck that cut through the spine, the Werewolf dropping to the ground like a sack of potatoes.

The other with a quick stab through the throat rather than the back of the neck as he intended. The Were turned at the last second, though not fast enough to swipe at Gaheris.

Pulling the last foot of steel free, the Knight slashed with his sword, removing the Werewolf's head. He didn't know if the Weres' ability to heal themselves quickly extended to the initial wound that he had given the beast, but he didn't want to take any chances.

Losing the element of surprise, several of the Werewolves having turned to face him, Gaheris allowed his instincts to take over.

Ducking.

Dodging.

Slashing.

Cutting.

Stabbing.

Relishing the fight.

Savoring what he viewed as a clean combat.

A clear goal in mind.

A necessary goal.

Unlike the several muddy excuses Arthur had given Gaheris during the last few years that the King Teg used to justify several of his assignments.

As he danced around his side of the hollow, it almost felt like old times. Fighting with Draig again as they reduced the number of Weres. Knowing that each beast killed brought them one step closer to victory.

A Werewolf howled a challenge, slashing at him from the side, forcing him to refocus his thoughts.

Gaheris ducked and spun, having been engaged with another of the beasts. As he pivoted away from his first opponent, he allowed his Grym-infused steel to slide across the beast's hip, earning an angry hiss that became a pained growl.

He didn't have time to judge how badly he had wounded the beast. The other Were that failed to take him by surprise was on him in a flash.

Gaheris glided back, weaving a web of steel in front of him as he put some space between him and the two Weres.

The wounded Werewolf didn't make a move toward him. The other did, surging forward, howling, eager for the kill.

Before the beast reached him, out of the corner of his eye Gaheris glimpsed the Berserkers in action.

He had never seen the like.

Bears fighting wolves.

The Werebears decimating the Werewolves.

The Berserkers tore into their foes with a bloody abandon, lost in the fight.

Unconcerned about their own injuries.

Desiring only the kill.

Seeking only to assert their dominance.

Gaheris lifted his blade, catching the Were's slash that was aimed at his face. He turned and took a half-step back, parrying another swipe at his hip. And then another targeting his ribs.

So it went for the next few seconds, the Were seeking an opening. Slashing with his claws. Snapping with his sharp teeth. Knowing that he would succeed eventually.

Gaheris knew it as well. Because though he was a Knight of the Round, the Were was stronger and faster than he was. He could maintain his defense for only so long.

So he didn't.

When the Were next swiped at him, rather than stepping back he ducked and stepped forward. Sword to his front, he punched the steel right through the beast's chest and into his heart.

The Were's growl became a whimper, the light leaving his eyes.

Sensing a movement to his right, Gaheris tried to pull his blade free.

Desperate to do so.

He couldn't.

Not quickly enough.

The dead weight of the Werewolf was pulling him down toward the ground and his steel was stuck between the beast's ribs.

Gaheris angled his head toward the oncoming threat. The wounded Were was almost upon him. Claw flashing toward his neck.

He didn't stand a chance.

He couldn't get out of the way in time.

He kept his eyes open, nonetheless, refusing to close them.

Needing to see until the very end.

Yet rather than his own death, he glimpsed a flash of white as a bolt of energy shot right by his face and slammed into the

Were, smashing the beast back against the crag, his body a burnt-out husk.

Sighing with relief, Gaheris pushed himself up and with a sharp twist pulled his sword free. Catching Draig's eyes, he nodded his thanks.

Not wanting to think about how close he had come to his own death, he jumped right back into the battle.

Only a few Weres remained standing on this side of the hollow.

He dispatched one of the beasts, the Werewolf so focused on attacking the Witch that he never realized Gaheris was behind him until the sharp point of the Knight's sword cut through his chest from behind. Heart ruptured, the dying Were collapsed.

And then Draig was next to him, Excalibur slashing through the air like a blazing torch, he and his former student pressing the few Werewolves still in the fight.

All of the Weres bloodied.

All of them battered.

All of them reaching one inevitable conclusion.

They had lost the battle.

And, if they continued, they would lose their lives as well.

A Were near the entrance to the hollow was the first to go. Because of the wounds to his legs, hobbling along the edge of the crag and then disappearing through the gap.

It wasn't long before another Were followed.

And then a few more as well.

Until there was only silence.

Splattered with blood, only a little of it his own, Draig surveyed the battlefield.

They hadn't dispatched all the Werewolves.

The beasts would come back eventually because of the blood debt.

But they wouldn't be back anytime soon.

The Renegades would need to pick a new leader. And they would need to rebuild their numbers.

Because there couldn't be more than a handful of Were-wolves left in what had once been the most feared pack in the country.

21

TIME TO TALK

"Why would Draig want to speak with the Knight?" Melissa walked next to Peggy Rose as they headed down the trail that would take them back to Kraken Cove.

"They're friends."

"Friends? I thought that the Knights had a kill on sight order for the Dragon."

"They did," Peggy Rose confirmed. "They still do, I believe."

Melissa didn't know what to make of the conversation taking place twenty yards farther down the path. Her curiosity almost pushed her to pick up her pace. A look from Peggy Rose kept her at the Sorceress' side.

She had met this Knight before he fought his way to her and Draig's side against the Werewolves.

Well, not really met. Melissa had seen him once before.

When she was called in by the King Teg and offered – forced to accept if speaking honestly -- the assignment that turned her entire life upside down, putting at risk her larger more personal objective. The Knight had walked in and whispered into Arthur Pendragon's ear before giving her a hard look and leaving.

"You seem worried, child. Is there something wrong?"

"No," Melissa replied quickly. Probably too quickly based on Peggy Rose's raised eyebrow. "I just don't understand how he could be friends with someone who's supposed to kill him."

"You forget, child. He was supposed to kill many of the Teg now living in Kraken Cove. And once many of those Teg wanted to kill him." Peggy Rose shrugged. "Circumstances change. So do Teg."

"I guess that's one possibility." Melissa's reply was noncommittal.

"You're not convinced?"

"I just don't understand how such deep animosity could fade away as if it had never been there to begin with."

"Sometimes it doesn't," Peggy Rose admitted, giving her a meaningful look.

"What do you mean?"

Peggy Rose's quizzical expression suggested that she didn't buy Melissa's purported lack of understanding. "Let's leave Draig and Gaheris to their conversation. There are a few matters that we need to discuss before we get back to town."

"Matters?" Melissa definitely was worried now.

"You. You and Draig."

"Anything to worry about?"

As Gaheris hiked next to Draig, he had no doubt that even though the three Berserkers, back in their human form, ranged ahead of them, his friend was searching their immediate vicinity with the Grym.

The Sorceress was deep in conversation with the Witch not too far behind them and likely searching around them as well. To say nothing of that hellhound of hers.

Strangely named Pinkie, he was nowhere to be seen. Probably staying close because Pinkie never strayed too far from Peggy Rose's side. And probably well aware of any potential perils as he terrorized the surrounding forest.

"No, the last of the Renegades are gone, a good thirty miles down the road."

"They shouldn't be a problem for a time. It will take them a good while to regain their strength and their numbers."

"True," Draig nodded, "and who knows? Maybe they'll run into some trouble that takes care of the rest of them."

"We can always hope," Gaheris agreed. "Did you have someone specific in mind?"

"Whoever paid them to come after me."

Gaheris nodded. Such a possibility certainly made sense.

"Yes, Morgase isn't very forgiving with those who fail her." The Knights of the Round were well aware that the King Teg's primary adversary used the Renegades on her more demanding, bloodier jobs, preferring not to employ her son's Paladins.

An interesting dynamic, Gaheris thought, though not unexpected considering the personalities, egos, and desires involved. Morgase and Mordred. Allies in the spotlight. Working together to undermine if not remove Arthur Pendragon. Yet in the shadows seeking to gain the advantage on the other. He could only imagine what it was like to sit down with them for a holiday dinner.

"Quite attractive, Draig." Gaheris nodded over his shoulder. "Dangerous as well."

"You mean because she's supposed to be dead?"

"Among other reasons," Gaheris chuckled.

Gaheris hadn't wanted to be with Arthur in the Dragon Vault during the latest confrontation between father and son, though not having any other choice as he couldn't ignore a direct order from the King Teg. All the while worried about the outcome and the consequences to follow. What some of the

Knights of the Round already were calling the Dragon rising from the ashes much like a phoenix.

Although watching the duel between Draig and Merlin that followed did prove useful. It finally gave Gaheris the answer to the question that had been pestering him for more than a decade.

How did Draig die at Belvedere Castle?

Or rather how did he disappear, because Gaheris never believed that Draig had died during the combat with his father in Central Park.

Merlin had been a part of that duel as well.

Gaheris had no doubt that the Sorcerer aided Draig in his escape then just as he assisted in making it seem like the Witch walking behind them now died in the Dragon Vault only a few days past.

"You know how it is," Draig replied with a shrug of his shoulders.

"With you, yes, I do."

"Should I be insulted?"

Gaheris chuckled. "Only a little."

Draig smiled. He had missed this interaction with Gaheris. The older Knight was his friend. His mentor. And in many ways, once he began training to join the Knights of the Round, his father as well.

Just like Merlin was for those aspects of his life that Gaheris couldn't understand or help him with. Because his father didn't have any time for him until he was older and could use him as he deemed necessary.

Arthur Pendragon viewing Draig not as his son, but as a tool. Another piece to be played.

"I take it that my father sent you."

"The King Teg did." Gaheris' eyes sharpened. "You must have assumed that he would send someone after what happened in the Dragon Vault." He laughed at the memory, shaking his head. "Arthur was quite shocked to discover that you were still alive."

"Some part of him must have known that I didn't die during our combat."

"Probably so," Gaheris admitted. "Still, he was likely hoping."

"I don't know how to take that," Draig murmured.

"I don't know either, so best to leave it alone." Gaheris clapped Draig on the back. "I didn't spend much time in Kraken Cove, Peggy Rose wrangling me before I could get a good look, but from what I saw, it's very impressive. A safe haven for the Teg who don't want to be bothered with the politics and machinations running rampant through our world ... or found by those who are seeking to do them harm."

"It's not what I intended."

"How so?"

"I needed a place to live after what happened in New York," Draig explained. "I liked Kraken Cove and set up shop there."

"Quite literally from what I saw. The bakery. The bookshop. The bar."

"My mother helped me. And for a few weeks it was quiet. Just the way I wanted it."

"Until ..."

"Until Peggy Rose arrived and set up her shop."

"And then the floodgates opened," Gaheris nodded.

"Exactly so. Cerridwen, Brigid, Hestia, and so many others. After the first year, Kraken Cove became ours. With the market in a downturn, it wasn't a hard thing to do. Rebuilding, revitalizing, renewing, all to ensure that the Teg arriving in town had places to live and ways to make a living."

"And now you're the mayor of a town that serves as a safe haven for any Teg seeking sanctuary." The spark in Gaheris' eyes suggested that he was proud of his protégé.

"Not the mayor," Draig clarified. "Just another business owner and sometime lighthouse keeper."

"Lighthouse keeper," Gaheris mused. "Certainly an appropriate role for you."

Draig shrugged. "You know how I need some time away from everyone."

"I do, and I also know that you never shirk your responsibilities when it comes to the people you care about."

"Do I need to worry?" Draig sensed the concern with which Gaheris offered his last statement.

"I don't know," Gaheris admitted. "Your father is not as he was. Or rather he's worse than he was when you were dealing with him last. Best to keep your eyes open."

"I always do, just as you taught me."

"Good. If I can, I'll send word if anything is coming your way. But you need to assume ..."

"That he won't leave me alone for long." Draig was disappointed by that, although not surprised.

"You know how your father is."

"Unfortunately, I do."

"It's been a pleasure to see you again, Draig. Even more to fight by your side. But now it's time to take my leave. I need to get back."

"It would have been better if you came alone."

"I didn't have a choice." Gaheris' eyes widened in alarm. "I hope you didn't kill any of them. Not that I'd shed a tear for some of them, but it would complicate my life and yours if you did."

"No, the Three Little Bears were quite gentle with them."

Gaheris' eyes grew even larger. "The Berserkers. After watching what they did to the Werewolves, now I am concerned."

"You have nothing to worry about. You'll find your squad a

mile down the road from the town line, on the right, a hundred yards into the wood. Exactly where you left them."

"In one piece, I hope."

"Safe and sound, probably still sleeping."

Gaheris smiled in appreciation. "Thank you, Draig. Be careful. You know your father. You know what he's capable of."

"That I do."

"And another word of warning?"

"Could I stop you if I tried?"

"No, you couldn't," Gaheris confirmed, patting him on the back again. "Beware the Witch."

Draig had heard much the same before. "Because she's hiding something?" After what he learned in the Circle, Draig finally had a sense of what that might be.

"In part, yes."

"You sense something more."

Gaheris nodded. "I do."

"You're not going to tell me?"

"I would if I could," he replied, giving his friend a grin.

"Another of your premonitions?" They came to Gaheris every so often. After working with the Knight for so many centuries, Draig had learned to trust them.

Gaheris nodded. "I'd tell you more if I could, but you know how it is."

It was Draig's turn to nod. He looked over his shoulder.

Melissa was deep in conversation with Peggy Rose. Although from what little he could see with that brief glance, it seemed more like a competition between the two.

That was to be expected. Speaking with either of them often was like that, and to have the two speaking to one another only added to the level of difficulty.

"You don't trust her?"

"Do you?" Gaheris asked, giving Draig a lift of his eyebrow.

Draig took a moment before replying. "I want to. But ..."

"You can't."

"I can't," Draig admitted. "Much like your premonitions, I just haven't figured out why."

"And you fear what will happen when you do. That it might be too late."

Draig nodded. "I do."

"WHERE DID YOUR FRIEND GO?"

When they reached the edge of town, Peggy Rose left Melissa. The Sorceress heading down another trail in the woods, Pinkie in tow.

Melissa was relieved. The conversation with the Sorceress had felt more like an interrogation.

She realized then that the Knight who had joined them in the battle against the Werewolves was gone as well.

"Gaheris understands that entering Kraken Cove on his own probably isn't the best idea. He went to get his men and then report back to my father."

"I was speaking with Peggy Rose about Gaheris," Melissa started. "I don't understand how you two can still be friends."

Draig didn't reply until they entered Kraken Cove, taking the path along the coast. It was there that the Berserkers appeared at the edge of the wood, each one offering a wave before striding back to the bakery.

"Why do you find that so strange?"

"After all the difficulties with your father?"

"A good point. My father does have a habit of creating difficulties."

"And you don't?" Melissa's sarcasm wasn't lost on Draig.

"Me as well," Draig admitted.

"And yet you and Gaheris are still friends."

"We are."

"Even though you two come into conflict on occasion. Probably more frequently than you would like, in fact."

"Yes, that's true."

Melissa lifted her hands, wanting to understand, quickly losing patience, Draig proving just as difficult as always. "Then explain it to me. How could you both still be friends?"

"Because we've known each other for a very long time."

"Time doesn't always help in situations such as these. In fact, sometimes it makes things worse."

"True," Draig admitted. "But you didn't let me finish."

"I didn't realize you had anything else to say since your responses are usually so clipped," Melissa replied, her sarcasm replaced with a snarkiness Draig had yet to experience from her. And he really didn't enjoy.

"Passive aggressive much?"

"I could do without the sarcasm in return," Melissa grumbled.

Draig chuckled softly, pleased that he could get her goat so easily. "Time is a factor, because in the time we've known each other, we've come to trust each other. That's why we're still friends. Trust."

Melissa thought about that, the harbor and marina, once difficult to see in the distance, now gaining greater clarity. "You make it sound simple. Much too simple in my opinion."

"Trust is anything but simple, wouldn't you agree?"

Draig gave Melissa a questioning look. She realized that he had quite deftly turned the focus of the conversation onto her.

Not knowing how to escape the predicament into which she had talked herself, she offered an honest response. "I would."

"And do you trust me?" Draig asked, not having the energy to beat around the bush after all that had occurred during the last few days.

Melissa didn't reply right away. "To a point. And do you trust me?"

"To a point," Draig replied.

Now they both knew from where they were starting. The question was, could they go beyond that?

Draig needed to find out, because the next steps he took would depend on the answer to that question.

"You didn't have to think about it for very long like I did," Melissa said with a smile, trying to infuse a little humor into what she knew was a very serious conversation and just as challenging, though for different reasons, than the one she had just engaged in with Peggy Rose.

Draig ignored her attempt to lighten the mood. "Arthur Pendragon shouldn't be a problem for you."

"Your friendly Knight saw me. He'll tell him I'm here."

"He won't."

"How do you know?"

"Because I asked him not to."

"And you trust him?"

"I do," Draig confirmed, his voice taking on a solemn note, "with my life."

"Then I'll just have to trust in that."

"Now we're making a little progress." What Draig said could have been taken as another attempt to lighten the mood, but he wasn't smiling. "We've dealt with Morgase's Weres."

"My thanks for that," Melissa nodded. She needed to give credit where credit was due.

"Yet you're still stuck between a rock and a hard place," Draig murmured.

"I am?" Melissa asked, although her mild protest rang hollow in her own ears.

"Please, Melissa, no more games. We don't have time for them. Arthur thinks you're dead, and he will think that for at least a little while longer. Morgase can't apply any direct pressure to you for the time being with the last of the Renegades fleeing with their tails between their legs."

"And I just thanked you for that."

"I'm not seeking your thanks, Melissa. I'm seeking the truth. Because the pressure you're under isn't just coming from my father and my aunt. Tell me."

"Draig, I ..." She shook her head, fearing that they would reach the crux of the matter between them, though she hoped not so quickly. Still not sure what to do next.

"Tell me, Melissa." His voice was quiet, calm, and also insistent.

Melissa hesitated, closing her eyes as they continued along the path. She really wanted to tell him. After all that Draig and his friends had done for her, he deserved to know.

Yet if she revealed her true motivation, what would happen to her ...

Trust was all well and good. But she had learned the hard way that when push came to shove, trust often flew out the window. More often than not, self-interest ruled.

Draig might be different with respect to that. In fact, she believed that he was.

She wasn't ready, however, to reveal all. To take that risk. Not yet. Not with so much at stake.

"I'm sorry, but I can't. Not now. Telling you any more than you already know helps neither of us, and it likely only increases the danger ... for us both."

"I can't help you if you don't tell me all that's going on."

Melissa retreated to her standard reaction when someone pushed her. A defensiveness masquerading as anger. "I told you before that I don't need your help."

Draig walked right through it. "If I didn't help you, where would you be? Taken? Dead?"

"Probably in a better place than I am now," she muttered. She heard the truth in his words. Still, she refused to acknowledge it, not knowing any other response when under pressure than to push back.

"Melissa ..." Draig's eyes flashed dangerously, not having any patience for the deflection.

"Draig, please." Melissa really wanted to tell him. Because he was right. She either would have been taken or dead if not for him. Still, that didn't matter. The only thing that mattered was that she was still alive and still free, and she could do what she needed to do. Because if she didn't, a worse fate awaited her. "You have secrets that you aren't willing to share. I have secrets as well that I can't and won't share. If I could tell you, I would. I can't. I'm sorry."

Draig didn't respond, although his expression hardened, his eyes blazing and revealing his anger.

"What did you see in the Circle?" Melissa was worried that Draig would lose his temper, not wanting to be the recipient after seeing what he could do to those who displeased him. But she didn't ask the question just because of that. She was beginning to understand what was driving him now. He had learned something atop Druid's Peak that was not only relevant to him, but also relevant to her. "Peggy Rose said the experience was unique to the individual Teg."

"More than I cared to," Draig replied in a quiet voice that was barely more than a whisper, his eyes never leaving hers, "yet still not enough."

"Did you have to practice to be this obscure or does it just come naturally?" Melissa teased, desperate to reduce the pressure that he was applying.

"A little of both," Draig admitted.

Melissa smiled. His eyes weren't burning as brightly as they had been just seconds before. A good sign. "It's like we already confirmed, Draig. We trust each other, but only to a point."

Draig nodded. He had hoped to gain the truth from her, but he had never placed much faith in hope. And he had been right to doubt that he could. Even after all that they had experienced together. A pity, though not a surprise. "That might not be good enough going forward."

"It might not, you're right," Melissa agreed.

They had reached the town green. The welcome smell of freshly made pastries from Tia's Bakes just a block to the west carried on the breeze, the beach and the ocean at their backs.

She reached out and grasped his arm. "I'm going to head back to the Safe Haven. I understand that you might want me to leave Kraken Cove." Draig stared at her, his fiery eyes not giving her a hint as to what he was thinking. "I don't want that, that's the truth, but I understand if that's what you want and think is best. Once you've made your decision, you know where to find me."

She leaned into Draig and kissed him lightly on the lips. Lingering for a few seconds before pulling back. Then she released his arm and strode across the town green, heading toward the inn.

She felt terrible leaving him in the dark. But she had pulled him in too deeply as it was. She couldn't ask any more of him.

Draig kept his eyes on her until she turned the corner and disappeared.

Why did he allow the Witch to do this to him?

Tangle him up in knots.

Worse, he didn't know if she was being sincere or just trying to play him.

22

INCOMPLETE REPORT

"That's all you have to report?"

Gaheris stood tall, back straight, arms clasped to his front. Calm. Completely at his ease.

Arthur sat with his legs crossed behind his overlarge desk that was crafted from a fragment of the Llangernyw Yew, the oldest tree in Europe. He was anything but calm, although he thought that he was doing an excellent job of hiding his agitation.

The setting sun illuminated the large office with a burnt orange that gave it a needed warmth until darkness fell and reminded them both of the reason for this meeting.

"It is." Gaheris had learned long ago to give Arthur no more than was absolutely necessary.

"Why do I get the feeling that you're not telling me everything?"

Gaheris had provided Arthur with a bare sketch of the town and not a word on the other Teg who might be living there. And more concerning, not a whiff regarding his son.

"I'm telling you all that I learned of Kraken Cove, my King. As I said, I wasn't in the town for more than a few minutes before the Sorceress took me aside. With so little time to explore, there was only so much I could discover."

Arthur's eyes flashed with anger. "You allowed the Sorceress to bundle you away like a swaddled child? You of all Teg, an original Knight of the Round?"

Gaheris didn't rise to take the bait. He knew better. "There are few who can stand against the Sorceress when she makes use of the Grym. I am not one of them, my King."

"Even though you had a squad of Knights at your back, you chose not to return to the town after that encounter with the Sorceress?"

Gaheris' decision in that regard bothered Arthur. It showed weakness on the part of his second in command. And if his lieutenant appeared weak, then by association he did as well. That could not be permitted. His rule was based on strength. Always strength. There was no room for anything else.

"I did not trust the Knights who were detained, my King. Bringing them into the town ..." Gaheris shrugged, a tinge of disappointment in his voice, "as I said, my King, better if I had been sent on my own. To take that squad into town after they allowed themselves to be hogtied so easily would have been a mistake."

"Because of the Sorceress?" Arthur filled his voice with a scorn that was difficult to ignore.

Once again Gaheris didn't rise to take the bait. He had served Arthur Pendragon long enough to interpret his moods and the consequences of getting swept away with them. "Yes, my King. One or six against the Sorceress ... it is much the same. None of us can use the Grym with the potency that would allow us to challenge her in any significant way."

Arthur stared at his second in command for quite some time. He couldn't fault Gaheris for the decision that he made, although he couldn't say that he was happy with it.

Finally, realizing that there was nothing more to be gained

by continuing with the interview, Arthur nodded, accepting Gaheris' report. "When next we go to Kraken Cove, we will need to take a full company. Perhaps two."

"Yes, my King," Gaheris agreed, "although I would advise against that."

"You would advise against that?" Arthur didn't understand his Knight's hesitation, which only fed his agitation.

"Yes, my King. In speaking with the Sorceress, it was made quite clear."

"What was made quite clear?" Arthur's eyes flashed dangerously, sensing the threat.

"If you go to Kraken Cove, the Sorceress warned that you would start a war."

"I can win any war I start, Gaheris. You should know that better than most."

And he did. Though Gaheris had begun to question many of those wars that Arthur had presided over. The stated objectives no longer appeared to be so clearcut, so necessary, as they had back then.

"I do, my King. I am simply relaying the Sorceress' warning."

"I get the feeling that there's more to it than that, Gaheris. Speak your mind."

Gaheris hesitated as he studied Arthur. He had known the King Teg since well before he first came to power.

Then, they had fought together for an ideal. To build a new reality. To create a better world for all the Teg.

Now that they had created that world ... he couldn't quite put what he was feeling into words, other than he was experiencing a deep sense of regret and remorse.

He remembered more the mistakes they had made rather than their victories. The mistakes that were now threatening to bite them in the ass.

"I have no doubt that you can deal with Draig and the other

Teg in Kraken Cove. However, I would advise against that at this time."

"Because of your past friendship with my son?"

"No, my King. Because Draig is not a threat, and we have more immediate challenges that we must address first."

Arthur glared at Gaheris for quite some time. His lieutenant didn't blink, staring straight ahead at some point just over Arthur's head. He didn't flinch. He stood tall, confident, even under the hard gaze of the ruler of the Teg.

Arthur finally nodded. "Leave me, Gaheris. We will talk of this later."

Gaheris offered a nod and slight bow of respect to the King Teg before turning and striding out of the office.

"What are your thoughts?"

Merlin stepped out of the shadows in the far corner of the office, taking one of the seats in front of Arthur's desk. He had used the Grym to hide himself in plain sight, as he often did, both when Arthur wanted him to and when he didn't.

"About what happened in Kraken Cove?"

Arthur nodded.

"It makes sense." Merlin shrugged, crossing one leg over the other. "Gaheris was right not to challenge Peggy Rose."

"And what would happen if I appeared in Kraken Cove with a few companies of Knights at my back?"

Merlin smiled, though it contained little warmth. "Gaheris was right about that as well. And we do have other matters that require our attention other than the rebirth of the Dragon."

"Allowing Draig to continue to do whatever he's doing in Kraken Cove makes me appear weak." Arthur said it quietly, although he bit off the words, clearly annoyed. "Some might even think me vulnerable."

"Addressing first challenges larger than your son does not make you appear weak, Arthur. It makes you appear decisive. More expansive as well, because those larger challenges that we face affect all of the Teg. You would be doing no more than was expected of you as the King of the Teg."

Merlin decided not to include in his reasoning that Arthur choosing to go after his son now would appear more self-serving than anything else and suggest a detachment and lack of concern for the well-being of the Teg, undercurrents of which already were roiling through their world and did not need to be stoked.

"I cannot just leave my son be, Merlin."

"I didn't say that you had to, Arthur."

Arthur waited, but Merlin didn't offer any more than that. "No additional advice? You always have more advice. Usually, I can't stop you from giving me advice."

"I didn't think that you wanted it." Merlin offered the statement in a soothing tone, knowing that if Arthur got more unsettled their current conversation could quickly devolve into another argument. And that would serve neither of their purposes.

Merlin watched and worried as Arthur struggled with his rising anger. It hadn't always been this way.

Arthur had shown so much promise when he pulled Excalibur from the stone and carved out his kingdom in Britain. And then from there doing the same in the Teg world.

He had demonstrated such skill. A deftness that few others had to bring enemies to his side. The resolve as well that was required to dispatch or remove those among the Teg who were unwilling to listen to reason.

Yet the many centuries of doing that had affected Arthur Pendragon in a way that Merlin never anticipated. Although he'd deny it if asked, Merlin believed that Arthur now saw himself not only as more important than the work that he was doing, but also that the work he was doing couldn't be done without him.

That was more than just disappointing. It was heart-breaking.

Arthur could have been so much more. He could have done so much more.

The conflict with Morgase and then Mordred didn't help. Nor did his getting involved with Gwennie.

Then all those other women who followed. Every single one seeking to use the King Teg, and Arthur sometimes allowing it to deal with his grief.

Though Merlin had believed that Arthur had the chance to chart a new course with Draig's mother. At least for a time.

But Merlin should have seen how that was going to end. A textbook case of self-sabotage, something that Arthur was demonstrating quite a knack for.

"Tell me, Merlin."

"If you really want to know what your son is doing, you can go talk to him." Merlin tried and failed to keep the exasperation from his voice. "You know where he is. Instead of peppering me with a bunch of useless questions or asking for advice that you don't want to hear, why don't you go do that? Why don't you talk with Axel and see if you can clear things up between the two of you?"

"My son betrayed me, Merlin." Arthur's voice was cold. That of a King and not a father. "If he wants to talk, he knows where to find me. And if he does that, then he's going to need to bend the knee before I listen to a word that he has to say."

23

DECISION TO BE MADE

"**S**he'd like you to visit again."

Riga walked along the beach, the lighthouse at her back, Draig's arm linked in hers. As was usually the case, several large ravens circled overhead.

"After the last time?" Draig chuckled softly. "I thought she'd want a break when she learned about that."

"In the past perhaps. Now she's beginning to understand more about you. About what you've had to do. What's been required of you. What you're doing now."

Draig nodded, knowing that Riga was the reason for that. "Thank you."

Riga squeezed his arm warmly then placed her head on his shoulder, pulling him closer for a few seconds. "The Witch is still here?"

"In town, yes. She's staying with Hestia."

"I warned you," Riga chided gently.

"You did."

"And yet you allowed her to stay."

"For a time," Draig admitted. "For a reason."

Riga smiled, pleased that he had taken her warning seriously and not surprised by his generosity. "You actually listened to me."

"I always listen to you, Riga. You know that. I just don't always do what you want me to do."

"Which is why we're still not together," Riga teased.

"Among other reasons," Draig clarified, offering her a small smile.

"Fair enough," Riga agreed, not wanting to relive their past. Enjoying much more the peace they had crafted with one another since they both realized that living together wasn't good for them or for their daughter. "And you're allowing the Witch to stay ..."

"Because of what I learned when I was in the Circle."

"Would you care to share?"

Draig did. He rarely felt the need to keep anything back from the Morrigan.

"What are you going to do?" Riga asked, mulling all that Draig had told her before asking her question.

Draig shook his head in frustration. "The piddly little conflict between my father and Morgase is nothing compared to what is coming our way. Their desire for power at the other's expense, their desire to rule the Teg, is putting all of the Teg at risk."

"You knew this would happen," Riga prodded.

Draig sighed. "I suspected."

"And yet you did nothing about it." Riga sought to push Draig, not make him angry, because she certainly wasn't in a position to question the decisions that he had made. If she had been in his place, she would have done much the same as he did.

"I did what I could for the Teg living in Kraken Cove."

"The Teg you truly cared about."

"Yes."

"And now?"

"Now, I need to think about all the Teg. There's a war coming."

"Among the Teg?"

"Among the Teg," Draig confirmed, "and with the Teg."

Riga nodded, having reached much the same conclusion based on what Draig had seen and experienced while in the Circle. "What are you going to do?"

"What would you suggest?" Draig had been mulling several options, concluding that only one got him where he needed to be, though it didn't really appeal to him.

Riga pulled Draig to a stop, turning him toward her. Locking eyes. Her expression hard. Measuring. The Celtic Goddess of War now standing before him.

"You must be who you were meant to be. The Dragon must rise once more."

Here ends *Duel with the Dragon,* Book Two of *The Fallen Knight Series*.

Axel Draig's story continues in *Beware the Dragon,* Book Three of *The Fallen Knight Series*.

Keep reading for the first two chapters of Book Three.

BONUS MATERIAL

If you really enjoyed this story and if you have a few minutes, consider writing a review.

Keep reading for the first two chapters of Book Three of *The Fallen Knight Series, Beware the Dragon.*

Order Book Three on my author website at PeterWachtBooks.com or on Amazon.

BEWARE
THE
DRAGON
THE FALLEN KNIGHT SERIES BOOK 3
PETER WACHT

Beware the Dragon

By Peter Wacht

Book 3 of The Fallen Knight Series

This book is a work of fiction. Names, characters, places, and incidents are the product of the author's imagination or are used fictitiously. Any resemblance to actual events, locales, or persons, living or dead, is coincidental.

Copyright 2025 © by Peter Wacht

Cover design by Ebooklaunch.com

All rights reserved. In accordance with the U.S. Copyright Act of 1976, the scanning, uploading, and electronic sharing of any part of this book without the permission of the publisher constitute unlawful piracy and theft of the author's intellectual property.

Published in the United States by Kestrel Media Group LLC.

ISBN: 978-1-950236-62-6

eBook ISBN: 978-1-950236-63-3

Library of Congress Control Number: 2024926948

❀ Created with Vellum

1. THE OCEAN DOESN'T FEEL RIGHT

Draig frowned, eyes narrowing. He gave a short wave as he pulled back on the throttle, the cabin cruiser slowing to little more than a drift. With a deft touch he turned the wheel just a hair to starboard then cut the engine entirely, guiding rather than motoring the craft into its slip in the Kraken Cove harbor.

The Safe Haven, Hestia's inn and his first destination that morning, was perched on the cliffs above.

Walking out to the bow, he threw the line to a scowling Seamus McCracken. The salty mariner caught it with barely a glance.

While Seamus tied the line to the cleat, Draig trotted to the stern then jumped to the dock, rope in one hand. In the other he held the blackthorn shillelagh that was never far from his grasp.

Once moored, he turned. Waiting.

His friend wouldn't be there unless he had cause to be. And, with Seamus, the cause rarely was a good one. But Draig understood that they needed to dance first, Seamus preferring to tiptoe before kicking him in the gut.

With a rare smile, Seamus stood there admiring Draig's

restored 1923 cruiser with its hull mahogany on oak and gleaming brass railings and cleats. It was more than sixty feet long. A fully extendable awning covered the aft deck. A real beauty.

"Still can't buy her from you?"

Draig shook his head. "Not until I'm done with her."

"When will that be?" Seamus already knew the answer.

"I don't know."

"Helpful as always," muttered the crusty seaman.

"I do what I can," Draig replied, cracking a small smile.

"To make my life difficult," Seamus muttered. "If you're not going to give her up, when are you going to name her?"

"When she tells me her name." A mysterious glint danced in Draig's eyes.

Seamus gave his friend a questioning glance. "She's going to tell you her name?"

"She will. When she's ready."

Seamus shook his head, only slightly amused. "Barely past breakfast and you're already irritating me."

"And you're here to greet me when you shouldn't be," Draig said, his smile gone. His countenance serious. Challenging. "You're supposed to be out on a job."

"I felt the need to get back to town sooner than I anticipated."

"This can't be good." Draig and Seamus walked farther down the pier, stopping in front of the *Kraken*, Seamus' deep sea fishing charter, which was just one slip over.

"You're not happy to see me?"

"Not with that expression on your face."

"My expression?" wondered Seamus.

Draig nodded. "Usually you're grumpy and dour, as if the world is about to fall on your shoulders."

Seamus wasn't offended, because Draig was correct. He lifted an eyebrow. "What do I look like now?"

"Grumpy and dour as always, but that the world already has fallen on your shoulders." Draig shrugged. "Either that or you've caught a case of the crabs."

Seamus snorted out a laugh. Unable to stop himself. "It's not the crabs. I'm careful about that."

"And for that I'm grateful." Draig studied his friend, Seamus' unease almost palpable. "So the world already has fallen on your shoulders."

Seamus nodded, not disputing the claim. "That might be a very good way to describe it."

"Describe what?"

Seamus ignored Draig's question, not yet ready to jump into the reason for his early morning visit. "Where are those mangy mutts of yours? Nasty beasts all three."

"I don't know that Butch, Cassidy, and Sundance would appreciate your description of them. You know how sensitive they can be."

"I do," Seamus admitted. "That's why I didn't say what I said where they can hear me. I'm more than familiar with their work and have no desire to be their next victim."

"They're not as bad as you think, Seamus."

"I don't know about that. As I said, I'm more than familiar with their work."

Draig smiled. This was one of Seamus' more common complaints, keeping in mind that he had many, and that he was more than willing to share all of them with Draig. Again and again and again.

Nevertheless, Draig sensed why Seamus had chosen to start with this one.

He was nervous, which was exceedingly rare for him.

Just as rare, his friend also was ... concerned.

For Draig. Even more so as to why Draig's dogs, who were overly protective and quite handy in a scrap, weren't with him.

The most obvious source of Seamus' worry would be the

events of the last few days. Draig didn't believe that was the cause, however. There was more to it than just that.

Rather than going straight to the heart of the matter that Seamus wanted to raise, Draig understood that it was better to allow his friend to get to it in his own time. It would slow things down, true, but he had learned through experience that it was better not to press.

Seamus didn't like to be rushed. If he was, he became even more difficult than he usually was.

"You just need to spend some time with them, Seamus." Draig gave his friend a smile, his reddish-orange eyes sparking with amusement. "Get to know them. They like you."

"They like me?" Seamus was surprised by that comment. Usually, he and Draig's dogs kept a wary eye on one another. Trusting, but only to a point.

"They do," Draig confirmed. "Almost as much as they like their favorite chew toys."

"Funny," Seamus muttered, shaking his head in feigned irritation while trying not to smile. "That makes sense, actually. Usually, I don't do well with your kind. That alpha response has a tendency to get in the way."

"My kind?" Draig wondered. Not concerned or offended by Seamus' comment. More that his friend was taking so long to get where he wanted to go. Clearly, something or someone had spooked Seamus. And it took a great deal to do that. "We're friends, aren't we, Seamus?"

"We are," Seamus admitted, "albeit reluctantly."

Draig chuckled at that even as his eyes narrowed. Seamus was grouchier than usual. That wasn't a good sign. This definitely wasn't the way that Draig wanted to start his morning. Adding another challenge to his already long list.

"You're not just here to start my day off on a good note." Seamus didn't miss Draig's sarcasm. "What's up?"

Seamus sighed, then kicked at an imaginary pebble on the

dock. "Normally I wouldn't bother you with something like this."

"But clearly this something is bothering you. Spill it," Draig prodded.

Seamus frowned, still trying to figure out where he wanted to start. He opted for the longer way around. "I was coming down the coast from Canada early this morning."

"Another smuggling run?"

"Just business," Seamus replied, giving Draig a deceptive smile and a shrug.

Draig wasn't taken in by the poor attempt at subterfuge. With Seamus, smuggling and business were one and the same. Feeling the press of time, he tried to nudge his friend along. "You were sailing down the coast from Canada ..."

"I was," Seamus confirmed.

"Then what's the problem?" Draig didn't understand why Seamus was hesitating. Usually, he had no problem telling him what he thought. About anything. Even when Draig told him that he didn't want to hear it. "You've made that run hundreds of times."

"True, but never like this."

"Seamus, you're dancing around like a middle-school boy too frightened to ask a girl to dance." Draig's tone demanded an answer. "What's the problem?"

"I don't know if it is a problem."

"If it's not a problem, then why did you wait for me to get here this morning?"

"That's a good question," Seamus admitted.

"Seamus." Draig's tone hardened in an instant, his eyes flashing dangerously. "I didn't get a lot of sleep last night, I've got more to deal with today than I want to, and I'm beginning to lose patience."

Seamus held up his hands, seeking to stave off Draig losing his temper. Knowing what that could look like and not wanting to bear the brunt of it. "I just don't want you to think that I'm crying wolf. That's all."

His friend's comment stopped Draig from pushing harder. The Werewolves were well out of Kraken Cove when he came down from the mountain yesterday and should be gone at least for a time, but he hadn't checked on them since late last night.

Draig did so then. Reaching for the Grym, he used the Power of the Ancients to extend his senses in all directions around the seaside town. One mile, then two. Five. Ten. Twenty miles. Fifty.

Nothing.

Just as he hoped and expected. The Renegades turned tail and fled after he killed Raik. In fact, he couldn't sense a Werewolf in the state. A good result. Those Weres wouldn't be coming back anytime soon, which meant he wouldn't have to worry about the blood debt between them until the pack rebuilt its strength. And that would take some time.

"Instead of beating around the bush, Seamus, just tell me what it is that's bothering you. Then I'll judge if you're crying wolf or not."

"I just don't want you to give me that look."

"What look?"

"The one that suggests that I'm full of it."

"You are full of it, Seamus," Draig replied more sharply than he intended. "You know it just as well as I do."

Seamus stared at his friend, his eyes shifting in color. From a deep ocean blue to a dark grey. At the same time, the mariner flexed his fingers and lifted himself up onto his toes. The energy flowing within him began to seek a release. To take shape.

He prevented the shift from occurring, although his glare continued for several seconds more before Seamus took a deep breath and settled back down onto the soles of his feet. He took several more deep breaths, pushing the air out through his nose, to calm himself.

"Only you can get away with doing that to me," Seamus grumbled once he was certain that he was back in control of himself.

"I'm honored." Draig grasped Seamus' shoulder and gave him a friendly squeeze, a form of apology for almost setting off his friend. "Now what's got you all hot and bothered? Not another mermaid I hope."

Once again Draig's humor made Seamus smile. It also helped him to relax just a little bit more.

"If only," Seamus mused. "Did I tell you about that time I found that mermaid ..."

"Seamus."

The mariner nodded, realizing that he couldn't delay any longer. So he just said it. "The ocean doesn't feel right."

Draig nodded slightly as he thought about what Seamus told him. Not out of concern. Rather curiosity. Understanding just how hard this was for his friend. "The ocean doesn't feel right?"

"That's what I said," Seamus confirmed.

"What does that mean? The ocean doesn't feel right."

"I'm sorry, but that's the best that I can explain it." Seamus shrugged, hoping that the movement of his shoulders explained to Draig why he was so hesitant to mention this to him in the first place. "It's just a feeling, no more than that. I wish I could tell you more, but I can't." Just then a cold gust of wind swept off the water of Kraken Cove, sending a chill through the both of them. "The ocean doesn't feel right. That's all that I wanted to tell you."

"And that's why you were here to greet me? That's why you returned sooner than you planned?"

Seamus nodded and shrugged again, hands now in his

pockets. Looking for another imaginary rock to kick into the water. "Yes."

Draig didn't say anything for a time, thinking about what Seamus had told him. Even more, examining his friend, who appeared to be more than just a little out of sorts. Seamus never would have interrupted a run up the coast unless he believed that it was absolutely necessary. Not with the profit to be made.

"When you say the ocean doesn't feel right, do you mean like a storm coming in?"

Seamus considered Draig's question, his head moving slightly up and down as he considered the possibility. "That might be the best way to put it."

"But?" Draig caught Seamus' hesitation.

"But it's not an actual storm."

"A metaphorical storm?" Draig prompted.

"What do you mean by metaphorical?"

Draig didn't bother to reply. If he tried to explain it he'd just end up down the rabbit hole.

"A premonition, perhaps?" Draig suggested, trying hard to understand when Seamus didn't seem to understand himself.

"That's an even better way to describe it." Seamus smiled, then chuckled softly, an uncommon event for him. If Draig hadn't struck gold, he had come close.

"Talking with you can be like pulling teeth," Draig grumbled.

"One of my better qualities," Seamus said with a wink, apparently feeling better now that he had told his friend what he wanted to.

"Have you ever had a feeling like this before?" Draig was still trying to get a better sense as to what Seamus was so worried about.

Seamus usually wasn't worried about anything. Especially when he was out on the water. Because on the water, there was little that could challenge him.

"Only a handful of times," Seamus replied. The mariner's eyes took on a glazed cast, seemingly captured by memories that he would have preferred to keep buried.

"What happened when it did?"

"Nothing good, I promise you that."

"Can you be any more specific, Seamus?" Draig was working hard to maintain what little patience he had left. "Anything you can share could prove helpful."

"The eruption of Krakatoa comes to mind," Seamus muttered, images of that event flashing through his mind. "Death. Destruction. Devastation. Mayhem. On more than just a massive scale. A global scale. And bad news for all the Teg." Seamus shivered as he came back to himself. "Nothing good for the Teg, that's all I can tell you. I don't know why I felt it. All I can tell you is that I did."

"Not a pleasant picture you're leaving with me," Draig admitted.

"It wasn't meant to be. I'm sorry. But you asked."

"Why are you telling me this now, Seamus?"

"This feeling that I get ..." Seamus' voice trailed off, then he shook his head as if he were trying to clear it of thoughts and memories that wouldn't leave him alone. "Whenever the ocean has felt like this, whatever the cause, it's never taken long for that cause to be revealed."

Draig's frown deepened. So a potentially catastrophic event and Seamus could tell him little more than that, other than it was imminent. Wonderful. Definitely not how he wanted to start his morning. "Thank you, Seamus. I appreciate you telling me this."

"I had to, Draig. We're friends after all, albeit reluctantly as I said." Seamus grinned, though that grin quickly was replaced by his more common grimace, which was caused by what he wanted to say next. He started and stopped several times, requiring a good bit of effort to put his concerns into words. "I just wanted to warn you. This feeling ... it's coming from my world, from the ocean, but I don't know the cause. I do know – and don't ask me why because I can't tell you – that it relates to you directly."

Recognizing his friend's discomfort, rather than pressing Seamus further, Draig nodded. He doubted that Seamus would be able to offer any more detail than that.

Still, what Seamus had revealed was quite helpful. It served as additional confirmation as to what he had learned in the Circle atop the Druid's Peak and the decision that he needed to make. A decision that he didn't want to make.

"Thanks Seamus." Draig clapped him on the back. "You're a good friend."

Seamus nodded. "Don't go spreading that around. I have a reputation to maintain." He jumped over the railing and landed on the *Kraken*, feeling better once he was floating atop the water. "If you need anything, you know where not to go."

Draig smiled. Grouchy and dour. Crusty. Certainly antisocial. But still a friend. Seamus was ready to assist despite his words to the contrary.

Draig reached for the Grym again, searching once more, taking more time, focusing on Kraken Cove and the town's surrounding environs. Extending his search all the way to the Druid's Peak to the west and then past his home, Raptor Bay Lighthouse, to the east. Well out into the Atlantic Ocean.

Nothing.

All seemed to be well.

There was no reason for him to be concerned.

At least none that he could identify.

Of course, that didn't mean that he shouldn't be worried.

Seamus was many things. But Peter from the fable he was not.

2. NO ROOM AT THE INN

Seamus' warning kept playing through Draig's mind as he climbed the stairs that led up the cliff from the beach to the Safe Haven.

"The ocean doesn't feel right."

Draig shook his head, unable to contain his smile that was a mix of both humor and frustration. Just as clear as always with Seamus. And just one more thing for him to worry about.

Still, despite Seamus' lack of specificity, Draig couldn't ignore the warning. Even as he turned his focus to that morning's primary task.

He had tried to get the information he wanted from Melissa yesterday evening on the way back into town after defeating Raik and sending what was left of his Werewolf pack running with their tails between their legs.

Melissa had been less than accommodating. Revealing some but not all of what she was dealing with, and by association what he was dealing with, since he had given in to his need to dig deeper into the mystery and helped the Witch.

After Seamus' warning, which he believed was connected in some way though he had no evidence to support that claim, he had to make Melissa understand that her withholding critical knowledge put them both at risk.

Draig knew that Melissa was hiding from him pieces of what she was truly about. And he knew that she knew that he knew she was hiding those pieces from him.

Yet she still refused to reveal any of it despite all the problems that she had caused for him and several of his friends.

Selfish. That was the only way to describe her actions.

He couldn't ignore that. Although it was a sign of desperation as well.

He had seen it many times before, and he could thank his father for that last. A natural result of the work that he had done for the King Teg for so long.

Draig needed to know what Melissa was hiding from him. He suspected, but with what he had in mind for dealing with what threatened him and those Teg residing in Kraken Cove, that wasn't enough. He required confirmation. Preferably before he put his plan in play.

And if he didn't get that confirmation?

The result he expected based on Melissa's remarkable obstinance and didn't want. Nevertheless, if it came to that, he would do what he needed to do, just as he had done in the past.

He didn't want to do that. He wouldn't enjoy it. But he wouldn't have a choice.

Draig stopped abruptly, halfway through Hestia's rose garden that ran along the northern side of the inn.

All the garden gnomes placed here, several dozen in fact, faced the Victorian house built on the edge of the cliff.

That was strange.

He had never seen that before.

A mistake perhaps?

He doubted it. Hestia didn't make mistakes.

Draig continued through the garden to the front of the bed and breakfast. All of the gnomes set in the garden beds that ran all the way down the driveway to Market Street were facing toward the Safe Haven.

More than strange now. Worrying.

Draig trotted up the steps.

The front door was open.

Hestia never left the front door open.

Ever.

Grasping his shillelagh in a tighter grip, he pushed the door open with his walking stick and stepped into the foyer. The counter greeted him, half the keys to the various rooms still hanging from their hooks.

Melissa was still here. Her key wasn't on its hook.

Draig peeked into the dining room. No breakfast to be had.

That didn't surprise him. It was just after eight.

In the Safe Haven, if you weren't down for breakfast by eight, you didn't get breakfast.

Hestia never failed to leave for her morning hike right after that.

So all seemed to be as it should.

Then why did it feel otherwise?

Draig stepped around the counter and glanced through the door into the small office that butted up against the stairs.

Not a piece of paper out of place on her desk. Not a speck of dust to be seen.

Just as was always the case.

But Hestia never, ever left the front door open.

Draig reached for the Grym for a third time in just the last few minutes, extending his senses throughout the Safe Haven. He couldn't do it from outside the inn because of Hestia's many wards.

Draig's shillelagh flashed. The illusion fading and revealing his gleaming sword, he raced up the stairs two at a time.

~

"Perhaps you could put some clothes on. It's time to go."

Melissa jumped a few inches off the ground at the quiet, insistent voice. Walking out of the bathroom wrapped in nothing but a towel, she had been drying her hair, eyes on the carpet.

"Who in all the hells are you?"

She removed the wet towel from her head, trying to understand how someone had gotten into her attic room without her permission. Hestia had said that was impossible.

Yet Melissa could barely contain her shock at finding a woman sitting comfortably in front of the bay window, legs crossed, one arm draped over the back of the couch, as if it were Melissa who had invaded her space.

"Who I am doesn't matter. What matters is that I'm here."

The intruder pushed herself up and took a few steps toward Melissa, who naturally stepped back closer to the bathroom door. She wanted to keep some space between them. If she didn't, Melissa would have fewer options than she already had.

She didn't get very far.

Two men she hadn't noticed appeared behind her, blocking her path. She could have sworn the pair hadn't been there before. It was almost as if they materialized out of thin air.

And maybe they had.

Three more men appeared right in front of her. One by the door to her room. Two others standing in a position that ensured she was boxed in with no avenue for escape.

The men looked quite similar in appearance. Nondescript. Normal if she could use that term with Teg who appeared and disappeared in a flash. Barely noticeable because they seemed barely there.

So much so that Melissa had a hard time seeing them even when she was staring directly at them. It was easier when they moved, but negligibly so. More like a flicker of motion that the eye still wanted to ignore.

She had heard of men such as these. How could she not since she traveled on occasion along the darker lanes among the Teg? But she had never come up against them until now, and gratefully so.

Warlocks.

The small mark that resembled an evil eye and was tattooed just above their right cheekbones confirmed it.

Seers of things in the dark that any sane Teg sought to avoid. Unseen unless they chose to be seen.

Using the Twisted Grym to blend themselves into their surroundings so that they were all but invisible.

The perfect assassins, preferred on certain jobs by those of the Tylwyth Teg who could afford their outrageously priced services.

"Get dressed, please."

Melissa pulled her eyes away from the Warlocks standing to her front and shifted her focus to the woman. Taller than her by a few inches. Wearing all black. Dressed like a runner. Her black hair kept out of the way with a ponytail.

A good disguise for Kraken Cove, but Melissa could see beyond what the woman wanted her to see.

A Witch, just as she was.

Stronger than she was, Melissa feared, though there was only one way to find out.

"I wouldn't do it if I were you," the woman said, seemingly reading Melissa's mind. "It won't end well for you."

"Do what?" Melissa filled her voice with as much innocence as she could muster.

A woman used to being in command, used to killing or kidnapping, so clearly this wasn't the first time she and her Warlocks had been used on a job like this.

Melissa detected the power that radiated from her. Maybe not a Witch. The power reminded her of ...

"Get dressed. Now," the woman ordered. She smiled,

though her eyes didn't. "You have two minutes. Then we leave. Clothed or in a towel. Your choice."

Melissa searched for some way to extricate herself from a situation for which she was sadly unprepared. "Just let me grab the clothes I left in the bathroom."

She made a move toward the open door, steam still wafting out from her hot shower and into the colder attic room.

The two Warlocks at her back closed ranks.

"Take what you need from your suitcase. You can get dressed right here."

"You expect me to change in front of them?" Melissa barked, hoping that the shock she infused in her voice might gain her some leeway.

It didn't.

"Take it or leave it," the woman shrugged. "I don't care if you're dressed in a towel or clothes when we leave. I only care that we leave. Time is pressing. You have two minutes as I said."

"I can't believe that you would ..."

The woman cut off Melissa's protest. "Ninety seconds."

Seething with anger because she worried about what would happen if she gave free rein to her fear, Melissa dropped the towel that she had used to dry her hair. Then she reached for the pile of clothes on top of her travel bag.

She got dressed as quickly as she could while still trying to maintain her modesty, not allowing the towel wrapped around her to fall until she had only her socks and running shoes left.

"I can't believe that you couldn't give me just a few minutes in the bathroom."

"We know who you are ... Witch," the woman said.

"Takes one to know one."

"That it does," her kidnapper replied, offering her a brief nod of respect.

"And who am I since you know me so well?" Melissa bent down. Pulling on her socks and then her shoes, she tied the laces. All the while her thoughts focused on how to make her escape. Various ideas running through her mind. None of them all that appealing.

"You're the Witch who has caught the eye of my Dragon."

Melissa pushed herself back up, giving the woman a quizzical expression. "Your Dragon?" She didn't quite understand, until she did. "You mean Draig?"

The woman's dark eyes flashed, hints of anger in the back. Or perhaps jealousy. Melissa couldn't tell for certain, the woman closing herself off just as quickly as she revealed herself.

"My Dragon, yes."

"That's why you're here? Because of Draig?"

"Unfortunately, no," the woman replied with a smile that threatened to curl Melissa's toes. "If only I was. I have such good memories of spending time with him in this very room."

"Good memories?" Melissa wasn't quite sure what the woman was talking about, but she could guess, and she really had little desire for details. Although she did want to extend the conversation. Every second she gained might be another second that she could use.

"Very good memories indeed. And a good thing for you that I didn't find him here with you."

Melissa nodded, remembering that flash in the back of the woman's eyes. Jealousy for certain. Perhaps she could play off of that.

"Well, I'm sorry to say that you just missed him." Melissa offered the woman a sly smile and then a wink.

The woman's eyes narrowed. "Is that so?"

"It is," Melissa replied, crossing her arms in front of her chest. "He left no more than thirty minutes ago." Her smile widened. "After his shower." She tilted her head down, as if she was sharing a secret with the woman and trying to keep it from the five Warlocks pressing in close. "He was dirty. Very, very ... dirty."

Her kidnapper's jaw tightened as her eyes flashed. The woman clenched her right hand into a fist then reached for her. "You little bit ..."

Getting the reaction that she wanted, Melissa didn't hesitate. Calling on the Grym she sent a blast of energy right at the woman's feet.

Melissa turned away and closed her eyes, seeking to avoid the full effect that the blinding power would have. The woman and her Warlocks, if they survived, would be dazed and disoriented, if not unconscious, unable to stand against the force she employed.

If she had learned nothing from Draig in the last few days, it was that it was better to provoke and then attack, because it was always better to attack than defend.

She could ask questions later. Although she really didn't have any questions for this lot. She just wanted to get away from them.

And her surprise attack should give her the chance to do that.

The flare of bright energy fading, Melissa turned back around and opened her eyes.

Her jaw dropped, smile disappearing, replaced by a look of dejection.

The woman laughed at her crestfallen expression. Other than the scorched carpet where the blast struck, nothing had changed.

The Warlocks still surrounded her, and they appeared to be even less pleased than they had been before her attack. The shield of protective energy continued for several seconds more, the woman wanting to show Melissa the real power that she was up against, before she released her hold on the magical construction, the energy flickering a few times before disappearing.

"That was a big mistake, Witch," the woman murmured, shaking her head in mock disappointment. "Although I can't say that I'm surprised. We were warned that you were less than trustworthy."

"Look ..." Melissa sought desperately for some other way to extricate herself from her dilemma, but nothing was coming to mind, and clearly the woman's patience, little there to begin with, had run out.

"We were told to take you, Witch. What condition you are in when we deposit you where you need to be was never discussed." The woman nodded as she studied Melissa, clearly thinking of revenge for the failed attack ... even more for her alleged indiscretion with her Dragon. "I think we'll have a little fun with you first. So you can't give us any trouble along the way."

"I was hoping that I wouldn't see you for several more decades, Callie."

Draig stood in the doorway, sword in hand.

And he was less than pleased.

In fact, he was pissed.

THE END OF CHAPTER TWO

I hope you enjoyed the first two chapters. To keep reading *Beware the Dragon*, Book Three of *The Fallen Knight Series,* order your copy today at PeterWachtBooks.com or on Amazon.

MORE BY PETER WACHT

THE FALLEN KNIGHT SERIES

The Death of the Dragon (short story)*

The Dragon Awakens

Duel With a Dragon

Beware the Dragon (Forthcoming)

The Dragon Returns (Forthcoming)

THE REALMS OF THE TALENT AND THE CURSE

THE TALES OF CALEDONIA

(Complete 7-Book Series)

Blood on the White Sand (short story)*

The Diamond Thief (short story)*

The Protector

The Protector's Quest

The Protector's Vengeance

The Protector's Sacrifice

The Protector's Reckoning

The Protector's Resolve

The Protector's Victory

THE TALES OF THE TERRITORIES

Stalking the Blood Ruby (short story)*

A Fate Worse Than Death (short story)*

Death on the Burnt Ocean

Monsters in the Mist

The Dance of the Daggers

Bloody Hunt for Freedom

A Spark of Rebellion

Shadows Made Real

Shadow's Reach

Storm in the Darkness (Forthcoming 2025)

THE SYLVAN CHRONICLES

(Complete 9-Book Series)

The Legend of the Kestrel

The Call of the Sylvana

The Raptor of the Highlands

The Makings of a Warrior

The Lord of the Highlands

The Lost Kestrel Found

The Claiming of the Highlands

The Fight Against the Dark

The Defender of the Light

THE RISE OF THE SYLVAN WARRIORS

*Through the Knife's Edge (short story)**

* Free stories can be downloaded from my author website at PeterWachtBooks.com. My books are also available on Amazon and other online retailers.

YOUR FREE SHORT STORY IS WAITING

THROUGH THE KNIFE'S EDGE

This short story is a prelude to the events in my epic fantasy series *The Sylvan Chronicles* and is free to readers who receive my newsletter.

Sign up and get your free copy at PeterWachtBooks.com